Praise for Faye Kellerman and her Peter Decker and Rina Lazarus mysteries

"Bold, taut, with an artful fusion of the down-and-dirty with characters whose personal lives we care about and whose spiritual and emotional growth are as compelling as the events themselves."
—SUE GRAFTON

"This couple's domestic affairs have the *haimish* warmth of reality."
—*The New York Times*

"Brilliantly etched and unforgettable."
—JAMES ELLROY

"Rich in mood and color . . . Touching as well as taut with suspense."
—*The Cleveland Plain Dealer*

GRIEVOUS SIN

A Peter Decker/Rina Lazarus Mystery

Faye Kellerman

FAWCETT GOLD MEDAL • NEW YORK

A Fawcett Gold Medal Book
Published by Ballantine Books
Copyright © 1993 by Faye Kellerman

Library of Congress Catalog Card Number: 93-12344

ISBN 0-449-14839-4

This edition published by arrangement with William Morrow and Company, Inc.

Manufactured in the United States of America

First Ballantine Books Edition: September 1994

10 9 8 7 6 5 4 3

For Jonathan
For the Three Musketeers—Jess, Rachel, and Ilana
And for my D'Artagnan—Aliza Celeste

Special thanks to Dr. Lawrence Platt
and Dr. Irwin Frankel.

ONE

HER FIRST SOUND WAS MORE BLEAT THAN WAIL, BUT SHE had ten fingers and ten toes, and that was all Decker cared about. Wrinkled and red, her skin covered with something akin to cold cream, she seemed perturbed by the world rather than scared by it. Decker watched as Georgina, the labor nurse, scooped his daughter from the obstetrician's arms into her own. After rubbing the infant with a towel and giving her a quick exam, the nurse swaddled her in a blanket. The baby was finally presented to Papa for inspection.

She had a mottled face, her nose scrunching as she beeped rather than cried. Her eyes were closed, lids as thin as onionskin. Downy fuzz covered her scalp. Decker took a gloved index finger and placed it on a tiny palm. Slowly, soft pink digits encircled his finger. It brought tears to his eyes.

"Is she okay?" Rina's voice was anxious.

"She's perfect, darlin'," Decker answered. "Just . . . *perfect*."

"Of course she's *perfect*!" Georgina folded thick arms across her bosom. "We only deliver perfect babies here."

Decker shifted his attention from his daughter to his wife. Rina's eyes were red-rimmed, her lips moving in silent prayer. Damp black tresses lay across her forehead. Never had she looked so beautiful.

"She's perfect, Rina." Decker's throat was clogged. "Just like you."

Rina gave him a weak smile, and Decker suddenly became aware of her exhaustion. But he knew such fatigue was normal after childbirth.

"You did *great*, Madame Decker!" Georgina's stubby finger stroked Rina's arm. "Just hang in a little bit more, and then you take that much deserved nap."

"Close your eyes, Rina," Decker said.

She nodded as her lids fell shut. Then she jerked them open and started breathing rapidly.

"Everything okay, Dr. Hendricks?" Decker asked.

"So far," the obstetrician answered. "She's expelling the afterbirth now. The contractions won't go away until she does."

Then Rina stopped panting as suddenly as she'd started. Decker watched Hendricks as he tended to Rina. Most of the doctor's face was hidden behind the surgical mask, but his eyes were visible and clouded with concentration. He placed his palms on her abdomen and pushed down. "Rina, do you feel strong enough to nurse the baby?"

Rina whispered yes. So *frail*.

"That's great, doll," Hendricks said. "Let Nature help us along."

"Help with what?" Decker asked.

The doctor didn't answer. Georgina took the baby from Decker's arms and placed her on Rina's chest. Cradling the infant, Rina watched a little wet mouth bob along her breast until it found the nipple. With a little encouragement, the baby pursed her lips and began to suckle.

Rina closed her eyes again, beads of sweat dotting her brow. At the bedside, Decker dabbed her face with a washcloth. He glanced around the labor room, taking in the surroundings for the first time. The place was papered in a chintz print—some sort of small vining flower. A hand-loomed rug had been thrown over an institutional tiled floor. The hospital bed was framed in wood, stained to match the wicker of a Sydney Greenstreet chair planted across the room. The homey decor was supposed to give the illusion that the woman was giving birth in her bedroom. But Decker couldn't block out all the medical machinery standing idle against the wall, the I.V. stand tucked into the left-hand corner.

Definitely a hospital.

He had been there for nineteen hours that had somehow been compressed into minutes. Now time was moving in slo-mo. The hands of the wall clock showed him only ten minutes had passed since his daughter had been born. The baby was still sucking on Rina's breast, but her eyes were closed—nursing in her sleep. Pink heart-shaped lips working Mama's nipple as thread-sized veins pulsed in her temple. Decker knew he was biased, but she *was* a beautiful baby.

His eyes drifted to Rina's face. Her lips were pale and parched.

"Can Rina have something to drink?" he asked.

"Not quite yet," Hendricks said, talking under his mask. Once more he pressed on Rina's stomach.

"Can she at least suck on some ice?"

This time the doctor didn't answer. Decker felt a headache coming on. Maybe he was just hungry—ten hours since he'd last eaten. Again Rina went into her Lamaze breathing. Decker held her hand, offered words of encouragement. Before the arrival of the doctor, he'd felt particularly needed. Now he was an appendage—useful but not indispensable. Rina stopped her labored breathing and wearily closed her eyes. Her voice was a whisper.

"I'm very tired."

"I bet you are," Hendricks said. "How about we give you a rest? Georgina, put the baby in the incubator and wheel her into Infant Recovery." He looked at Decker, and smile lines appeared at the corners of his eyes. "You've got a beautiful, healthy daughter, folks. She shouldn't be in Recovery more than an hour or so. Then they'll move her to the nursery and you'll be able to show her off to the family."

"That'd be nice," said Decker, smiling.

"Grandparents all excited?" Hendricks asked.

"Yeah, they haven't held a newborn in a while."

Neither had he, he thought. *Nineteen* years. My God, it seemed like yesterday since Cindy was born. And then, sometimes, it seemed like a thousand years. Georgina loaded the baby in the incubator. "Be back in a minute."

Decker nodded, and the room turned quiet. Rina's eyes were closed, her mouth slightly agape. Decker wanted to tell her how much he loved her, but he didn't want to disturb her rest. A few minutes later, Georgina returned. She placed a hand on Decker's shoulder.

"How're you holding up, Pop?"

"Not too bad for an old guy," Decker said. "Mom's resting."

"Yeah, she needs some peace and quiet."

Hendricks said, "Georgina, set up a twenty-milligram Pitocin drip, please."

Anxiously, Decker looked up at the labor nurse. She flashed him a smile of crooked teeth, but the expression wasn't cheery. Then she liberated the metal stand from the corner and opened a cabinet door. Out came a plastic bottle that hung on a rack. Georgina hooked the I.V. line up to Rina's left arm, then adjusted some valves. A moment later, Decker saw clear liquid run through plastic tubing. Again the doctor pushed on Rina's abdomen. A soft moan escaped from her lips as she attempted to control her breathing. But fatigue was taking its toll. She cried out. Decker looked at Hendricks.

"I'm pushing with some pressure," the OB said calmly. "It doesn't feel comfortable, but it should help Mom along. Georgina, increase the rate of the drip."

"Right away, Doctor."

Decker didn't like the military cadence in the labor nurse's voice. It had gone from jocular to professional. He felt his heart race.

"Is everything okay, Doctor?"

"She's having a bit of trouble expelling the placenta."

Hendricks paused. "I can feel it, but . . . the Pitocin should help. Does it hurt, honey?"

Again Rina nodded.

"Honey, I need to keep pressing on your uterus. Just keep on with your Lamaze breathing." He turned to Decker. "Just help her like you did in labor."

The doctor compressed her stomach wall. Rina's face contorted with pain.

"Try to breathe, Rina," Hendricks said.

"I can't—"

"Breathe, Rina," Decker said. "Squeeze my hand if it hurts."

Rina took his hand. Her fingers held no strength, and her complexion had become wan. Hendricks clucked his tongue and shook his head. Decker felt his stomach drop.

"Georgina, get a gurney and see who's available for OB Anesthesiology," Hendricks said. "Also, get me point two-five milligrams of Methergine and a BP cuff."

"What's going on, Doc?" Decker said.

Hendricks ignored him.

"What's going *on*?" Decker repeated.

"In a moment, Peter."

Decker was silent, his gut a tight, wet knot. His body ached with tension. He forced himself to rotate his head, releasing a symphony of creaks and pops from his neck. Georgina returned, carrying a metal tray with a needle on it. Hendricks took the syringe and injected the medicine into Rina's shoulder. She didn't even wince.

"I love you, Rina," Decker whispered.

A nod was her answer.

A petite woman in scrubs entered the room, a gurney in tow. Hendricks pushed the gurney until it abutted Rina's bedside.

"I'm going to move you to a delivery room, Rina," Hendricks said. "At the count of three, I want you to slide your backside onto the gurney. Think you can do that?"

Rina moaned a yes.

On three, Rina raised her body as Hendricks and Georgina lifted her onto cold, brushed metal. Up went the side rails, Georgina locking them into place. The flaps of Rina's hospital gown had unfolded, exposing her breasts. Decker drew them back together and wiped Rina's forehead with the washcloth.

"Peter, I want to keep a close eye on Rina until she delivers the afterbirth," Hendricks said. "It may take a while. At this point, it's no emergency. But she is bleeding a tad more than I'd like to see. I'm sorry, but you won't be able to be with her now. Don't worry. And get some rest."

"Why can't I come with her?" Decker said. "I'm already suited up—"

"No, I'm going to have to insist you remain here." Hendricks's voice was firm and taut. "Georgina, could you please escort Sergeant Decker back to the waiting room."

Before Decker could get words up from his throat, Rina was whisked away. He felt a sudden chill and shuddered. Pressure on his elbow—Georgina's hand.

"This way, Sergeant."

"Why . . . why is he—"

"Just like he said, Sergeant. He feels safer if she's in a delivery room—"

"You mean an operating room."

"Whatever."

"*Why* is he taking her there? Can't he deliver a placenta here?"

"It's a precaution."

"Precaution for *what*?" Decker shouted.

"Sergeant, would you like to come this way, please?"

"No, I would *not* like to come this way, please! I'd like to know what the *hell* is happening with my wife!"

Georgina said, "Sergeant, you know as much as I do."

"Aw c'mon, lady, you work here. Surely, you have some inside *dope*!"

Georgina was quiet. Decker began to pace.

"I'm sorry."

"It's fine, Sergeant. I understand."

Decker trod the floor. "He said something about her bleeding. Does he mean *bleeding*? Or does he mean *hemorrhaging*?"

"Sergeant, I don't know."

The room became still. Decker covered his mouth and blew out air. His eyes began to burn, and he rubbed them vigorously. Georgina managed a tepid smile and placed a fleshy hand on his shoulder.

"Come."

Decker remained rooted. "When will I know what's going on?"

"Sergeant, I'm sure the doctor will speak to you just as soon as he can. These changes in plans happen all the time. It's usually nothing."

Decker bit his thumbnail. "You know, in my profession, I give that kind of bull . . . that kind of line all the time. I see a distraught parent whose kid is missing. I say, 'Hey, it happens all the time. Usually, it's nothing.' But sometimes, it's something."

Georgina didn't answer.

"Right?" Decker raised his voice. "Sometimes it is something, isn't it?"

Georgina lowered her eyes, then looked up. "Yes, sometimes it is something, Sergeant."

"Well, if it would be something, what . . ." Decker cleared his voice. "What could it be?"

"Sergeant, I'm just not qualified to diagnose your wife's condition."

Decker was silent.

Georgina sighed. "Sergeant, do you have any family with you?"

Family. Rina's parents. The *boys*. Decker felt his knees go weak. He sank into the Sydney Greenstreet chair and ran his hands down his face. Wordlessly, Georgina handed him a glass of water. He downed the glass too quickly and felt his stomach rock with nausea. His skin felt prickly and gelid. It took him a minute to find his voice.

"They're waiting in the lobby . . . my daughter, Rina's parents . . ." Decker swallowed hard. "Rina's sons, too. What should I tell them?"

"I'll walk you out and talk to them."

Decker shook his head. "No, it'll scare them—the boys. Their father died about four years ago."

"Oh dear, I'm very sorry."

"You can understand why I don't want to alarm them."

"Absolutely. I didn't realize . . ."

Decker stared at his empty glass. "How about a little guidance here?"

Georgina thought a moment. "Be low-key and tell them the truth. That the doctor is still with Rina but just as a precaution. She's having a little trouble expelling the afterbirth." She patted his hand. "I know this is going to sound a little cavalier, but you're getting worked up over nothing, Sergeant."

"What happens if she can't deliver it?" Decker asked.

Georgina frowned. "You're very persistent."

Decker shrugged helplessly.

Georgina sighed. "I shouldn't be telling you this, because I don't know your wife's individual situation—"

"But?"

"But sometimes the placenta has an obnoxious habit of sticking to the uterine wall. Sometimes to get it all out, the doctor has to go in and do a D and C. It's done under anesthesia, and that's probably why Dr. Hendricks wanted an anesthesiologist."

"Oh." Decker felt his shoulders relax a fraction. "A D and C's kind of a routine procedure, isn't it?"

Georgina paused. "I shouldn't be telling you anything. Pretend we didn't have this discussion, okay?"

"All right," Decker blew out air. "Thanks. Really, it helps." He ran his hand through thick ginger hair. "Is there any way you can peek in and—"

"No, Sergeant."

Slowly, Decker rose to his feet. "I'm okay."

"You're sure?"

Decker nodded. Georgina gave him a bear hug.

"Now you go in there and smile. Your wife's in very good hands. You go tell the family the good news about your new little daughter."

His new little daughter. Decker had forgotten about her.

Two

SIX PAIRS OF BEAMING EYES GREETED HIM. EVEN ACROSS
the third-floor lobby, Decker could see their excitement and
expectation. It was all he could do to keep from gagging,
but that was probably him. Worried over nothing. But now
he had to think of the boys. Not to mention Rina's parents,
who had already gone through hell fifty years ago. No need
to set everyone in a panic over a little medical problem.

He took a deep breath, ran his hand along the surgical
blue pants, and put on the smile. To make it genuine, he
thought about his new little daughter. He did a slow lope
across the waiting room, dodging couches and chairs upholstered in houndstooth wool and coffee tables sprouting
Styrofoam cups. The room held a few lone souls reading
paperbacks and checking their watches as well as one other
small grouping similar to his own clan—a family expecting
to hear news soon. He approached his entourage.

"Well?" his mother-in-law asked.

Her "Well" came out *"Vell."* The Eliases were Hungarian. Stefan was strong and squat in contrast to Madga, who
was lean. Her dress and accent reminded Decker of a dark-
haired Zsa Zsa Gabor.

"A healthy little girl," he announced.

"Ah, Akiva, *mazel tov!*" She stood on her tiptoes and
kissed his cheek. "Boys, you have a new little *sister!*"

And for a moment, Decker did feel good, caught up in the hugging and well-wishing. Sammy pumped his hand and said that a sister wasn't the bar mitzvah present he had in mind. Jake whooped like a crane. Cindy simply slapped his back and told him "Way to go!"

It was Marge who held back. When he caught her eye, she smiled and winked at him, but Decker could feel her studying his expression. She *knew*: the way it is with partners. Quickly, he held a finger in the air—a sign to her not to push it. She understood.

"And how is my little Ginny?" Stefan asked. "When do we see her?"

His little Ginny, Decker thought. The Eliases called Rina by her English name, Regina. Ginny for short.

His little Ginny. His little daughter!

Remain calm, Deck.

"Akiva?" Magda asked. "Everything is okay, yes?"

Decker bit his lip. Damn it, he couldn't keep the anxiety in check. Cut to the chase.

"Well, Magda, she has a teeny problem. She's still with the doctor."

Magda brought her hand to her chest and fired out a series of foreign sentences that sounded like questions.

"Magda, I don't understand Hungarian," Decker said.

Stefan said, "What do you mean, a problem?"

"She's having a little trouble expelling the afterbirth. I'm sure it's noth—"

"But she's okay, no?" Magda interrupted. "Where is she?"

"With the doc—"

"How long will she be with him?" Magda said.

"I don't know, Magda," Decker said. "The doctor didn't tell me. So why don't we sit down and relax while we wait."

"There's no one we can talk to, Akiva?" Magda said.

Decker glanced at his stepsons, then shot a meaningful look at his mother-in-law. Though upset, Magda took a deep breath and smiled at the boys. Then she placed her hand over her mouth—as if her fist would muzzle her apprehension.

Decker winked at his stepsons and received scared expressions. He knew he should say something reassuring, but he was afraid that the words might sound hollow. Instead, he took a position on the arm of the couch, drawing Sammy under the wing of his right arm.

Magda paused, then perched herself on the edge of the sofa. She brushed imaginary specks off black wool pants and camel jacket. Rina had inherited her mother's coloring—the dark hair and light eyes—but Magda was thinner, bonier, than her daughter. Stefan cuddled Jake next to his muscular chest. He was dressed in a gray shirt that matched his hair, and black pants. On his feet were orthopedic shoes. Something new, Decker realized. Cindy stood behind him and placed a hand on his shoulder. Decker turned around and gave her a weak smile. At nineteen, his daughter had turned into a young woman—tall, with radiance in her expressive brown eyes. Her face had lost its adolescent roundness and now had the bone structure of a newly crowned adult along with a tan from the summer sun.

Magda blurted, "Does doctor say this is a big problem?"

Decker said, "No, he was pretty casual about it. Just wanted to watch her as a precaution."

Hell if he'd tell his mother-in-law about her daughter bleeding a *tad* more than Hendricks liked. And it *was* probably no big deal. Decker remembered his first wife having a D and C after the birth of their second child. Jan had been just fine. Unfortunately, the baby had been stillborn—a boy. Morbid, unwanted thoughts began to invade Decker's brainspace. He tried to shake off the nightmarish memory.

"But she's all right, my Ginny?" Stefan said.

"I'm sure she's fine."

"They didn't want you with her, Akiva?" Magda asked.

"No . . ." Decker hesitated. "No, they wouldn't let me stay with her. But everything'll work out. It always does."

The group was silent.

"Where is she now?" Stefan asked.

"They took her into a delivery room."

"But she delivered okay?" Magda said.

"Like a trouper." Decker stood. "Doc just wanted to watch her."

"That's what you're paying him for, Pete," Marge said.

Decker stared at his partner—the voice of reason. But he didn't feel rational. He stood and rocked on his feet. "It happened so fast. One minute she delivered a gorgeous little girl . . . the next . . ." He caught himself. "It's just a precaution. Don't worry." Again he tried a smile for the boys. "Hey, your mom's an iron woman."

"The doctor looked worried?" Magda said.

"Just concerned."

"But not worried?" Magda said.

"Maybe a little worried."

"But not a *lot* worried," Magda said.

"A little, a lot," Stefan said. "Magda, you're driving everyone crazy."

"I want to *know*." Magda began to chide her husband in Hungarian, then stopped herself. "I worry." She smiled at her grandsons. "You know your *omah* is a worrier. I worry about everything."

Decker took his mother-in-law's hand and gave it a gentle squeeze.

"Why is she still with the doctor?" Magda asked.

"Magda, I honestly don't know," Decker said. "They kicked me out."

"Is she going to be all right, Dad?"

Decker regarded Sammy—an adolescent face with eyes that held a child's fear. As Decker searched for the right explanation, his father-in-law picked up the slack.

"Sure, she'll be fine, Shmuli," Stefan said. "Your *eema*'s a strong girl. You want something to eat?"

Sammy shook his head.

"Nu, and you, Yonkel?"

"No, thanks, *Opah*."

With resolution, Stefan slapped his hands onto the pillow cushions and hoisted himself upward. "Then we go to the gift shop." He checked his pockets. "Buy some comic books maybe. Something nice for *Eema*'s room. Come on, boys. Do you have a twenty, Magda?"

"It's okay, *Opah*," Sammy said. "I'll just stay here."

"No, you come with me, Shmuli," Stefan said. "I don't know what comic book you like. Only the cat who eats lasagna."

"Garfield," Cindy said.

"Yes, Garfield. And who is the other? With the tiger?"

"Calvin and Hobbes," Jake answered.

"Calvin and Hobbes," Stefan repeated. "You come, too, Yonkel."

Slowly, the boys got up and walked over to their grandfather's side. He tousled the boys' hair above the napes of their necks, careful to avoid knocking off their new leather yarmulkes. Jake leaned into his grandfather's side, but Sammy kept his distance. Hands in his pockets, eyes cast on the floor. Decker felt the onslaught of parental failure, disgusted that he couldn't put aside his own nervousness to comfort his son.

"Thanks, Stefan," Decker said.

Stefan patted Decker's back softly. "You just like my wife, you worry. You think you hide it, but I can tell. I just talked to God. He tells me she'll be fine. So relax, nu?"

Decker marveled at how well the old man coped. Was it a skill he picked up because he survived the camps, or did he survive the camps because he had the skill? Decker sometimes wondered how he would have done if he'd been forced to live through the torture. Probably would have fallen apart, if the present was any indication.

"You go down to the gift shop with your *opah*, boys. I'm going to try to find out what's going on."

Marge said, "Let me ask—"

"No, I'll ask—"

"Pete—"

"Marge, let me handle it my way."

"I'll come with you."

"That's not neces—"

"C'mon, Pete. Let's go."

"Marge, maybe you should stay with Magda."

"No, you go ahead with her, Akiva." Magda stood and brushed off her pants. "When Stefan says God say she'll be okay, she'll be okay. Cindy and I maybe go see the baby."

Cindy's face suddenly became animated. It was wonderful to see her spontaneous burst of joy. It reminded Decker that this was supposed to be a happy occasion. "Can we really see the baby?"

"I don't know, Cindy." Magda hooked her arm around Cindy. "We find out."

"You can't go behind the double doors," a middle-aged woman in a white uniform told them. "I'm sorry. Staff only."

Marge took out her badge. "Police, ma'am."

The woman backed away. "Oh . . . okay. I thought . . ."

Decker didn't give her a chance to fill in the blank. He took off down the long corridors and didn't stop until it dawned on him that he didn't know where he was.

"Is this Maternity, Pete?"

"I don't know." He grabbed his head. "God, I don't know what the fuck I'm doing. I'm freaking myself out."

"When was the last time you ate?"

"Margie, my stomach feels like vinegar." He bit on the ends of his mustache. "They took her into a delivery room."

"We can't exactly waltz into delivery rooms making inquiries, Pete."

"That wasn't my *intention*, Marge."

"I know. I didn't mean to sound snide." Marge stopped a young kid in scrubs and asked for directions to Maternity. Down the hall to the right.

Decker left without thanking the kid, forcing Marge to trot just to keep up with him. But Decker knew she was smart enough not to say anything about his behavior. The woman had picked up some salient points after working with him for six years. Decker found the set of double doors leading to the labor rooms and went inside. The flooring had gone from carpet to linoleum with geometrical designs, and felt cold under his paper-muled feet. Still gowned up, for all the nurses knew he might have been an expectant father on a coffee break instead of an interloper.

The nurses' reception area was empty, except for a woman in blue scrubs in the back office talking to someone holding a broomstick—either a janitor or a witch. The corridor was devoid of people, which surprised him. When he'd brought Rina in, the hallway had been well populated. But that was during the daytime. It was almost nine, and most of the ancillary staff went home by five. The nighttime floor nurses must be occupied with women in labor.

Next to the nurses' station was a lab room, its counters stocked with scopes, slides, and vials. A large industrial sink was mounted on the wall—stainless steel with a deep bowl like the ones at the morgue. The recollection made him shudder. Past the lab, down the hallway began a series of doors leading to the labor rooms. He peeked through one of the windows, feeling a little voyeuristic, and saw a woman, her bloated belly hooked up to machines, face contorted in pain. Through the closed door, he could hear panting, then an agonizing moan.

Stretches of empty pale pink corridor, the smell of antiseptics, hallways echoing feral growls—a real house of horrors. Maybe this was a nightmare. He was going to wake up any minute and find Rina safe, asleep at his side. A tap on his shoulder made him jump, reminded him this was all too real.

Georgina—her eyes on Marge.

"Excuse me, miss, but this is a restricted area."

"I'm just accompanying Sergeant Decker. He's wondering what's going on with his wife."

"I'll be happy to help Sergeant Decker," Georgina said. "Would you like directions out of here? It can be a maze."

Marge nodded. Georgina directed her down the hallway and told her to follow the Exit signs. They'd lead her back to the lobby. Marge thanked her, threw Decker a sympathetic look, turned, and walked away.

Decker managed a sidelong glance at Georgina, feeling

assertive and sheepish at the same time. "I was just wondering . . ."

Georgina took his arm. "Let's go talk somewhere else. Hallways aren't conducive to conversation."

She took him inside the nurses' station, giving him a seat at the front desk. The woman in the blue scrubs and the woman with the broomstick were still deep in conversation. There was a series of numbered monitors against the back wall, each one making audible beeps at different tempos. At least the pitch was the same. Hanging on the right wall was a blackboard with the labor rooms' numbers, the name of the patient, doctor, and any specifics. Decker found Rina's number. After her name was DELIVERED, then the letters OR along with the names of three doctors.

"She's still in the operating room?" Decker asked.

"Yes, she's being operated on," Georgina said flatly. "I don't know the nature or the extent of the procedure. All I know is they called in a couple of scrub nurses and an anesthesiologist. I'll let you know more—"

"Are they doing a D and C?"

"I don't know exactly—"

"Is she still bleeding?"

Georgina gave that all-too-telling pause. "I'm sure everything's being done to control her situation."

"Is she in imminent *danger*?"

"She's in good hands—"

"That's not what I *asked* you." Decker stood, then felt his knees buckle. "God, I'm going to be sick."

Georgina helped him back into the chair. She heard a high-pitched continuous beep and turned to one of the monitors. "I have to check on someone. You just sit there, okay? I'll be back in a few minutes."

Decker nodded. Head down, he watched spots of light dance on his lap. He raised his chin, felt his head swim. Catching sight of something in blue paper garb marching down the corridor, he leapt up and caught her by the arm. The woman immediately backed away. Her head was still covered by a cap, but her face mask dangled by strings

around her neck like an undersized bib. Her name tag said
DR. WALLACE.

"Are you with my wife?" Decker whispered.

The woman looked at her arm still in Decker's clutches.
"Who's your wife?"

"Rina Decker."

"Yes, as a matter of fact, I am."

Decker released the woman's arm. "My God, I'm sorry."

"It's okay, Mr. Decker, I understand."

Decker regarded her eyes—intense and purposeful, but
not the kind of eyes that were about to deliver tragic news.
Man, he'd seen *that* look before.

"Your wife is being operated on—"

"I know that. How is she?"

"She's holding, but she's lost some blood, Mr. Decker.
We already gave her a pint of her own blood. She was
smart enough to donate autologously before she went into
labor. But she's going to need more—another couple of
pints. Before we start with the banks, we were hoping she
might have a blood relative who can donate. Matched relatives are always your best bet for good takes on transfu-
sions."

"Her parents are here."

"Then let's go test them."

Decker started to walk, but stumbled. This time it was
Dr. Wallace who caught his arm. "Do you need to sit?"

"No." Decker cursed his weakness and commanded his
legs to be steady. "She has her sons out there. I don't want
to scare them."

"Frankly, this could scare them."

"It's *bad*?"

"Don't panic, Mr. Decker, I just don't have anything definitive to tell you right now. Uncertainty is very scary for
little kids. For you, too. But Dr. Hendricks is the best. And
he's as cool as a cucumber, in total *control*."

Decker felt his throat clog. He picked up his pace, trying
to keep step with Dr. Wallace. "What should I do about my
boys? They're perceptive."

"How about if I talk to the parents, and you occupy your boys?"

"They're going to want to know what's going on. What do I say?" Decker ran his hands over his face. "God, I can't believe . . ."

"She's in very good hands."

"If I hear that one more time, I'm going to throw up! How *serious* is her condition?"

"It's serious."

"Life-threatening?"

"It's serious. Let's leave it at that for now."

"God, this is just a *nightmare*." He heard his voice crack. "Is this unusual?"

"Not as unusual as you might think."

They had reached the lobby. As luck would have it, the group was all there. Stefan had returned with the boys from the gift shop. Cindy and Magda were deep in conversation. Marge was leaning against the wall next to the complimentary coffeepot. She was the first to notice and pointed the others in his direction. Again he was met with expectant faces. But this time there were no smiles. Decker took Dr. Wallace over to the group.

"She need . . ." Again his throat swelled. "She could use some blood from a relative."

Slowly, Rina's parents rose. "Where do we go?" Stefan asked calmly.

"Come, I'll take you," Dr. Wallace said.

Sammy spoke up. "I want to come."

Dr. Wallace said, "You have to be seventeen to donate blood."

"I *am* seventeen," Sammy persisted. "I'm small for my age. I already have a complex. Don't make it worse."

"I want to come, too," Jake piped in.

"Boys, just stay here," Decker said weakly.

Sammy yelled, "I want to help my mother, damn it!"

Decker was taken aback by the force of Sammy's voice. Magda took him under the crook of her arm. "He can come with us, no?"

Dr. Wallace sighed. "You seem big enough. Won't hurt to give you a pinprick." She looked at Cindy.

Decker said, "She's my daughter . . . Rina's stepdaughter . . . not a blood relative."

Dr. Wallace said, "So you'll watch your pop for me?"

Cindy nodded.

"Come along. Let's go help your mom." Dr. Wallace started her speed walk. In the distance, Decker heard her ask what the boys' names were. He couldn't hear if they answered her. Either they were too far away or their voices were too weak.

Slowly, Decker lowered himself onto the couch. Marge sat at his right, Cindy at his left. She held his arm and kissed his bicep. Decker turned to her and tried out a smile.

"It'll be okay, Dad," she said. "Do you need anything?"

His initial reaction was nothing, but then he gave the matter some thought. "Princess, would you mind getting me something to eat? I think there's a vending machine with fruit on the first floor. How about an apple and a banana?"

"Got it." Cindy stood. "Do you want anything, Marge?"

"An apple sounds great."

"On the double."

Cindy did a jog to the elevator. When she was out of sight, Decker slumped back on the couch and closed his eyes.

"Do you want some coffee, Pete?" Marge asked.

"Nothing, thanks."

"What did the doctor say?"

"It's serious, Margie . . . I'm scared."

He swabbed his wet cheeks with his fingers. She hugged his shoulder but didn't speak. Decker was grateful for the silence.

THREE

IT WASN'T AS IF SHE WAS NARCISSISTIC OR ANYTHING AS PSY-chologically disturbed as that. It was just that hers was a body worth looking at. Like admiring a work of art.

Because that was what she was—a work of art.

Stripped down naked, sweat glistening from smooth, bronzed skin, she regarded herself in the mirror. Perfect round, pronounced breasts because of the developed pecs underneath. The just rewards of really *hard* work. She'd gained shape without gaining an ounce of fat. She patted her flat abdomen, did a couple of arm rolls, then ran through a couple of poses—all sleek, defined muscle.

Definitely, she had developed the definition—the *cut*!

She swiped her damp body with a thick white Turkish towel, then wrapped it around her trunk, eyes never leaving the mirror. Short wisps of downy-fine facial hair ran down her cheek parallel to her ear—peach-fuzz sideburns. It went with the territory. At least it was blond. Good thing, because her coloring was naturally dark.

She unclipped her hair, and black satin fell to her shoulders.

Exotic. That's what everyone had said about her. She was exotic-looking.

Again she studied her reflection in the silver glass.

In only two years, she had turned from a nothing into a

something. From a tall, shapeless form to a Greek sculpture. But she was so much *more* than just a perfect body. With the discipline had come the control—*real* control. Not the artificial kind that comes when the mind is altered by chemicals. Drugs that hide but don't cure. Now *she* was in control. Her mind was as disciplined as an army general's, as meticulously organized as a dictionary. She was master of her destiny. There was nothing she couldn't conquer, nothing she couldn't overcome.

Best of all, the voices had stopped.

The door opened and closed. In the mirror, she saw him coming at her. This time it was Eric. He was naked, his biceps like veined footballs. He duck-walked to her, his thighs so buffed they had rubbed the inner skin raw.

She didn't bother to turn around, just dropped on all fours.

He stood behind her, then dropped to his knees and slapped her rear.

"Are you ready for it, babe?"

"Ready, willing, and able."

"You really want it?"

"I really want it."

"Say it again."

"I really *want* it!"

"Say it with *conviction*!" Again Eric slapped her ass, his leathery hand stinging her hide. "I want to hear *conviction*!"

She smiled. She liked Eric. He was gentle.

"I said I really, really *want* it!"

"Get *mean*, Tandy! I want to hear *mean*!"

"I really, really *want* it! Give it to me *now*, or I'll blow your toes off!"

Eric laughed. "Blow my toes off?"

"One! At! A! Time!" she yelled. "*Give* it to me, Eric!"

"I can't *hear* you!"

"Give it to me *now*!"

"Still can't hear you!"

"Give it to me!" she screamed, feeling the heat in her face.

"Still, still can't hear you!"

"GIVE IT TO ME, DAMN IT! GIVE IT TO ME, *NOW*!"

"*Atta* girl, babe! Now that's *conviction*!"

She closed her eyes, then held her breath until she felt the quick thrust of the needle in her butt. Slowly, she blew out air, feeling the surge in her body.

In control.

She grinned.

Life was good!

FOUR

IT TASTED LIKE WET SAND. DECKER DIDN'T KNOW IF IT WAS the apple itself or his taste buds, but he ate it just to be polite. Cindy was worried about him, so he wanted to exhibit some normal behavior. As if doing routine things might suddenly turn the ordeal into something routine. His daughter and partner watched him chew. He became aware of the workings of his jaw, and it made his teeth hurt. He swallowed dryly and took his daughter's hand.

"Thanks, princess."

Marge stood. "You sit. I'll get you some coffee."

Decker nodded. Passivity was a role he seldom played, but he couldn't summon enough strength to think on his own.

"This is the worst part, Daddy. The waiting." Cindy hesitated a beat. "Maybe I should check to see if the baby's been assigned to a nursery yet?"

"That would be great."

"I'll be back in a minute."

"Thanks, sweetheart."

Marge came back with the coffee.

"She's a good kid, your daughter."

"The best."

"How was it having her for the summer?"

"Terrific. I think being needed has done wonders for her self-confidence. She's been an enormous help to Rina these past couple of weeks ... drove the boys all around. I'll be sorry to see her leave."

"How did she like her first year away?"

"She liked Columbia enough to go back. I think she enjoyed herself."

"The typical college experience, huh?"

"Yeah, complete with bouts of exhilaration and depression—usually one right after the other."

"Does she have a major?"

"Not yet. But she mentioned something about criminal sciences or whatever they call it back there."

"Wonder where that came from?"

"As long as it's not direct fieldwork, I'm all for it."

"Sexist."

"Parentist. I wouldn't want my boys to be cops, either." He ran his hand over his face. "God, this is just *hell*! What's keeping the others? How much blood could Rina possibly need? Maybe I should look for them."

He started to rise, but Marge pushed him back.

"Don't spin your wheels, Pete. Stay here in case someone has some news for you."

"I can't believe this is happening." Decker's stomach juices were an ocean of nausea. "What's taking them so goddamn long?"

He bounced up and began to pace. Marge didn't try to stop him. At loose ends herself, she picked up a hospital magazine on parenting and absently flipped through the pages. All these pictures of smiling parents holding their newborn tykes. It made her feel very old and very single. She read an article on infant jaundice, learned more about the liver and bilirubin then she ever wanted to know. She had just about read the periodical cover to cover when Cindy returned, sporting a wide grin. Pete didn't even notice her. Too busy flattening the carpet nap.

"What's up, kiddo?" Marge asked.

"God, she's huge!"

Decker stared at Cindy. It took him a moment to realize where he was. "Who's huge?"

"Your daughter, Daddy. She's at least twice the size of any of the other kids in the nursery. And she's definitely the most *alert*—eyes wide open. You want to see her?"

"Now that sounds like a good idea," Marge said.

Decker shook his head. "I don't want the others to come back and find me gone."

"So I'll wait here," Marge said.

Decker shook his head. "I just can't . . . not now. Not . . . feeling the way I do."

"I understand, Daddy. I just wanted you to know how great she's doing."

Decker felt tears in his eyes and rubbed them away. "Thank you, princess. I appreciate it."

Cindy stuck her hands in the back pockets of her jeans. "You want to see her, Marge? She's in Nursery J."

"I think I should wait with your dad."

"No, go ahead, Marge," Decker said. "Tell me she's beautiful."

"She *is* beautiful," Cindy said.

"No, Pete, I'll wait with you," Marge said. "Watch you run a track in the carpet."

"It's better than punching out walls," Decker said.

"Infinitely," Marge said.

Cindy tapped her foot. "Well, if I'm not needed, maybe I'll go back and visit the baby again. If the nurse'll let me near her. She's real *weird*!"

"In what way?" Marge asked.

"Actually, it was sort of my fault. I was so excited to see the baby. She's right in the front of the window. I was playing with her, tapping on the glass. Then all of a sudden she started crying . . . all alone." Cindy pouted. "So I went inside the nursery and asked if like, maybe someone could pick her up. For no reason, the nurse started *screaming* at me that she wasn't anyone's personal nanny, and if I didn't leave instantly, I was going to infect all the babies. She made me feel like Typhoid Cindy. I wasn't even *near* them!"

"Nurses sometimes get a little territorial," Marge said.

"Yeah, you should have heard her rant when I asked if *I* could hold my sister. She started *interrogating* me: Just who was I, and what was my business with the baby anyway?"

"They have to be cautious, Cindy."

"Yeah, I know. That's why I figured if Dad came and said I was okay . . ." Cindy shrugged. "It's not the right time. I'll just go back and play with her through the window . . . if *Marie* doesn't boot me away."

"Marie's the nurse?"

"Ms. Prune Face in white."

Decker came over to them. "Ms. Prune Face in white?"

Cindy said, "The nurse who gave me a hard time about holding my sister."

"What?" Decker said. "When was this?"

"Just a moment ago."

"Why'd she give you a hard time?"

"Because she's a weirdo."

Marge said, "Cindy went into the nursery without being suited up. The nurse might have overreacted a little."

"I wasn't in the actual part where the babies were."

"Cindy, please don't make waves," Decker said. "Not now, hon, okay?"

Cindy nodded and kissed her father's cheek. "You really should see your new daughter, Daddy. She's beautiful—all pink and bundled. And she has a loud, healthy cry. I could hear it through the window."

"Wonderful," Marge muttered.

"Keep an eye on her for me," Decker said. "Just . . ."

"I know," Cindy said. "I'll keep it muzzled until we're all back to normal. I can swim with that."

Magda was carrying an armload of cellophane-wrapped snacks. Sammy was sandwiched between his brother and grandfather, his head resting against the old man's side. Stefan had his arm around Sam's waist. Sam's complexion was pasty; his gait was slow and clumsy. Decker ran over and swooped the boy in his arms.

"Good Lord, what's wrong?"

"I *alone* gave blood," Sammy whispered. "That's because I'm a manly, manly man."

Decker smiled. Since his bar mitzvah, whenever there was a task requiring some physical strength, Sammy would always volunteer to do it, claiming that now he was a manly man. Decker placed his stepson on the couch.

"If you're Dracula, I already gave at the office," Sammy said.

"Very funny." Decker brushed chestnut-colored bangs off the boy's forehead. "What took you so long?"

"They wouldn't let him go for a half hour," Stefan said. "I think they really didn't believe he was seventeen."

"He isn't seventeen!" Decker heard the raw anxiety in his voice. "Why'd you let him do it?"

"They had no choice," Sammy said. "I insisted."

"Nu, the boy has a mind of his own," Stefan said.

"He needs to eat things with sugar, Akiva," said Magda. "He don't drink. Tell him to drink."

Decker propped up his son's head. "Drink, Sammy."

"I'm full."

"Then eat cookie," Magda insisted.

"It's not kosher," Sammy pronounced.

"It's made with vegetable shortening—"

"It doesn't have *hasgacha*."

Decker said, "I don't care if it's made out of pig's feet, Sam, eat the damn cookie! Got it?"

"Yes, sir." Sammy took the cookie and began to nibble on the edge. His face had suddenly regained a smidgen of color, and he seemed calm. Decker wondered if his sudden stern command had given the kid a sense that he was in control.

Stefan said, "We buy a pack of cards. Jake and I play poker. You want me to deal you in a round?"

"No thanks, Stefan," Decker said.

"Then just we two play." The old man looked at Jake. "What do we use for betting, Yonkie? I have box of Raisinettes."

"Raisinettes are fine, *Opah*," Jake answered back.

Magda said, "You don't hear anything, Akiva?"

Decker shook his head.

"Where's Cindy?"

"She went to visit the baby," Marge said.

"The baby's in the nursery?" Magda said.

"Yeah. Would you like me to take you there?"

"That would be nice."

Marge smiled to herself. Mrs. Elias's words came out *Tat vood be nice*. Her accent, along with the coiffed blue-black hair, heavy gold rings, and expensive clothes, suggested something untouchable. Perhaps under other circumstances, the woman would be aloof. But now she exuded an unmistakable warmth.

"Let's go," Marge said.

Magda said, "You feed Sammy, Akiva. Make sure he drinks."

Decker said he would, noticing a gleam in his mother-in-law's eyes. She was excited about the baby, and that was good. But his moment of relative quiescence was cut short by a figure draped in surgical greens coming through the double doors. The man's step was quick and determined. His feet shuffled against the carpet. He threw his hand behind his neck and undid his mask as he walked. Decker recognized Dr. Hendricks and felt his knees buckle. Marge grabbed his arm.

"Sit down, Pete. It's okay. She's okay. I can see it in his eyes."

The doctor was close enough to have heard her and seemed surprised by her confidence. "Yes, she's going to be fine."

The full report was interrupted by a host of *baruch Hashems* and *mazel tovs*, by hugs and tears and words of encouragement. The doctor waited until the excitement died down and then invited them to sit. The formality of his manner made Decker take note.

"What is it?" he asked.

Hendricks said, "Rina lost blood and is still heavily sedated—"

"When can I see her?" Decker broke in.

"When she's out of Recovery. But she's going to be there for a while. I'm going to put her in an ICU until I feel she's strong enough and her blood count is elevated. But I'm extremely pleased. She's doing remarkably, considering." Hendricks looked at Sammy. "Last time I saw you in the flesh, you were six weeks old. I'd say there's been a little growth since then. Maybe not seventeen years' worth . . ."

Sammy smiled. Hendricks placed a hand on the boy's shoulder. "You did a great service for your mother. She has an unusual blood type, and yours was as perfect a match as they come. You always hope your kids'll be there for you, and, my boy, you sure were. You really should be proud of yourself."

The boy looked at his lap and nodded gravely. Hendricks smiled at Jake. "And you've changed a bit, too. Thanks for helping out, too, Jacob."

The younger boy smiled back. Hendricks looked at the clock, then at Mr. and Mrs. Elias. "It's almost ten. Visiting hours are just about over, but I'm sure if you're quick, you can sneak in a peek at that beautiful granddaughter of yours. Then I want you all to go home and relax."

"I can't leave," Decker said.

Hendricks frowned. "I won't press you, Sergeant. I know you're going to want to see Rina as soon as she comes out. But you really should try to rest." To Mrs. Elias he said, "Take the boys home and get some sleep. You're going to need to relieve him in the morning."

"I will, Doctor." Magda paused. "She's really *okay*, my daughter?"

Dr. Hendricks took her hand and held it. "She's really okay."

"We just love her. . . ."

Tears formed in Magda's eyes. Stefan took his wife's hand, squeezed it, then turned to Decker. "You come see your baby, Akiva. Just for a moment."

"Go, Sergeant," Hendricks said. "You could use a little joy."

Slowly, Decker stood and blew out air. He didn't want to go. What he wanted more than anything else was to see Rina. He wanted to hold her hand and kiss her long, slender fingers. He wanted to tell her how much he loved her. He didn't want to be ecstatic while she was suffering. He didn't want to do anything without her. Because *nothing* was as joyous as when they shared the moment *together*. But he decided to go see his daughter anyway. Because a little joy was better than none.

FIVE

CINDY WIGGLED HER FINGERS AT THE PINK BUNDLE WITH the saucer eyes, thinking the witch had purposely put the baby all the way in back. But it didn't matter. Baby Girl Decker was so big and alert, she'd be visible wherever she was. The two layettes that abutted hers belonged to Baby Girl Rodriguez and Spencer Dole. BG Rodriguez was a teeny little thing with a head no bigger than a navel orange.

She had thick black hair and wrinkled skin. Spencer had a fat, squat face and howled constantly. But BG Decker seemed unbothered by her roommates' perplexities, preferring to drool on her paper bedsheet while trying to suck her thumb.

The nursery was a full house tonight—layettes filled with whites, blacks, Hispanics, and one Asian named Baby Boy Yamata who never cried. Rows of innocent babies out of Central Casting. Baby Girl Decker was living in a veritable pint-sized UN. A moment passed, then Baby Girl Jackson, representing the African-American contingent, opened a toothless mouth and let out a silent wail.

Nose to the glass, Cindy made silly faces at her sister, wishing she could hold her, hoping that Nurse Marie Bellson would go off shift and let her alone. The woman was intimidating, lean with knobby, rakelike fingers. Bellson was a deciduous tree in the wintertime—thin and barren. She had a way of making you feel guilty even if you hadn't done anything.

Cindy's eyes moved to the wall clock—visiting hours were almost over. She knew she'd have to leave any minute. As if to prove herself correct, she saw Bellson come out of the nursery. The woman was pure no-nonsense. She wore little makeup, and practical jewelry—a class ring, two gold stud earrings and a gold cross above her uniform breast pocket. She had attractive eyes, though—bright green spotted with brown. They'd be even prettier if they didn't look so angry. Cindy put on her nicest smile.

"One more minute?"

Bellson shook her head. "You're getting too attached to the baby. You're her sister, not her mother." She flicked her wrist. "Visiting hours are officially over. Good night."

Cindy sighed, looked down the hallway, then broke into a grin. "That's my father and my stepmother's family."

Bellson put her hands on her hips and shook her head again. Cindy jogged down the corridor and gave her father a bear hug.

"Rina's okay?"

Decker linked arms with his daughter. "She's out of surgery. Sammy gave her a pint of blood, God bless him."

"But everything's okay?"

"Not out of the woods yet, but I feel a lot better than I did an hour ago."

"You look beat, Dad. You need rest."

Decker knew she was right, but that was immaterial. He wasn't going *anywhere* until he saw Rina. "Are you our personal escort?"

"Absolutely, if Bellson doesn't kick us out. She just told me to leave." Cindy frowned. "Here comes the Wicked Witch of the West now."

A thin woman in white approached them. She had surface wrinkles trailing down the corners of her eyes and mouth and a set of wavy lines across her forehead—the kind of wrinkles that usually come from overtanning, except this woman held a proper Victorian pallor. Her hair was clean, but the color was dingy—pipewater from old plumbing. Her eyes were her saving grace—Kelly green sprinkled with coffee brown. They were clear and perceptive. She wasn't pretty, but she managed to strike an attractive pose. Decker put her age at around forty. She held out her hand, and Decker took it.

"How is your wife, Mr. Decker?" Bellson asked.

"She's still in Recovery."

The RN nodded. "We've got the best post-op care in the country. So try not to worry. I'll let you folks take a quick peek at the baby before I boot you out. Not my idea, but the babies are being transferred from the nurseries to their mothers for the ten o'clock feeding. We don't like outside people in the wings while we're wheeling them down the foyers. Who knows what kind of bugs they're harboring."

Magda said, "We be quick."

"Come." Bellson's walk was brisk. "You're the grandma? You look too young." She stopped at the glass window. "She's all the way in back. I'll put her in front for you."

Cindy watched Bellson disappear behind the nursery doors, amazed by the woman's transformation. From sneers to smiles, she'd become all-accommodating. It made Cindy feel funny. Why was Bellson so mean to her and nice to everyone else? She shrugged. At least Dad was happy. His smile was genuine—first one she'd seen tonight. She went over and leaned her head against his arm. Together, they watched Bellson—who had donned a blue paper gown, gloves, and a face mask—rearrange the layettes until BG Decker was in front. Then the nurse picked her up and gave them a front view of the bundle. Cindy noticed that her father was holding back tears. He'd always been good at damming his emotions. It was one of the reasons why tonight seemed surreal. She had never seen him scared.

She said, "She looks like you, Daddy."

"No, no, no," Magda said, rapping gently on the glass. "She look like Ginny, but she has Akiva's coloring—the red hair and fair skin."

"Poor kid," Decker said. "Another lobster in the sun."

"Suntanning isn't good for you anyway, Daddy," Cindy said. "And if that's not a cheap rationalization . . ."

"Grandma's right," Marge said. "She does look like Rina."

"Of course she does," Magda announced. "I'm good at faces. Nu, Stefan, tell them."

"She's good at the faces," her husband stated.

Decker turned to his sons. "What do you think?"

"I think she's funny-looking," Jake said. "She's all red."

Magda gently hit his arm. "You were red when you were born."

"No, no, no," Stefan said. "Yonkie was never red. Shmuli was red."

Decker regarded his elder stepson, still pale but steady on his feet. He seemed lost, his eyes unfocused. "Are you okay, Sam?"

"Huh?"

Decker put his arm around the boy. "What are you thinking about?"

"I wish I could see *Eema*. You know . . . just *see* her."

"Boy, I know how you feel."

"She'll be okay, won't she?"

"Doc assures me she'll be fine. I believe him, Sammy."

"When do you think you'll see her?"

"I don't know, Sammy. Soon, I hope."

"Will you call us after you see her?"

"Depends on the time." Decker hugged his shoulder gently. "I'm not going to call you at three in the morning."

"No, you *call* us, Akiva," his mother-in-law said. "I don't sleep much tonight anyway. You call us as soon as you see Ginny. I want to know." She wiped her eyes. "Please, you call."

"I'll call."

"Maybe you call Rav Schulman in the morning," Stefan suggested. "Ginny would want you to call him."

Decker nodded, thinking it was a good idea. Over the years, the old rabbi had become more than Decker's teacher, had become even more than a spiritual adviser. More than anything, Rav Schulman had become a wise and treasured friend. Decker could certainly use a little wisdom now. He watched Marie Bellson resettle his daughter back in the layette. To Cindy, he said, "The nurse seems okay."

"To *you*." Cindy shrugged. "Maybe I just rubbed her the wrong way. I didn't mean anything. But sometimes I guess I get a little overexuberant."

"Thanks for your help, Cindy."

"You like your daughter?"

"I like both my daughters."

Cindy stepped on her tiptoes and kissed her father's cheek.

Nurse Bellson came back and placed her hands on her hips. "I'm sorry, but I'm going to have to ask you all to leave. I've *got* to get these babies to their mothers. We don't want any hungry infants."

"Who's going to feed our baby?" Cindy asked.

Decker noticed an immediate narrowing of Bellson's eyes. The expression was subtle and fleeting, but it was strong enough to set his antennae quivering.

"I'm going to feed her *personally* just as soon as I finish wheeling the babies to their mothers," Bellson said.

"Can I feed her?" Cindy asked. "I'll gown up. Please?"

Decker cut in before Bellson could speak. "I think it would be a good idea if Cindy ... I know my wife would like it. If you wouldn't mind, Marie. I don't want to upset any rules, but . . ."

Decker watched Bellson rock on her feet.

"It's unusual," she said.

"I promise I won't get in your way," Cindy said.

"That'd be a first," Bellson muttered under her breath. Then she smiled. "I suppose I could allow it this one time. Go inside the nursery, but don't go past the yellow line. I'll suit you up in a minute."

"Thank you very much, Marie," Decker said. "I appreciate it."

"You're welcome." Marie checked her watch again.

Decker said, "We're leaving. Thanks."

Marge hugged Decker. "Baby is just beautiful, Pete. I'll call you tomorrow."

"Thanks for coming down, Margie. Get some sleep. Some people have to work in the morning."

"Three weeks to go, then it's big time." Marge gave him a quick salute. "See you in Homicide, big guy."

"You *call* us, Akiva, when you see Ginny," Magda reminded him. "I just want you to tell me she's okay."

"I promise, Magda."

Decker knelt and drew his sons near him. "I want you guys to get some sleep. It's been a long, torturous day, and we all need our rest."

They nodded weakly. It was late, and anxiety had sapped their strength.

"Where you go now, Akiva?" Stefan asked.

"Back to the OB lobby. They promised they'd tell me as soon as Rina was out of Recovery. Come on, I'll walk you to the elevators. Cindy, you're staying here, right?"

"Yeah."

"Tell me when you're done feeding the baby. Don't you dare walk to your car by yourself."

"I know, I know—"

"Don't shine me on, Cynthia. I'm serious."

"I promise I'll check in with you."

"Good."

"Daddy?"

"What?"

"Does the baby have a name?"

"I think Rina wanted to wait until we named her in synagogue."

Cindy hesitated. "It just might be nice to call her something. But I don't want to ruin your tradition."

Decker thought a moment. "I think Rina mentioned something about naming her Channa Shoshana—Hannah Rose in English."

Magda erupted into tears. "That was my *mother*'s name. My mother, Channa, and Stefan's mother, Shoshana, *aleichem hashulom*. Gottenu, I hadn't thought about . . ." Again, the flood of tears. "Our other granddaughter was named after *their* side, so this be the first name for my mother." She hugged her husband. "They'd be so *proud*, nu, Stefan."

"Very proud."

Decker spotted Nurse Bellson's impatient eyes. They had narrowed, and only part of the green irises were visible. *Panther eyes.*

"We're holding up the show," he said. "Thank you, Marie. Let's go." He kissed Cindy's cheek. "Bye, princess."

"Bye, Daddy."

Cindy watched them go, her father holding the boys' hands while Magda sobbed on her husband's shoulder. As soon as the group was out of sight, she felt the heat of Bellson's glare. The nurse had her twiggy arms twisted across her chest.

"Well, you engineered that one nicely."

"Can we please be friends?" Cindy asked.

"You don't trust me to feed the baby?"

"Of course, I trust you, Ms. Bellson. I just feel so *sorry* for her, her mom being operated on and everything. My father was a basket case about a half hour ago. She's my sister . . . my first actual sibling. I'm just trying to help."

"You're getting in my way."

"It's unintentional. Honestly."

"Unintentional." Bellson snorted. "Haven't you something better to do with your life than hang around here?"

"I'll be back in school in a week. How's that?"

"Where?"

"In New York. Columbia University, specifically."

"UC system isn't good enough for you?"

"Who can get into UCLA?" Cindy forced herself to smile. "Besides, I'm trying to give my poor mom a break after all these years putting up with me."

"You don't get along with your mom?"

Cindy waited a beat before speaking. She sensed that the nurse was hoping she didn't get along. "Actually, I'm close to both my parents. They lead very different lives, but they're both good people. I do the best I can."

Bellson hesitated, then shook her head once again. Her eyes suddenly softened. "I suppose it's nice what you're doing for your father. Just don't step on my toes, all right? I've been charge nurse of this unit for ten years. I don't appreciate people barging in, demanding that I cater to them."

"I didn't mean anything. I'm sorry."

"S'okay." Bellson uncrossed her arms, letting them slowly drop to her sides. "I do get testy, especially when I'm overworked and understaffed." She played with a gold class ring on her left hand. "My profession means a lot to me. I put my heart and soul into my babies—all of them. You notice that little Rodriguez baby?"

Cindy nodded.

"Mama's only fifteen years old—a child with a child. I've spent hours with her just teaching her the basics. How to hold her baby, how to feed her, how to change a diaper. Letting her know that what she's got is a *baby* and not a *doll*."

"That's very nice of you."

"It's because I care. I care about that skinny little thing." Bellson furrowed her brow. "She was low birth weight because her mother smoked during pregnancy." She dropped her voice a notch. "And I bet she smoked more than tobacco."

The nurse smoothed her paper gown.

"Anyway, it's not my position to judge. We've all done things we're not proud of. But it is my position to *help*. I don't want that poor little thing going home with an untrained mother. They're the ones who do damage. One of the things I always tell the mamas: If they don't want what the good Lord blessed them with, there are hundreds of nice families who'd gladly take the baby off their hands. They should quit their eternal griping and thank Jesus they have a healthy baby."

Cindy nodded solemnly, thinking that Bellson would have been a great Puritan. She could picture the woman in a Pilgrim's hat, her reedy body covered by a black dress with a starched white apron, fingers kneading stiff bread dough in a one-room shack heated by a black iron cauldron. Pilgrim Bellson would be an attentive mother—caring—but she'd never crack a smile. The Pilgrim glanced at her watch—the timepiece an anachronism that brought Cindy back to the present.

"I'm running late," Bellson said.

"My fault, I'm sorry," Cindy said. "I'll wait in the nursery and won't go past the yellow line."

"Good." Bellson played with her ring again. "It's nice what you're doing for your sister. As long as you remember you're not the infant's mother. I hope your stepmother takes your place soon."

"I hope so, too," Cindy said. And she meant it.

Six

THE KICK AROUSED HER FROM A DULL SLEEP. SHE OPENED her eyes and was staring at loin-clothed crotch. She couldn't even tell who the crotch belonged to, because the wall of chest muscle hid the face. The voice told her to get the hell up. For a moment, she panicked. Her heart began to pound, awakening her out of her stupor.

The low one's come back!

But then the voice was familiar in a positive way.

Mack.

The voice belonged to *Mack*.

She relaxed.

Back in control.

It was Mack.

Eric was better, but Mack was okay.

"Are you just going to lie around and gather dust like a rug? If you're a rug, maybe I should take you out and beat you."

The floor was cold and hard. His intimidation was working. She was feeling appropriately hostile. Lifting heavy weights required the rush, and nothing gave you the rush like hostility. "Shut up!"

"So are you ready to work or what?"

"I'm ready."

He held out his hand. She took it, and he hoisted her to her feet. He threw a bundle at her.

"Put some clothes on."

She nodded and dressed quickly.

"How much time do you have?" Mack asked.

"Two hours."

"Two hours? Tandy, we can't do *anything* in two hours."

"Well, that's all the time I have, Mack. Take it or leave it. Help me with my weight belt."

"You should get a better-quality belt." Mack slipped the leather straps through the metal loops and pulled tightly, enjoying the sound of her curses. "After two years of pumping, you're no virgin, you know. You want to make progress, you need the right gear."

"I'm a little tight on cash at the moment."

"Hey, are you serious about building or what?"

"Of course I'm serious."

"Then find the cash, Tandy. If you're gonna do, do it right."

"It's too tight, Mack!"

Again Mack pulled on the straps.

"There! *Now* it's too tight."

"You are such a sadist!"

"Fuck you! What's this two hours crap? Are you committed, or are you playing games? We don't have time for games."

"I told you I'm committed."

"That's what you say, but that's not how you act," Mack snarled. "Two hours . . ."

"How about the pecs? We could do the pecs in two hours, Mack."

"Yeah, we could probably do the pecs," Mack said. "Be better if we had three hours."

"I have to work. I'm pulling the graveyard shift." She attempted a deep breath, but the belt was too tight. All she could so was exhale short little puffs. "I'm going to need something, Mack."

"What? Like some B-six?"

"Something stronger."

Mack paused. "It can be arranged."

"You're a doll—"

"Hey, I don't want to ever hear that kind of *shit* before a session!"

"Okay, you'd be a doll if you weren't such a dumb jerk!"

"Much *better!*"

Mack slammed her back into his granite-hard chest. He reached around her body and felt her breasts. "I hate to say this. But you're coming along nicely."

She felt herself smiling. "Thanks. Or shouldn't I say that?"

"You shouldn't say that. You should say, 'Of course I'm coming along, *asshole!*' You've got to learn to get your body to deliver the *rush*. Pumped up means more than just the physical body, you know."

"I know."

He felt her again. "Yeah, you're doing well. Of course, there's always room for improvement. Your pecs have good tone, but no bulk."

"What are you *talking* about! My chest is getting bigger all the time, and not a drop of it is due to fat."

"Not enough." Mack shook his head. "I'm going to increase your weights. What are you at?"

"Twenty each arm free weights."

"How many reps?"

"Twenty."

"How 'bout we use twenty-five weights, but we'll drop the reps to ten. Try to bulk you up."

"Whatever you think."

"Tandy, get *mean!*"

She turned around and smiled. Then she punched his stomach as hard as she could. Her entire hand went numb from the impact, but it did the job. Mack had sucked in air from the surprise punch. Not a lot of air—not more than a little gulp—but she had actually caught him *off guard*. Mack shook his head, laughed, then pinned her against the wall. They went nose-to-nose.

"You ever try a stunt like that again, I'll *kill* you!"

She spit at him. He spit back. Then they both laughed.

Mack said, "No good. Can't pump and laugh at the same time." He stared at her, then squeezed her arms with his massive claws. He thought he was being scary. But nothing, *nothing* physical, could be as scary as the mind out of control. She bit back the pain and kept eye contact.

"Good," Mack whispered. "That was real good, Tandy."

She felt him slowly easing the pressure off her arms, then he ran his hands over her breasts. Tandy closed her eyes. It felt good. In another world, she might have delved further. But that wasn't where she was at now. Mack knew it, too. And really that wasn't where *he* was at, either. It was just the touching. Gorgeous bodies like hers and his ... they were meant to be touched by those who could truly appreciate them.

"You ready to *sweat*, girlie?" he said.

"Always."

SEVEN

THE SHAKING OF HIS SHOULDER BROUGHT DECKER INTO A groggy state of consciousness. He leaped up, then felt unsteady on his legs. He could feel an arm giving him support. He rubbed his eyes and focused on a round, fair face. A body garbed in slacks, sports shirt, and a white coat—Dr. Hendricks. No more scrubs. Decker took that as a very good sign.

"Are you all right?" Hendricks asked.

"I fell asleep. I can't believe I did that."

"Happens to the best of us." The doctor felt the stubble on his chin. "Rina's progressing well. I just finished putting in the order to move her to the ICU. I don't expect she'll stay there long. I just want to make sure we have everything under control. You can see her now. She's still heavily sedated, so don't count on a lot of witty repartee."

Decker smiled.

"She was oriented when I spoke to her. Her vitals are good. All indications are she'll be just fine."

"Thank *God*!"

Hendricks placed a hand on Decker's shoulder. "I'll be around for the next hour or so. I'll need to talk to you, but I know how anxious you are to see Rina. Peter, I don't want you shocked by her appearance."

"Doctor, I've seen everything in any kind of condition imaginable."

"It's different when it's your wife."

Cerebrally, he was prepared. Emotionally, he wasn't. Her complexion was chalky gray, lips so pale they blended with the rest of her skin tone. Her hair had been pulled off her face. What strands did show were limp with perspiration. Her left arm was attached to a board on the bedrail, the underside bruised and milky white. An I.V. was held in place by big white bandages at her wrist. The rest of her body was covered by a bedsheet. Her sleep seemed deep—not a hint of movement under her delicate lids. He'd seen stiffs with better color. That thought gave him a chill.

He was afraid to touch her, afraid she might turn to dust like an antique document. Carefully, he edged his hand toward her cheek, letting it rest above her mouth for just a moment, felt her sweet breath upon his palm. He inched his fingers to her lips, then quickly removed his hand. Biting his lower lip, he pulled a chair by her bedside and broke into the shakes. He knew he should call Rina's parents, but he needed time to convince himself that she was really okay.

He hugged his body and watched his wife sleep. Forcing himself calm, he took her hand in his, encircled his fingers around hers. She didn't stir. He didn't remember how long he sat like that. The next thing he knew, the doctor was waking him again. His eyes went to the wall clock. It was after twelve. Slowly, he extricated his hand from Rina's. She hadn't changed position.

Decker stood and the doctor put his arm around him. He whispered, "Let's go in my office."

"It's okay to leave her?"

"Yes, she's fine."

They stepped outside the ICU into a brightly lit hallway, eerie because it was so empty. Then Decker stopped.

"My daughter!"

"Your baby's doing great, Peter. Pediatrician'll be in tomorrow if you want to talk to him."

"No, my other daughter," Decker said, "She's nineteen. She was with the baby. I told her to check in with me before she left. If she walked by herself to the parking lot, I'll wring her neck. You keep thinking there'll come a time when you'll stop worrying about your kids. . . ."

"Nah, it never comes," Hendricks said.

"Do you mind if I find out where she is?"

"Go ahead. My office is room six-seventy-eight B. I'll wait for you there."

Decker asked Hendricks how to get to Nursery J. As he listened to the doc's words, he was acutely aware of the fact that his ears were hearing, but his brain wasn't processing. Although Hendricks had pointed him in the right direction, Decker didn't know where he was going. He was senile from worry and lack of sleep, walking in a stuporous state down long plush corridors that seemed to meld into other hallways that led nowhere.

After a couple of false starts, he somehow reached the correct nursery. He peeked in the window—two rows of layettes containing bundles topped by little fuzzy heads. As his eyes danced over the tiny faces, Decker suddenly realized that his own infant daughter's bassinet was gone. That jolted his heart and cleared his brain.

He knocked on the entry to the nursery but didn't wait for an answer. Instead, he turned the knob just as a scrub-suited woman opened the door from the other side. She was middle-aged and petite, her face small and pinched. She was wearing a hair cap. Her name tag said DARLENE JAMISON, RN.

"I'm Peter Decker. I was just wondering where my baby was. My baby daughter . . . and my other one, too. Both my daughters. Did you happen to see—"

"You're Cindy's father. Can tell 'cause of the hair. Relax. She's fine . . . in the back with the baby. They're both sleeping." Darlene broke into a grin and shook her head. "Come in. If you want to see your dynamic duo, you're gonna have to put on some protective clothing. And you'll have to take your shoes off, too."

Decker stepped inside the waiting area of the nursery, the anteroom so brightly lit it hurt his eyes. Instantly, his ears were assaulted by high-pitched squalls and protests. His eyes drifted over to the layettes. Baby Girl Jackson seemed to be making most of the noise. Her mouth was wide open, and she was howling up a storm. She sat between Baby Girl Rodriguez, who was beet red from her wailing, and Baby Boy Yamata, who seemed above it all. His big eyes were open and staring at the ceiling as if to say, Lord, what is wrong with all these people?

Decker couldn't help but smile. A big yellow line set out the perimeters of where he was allowed to place his feet. Beyond the line was a glassed hallway on either side, doors leading to the nurseries. As far as Decker could see, Darlene was the only person tending sheep.

"My daughters are okay?" Decker said.

"Dandy." Darlene chuckled. "Hope you realize your big girl's a real mama lion. She's *very* attached to the baby. When things settle down, you might want to gently remind her that she's the sister, not the mother."

Decker ran his hands down his face.

"Not what you wanted to hear, huh?" Darlene patted his shoulder. "Sorry. Cindy'll be fine. How's your wife doing?"

"She's pretty wiped out. Her doctor's waiting to talk to me. Do you want me to talk to Cindy now?"

"No, not at all. I don't mean to say that Cindy is a problem. She's a great kid, full of spunk. I think it's kinda cute. 'Course, I'm a little hang-loose. Single mother of three, five years on the graveyard shift, you learn to relax and smile if you want to survive. I'm pretty much my own boss. No one bothers to come down and check things out at one in the morning. Marie's the one with all the pressure."

"Did Marie and Cindy get into any kind of conflict?"

"Well, it's not that Cindy's gettin' in the way, it's . . . I think it's a turf problem. Marie's an institution here. She's used to postpartum moms—tired, anxious, and willing to hang on to everything Marie's got to say. Now a kid like Cindy comes along—full of energy. Marie's just not used to that. Marie told me to kick Cindy out when I came on shift at eleven. But, heck, she really seems like a good kid. Talks nicely about you, her mom, her stepmom and stepbrothers. I know this is her first sibling, and she's so excited. I just didn't have the heart. And then she fell asleep. . . ."

"I'll talk to her."

"You don't have to do it now, Detective. . . ." Darlene paused. "Is that the right title?"

Technically, it was Detective Sergeant, but Decker told her Detective was fine.

"I don't care really," Darlene said. "I like Cindy. But Marie's the boss. You'll have to work by her rules."

"I understand." Decker took an Advil from his pocket and popped the pill in his mouth. "Let me talk to the doctor, then I'll come back."

"You've got two lovely daughters," Darlene said. "And I know you've got some stepsons, too—a real nice family. Congratulations."

"Thanks. Do you have any idea where six-seventy-eight B is?"

Darlene laughed. "Place is a maze, isn't it? I'll at least get you to the elevator and give you directions from there." She crooked a finger. "This way."

Decker followed her, an obedient robot wondering why

the hair on his neck was standing on end. It wasn't because he was tired. It wasn't because Darlene had told him that basically Cindy was being a pain in the neck. It wasn't even because of Rina. It wasn't until he was standing in front of the door to room 678B that he figured out what was bothering him. It was Darlene Jamison, RN. She was the only one Decker had seen actually in Nursery J. And she had left the babies alone to walk him to the elevator.

Hendricks's hospital office was designed strictly for function. Into the small space were crammed a standard institutional-issue metal desk, a low-back secretary's chair, and two waiting-room chairs that had seen better days. On the walls were metal shelves holding reference books, medical tomes, and an old coffeemaker. Decker recalled the doctor's private-practice office—decorated to the hilt. But for some reason, Decker felt Hendricks was more at home here. He seemed more relaxed. Maybe it was just fatigue.

"Have a seat." Hendricks opened a chart on his desk. "Did you find your daughter?"

"She was with the baby in the nursery. Apparently, she's becoming quite attached to her."

"It's her first sibling, isn't it?"

"She has stepbrothers, but this is different."

"Is she close to her stepbrothers?"

The questions seemed out of place—too personal. Must be trying out some rapport-building, Decker thought. The guy had something on his mind but didn't want to jump into it.

"She likes her stepbrothers, but the relationships aren't close ones. Not a lot of history between them."

Hendricks shifted in his seat. "Are you close to your stepsons?"

Decker paused, thinking what a *weird* question that was. Maybe Hendricks was worried he was going to show favoritism. He shouldn't have been concerned.

"I'm very close to them. I consider them my own sons, and I love them dearly."

"Are you their legal father?"

Now Decker was genuinely taken aback.

"Uh, no, not yet." His heart began to race as he moved to the edge of his seat. "Why? Is Rina in danger—"

"No, no, no. Nothing like that. I didn't mean to scare you."

Decker sat back and blew out air. "I'd adopt them if they wanted. I didn't want to take away their father's identity. I'm ready for it. But I don't know if they are."

"Very sensitive of you."

Decker didn't answer, trying to assess where Hendricks was coming from. The doctor looked down at the chart, clearly uncomfortable. Decker wished he'd get on with it.

"So your daughter's taken a shine to her new little sister," Hendricks said. "That's nice."

"Do you think it's a bad idea for her to become attached to the baby?"

"Only if it's to the exclusion of her normal activities. Why? Is there a problem?"

Decker rubbed his face. "She seems to be having some conflict with Nurse Bellson, getting in her way, that kind of thing."

Hendricks rolled his eyes. "Marie's a damn good nurse, but she does get a bit possessive."

"Not the first time there's been a conflict?"

Hendricks shook his head. "You want me to talk to Marie for you?"

"No, no, no. I'll handle my daughter."

"Isn't she going back to college soon?"

Decker nodded.

"So it should work itself out," Hendricks said.

"Yeah, you're probably right."

Hendricks yawned. "Sorry. It's been a long night—a busy night. Not just Rina, others as well. Having babies must be in the air. But I did want to talk to you before I left, tell you what happened . . . explain a few things."

Decker waited.

"Rina developed a condition known as accreta." Hendricks sighed and spelled it. "Basically, the placenta didn't come out on its own. This can happen for a lot of different reasons, the most common being that the placenta adheres to the uterus. When this occurs, we have to go in and physically remove all of the tissue. Sometimes we can do it with a simple D and C. We go in and scrape the uterus . . . clean everything out."

"There's a 'but' to this, isn't there?" Decker said.

Hendricks's eyes went from Decker to the chart. Decker felt his stomach churn.

"What?"

"Rina's hemorrhaging was quite severe; her blood pressure was beginning to drop precipitously. We had no choice but to operate. Once we did, we found out what the problem was. The placenta had grown through the uterus, and that's what caused all the hemorrhaging. I'm sorry to tell you this, Peter, but Rina had a hysterectomy."

His words hung in the air. Decker was too stunned to respond. The room suddenly seemed to take on motion, walls pulsating, the bookshelves undulating. Nausea crept from his stomach to his throat. He swallowed to keep from retching and covered his mouth with his hand.

Hendricks fiddled with the chart. "I know this must be quite a shock to you—"

"Couldn't you just have *cut* it out?" Decker blurted. "The placenta . . . couldn't you have surgically removed it?"

"No—"

"You had to take the *whole* uterus out?"

"Yes."

"I don't understand—"

"Peter—"

"I mean, isn't that what surgery is? Cutting things out? Cutting *selective* things out?"

Hendricks didn't answer.

Decker said, "I just don't understand why . . ."

"Peter," Hendricks said softly, "her placenta was like an open hose of blood. The more I tried to remove it, the more she bled. I had no option whatsoever. I know how Rina feels about children. I delivered Samuel and Jacob, and I held her hand after all three of her miscarriages—"

"I thought she miscarried because her husband was so sick. That's what she told me."

Hendricks was silent.

"No?" Decker's voice sounded desperate.

"Peter," Hendricks began, "who knows why she miscarried? Needless to say, I was delighted when she carried this baby to term. Throughout this ordeal, please try to remember, she did give birth to a beautiful little girl. You have a healthy daughter. Good heavens, I know Rina wanted a slew of children. And this is going to hit her very hard. That's why I asked you how close you are to her sons. Some men get idiotic with the idea of having a boy—"

"No . . ." Decker shook his head. "No, it's not a problem." He felt his eyes go wet and shut them a moment. When he opened them, the horror hadn't gone away. "What . . . what do I say . . . ?"

"I'll tell her. That's my job."

Again Decker shook his head. "I can do it."

"Peter, I'm sure in your line of work, you have had to deliver a fair share of bad news. Let me be the bad guy."

"No, I can't . . . I can do it." Decker looked down, then looked up. "When should I tell her?"

Hendricks sighed loudly. "If you insist on doing this, I suggest you mention it to her as soon as she has some of her strength back. I'll let you know when her blood count stabilizes."

Decker lowered his head and nodded.

"She's a strong woman, Peter. She's going to recover very quickly. The actual operation was . . . God, how do I say this without sounding like an insensitive jerk?" Hendricks paused. "The operation itself was routine. Rina's ovaries were left intact, so hormonally, she'll be as regulated as any other woman her age. And she'll be able to nurse. Just as soon as she's stabilized, she'll recover in a snap."

"I love her so much," Decker whispered. "She's going to be devastated."

"And you?"

"Truthfully, I'm not feeling too good, Doc." Again

Decker dragged his hand over his face. "But I'll be fine. It's Rina . . ."

"It's a loss, Peter," Hendricks said. "Not like a death of a baby, thank God—" He caught himself. "You already went through that with your first wife, didn't you?"

Decker nodded.

"That must have been hell. This is hell, too. Something you both are going to grieve over. There's no getting around it. If you're determined to tell her yourself, I won't stop you. But if you need anything, pick up the phone, call the exchange, and say it's an emergency. I'm here for both of you. For Rina and you and for the family—the boys, the grandparents. Just give me a call."

All Decker could do was nod.

"I've ordered a cot for you next to Rina." Hendricks stood. "Try to get some rest, all right?"

"Thank you." Slowly, Decker got to his feet. "I've got to talk to my daughter."

"It can wait until the morning."

"I want to do it now."

"Peter, it can wait." Hendricks put his arm around Decker's shoulder. "Go to sleep. Doctor's orders."

"I've got to tell Rina's parents—"

"Don't tell them anything before you've told Rina."

"No, not this." Decker was finding it hard to talk, hard to speak without choking. "I promised I'd call them as soon as Rina was out of recovery . . . tell them she's okay. They must be worried sick."

Hendricks turned out the lights. "I'll call them for you. Give me the number."

It took Decker a few seconds to remember the order of the digits. "You'll tell them Rina's doing okay?"

"Yes, I will. Because Rina *is* recovering well." Hendricks pulled out keys from his pants and locked the door. "Come on. I'll walk you back to the ICU."

Decker didn't argue. He felt like a child being put to bed. He didn't want to go, but he was just too exhausted to protest.

EIGHT

CINDY WOKE UP WITH A START, HER BODY PINCHED FROM sleeping in a chair. Beside her was Hannah's layette, the baby lying on her stomach, eyes closed, the little pink face molded into the mattress. It had been almost three hours, and Hannah hadn't uttered a peep. A big kid, her birth weight almost nine pounds, she probably had a bigger stomach than most of the other infants. Good for her and lucky for Rina. Hannah would probably sleep through the night at an early age.

The wall clock said 1:05, and Cindy assumed it was A.M. For how brightly lit the nursery was, it could have been P.M. Kind of like the Vegas casino she had visited a year ago—a fixed internal environment that scorned the passage of time. She stood and stretched and crossed over the yellow line to the nurses' station. Through the glass, Cindy could see Darlene talking animatedly to a big-boned black woman, waving her arms as if conducting. Cindy knocked on the door. Darlene looked up and beckoned her in.

"Hi," Cindy said.

"Take off your mask," Darlene said. "Can't understand a darn thing with that on. Everyone sounds like they're talkin' with marbles in their mouth. How's your sister doing? Did you feed her yet?"

"She's still sleeping," Cindy said.

51

"You let her sleep past her twelve o'clock feeding? Uh-oh, Mom's not going to like *that*. Gotta get her on a schedule. What kind of marine are you, anyway?"

There was a sparkle in Darlene's eyes, a gentle tease in her smile. Cindy smiled back. "Should I feed her?"

"Well, since you already messed her up, you might as well let her wake up naturally. You first-time big sisters just can't do a darn thing right." The head nurse glanced at her watch, then turned back to her heavyset charge. "Lily, start wheelin' the babies back into the nursery from their twelve o'clock feeding. Do rooms three-fifteen through three-thirty. I'll do the rest. Be sure to check the chart and see who has rooming in. Don't take the rooming-in babies back."

"I won't," Lily said solemnly.

Darlene said, "But do check in and see if everything's okay. Any questions?"

Lily gave a nervous smile. "Not a one!"

"Then either I'm doing something very right or something very wrong," Darlene said. "And relax, Lily. Try to have some fun. As long as you're doin' some work."

"Thanks a lot, ma'am." Lily laughed anxiously and turned to Cindy. "She's a real slave driver."

"Is that nice, Nurse Booker?" Darlene pouted. "After all I've done for you?"

"But a real nice slave driver," Lily said. "Watch out for her when you're a trainee."

"A trainee?" Cindy asked.

"Darlene has big plans for you."

Cindy laughed but was confused.

"Nurse Booker, kindly remove yourself and go do some work," Darlene said.

"Yes sir, ma'am." Lily saluted, waved at Cindy, then left.

Cindy waved back, watching a big rear fill out the backside of her uniform. Despite Lily's girth and size, she looked young—early twenties, maybe. Probably a recent graduate of nursing school, and this was her first real job.

"She seems really nice," Cindy said to Darlene.

"She's going to be a darn good nurse," Darlene said. "Know why? 'Cause she's conscientious and *caring*. She worked herself up from *nothing*, 'cause her dream was to help people. Shows what you can do when the motivation is there. Have you ever thought of nursing as a career, Cindy? You seem pretty darn caring yourself."

Cindy felt heat in her cheeks. Seemed like Lily and Darlene had been doing some talking. "I haven't made up my mind yet, but I'm leaning toward criminal sciences."

Darlene made a face. "The nursing profession could use caring people. Think about it." She straightened her spine and did a few arm circles. "You calling it quits tonight, you slacker?"

Again Cindy smiled. "I thought I'd just wait until Hannah wakes up so I could feed her. Then I thought I'd go home. Maybe come back later in the morning. Is that okay?"

"Okay by me, kid. Just don't get in Marie's way."

Cindy frowned. "Marie's going to be on shift again?"

"Doing the three-to-eleven, plus all night here with me—double duty. The other night charge nurse is taking the night off." Darlene furrowed her brows. "Marie's a *good* nurse, Cindy. Very dedicated and patient with the moms and the babies. She just doesn't have a lot of leftover patience for anyone else, especially young kids like yourself who're self-confident and able-bodied. You're gonna have to learn to deal with all sorts of people in your life."

"I don't say a word to her," Cindy said. "I try to mind my own business. She just doesn't like me hanging around Hannah."

"You know how to bake?" Darlene asked.

"Yes."

"Tell you what, Cindy. When you come back, bring her some home-baked chocolate-chip cookies. Marie'll appreciate the gesture. That's all she wants. A little appreciation."

"Hey, if that's all it takes, I'll even wrap them up in a basket with ribbon."

Darlene said, "I gotta go fetch some babies, start doing my blood work."

Cindy drew her paper-covered foot across the ground. "Was my dad around here at all?"

" 'Bout an hour ago. I told him you were with Hannah and both of you were asleep."

"I should go let him know I'm alive." She looked at the clock. "I think I could make it back and forth before Hannah wakes up."

"Probably," Darlene said. "Hon, do me a favor. Before you go, check and make sure Angela or Chris is in the back room. Nursery C and D called them away 'bout an hour ago 'cause we're so short-staffed. Budget cuts. Seems the whole nursing staff is a few old-timers and a bunch of temps who don't know a darn thing. I told them they could float for a while, but sometimes when you get busy, people forget to look at the clock. Someone should be in the nursery at all times."

"And if they're not?"

"Wait for me, and I'll call someone in."

"I can visit my father later. Do you want me to wait here until you're done wheeling back the babies?"

Darlene wrinkled her nose as she thought. "If you wouldn't mind, that would be convenient. All these budget cuts . . . make you wonder if hospitals are really for patients anymore." She clucked her tongue and handed Cindy her beeper. "Just push the red button if you think you got an emergency. I'll be right on the floor."

"No problem," Cindy said. "Do you want me to check in on the other babies?"

"Only if you want to visit," Darlene said. "Thanks for your help, Cindy. And think about nursing, missy. You're a natural."

Cindy's eyes went to the ceiling. "Uh, I'll be with Hannah. See if she's awake and ready to eat."

As Cindy started to leave, Darlene called out her name. "Aren't you forgetting something?"

"What?" Cindy asked.

Darlene pointed to her face mask.

"Sorry." Cindy slipped the mask over her mouth and nose and tied the strings. "Better?"

Darlene frowned, then broke into a big grin. "You either

said 'better' or 'butter.' Yes, it is better—or, no we don't have any butter."

Bottle in hand, Cindy heard the knock and looked around. Darlene and Lily were still out fetching the babies. Cindy looked down at the bundle in her arms. Hannah had closed her eyes, a small line of drool creasing a perfect chin. She needed to be burped, and Cindy wanted to do it before her sister was deep asleep. But someone kept hammering away at the nursery door. The noise was no doubt disturbing the other babies. Carefully, Cindy lay Hannah in her layette and went to the front part of the nursery. Through the glass windows, she saw her father. His face was ravaged with exhaustion, his eyes lolling in their sockets. Quickly, she opened the door.

"Are you all right?" She started toward him, then moved back. "I can't hug you, 'cause I'm all suited up."

"S'right." Decker was having trouble focusing. "I just woke up and realized I hadn't seen you yet. I wanted to make sure you were okay."

"I'm fine, Daddy. Go back to sleep."

"What're you doing?"

"I just finished feeding Hannah. She needs to be burped. If you want to do it, you'll have to put on a gown. You can't cross that yellow line unless you have a gown on."

Decker took a step away from the walless barrier. "I'd love to burp her, except I'm so tired I'm afraid I'd drop her. How's she doing?"

"Great."

Decker felt himself smiling. It must have been a reflex, because every muscle in his face was too numb to move voluntarily. "Thanks for taking care of her. As soon as Mrs. Elias comes here, I want you to go home and get some rest. I know you teens think you're immortal, but you need sleep."

Cindy stared at her father. "It's not because you think I'm too attached to Hannah, is it?"

Decker paused. "Who gave you that idea?"

"Nurse Bellson," Cindy said. "She thinks I am. She's

worried I'm going to feel jealous when Rina's well enough to take care of Hannah. It's not true. I'm only trying to help."

"I know you are."

"So you're not upset with me?"

"No, sweetheart. I love you very much. Just if you could try to avoid butting heads with the staff—"

"You mean Nurse Bellson?"

"If that's who you're butting heads with, then yes, get along with Nurse Bellson. Even if it's her problem."

"Daddy, you're dropping on your feet. You look real sick. I think you should sit down."

"No, I'm okay." Decker stifled a yawn. "I have to get back to Rina."

"How is she?"

"Still sleeping." Decker forced his eyes open. "Cynthia, I really do appreciate all your help. But you *do* need your rest."

"Look, if you want me to go home now—"

"No." Decker was surprised by the sudden strength of his voice. "No, you can wait until Mrs. Elias gets here. If you don't mind."

Cindy looked quizzically at her father. "Where did that come from?"

"What are you talking about?"

"Why do you want me to wait for Mrs. Elias?" Cindy widened her eyes. "You don't trust Nurse Bellson either, do you, Daddy? Do you have something on her?"

Despite his fatigue, Decker laughed. "You've been watching too many bad movies, sweetheart."

"You're not being honest with me, Daddy. Why don't you trust her?"

Decker sighed. "It's not Marie Bellson. It's the night nurse, Darlene—"

"*Darlene?* She's a living angel."

"Cindy, she left the babies alone to walk me to the elevator."

"Are you sure, Daddy? Maybe there was someone in back, and you didn't notice."

"Oh." Decker hesitated. "Shows you what I know. Is there someone in back now?"

It was Cindy's turn to hesitate. "Well, Darlene kind of told me to wait for her *specifically* because she didn't want the babies left alone. She and Lily—that's her newest trainee—they were collecting the babies from the moms after the twelve o'clock feeding. It's taking a little longer because Darlene volunteered to help out in the adjoining nursery. They've been shorthanded lately 'cause of budget cuts."

"So Darlene left *you* in charge?"

Cindy's eyes went to the ceiling. "She's right here on the floor, Daddy. I have her beeper, but it isn't even necessary. She comes back every few minutes. Says she'll finish up real soon. She's doing the best she can."

"Cindy, you're a peach, but Darlene doesn't know that. You could be *anybody*. Did you ever see Marie leave the babies alone?"

Cindy shook her head. "I guess Darlene is very trusting."

"It's dumb. She's asking for a tragedy and a lawsuit." Decker put his hands in his pockets. "I'm very grateful that you're watching Hannah. And truthfully, yes, Marie does tweak my nose. If Rina weren't so . . . so laid-up, I'd check my whole family out of here. But as of now, I'm stuck. So if Mrs. Elias wants to take over for you for a while, *let* her. Marie'll probably be more tolerant of her than you."

"I ask you, Daddy, is that right?"

"No, it isn't right, but frankly I don't care. I'm looking for what'll work. So help me out. You can come back when Mrs. Elias has to go home to tend to the boys. Okay?"

Cindy nodded.

"And please don't make *problems*. I want you here in the nursery, Cindy, because I *do* trust you."

"Thanks, Dad. It's nice to hear that."

"You're welcome." Decker rubbed his eyes. "Go burp your sister. Give her a kiss for me. Tell her I love her and hope to burp her very soon."

"She'll be waiting for you, Dad. Sorry if I'm being a bit of a pain."

"Nah, you're never a pain. You're a great kid, Cynthia. The best. God knows, your mother and I have had differences, but she did a fabulous job."

"You had a little to do with it."

"Not as much as I should have." Decker raised his brow. "Probably why you turned out so good."

NINE

AFTER SHE VOMITED, SHE FELT MUCH BETTER. MACK WAS nice—helping her into a chair, then wiping her mouth. He took out a Rubbermaid quart container and peeled off the blue lid. Dipping a tablespoon into the hard plastic, he fished up some tan mush.

"Open up."

"I'm sick."

"Open up, Tandy. You need your calories."

She didn't move.

"You're really infuriating, you know?"

Mack pried her jaws apart with his thumb and forefinger. She was fighting him, but it was a losing battle. Such unbelievable strength in *two* little fingers. She couldn't help but be awed. He force-fed her some mush, pushing the oversized spoon into her mouth. In her different life, she would have gagged. But now she was in control.

Pureed chicken. Wasn't half bad.

"Come on, Tandy, open all the way up."

Passively, she complied.

"That's a good girl."

Another spoonful.

"How much do I have to eat?"

"The whole thing."

"Mack—"

"If you want to look right, you have to eat right. Now shut up and open up!"

She paused. "I don't think that's physically possible."

Mack laughed and fed her another spoonful. "You did fair tonight. I've seen you do better."

"I wasn't at my best."

"Something on your mind?"

She shrugged.

"What?"

"It's just work, I guess."

"Bitches giving you problems?"

"Always."

"Open up, Tandy. I refuse to let you leave until you've had your proper caloric intake. How the hell are you going to build muscle if you don't give your body fuel?"

"A month ago, Leek put me on eight hundred calories a day for two weeks."

"A month ago, you were working for the cut. We're not working for the cut right now, Tandy. We're going for bulk."

She sighed but obeyed. After she swallowed, she said, "All this back-and-forth. One minute I feel like a pig, the next minute I'm starving myself."

"Hey, are you going to let your body control you, or are you going to control your body?"

She was silent.

"Know what I'm saying, Tandy?"

"I know. Rest assured I'm in total control."

"No one said this was easy. You want easy, don't come here. Go to the Golden Hotshot Spa and pay a million dollars a day to do it all wrong."

"I'm not looking for easy, Mack." She licked her lips. "I've never looked for easy. Easy is unhealthy. Maybe it is my work. My other work. I do so much, and no one ever says anything. They take me for granted."

"The docs, too?"

"No, the docs *love* me. They know I'm great. It's the people I work with . . . the nurses . . . the head nurses."

"They're just jealous, Tandy. They can't stand the fact that you *know* more. Probably galls them that you look so good, too."

She nodded.

Mack presented her with another spoonful. "So don't pay any attention to them, okay? They're just laying a trip on you."

"Sometimes I wish I didn't have to work."

"So move in with me or Leek or Eric. We have group grunts. They really get the competitive spirit going." He paused. "We could set you up with some *easy* nursing clients. No bureaucracy and lots of side benefits."

Right, Tandy thought. She knew all about the *side benefits* à la Leek. Penny-ante stuff. Such mundane fools. "Not for me. But thanks for the offer."

"Welcome. Open."

She swallowed the puree. It tasted like gritty soup.

"Besides, my work *is* important, Mack. People *rely* on me. I just don't get any appreciation from the people I work with."

"Like I said, they're jealous."

"But my patients . . . I'm really important to them."

"I can dig it."

"The doctors don't have the time. It all falls on the nurses."

Mack began scraping the sides of the container. "People at the hospital ever notice how good you look?"

Tandy twitched. He didn't *understand*. Talking to Mack was like talking to wood. But at least he was real. She knew that much.

"Uniforms hide a lot."

"Uniforms hide these?"

He squeezed her breasts. She yelped with pain.

"God, don't *do* that! I'm so *sore*."

Gently, he began to touch her, walking his fingers over her breast tissue. But it was more medical than erotic.

"You definitely are swollen."

"I'm really going to feel it tomorrow."

"That's okay. You can only tolerate pain if you have pain."

"No more." She pushed aside the spoon and stood. "No more. I've got to go to work. Did you get it?"

"Yeah. I mixed it with a little something to take the edge off. I mean, you're still going to feel sore—gotta feel the soreness—but not like a truck ran over you. How do you want it?"

"Usual, I guess."

She sighed and dropped on her hands and knees. She felt him pulling off her panties.

"God, you have a wonderful ass."

"You mean a wonderful pincushion."

She felt him kissing one of her buns, running his mitt-sized hand over her firm flesh. Mack's voice had dropped to a whisper. "It's been a long time since I've had a woman."

"I can't, Mack. Besides, it won't work. You know that."

"What a loss. . . ." His voice was low and wolfish. "For both of us."

Kill him.

Tandy jerked her head up, her eyes snapping open. The suddenness of her motion startled Mack.

"You all right, Tandy?"

Beads of sweat ran down her face. The low one. Or was it? Did she *really* hear it? Tricks upon tricks upon—

"Tandy?"

"I'm . . ." She took a deep breath and let out a forced laugh. "I'm . . . fine. Let's get on with it. I've got to go."

Gritting her teeth, she didn't even flinch as she felt the bite of the hypodermic. She rose slowly, her muscles aching. Like an old woman, she hunched her way to the corner, pulled the uniform off the coatrack, and stepped into the white dress.

She looked in the mirror, straighted her collar, and

tugged on the hemline. Her developed chest was pulling the dress upward, showing off her long, shapely legs. She flexed and pointed her toes several times, watching her calves expand and contract with each movement.

So graceful. Like a ballet dancer.

Her face had lost some of its color. She steadied her hands and pulled out blush, dabbing her cheeks with a touch of red. She dropped the compact back in her purse and pulled out a brush. Gathering her hair into a ponytail, eyes on her reflection, she knew she was beautiful. It wasn't Mack's fault. Mack just couldn't help himself.

Again she straightened her posture. She was now a model of efficiency in her uniform. She knew she could inspire trust.

That was important. Trust.

She glanced at her watch.

Time to go to work.

TEN

DARLENE EDGED THE LAST OF THE LAYETTES INTO ITS SPACE in Nursery J, then placed her gloved hands on her hips. Her eyes traveled to the babies, ten of them—two blacks, four Hispanics, three whites, and one Asian—as varied as L.A.'s own population. Each had its own personality, even at this age, but all of them were as precious as an angel's song.

Not that they sounded like angels. Baby Girl Rodriguez

and Baby Girl Jackson were squalling up a storm. Now Baby Boy Yamata . . . there was a good baby. Quiet. Like his parents.

Squalling up a storm.

The expression made her smile. No one knew squalls like she knew squalls. The late November winds on the lake . . . a cold so bone-chilling it froze your teeth numb.

Baby Girl Decker was missing . . . probably still with Cindy in the back room. Darlene thought about Cindy—a real good kid. Not too many sisters were that devoted. Not a lot of devoted people, period. That's what Darlene liked about nursing. You gave to others, actually *helped* them. Helped them more than the *doctors*, if the truth be known.

She watched the infants for a few minutes without doing anything, observing wide-open mouths and scrunched-up eyes. Baby Girl Rodriguez had cried herself lobster red, fingers balled up into tight fists as she cried to be held. Too bad Darlene had only two arms. Shame women weren't born octopuses.

Rubbing her arms, she threw a furtive glance over her shoulder. Slowly, her hands reached toward Baby Girl Rodriguez. Teeny little thing. Darlene had cooked chickens that weighed more. But the baby was fully formed and doing well. Cute coffee-bean eyes hidden by locks of silky black hair. The baby quieted as Darlene nestled her into her bosom, patted her little back. Tiny, fragile bones. All of the babies, so small yet perfect human beings. The wonderment of new life. It never failed to amaze her.

She undid BG Rodriguez's blanket, and the cold blast of air suddenly sent the little girl into another episode of hysterics. Quickly, the nurse took the unclad baby over to the scales.

"Now this'll only take a minute, honey," Darlene cooed as she slid the poise over the indicator numbers. BG Rodriguez was still a little under two kilos: She'd need at least another couple of days of hospitalization before she'd weigh enough to go home.

"Stop your bellyaching. We ain't even at the hard part yet."

With a firm grip, Darlene lifted the infant from the scales, placed her on the table, and rewrapped her in her blanket. The baby's loud outbursts quieted to whimpers. On the table was a tray of instruments and a stack of charts. Placing a firm hand on the infant's stomach, Darlene scanned through the pile until she found BG Rodriguez's records. She flipped through the papers, looking for additional instructions or orders from the pediatrician. Finding nothing of significance, she wrote in the time and the latest weighing.

The baby was now fully awake, black eyes trying to focus, legs kicking under the covers. Darlene chucked her chin, then carefully liberated a little foot from the swaddle of the blanket.

Tiny foot—as small and soft as a ladyfinger. Little red toes.

Again Darlene took a quick peek over her shoulder. She felt her shoulders tighten as she reached for the instrument tray. It was always tense with the first one. Holding the foot firmly in her grasp, the charge nurse held her breath as she jabbed a razor-sharp needle into the pad of the baby's heel.

Decker's own snoring woke him up. He heard himself snort and grunt, then he shook his head in a weak attempt to dislodge his stupor. His bones hurt; his muscles ached with rigidity. He managed to open his eyes, light flooding his retinas. It took him a moment to focus, and when he did, he was shocked to see Rina's eyes upon him. Quickly, he sat up, swinging his stiff legs over the edge of the cot. He took her hand and kissed it.

"Morning, darling." He looked at the wall clock. Five fifty-two—morning only in a technical sense. He leaned over and kissed her cheek. It was hot and dry. "How do you feel?"

Rina's lids fluttered, but she kept her eyes open. "How's . . . our baby?"

"Gorgeous!" Decker tried to sound upbeat. "Beautiful just like you."

"Tell me."

"Well ..." Decker cleared his throat. "She's big and robust and beautiful and alert. Definitely the best kid in the whole hospital."

Rina's lips formed a weak smile. "I want to hold her. Hold my baby." Her eyes grew wet. "But I can't, can I?"

"Of course you can *hold* her. You'll spend hours holding her. But first you've got to recuperate."

"From the surgery," Rina whispered.

"Yes, from the surgery," Decker said. "Go back to sleep, honey. It's the best thing for you now."

Rina turned away, then faced him again. "Something's ..." She swallowed hard. "Something's wrong, Peter."

"I'll call the nurse—"

"No," Rina cried hoarsely. "That's not what I meant."

Decker felt his head spin. "Doctor says you're going to be fine, Rina. But you need to rest ... relax. The only thing you should be concerned about is getting your strength back. Now I'm ordering you to close your eyes and go back to sleep."

Rina attempted a deep breath, her face contorting from the effort. "I'm not bleeding normally. Not like the others ..." She winced. "And the miscarriages, too. It's not normal."

Decker squelched a wave of nausea. "Rina, you're so tired. Go to sleep, honey." His voice was making tinny echoes in his ear. "I'll be here when you wake up. You'll feel better after you sleep."

"Your face." Her voice was *so* raspy. "You're not looking at me. Tell me."

Decker couldn't talk, paralyzed by exhaustion and fright.

"What's wrong with me, Peter?"

"Nothing's wrong, honey."

Immediately, he regretted the false words. He had to tell her. He couldn't let her think she was the same as before, only to have her psyche destroyed later on. She'd never forgive him. As much as he dreaded the task, he knew he had to confess. He forced himself to look in her eyes. They'd become deep blue pools.

"I love you, baby."

"What is it, Peter?"

He kissed her hand again, then whispered, "Rina, you had a hysterectomy. That's the reason you're not bleeding normally."

She didn't react.

After some false starts, he finally found his voice. "Rina, we have a lovely, lovely family. A beautiful new baby . . . a real gift from God. We have to remember that."

She said nothing, her eyes resting blankly on his face.

"I know how you must feel . . . no, I don't know how you feel. I don't know what I'm talking about."

He kissed her hand again.

"Rina, the truth is, I'm an old man. I mean, who wants to be playing sandlot ball when you're fifty, right?"

Her expression reflected his stupidity. He knew he should just *shut up*, but the jitters kept his vocal cords humming overtime.

"I know how you feel about kids, honey. And I love kids, too. We've got to look at it this way. We have three beautiful, healthy children; I've got a nearly grown daughter. Babies are *wonderful*, but it's nice when the kids grow up and are big—on their own. Give us a little special time . . . we haven't had a lot of that, you know?"

Nothing.

"Rina, four kids can be a real stretch on the pocketbook. Private schools, then college. Man, I can't believe what it cost to send Cindy through one year of Columbia. . . ."

He was babbling. But it didn't matter, because none of his words were really registering with her.

"Honey, I know it's hard to have perspective. But . . . but try to think about how blessed we are to have a beautiful, healthy baby daughter—"

"Peter, I'm only *thirty* years old!"

And then came the tears, the sadness so pure and honest it mercifully muzzled his moronic ramblings. He brought her face against his chest, and she sobbed on his shoulder.

"It stinks, Rina," he whispered. "I'm so sorry, baby. I'm so, so sorry!"

The information was too devastating to handle consciously. Eventually, she cried herself to sleep.

Holding his daughter, Decker felt comforted. There really was something to be grateful for. If only Rina could *hold* Hannah. He knew the contact—the *bonding*—would lift her spirits.

The baby slept as he rocked her—a perfumed package tucked in the crook of his arm. Decker kissed her forehead through his mask, his coffee-laced breath recirculating through his lungs. It wasn't unpleasant—beat the early-morning sourness in his stomach. Rabbi Schulman had come as soon as he called. He was with Rina now, watching her sleep, giving Decker a chance to see his daughter without worrying about his wife.

Decker hadn't out-and-out told the rabbi what had happened to Rina, but the old man had figured it out by what *wasn't* being said. Decker felt bad discussing Rina without her consent, but he made a judgment call, hoping it was the correct decision. In the past, the old man had always been a source of comfort for both of them.

Cindy pulled up a chair beside him. "She's beautiful, isn't she?"

Decker smiled under his mask. "I only make beautiful girls."

Cindy gave a soft laugh. "You look . . . serene, Daddy."

"Babies do that to you. Brings back lots of memories of when you were born, kid. It was hot and muggy, and I remember thinking your mom was going to dehydrate if I didn't get her to the hospital. I can't believe that was nineteen years ago. Where does the time go?" Decker chuckled. "That's swell. Now I'm sounding like an old geezer. Stop me before I become my father."

Cindy laughed. Decker looked at his elder daughter's face, at the dark circles under her eyes.

"You didn't go home last night, did you?"

"I fell asleep. I rested."

"Go home, princess. Rabbi Schulman is with Rina. I'll wait for Rina's parents to take a shift."

"They just arrived with the boys not more than five minutes ago. They're waiting to see the baby. You should put Hannah in the layette so Nurse Simms can wheel her into the window area."

"Oh, sure." Decker stood, then settled the sleeping infant in her cart. He draped an arm around Cindy. "Did you ask Mrs. Elias if she'd stay with Hannah?"

"Yeah. She said she'd be delighted." Cindy lowered her head. "Guess I'm not needed anymore."

"Princess, you've been an enormous help these last eighteen hours. I couldn't have done it without you."

"If you want, I'll come back after Mrs. Elias leaves."

"Yes, I'd like you to very much. You and Nurse Bellson work things out?"

"Not really. She still hates me. I can't figure out why."

"Don't bother. It's her problem, not yours."

Cindy smiled, but she was clearly troubled.

"What's wrong?" Decker asked.

"Daddy, did you know that Nurse Bellson pulls double shifts an average of twice a week?"

"Where'd you find this out?"

"Darlene. Doesn't it sound like she's overinvolved with the babies?"

"Sounds to me like Darlene shouldn't be gossiping with you."

"Darlene didn't say *she* thought Marie was overinvolved. That's *my* observation. And it's not just the babies, it's the *mothers*, too. I happened to overhear her lecture this teenaged mom on how to care for her baby. She was very bossy. 'Do this, don't do that.' And then you know what she did?"

"No. Why don't you tell me?"

Cindy smiled. "She asked a couple of moms to pray to Jesus with her. Don't you think that's completely inappropriate?"

Decker was quiet, taking in Cindy's words. "Yes, as a matter of fact, it is."

"I think we should say something to her boss."

Decker exhaled forcefully. "Cindy, while I appreciate your sense of propriety—"

"I should keep my mouth shut, right? At least while Hannah's under her care."

Decker didn't answer.

"Maybe we should move Hannah to another nursery," Cindy suggested.

"They're going to ask why," Decker said. "Then what do I tell them? Because my daughter doesn't get along with your top charge nurse who has worked here for over a decade? A nurse who was nice enough to let her hang around even though it's bending the rules? If Marie had really wanted, she could have kicked you out. But she hasn't done that. That's worth something, Cynthia."

"Then why does she have such hostility toward me?"

"Probably because you're treading on her turf. It's irrational. From what you've described, I'm not saying the woman's without problems."

"Maybe she resents you and Rina because you're not Christians."

Decker shrugged. "I don't think so. I think she's just territorial."

"Darlene isn't like that at all."

"Are we talking about the same Darlene who left you in charge of a dozen newborns?"

"She didn't leave me in *charge*."

"Cindy—"

"Daddy, better I be in charge than some of the staff during the graveyard shift. It gets real *weird* here at night."

Again Decker paused. "What exactly do you mean by weird?"

"Darlene said because of the budget cuts, the hospital is forced to use a lot of temporaries and floaters. Some of them are very strange. Believe me, we're very lucky to have Hannah under Darlene's care."

"Well, that was confidence-inspiring." Decker bit the ends of his mustache. "Maybe I should check Hannah out today. The pediatrician told me medically she could be discharged. But I really wanted her to stay overnight. It's going to be another day before Rina can come home, and I wanted to give her a chance to hold Hannah. I didn't want her to feel isolated from everything. But you're a sharp kid. If you say it's weird, I'll take both of them out of here."

Cindy looked pained with the responsibility of decision. "Dad, I'm real tired. Maybe I'm exaggerating."

Decker sat back down. "Good Lord, do I know that feeling."

"Daddy, *I'll* watch Hannah again tonight. Last thing I want is to take the baby away from Rina." Cindy hesitated. "How's she doing?"

Decker didn't answer.

"Daddy?"

Decker ran his hands over his face. "There've been a few complications, but she'll be all right."

"Serious complications?"

"She'll be all right," Decker said again.

"You're hiding something from me, aren't you?"

Decker looked at his daughter. "I just don't like talking about Rina when she's not around."

"You're right. I don't mean to be intrusive."

Decker put his arm around his daughter. "Princess, go tell the nurse to wheel the baby out. Then I want you to go home and get some rest. Come back here when you're refreshed. I really do need your help."

"Daddy, it's *my* pleasure being able to help you." Cindy ran her toe along the ground. "Being able to be with you like this has been really nice. You and I talking like friends. I know you're my father first. But it's nice to be friends with your dad, right?"

Decker tousled Cindy's rust-colored hair. "Yes, it's very nice."

They had moved her to a regular hospital room—an indication that she was no longer in danger. Now she was just a mere patient. They'd look after her for a day or maybe two, then she'd be released. No matter that she'd leave a shell of what she'd been. That didn't *concern* the hospital.

As long as her heart was beating and her breathing was steady, she'd be sent home.

She didn't look at Rabbi Schulman. From a single glance, Rina knew Peter had told him. One part of her felt angry and betrayed. But the other side whispered relief. The emotional pain was too much to bear alone, too much to comprehend. Why was happiness always ripped away from her? After Yitzchak had died, she thought she'd never love again. But *Hashem* knew better. She met Peter, and she did love again. It was a miracle.

Then this.

Why did He feel the need to constantly *test* her? Wasn't her unwavering faith enough?

Without her realizing it, tears had formed—hot and bitter. Still staring at the wall, she said, "He shouldn't have told you. It wasn't his place to tell you."

"I knew something was very wrong, Rina Miriam," the *rav* said softly. "Akiva simply told me the specifics." He paused. "Perhaps it was my fault. I asked Akiva detailed questions. I apologize for prying into your life."

Rina didn't answer. Now, instead of being angry, she felt guilty that she had made Rabbi Schulman apologize. Weak and sick, pain encircling her like a tight girdle, she wanted to sleep for a hundred years.

Schulman said, "I would like to wish you a *refuah shelenah*, Rina Miriam—a very speedy recovery. I am sorry for your pain. It is confusing when unfortunate things happen to nice people. It puts us at odds with our sense of justice."

Rina turned to the *rosh yeshiva*. The man was in his late seventies, and his age was finally beginning to show. His skin was wrinkled and mottled, but his dark eyes were as clear as ever. He sat stoop-shouldered, legs crossed, his liver-spotted hands clasped and resting on his knee, fingers holding the rim of his homburg. He wore his usual black suit and tie and a starched white shirt. His beard was white, as was his hair. Atop his head was a black silk skullcap.

Rav Schulman was a calm man, a *calming* man—his voice, his presence. No matter what life demanded of him, he always had enough time for those who needed him. Rina said, "I suppose this is a minor setback in the scheme of things." She sighed, then grimaced as her wound throbbed. Her voice had come back, but her throat still felt raw. "It isn't the Holocaust."

"No, it is not the *Shoah*. But that doesn't mean you aren't entitled to your grief, Rina Miriam. I lived through the *Shoah*; I lost my only son. Yet I still become frustrated when I misplace my wallet. So what does that say about human nature?"

Rina sank into her pillow and stared at the ceiling. "I feel petty for feeling so . . . bitter."

"Your operation was far from petty. Your bitterness is very understandable." Schulman licked his lips. "Are you in pain? Do you need anything?"

Rina looked at the I.V. in her arm. "Nothing, thank you. My doctor told me I can eat solid food for lunch. Not exactly heart-stopping news. But it is the only news I have."

"I'm glad you are recovering nicely."

"Thank you for coming down, Rav Schulman. You have always been a rock of support for me and my family."

"You're welcome, Rina Miriam. Have you seen your baby?"

"They won't . . . I'm still running a fever, and they don't want the baby to contract anything."

"It will help when you can hold your baby."

Rina continued to stare at the acoustical ceiling tiles, wet streaks down her cheek. "I have three *healthy* children, *baruch Hashem*. I should be doing *better* than this."

"You needn't reproach yourself for showing human emotion. Nowhere in the Torah does it say we cannot feel sadness or happiness or anger or even *doubt*. Sarah laughed when *Hashem* told her she would conceive at the tender age of ninety. Some say it was the laughter of joy. After nine decades of being barren, she was elated at the prospect of having a child. But others say it was laughter of disbelief." Schulman paused. "Not so hard to imagine her disbelief, nu?"

Rina nodded.

"*Hakodesh Baruch Hu* Himself tells Sarah of such a miraculous, wonderful event," the *rav* continued. "The same *Kodesh Baruch Hu* who *created* the world. Is nothing beyond Him? Is there anything that He cannot do? Yet Sarah—a *prophetess*—still could not think beyond *her* earthly limitations, and laughed at *Hashem*'s prophecy. So if she could be human, so can you."

"I'm angry at God," Rina whispered.

"I, too, have been angry at God. He is strong. He can take your anger without feeling personally affronted."

Rina surprised herself by smiling.

Schulman said, "You are not without insight, Rina Miriam. You should be grateful for your three healthy children. And you *are* grateful. But while I don't want to put words in your mouth, I would imagine you are saddened by the fact that your family size was determined by a surgeon rather than you. In reality, how much control do we actually have over our lives? Life is a loan from *Hashem*. We are put here by His design; so shall we leave by His design. So if death, like life, is part of the Eternal's plan, why do we say *tehilim* for the sick? Do we really think that our prayers will alter *Hashem*'s design?"

The rabbi held his finger up in the air.

"The answer for me is yes, they can. We believe in a personal God—a God who at least *listens* to our prayers. We don't understand *Hashem*'s ultimate design. But that doesn't mean we can't *ask*. King David knew his first offspring with Batsheva was a child born from sin. He knew from prophecy that the child wouldn't live. The words came directly from the prophet Natan's lips. Yet David, *Hashem*'s own anointed, fasted and prayed to *Hashem* to spare the child."

"It didn't work," Rina said.

"No, it didn't. But David gave it a try. There are times when *Hashem* is willing to deviate from His original plans, times when He has forgiven the most grievous of sins. Our prayers are not empty words, Rina Miriam. Though the world may seem very dark now, *Hashem* has an open ear for you. You may ask. You may not get, but you may *ask*."

Rina's hand fell upon the clamp that closed her surgical

incision. To spare her own life, they had taken away her ability to create life. "I don't want ... well, I want but I don't expect miracles. I know ..." Her eyes moistened. "I know I can't have a magical transplant. I can't have any more children. I ... will learn to accept that. But right now, I want the rage to go away. It hurts to be so angry."

"You will not be bitter the rest of your life. You are a strong woman. You will go on with your life. You will laugh again. You will enjoy your beautiful family. Just give yourself time for reflection and thought...."

Rina held back tears. "I'll try."

Schulman patted her hand. "You are very tired. Rest while you can. It hasn't been so long that you can't remember how much energy it takes to care for an infant."

"Rav Schulman?"

"Yes?"

"That *pasuk* about King David? It has always bothered me."

"How so?"

"David wept and fasted and prayed and wailed *before* the baby died. As if he were anticipating his mourning."

"This is very true."

"But then *afterward*, he got up and washed and dressed and anointed himself. Wouldn't you have expected some kind of ritual mourning *after* the baby died as well?"

"Yes, you would. And David's behavior puzzled his servant as it puzzles you. There have been several commentaries on the issue. The first: A child isn't considered a full life until after thirty days, so it would have been improper for David to sit *shivah* for him. Second: King David actually *did* sit *shivah* for his son. The passage 'and he arose from the earth' meant he came up after the traditional seven days of mourning."

The rabbi took a breath and twirled the tip of his beard around his forefinger.

"The third interpretation was made by the radak—Rav David Kimchi—and it is what we just talked about: that David's fasting before the child died was a prayer to *Hashem* to spare the child. Once the baby died, David saw that this was the will of God, and his rising from his mourning—the anointing, dressing, and washing—was to show his kingdom that he accepted the will of *Hashem*, no matter how painful."

"So I should get up and wash and go buy myself a new dress, huh?"

"Not a bad idea, even if you mean it allegorically. Rina Miriam, you should do whatever *you* need to do to get you over this difficult time. If you need to grieve, grieve. If you need to be angry, be angry. If you want to put it behind you, you can do that, too. Judaism has a lot of rituals, a lot of nonnegotiable behaviors. But we also allow for a great deal of personal freedom. Personal freedom and its sister trait, personal responsibility, are what make the religion so hard. But they are also what make the religion so satisfying."

ELEVEN

LIKE THE OLD DANCE MARATHONS, IT WAS AN ENDURANCE test. Cindy stayed awake out of sheer stubbornness. Though queasy and off-balance, she knew she'd make it through the night. She'd had lots of prior experience from cramming for finals.

A little past one and all was well. Up for hours upon hours. As she flipped through her memory file, she seemed to recall her father doing consecutive shifts at work for two, even three days in a row . . . her mother complaining about it, some of her annoyance stemming from worry. How did Dad operate on such little sleep? But Dad was always driven.

Cindy contemplated a catnap—Hannah had just fallen asleep and wasn't due to be fed for two more hours—but she had decided against it after talking to Dad about Marie . . . and about Darlene, also. Hannah was just too important for her to be asleep at the wheel.

At this point, Cindy didn't really trust *anyone* on duty. So many weirdos coming in and out of the nursery, all of them hidden under surgical masks. Not that Cindy really *knew* they were weirdos. It was the time of night. Everyone looked fun-house distorted.

Just make it through the next six hours, and Hannah would no longer be her responsibility. Rina would be going home in the morning, the baby with her. Dad had even hired a baby nurse named Nora. Even though Cindy had told him that she'd take care of Hannah until Rina was well enough. But that was Dad. Worried that she wasn't having enough fun. And then when she tried to have some fun, he'd worry for her safety.

It was an occupational hazard of his job, always seeing the world as a battlefield. That's why she decided to study criminal science from an academic viewpoint. Still, it must be thrilling to be tossed in the thick of it. A rush that did strange things to your head.

Like right now. She thought of herself as kind of an undercover cop, analyzing Marie and Darlene while trying to appear casual. Silly, but it helped pass the time.

One-fifteen A.M.

All the babies from Nursery J had been wheeled back home, an earful of noise coming from the other room. Cries in counterpoint harmony. *Symphonie aux Bébés*!! From all the fussing and yelling, it was a sure bet that Marie was doing checkups. Not that Marie was particularly heavy-handed, although Cindy thought Darlene was better, but the babies didn't like the procedures. They didn't like the weighings because the nurse had to unwrap them, and the cold air on their tummies made them cry. They didn't like the measuring because they were on their backs, their little leggies all stretched out. All the probing and poking. And then there were the blood tests taken from their teeny heels. That was always good for a yelp or two.

The stuff you pick up hanging around a hospital.

The crying seemed a little louder tonight. Maybe it was just her. Sound magnifies when one is sleep-deprived. Something she'd learned in one of her psych courses.

Cindy glanced at the clock again. The big hand had moved two minutes.

Too tired to read, she scanned *Scientific American* and looked at the pictures. Multicolored graphs and schematics that looked like stacked Tinkertoys. They were supposed to represent the cellular makeup of a rare tree lichen. She closed the magazine and placed it on her lap. Then she stood and put the magazine on the chair and peered inside the layette.

Hannah was snoozing like the proverbial baby.

Cindy didn't want to bug the nurses, but she was so damn bored staying up with no one to talk to. Maybe she could help Darlene. Darlene was always willing to give her something to do. Part of it was propaganda: showing her the wonders of nursing. Every time Cindy did something, Darlene would praise her to high heaven and tell her what a wonderful nurse she'd make, how the profession needed smart, dedicated people like herself. Cindy took the compliment but tuned out the message. Though she'd learned that nursing was a lot more than changing bedpans, she'd also sensed that the profession was a lot of hard work and responsibility for the compensation. Always under a doctor's orders . . .

Not that power and money were important to her. But passion was. She didn't feel passionate about nursing, not like she did about criminal sciences.

Cindy blinked several times, then stared out the window to the nursery. Lightly, she massaged her temples, trying to rub away the small throbs of an upcoming headache. Headaches just like Dad's, only sometimes hers turned to migraines. Dad said he had them in his younger days. The wonders of genetics. It was all the noise. The babies going at it without coming up for air—so *loud*.

Carefully, she tiptoed to the main section of the nursery, her eyes falling on the layettes aligned in teeth-comb order. No one was around—not Marie, not Darlene, not any of the other nurses. Distressed-infant cries were echoing off the walls.

Cindy felt strange and suddenly cold.

She called out a hello, projecting so she could be heard over the squeaks and wails.

No answer.

Wrapping her arms around her chest, she walked over to the layettes. Baby Girl Jackson's diapers had leaked onto the blanket. Spencer Dole had become completely un-tucked, the blanket loosely covering the infant's face. My God, even Baby Boy Yamata was crying. He had spit up on his blanket, black hair wet and sticky.

Cindy pulled the coverlet off Spencer's face and placed the red-faced little baby boy on his stomach after reswaddling his body. Comfortable and cozy, the infant im-mediately fell asleep as he sucked on his fingers. She cleaned Baby Boy Yamata's face with a sterile wipe, wrapped him in a clean blanket, and placed him on his stomach. That was his position of choice. He closed dark eyes and drifted off to baby slumberland.

She looked around. Alone and anxious, she changed Baby Girl Jackson's diaper, hoping no one would walk in and think she was molesting the infants. She knew she had no business touching the babies, but no one was in sight.

Something was wrong.

She looked inside the glass window of the nurses' station for Nursery J.

Empty.

Where the heck were Marie and Darlene?

Cindy looked at the clock, looked at the window, looked at the babies, her mind dizzy with indecision. She started toward the yellow line, but realized she was suited up. If she crossed the border, would she have to regown in order to get back to Hannah? She didn't even know where the nurses kept the gowns.

Then she saw the wall phone and a directory posted to

the phone's immediate right. She dialed the exchange for Front Desk. The phone rang and rang, and no one answered. Then she tried the hospital operator, who answered after ten rings. Cindy explained the situation to the operator and was then connected back to the front desk. Again no one answered.

Darlene had said there had been some major cutbacks at the hospital, but this was *ridiculous*! Suppose Cindy was a sick person who needed help? Or suppose she was calling for one of the *babies* who needed help? What a disaster that would be. Her mind was suddenly besieged with worst-case play-outs.

The clock read 1:45.

All of a sudden, time was moving quickly.

Two experienced nurses supposedly on shift, and there wasn't a soul in sight.

What to do, what to do?

Give it another five minutes.

And then what would she do?

At two, she tried the front desk again.

No one.

Where *was* everyone? A baby could be choking or something.

Now she was thinking like Dad.

Dad!

Good old Dad!

She could call him, but she didn't want to wake up Rina. Nor did she want Rina to know about the lax care at the nursery. Daddy was right. Darlene *was* weird to leave the babies alone. And Marie was weird, too. But at this moment, she would have given a lot to see either of their faces.

What on earth was *going on*?

As soon as the clock clicked 2:10, Cindy put her foot tentatively over the yellow line. Walking swiftly, encountering no one in the halls, she went directly to Rina's room and knocked softly on the door. When no one answered, she opened it and stepped inside.

Dad was sleeping in a cot next to Rina's hospital bed. She went over and gently shook his shoulders. His arousal was so fast that he startled her. Then she remembered he was used to waking up on a moment's notice. He was wearing gray sweats and had on tennis shoes that looked as big as boats. His bleary eyes scanned her face. A glance and he knew something was wrong. He put his arm around her shoulder and led her into the hallway.

"What is it?"

"Hannah's fine, Daddy."

Decker took a deep swallow and brought his hand to his chest.

"I scared you," Cindy said. "I'm sorry. I just didn't know what to do—"

"Do about *what*?"

"There's no one in the nursery—"

"*What?*"

"For about forty-five minutes," Cindy said. "I tried calling the operator and the front desk, but no one ans—"

"Who's with the babies now, Cindy?"

"No one—"

"Good God!" Decker started jogging. "You left Hannah *alone*?"

"I'm sorry, but I just didn't know—"

"Why didn't you *call* me?"

"I didn't want to wake up Rina—"

"Cindy, for God's sake, use some common sense! It's better to call and wake Rina up than to leave Hannah alone—"

"I'm sorry—"

"Jesus!"

"Daddy, you're going the wrong way." She tugged on his arm and steered him to the left. "This way."

Quickly, they ran down the common nursery hallway, nearly bumping into Darlene. The plump nurse looked at them wide-eyed, then started marching toward Nursery J.

"What's wrong?"

"Where *were* you?" Cindy asked.

"Nursery B," Darlene said defensively. "If you needed something, why didn't you ask Marie?"

"Because I can't find Marie."

"What?" Darlene exclaimed. "Then who's with the babies?"

"Good question!" Decker snarled.

"No one in there for the last hour maybe," Cindy said.

"That's *crazy*!" Darlene said. "I passed Marie a long while back. She said she was on her way back to Nursery J."

"Then she didn't show up," Decker said.

When they arrived at the nursery, Darlene stopped and said, "Detective, you're going to have to wait here, because you're not suited up."

"Cindy, go in and tell me Hannah's okay."

"Right away."

Darlene faced Decker. "I'm very sorry. I don't know how this hap—"

"It happened because you were careless," Decker snapped.

"I don't appreciate your *rudeness*, Detective."

"And I don't appreciate hospital negligence."

Darlene folded her arms around her chest. "I don't think there's any sense in pursuing this conversation."

"I agree," Decker said. "So why don't you forget about my manners and just get back to work."

Red-faced and shaking, Darlene opened and closed her mouth. Then she turned and disappeared within the inner sanctum of the nursery. Decker looked down at his sides and saw his hands clenched into fists. Slowly, he uncoiled his fingers. Cindy came back a moment later. She was breathless.

"She's fine, Daddy. Sleeping like . . ." Suddenly, Cindy broke into tears. "I'm sorry."

Decker hugged his daughter tightly. "No, *I'm sorry*, Cynthia. I shouldn't have belittled you like that. That was terrible." He laughed nervously. "A heap of thanks for all your help, huh?"

"But you were right," Cindy dried her tears on his sweats. "I shouldn't have left Hannah. I should have just called you."

"As long as Hannah's okay."

Cindy pulled away and nodded. "She's fine. I'll just go back—"

Decker pulled her back into his arms and hugged her again. "Cindy, thank you, thank you, *thank you!*"

She smiled. "It's okay, Daddy."

Decker said, "I'm checking Rina and Hannah out just as soon as Rina gets the final okay from her doctor. This place is a security nightmare. You better believe Rina's doctor as well as the administration are going to be hearing from me. Some heads are going to roll."

"Daddy, Darlene is a single parent—"

"I don't care, Cynthia. If this is a typical example of her competence, it stinks!"

"What about Marie?" Cindy said. "Isn't she at fault, too?"

"Cindy, as far as I'm concerned, the both of them aren't fit to run a chicken coop!"

Cindy broke off and whispered, "Daddy, you're shouting."

Decker stopped. "Dad on the rampage, huh?"

Calm down, Deck.

"I'm all right, Cindy." Decker gave her a forced smile.

And remember to unclench your jaw.

Sighing, Cindy hooked her arm around her father's. "I understand your feelings. I'd be upset, too. As a matter of fact, I *am* upset! I was panicked, seeing all those babies and not knowing what to do. Watching Hannah has really turned into an awesome responsibility."

Decker digested that. "You're right. It's not what you're supposed to be doing. It was just that Rina needed me very badly. But now, you and Hannah need me more. You go on home. *I'll* stay with Hannah."

"Daddy, I didn't mean *that*."

"I know. I just want you to go home and get some sleep, okay?"

Cindy looked down.

"Princess, it has nothing to do with trust. You're as capable as I am, we both know that. We also both know that I'm not going to be able to sleep a wink until Hannah is *out* of here. You know how I am once I get a bug in my brain. So humor me, okay?"

"I understand. Would you like me to look after Rina?"

"No, I'd like you to go home and get some sleep."

"I can sleep on your cot, Daddy. If Rina needs something, I can get it for her. Besides, I've gotten to know Hannah. Maybe Rina would enjoy hearing all about her. How often she sleeps, how often she eats, how many ounces she drinks, how often she *poops*."

Decker laughed. "That's really nice, Cindy. And yes, I think Rina would really like to hear all about Hannah."

"It's her first daughter."

"Yeah." Decker winked at her. "Something special about those first daughters."

Cindy smiled.

Decker said, "Go bunk down in the cot. When Rina wakes up, tell her we switched places. Don't tell her what just happened. No sense scaring her."

"I'll just tell her you were giving me a sleep break."

"That's good." Decker looked around. "I need a gown, don't I?"

"Yes. Oh, here's Darlene. Can you get my father a gown? He's going to spend some time with Hannah."

Darlene didn't answer. She looked dazed.

"What is it, Darlene?" Decker said tensely. "Is everything all right?"

"It's . . ." Darlene put her hand to her mouth. "I don't know where the devil Marie is. I've paged her and . . . this is . . . I . . ."

Decker regarded the nurse's face—as white and blank as an empty canvas. Her voice was unnatural; her hands were shaking. He said, "Sit down and tell us what's wrong."

She gazed helplessly at Cindy. "I've called Security. They're going to want to talk to you."

"*Me?*" Cindy felt her chest tighten. "Why do they want to talk to me?"

"What's *wrong*?" Decker said louder.

"It's crazy. . . ." Darlene muttered. "She came back at twelve-oh-five. She was on her way here when I left to help out in some of the other nurseries."

"*Who* was here?" Cindy said. "Marie? Marie hasn't been here for the past hour."

"I can't seem to locate . . . It's simply not . . . and Marie's not answering her page. It's crazy. In all my years as a nurse, I've never . . . I mean you *read* . . ." Again she faced Cindy. "*Somebody* had to have been here, Cindy. Someone must have been in the nursery."

"Maybe somebody was here, Darlene," Cindy said. "I was with Hannah. I wasn't in the main nursery—"

"So you *must* have seen someone. Who did you see?"

"I didn't *see* anyone. I was busy with Hannah."

"Why are you interrogating my daughter?" Decker said.

"I'm not interrogating. I'm just asking—"

"Why?"

"If only Marie . . ."

"Why does Security want to talk to my daughter?" Decker said forcefully.

"Because she isn't here." Darlene began to shake all over. "And Cindy was probably the last person to see her."

"But you said *you* saw Marie in the hallway, Darlene," Cindy said. "That would make you the last person to see Marie."

"No, not *Marie*!" Darlene burst into tears. "It's one of the infants! I can't find Baby Girl Rodriguez!"

TWELVE

NOSE PRESSED TO THE GLASS, DECKER STARED AT THE newborns—things no bigger than a rib roast, completely helpless . . . sinless. His heart went out to them, knowing that life would dish out a fair amount of dirt even if they were *lucky*. Baby Girl Rodriguez's safety net had unraveled just a few days into her existence. His eyes traveled over the infants of differing races and sexes until they landed on an empty layette. His heart began to pound.

"Hey, Sergeant."

Decker spun around, startled by the interruption.

Officer Brian Harlow. He'd been in uniform nearly three decades. He was still muscular and fit, but the years were there. Hair that was more silver than blond, a gut straining the buttons of his shirt. Vanity probably prevented him from admitting he needed a larger size. Harlow ran his fingers through his slicked-back hair.

"We've done three passes through the lots, through the immediate neighborhood, too." He shook his head. "No sign of the red Honda. It's still dark, not easy to tell colors, but we'll keep trying. Should be better when the sun comes up. In the meantime, do you want to put out an APB on the car?"

"Yeah, call it in."

Harlow clapped his hands together. "You got it."

"Any action by Bellson's apartment?"

"Just talked to the cruisers. Everything's quiet."

"No movement inside?"

"Nothing."

"Any lights?"

"Black as a well," Harlow said. "When do you think the warrant'll come through?"

"Probably take another hour or so," Decker said. "Hollander couldn't get through to the first two judges. Finally, he managed to locate a third and wake him up. He's on his way to His Honor's house as we speak."

"How's the baby's mother?"

"Lourdes Rodriguez," Decker stated. "Detective Dunn's with her now."

"I'll call in that APB." Harlow slapped Decker's back. "Congratulations on your kid, by the way."

"Thanks."

Decker checked his watch. Darlene had last seen Marie around midnight. If Marie had taken off with the baby, she'd have a big jump on them. He had sent some uniforms to watch her apartment. So far nothing.

Why would a woman who had worked with babies for years suddenly snatch a kid? A latent maternal longing? A fit of madness? Maybe she'd done it against her will. Some psycho sticking a gun to her temples and forcing her to take the baby. It was that very thought that scared Decker the most—Marie and the infant in the hands of a psycho.

Slipping his hands into his pockets, he glared at the security guard. Guy was pissed, probably felt usurped—too damn bad. He and his guard buddies had had their chance, and they'd blown it with a capital *B*. Not that TECH-WATCH Securities International wasn't working overtime, covering its butt, hoping to keep the liability down.

Good luck, pal.

Mom was hysterical now, not even thinking about litigation. But after a day or two, even if the baby was recovered safely, odds were that the security firm and the hospital would get phone calls from a heavy-breathing lawyer.

Marge walked over to him, notebook in hand. "How's it going, Rabbi?"

Decker stuck out splayed fingers and rotated his wrist back and forth. "How's Lourdes Rodriguez?"

"Sleeping."

"Get a chance to talk to her?"

"A little. She isn't married to the father, but they're together—boyfriend/girlfriend. She couldn't imagine Papa stealing their baby. Or forcing Marie to steal the baby. As a matter of fact, she grew hysterical at the prospect of telling him what happened. She's afraid of what he might do."

"To her?"

"To her, more like to the hospital." Marge raised her eyebrows. "Seems Matty likes to play with matches and owns a firearm or two—"

"Jesus!"

"If I were you, I'd get Rina out of here."

"She's leaving at ten this morning. We'd better put a watch on this guy once he's informed. What's his full name?"

"Matthew Luke Lopez."

"Did he Anglicize his name?"

"No, it's his legal name. He's American born but was raised in the barrio. Lourdes said he has a good heart, but a bad temper."

"Tell me something new," Decker said under his breath. "How old is he?"

"Seventeen, eighteen. Lourdes wasn't sure."

"Prime age for impulse."

"Yeah, I thought about that." Marge stopped talking. "In all fairness to Matty, Lourdes wasn't making a lot of sense. Doc upped her dose of sedatives. She's completely zonked out now, poor kid." She pushed wisps of hair out of her brown eyes. "Man, this is just horrible! So close to home. You must be *freaked*."

"Yeah, I'm a little . . ." Decker was quiet. "Did you get anything out of the Rodriguez family?"

"Mamacita is with Lourdes now. She speaks broken English, refers to her sons a lot."

"Lourdes's brothers are here?"

"Waiting for me in the lobby. I kicked them out of the hospital room early on. Which didn't endear me to the clan. But I couldn't get anything done with three mucho macho guys hanging over my shoulder. I did tell them to stick around, that I'd want to talk to all of them. That didn't set right with them, either. Guess their prior experiences with the police haven't been positive. At least I feel I'm earning my money. You want me to interview the nurse who was on duty?"

"Darlene Jamison," Decker said. "No, I'll handle her. I did a quick interview with her right when it happened. She wasn't making much sense, either. But she did give me an approximate timetable of her whereabouts. She was where she said she was. But I'm far from done with her."

"Where is she?"

"In the nurses' station, making arrangements with her baby-sitter to stay a little longer. I'm angry as hell at the woman, but I do feel for her. She looks genuinely shaken. And she's probably worried about her own derriere. She's got some liability in this." Decker looked at his watch again. "It's been about fifteen minutes. I'll give her another five minutes, then we'll go over it again."

Marge paused. "What do you want to do with Cindy?"

"She's with Rina. You can interview her just as soon as my ex–father-in-law gets in."

"Don't you think you're overdoing it by getting her a lawyer?"

"It's not her lawyer, Marge, it's her grandfather. Jack was adamant that she not say anything until he comes down. What the heck." He shrugged. "Do you want me to assign someone else to do the interviewing?"

"No, Pete, I'm comfortable with it," Marge said. "Cindy's a witness, not a suspect. As a matter of fact, I'll take over the entire case if you want. You still have time off. Maybe it would be better if you spent it with Rina. There'll be plenty of other cases to bust."

"I keep trying to tell myself that. That I shouldn't be working. But then . . ." He slammed his fist into his open palm. "Marge, it could have been *Hannah*! If Cindy hadn't been with her, who knows? I *owe* it to that little baby girl to find her. I owe it to her and to her *mother*."

"Pete, everyone's busting their chops with this one. The case is top priority. Hospital's sealed. We're going to interview anyone who passed through these hallways, anyone on duty, and anyone just hanging around. Cameras will be down for the morning news—we're gonna get the word out about this little girl in a *big* way. You owe something to Rina, too."

"You know what Rina will say, Marge."

"Find the kid."

"Find the kid," Decker repeated.

Marge gave up. "So how do you want to divide this?"

"I'll investigate Marie Bellson. Someone just brought up her work file from Personnel. After I'm done with Darlene, I'll go through that. I'll also call back Hollander and find out if the warrant came through. When it does, I'm planning to visit Bellson's place personally."

"Fine. After I'm done dueling with the Rodriguez boys, I'll go over the interviews the uniforms are doing on the staff. Find out who saw what. See if the blues missed anything. How many do we have assigned to do the job?"

"Twelve—two per floor. Mike said he'd help you just as soon as he's done obtaining the warrant."

"That's good."

"Go over the accounts with a magnifying glass, Marge."

"I'm *glad* you told me that, Pete. Otherwise I would have been slipshod."

Decker frowned. "How 'bout cutting me a little slack, partner?"

"Sorry."

"I was talking as much to myself as I was to you."

"I know." Marge patted his shoulder—the one without the old bullet wound. "Just relax and concentrate on this Bellson lady."

There was a moment of silence. Decker said, "Do I make a lot of condescending remarks like that?"

"Occasionally."

"You know I don't mean anything by it. I think you're top-notch."

"I know, Pete. It's okay." Marge rubbed her eyes and looked up. "Cindy's counsel's here."

Decker waved his ex–father-in-law over. Jack Cohen was in his midsixties but still walked and talked and dressed like a young man. He had a sprightly voice, bright blue eyes, and a quick comeback for every remark. He could be fun to be around because his aggression was tempered by wit. Not so his daughter. "Counselor Cohen," Decker said. "My partner, and Cindy's interviewer, Detective Dunn."

"We've met before, but it's a pleasure." Cohen shook hands with Marge. "Where's my girl?"

"She's with Rina," Decker said. "I'll call her now that you're here. Thanks for coming down, Jack. It's probably not necessary—"

"It can't hurt." Cohen tugged on his jacket lapel. "She sounded upset, Peter. Scared. It's good you called me. I want to be with her, not because she's in trouble, but because she's my granddaughter and I love her." He turned to Marge. "Let me talk to her for a few minutes, then we'll talk to you."

"Sounds good," Marge said.

Cohen shook Decker's hand. "Congratulations on your new little girl, Pete."

"Thanks, Jack." Decker looked down, then up, and smiled.

Cohen said, "You want me to tell Jan when she and Alan come back from Europe?"

"No, Jack, if she doesn't hear it from me, she'll make my life miserable." Decker thought a moment. "Of course, if she does hear it from me, she'll still be miserable. But at least she won't bear a grudge."

"She'll probably even send you a baby gift." Cohen smiled. "You want to know the truth, I don't give a damn about you two anymore. I got a terrific granddaughter out of the marriage, I'm happy. *Ciao.*"

Marge waited until he left, then said, *"Ciao?"*

"Jack can be kind of Hollywood."

"How long did you work for him?"

" 'Bout six months—trust-and-estate planning. Can you imagine me doing trust-and-estate planning?"

"Why didn't you work for the D.A.?"

"Do you know what starting deputy D.A.'s make?"

"They make more than starting cops."

"But I wasn't a starting cop. I was a seasoned detective. A deputy D.A.'s job would have meant a pay cut. Estate planning paid very well." Decker rubbed his neck. "No regrets. It all worked out in the end. I'd rather be solving crimes than plea-bargaining felonies to misdemeanors."

Darlene declined Decker's offer of another cup of coffee. "I'm okay, Detective. I'm just . . . stunned."

"Aren't we all. Everything work out okay with the baby-sitter?"

"Yes, she said she'd . . ."

The nurse lowered her head, chin resting against her chest, eyes focused on her lap. They were red-rimmed and puffy, her pinched nose pink and raw. Slight of frame to begin with, Darlene had balled herself up into something inconsequential.

Decker said, "I want to go over everything one more time. When you left Nursery J, you claim the babies were supervised."

"Chris was there, and Marie was heading back there." Darlene looked up. "And of course your daughter was there—"

"Cindy was not in any kind of supervisory role, Darlene."

"Yes, that's true, of course. But she was in the back with Hannah. I just thought she might have heard something."

"Someone else is talking to Cindy. For now, I'm talking to you. So you left Nursery J, and Chris was there and Marie was on her way."

"Yes."

"Then what happened?"

"I went to help out at the other nurseries. Lots of babies without a lot of staff. A couple of scheduled regulars didn't show, so we had to make do with floaters and temps. Maybe one of them—"

"Everyone's being questioned. Who is this Chris, specifically?"

"Christine Simms. One of our nurses."

"She was in the nursery when you left?"

"Yes, she was there. And Marie would have been there in a minute. Then a little later I saw Chris in the hallway on her way to Nursery C. She'd been asked to help out with the weighings since we were so short-staffed. I asked her who was at Nursery J, and she said Marie was still there, that Marie told her she could handle it by herself."

"But you told me you passed Marie in the hallway."

"I *did*. She said she was on her way *back* to Nursery J. Someone has to be supervising the babies at all times."

"Someone like my daughter?"

"That was only for moments at a time," Darlene said defensively.

"When you walked me back to the elevators, you left the nursery without leaving someone in charge."

Darlene bit her lip. "I do run out for a moment from time to time. It's wrong. I was . . . you're right, Sergeant, it was irresponsible. What can I say? But I *wasn't* in charge of Nursery J when the baby disappeared. After I left, there were going to be two people in that nursery—Marie, the head nurse, and Chris."

"Who was officially in charge of J that night?"

"Marie. She's the charge nurse of the entire unit. Each nursery is supposed to have two nurses. That's officially. In reality, we're lucky if we have a nurse per nursery. You have any idea how much work that is for a single nurse?"

Decker didn't answer, thinking about her words. Hospitals compromising care for money. When questioned about the staff-to-patient ratio, hospitals always gave the same stock answer. It was either cut back or close down.

"Have you ever seen Marie run out for a moment and leave the babies alone?" Decker asked.

"No."

"Never? Not even once?"

"Honestly, no."

Decker said, "Who do you think was in Nursery J around the time the baby was taken?"

"It could have been anyone working tonight, including temporaries or floaters."

"We're compiling a list right now. These floaters ... who exactly are they?"

"They're nurses who go where they're needed. We're getting less and less OB nurses to work OB. In the past year, we've only had three nurses who have had specific training in OB or neonate. Makes it hard to get things done when you don't have specialists for the job."

"Going back to the floaters ... are they hospital employees?"

"I think so. But I don't know for sure."

"How about the temporaries? Are they employed specifically by the hospital, or does the hospital get them from agencies?"

"I don't know."

"Do you usually see the same floaters and temporaries working?"

"Some of the faces look familiar. I've even learned a name or two. Detective, I'm so shaken ... maybe I'll do better the next time we talk. I'm so sorry."

Decker held back a yawn and finished up some notes. He'd pursue the status of the work staff with the administrators. They'd know about hiring procedure. Then he remembered Cindy's description of the weirdos who worked at night. He was willing to bet that the hospital hired as cheap as possible and wasn't always meticulous about checking out credentials. Chances were the administrators wouldn't be forthcoming about opening up their files. They'd probably state that divulgence of names was an unwarranted invasion of privacy or some other bull. For them, it was going to be *cover your ass royally* time.

He said, "I'd like to talk to you about Marie Bellson."

Darlene nodded. "Did they find Marie's car?"

"Not yet."

"I just can't believe that Marie . . ." Darlene met Decker's eyes. "It doesn't make *sense*, Sergeant."

"Did Marie seem agitated lately?"

"No."

"Worried? Preoccupied?"

"No."

"Did she seem unusually happy— like she'd won the lottery?"

"No. She was just plain old Marie." Darlene redirected her eyes to him. "I just can't believe . . . it doesn't make *sense!*"

"Okay, let me ask you this, Darlene. Do you ever remember Marie going through some hard times?"

"Everyone goes through hard times."

"Tell me about Marie's."

"I don't know, Sergeant. I found out that you're *Sergeant* Decker, right?"

"Sergeant's fine," Decker said. "*Think*, Darlene. There's a *baby* at stake."

"I *know!*" She started sobbing. "It's all my fault!"

"Darlene—"

"If I'd just been a little more careful!"

"Darlene—"

"I just *trust* everyone!" she cried. "I think everyone's good, and no one would ever hurt a little baby. Who would ever hurt a *baby*? And now a little baby is gone because I was too trusting!"

"Darlene, whipping yourself isn't going to help." Decker handed her a tissue. "Let's talk about Marie. Think about Marie now."

Darlene dabbed her eyes and told him to go on.

Decker said, "Do you ever remember Marie going through some stressful times?"

"At work?"

"At work or in her personal life—a breakup with a mate, a parent dying, trouble with the kids, something like that."

"Marie didn't have children. Matter of fact, I don't recall Marie ever having a special someone. As far as I know, her life started and stopped with nursing and God."

She asked the moms to pray to Jesus with her. . . .
Decker remembered the gold cross over her uniform
pocket. He had mistakenly thought it was a medical
emblem—like the Red Cross.

"God?"

"She believed in Jesus. But she wasn't obnoxious about
it."

"Cindy said she used to ask patients to pray with her."

"Only if she felt they wanted to. She wouldn't ever have
forced Jesus down their throats. She wasn't preachy."

"It wasn't routine?"

"No, not at all."

"It is inappropriate."

Darlene was quiet. "Yes, I suppose it is."

Decker tapped his pencil against the pad. "Marie was
single for as long as you've known her?"

"Yes."

"Did she ever mention regrets at not having kids?"

Darlene shook her head. "She liked the babies, but not in
a sick way. Marie was terrific with the little ones, but she
was even more terrific with the moms. Helping them adjust
to their newborns. And she was great as a nurse supervisor.
She *trained* me, Sergeant. She trained just about every
nurse who has ever passed through OB in the last ten
years."

"Was that part of her job? To train nurses?"

"Yeah, of course. But she took it even further, 'cause
deep down she really *cared*. She took a special interest in
every single one of us. She wanted us to *know* what it
meant to be a truly dedicated nurse. She was a busy
woman, Sergeant, but she always had time for our questions. Had time for the moms' questions, too. That's why it
doesn't make sense."

"What do you mean when you say she took a special interest in her nurses? Don't all head nurses answer questions?"

"Marie went beyond that. First week on the job, I got an
invite to her home. I was nervous, I can tell you that. I
thought it was like a test." Darlene shook her head. "She

was just being friendly. Asked me to talk about myself, asked me what I wanted out of nursing, if I had any problems I'd like to discuss with her."

"Doesn't sound like the Marie Bellson I've been told about," Decker said. "The one I've heard about was all business and pretty testy."

"Marie could be testy. We're all under a lot of pressure here. But she really *cares*."

Darlene suddenly looked puzzled. Decker asked her what was wrong.

"Only problem with Marie was . . ." Darlene seemed to collect her thoughts. "Seemed to me that once I'd learned the ropes, she cut the personal relationship . . . didn't ask me to her house, didn't accept any of my invites to my house. She was nice enough at work—nice but professional. The personal touch was gone."

Darlene sighed.

"But you've gotta understand Marie, Sergeant. She saved her energies for those that really *needed* her. She's a true nurse inside and out. And she has ethics, a belief in right and wrong. And she's God-fearing. That's why I refuse to believe that she'd ever lay a finger to harm a little baby."

"Who said she's planning to harm the baby? Maybe she just took the baby and wants to raise it as her own."

"No, I don't believe it."

"Did Marie ever have any miscarriages?"

"So far as I know, she was never married."

"She could have had miscarriages without being married."

Darlene blushed. "I don't know of any miscarriages, no."

"Any abortions?"

Again Darlene turned red. "Not that I know of."

"Did Marie ever lose a child?"

"I wouldn't know."

"How about a younger sibling?"

"If you're trying to give her a motivation to steal a baby, I think you're barking up the wrong tree."

"Then why would she steal a baby?"

"I don't believe she did."

"Then where is she, Darlene? And where's the baby?"

"I don't know." Darlene suddenly shivered and hugged herself tightly. "I truly don't know."

THIRTEEN

It didn't matter what *she* said.

It didn't matter what *he* said.

Past is irrelevant. So is the future.

The here and now.

The here and now.

What mattered?

Who cared?

She cared.

That's how it all started . . . because she cared.

They didn't, but she did.

She cared.

She *cared*.

Flowers took up every available inch of space—either a hospital room or a mortuary. Decker put down his cup of coffee and smelled a bouquet of yellow roses. He pulled a blossom from the arrangement and presented it to Rina. She took it and placed it on her lap. Her eyes were unfocused . . . far away.

When she'd come into the hospital, there'd been a blush

in her cheeks. Now they were pale and bony. Decker sat on the bed, then took her hand and kissed it.

"How're you feeling?"

Rina took in her husband's face—suffused with tension and worry. "I just saw the six o'clock morning news. They flashed the baby's picture on the TV screen." She looked down. "You know the newborn photo that the hospital takes when the baby is a day old? The blanket in the background was the same blanket they used for Hannah's picture."

Decker nodded.

"Oh, Peter! And here I was feeling *sorry* for myself." Rina blinked back tears. "I'm such an *idiot* for not appreciating what I have."

Decker squeezed her hand. "Rina, you've been through an awful ordeal. It's okay to feel bad. I feel bad for you. And in all honesty, I feel bad for me. I feel like we both got a raw deal."

"It's trivial compared to what that poor mother must be going through."

"Your operation wasn't trivial, darlin'. But if we're comparing hells, I'd rather be in our shoes than in Lourdes Rodriguez's." Decker saw his Rina's face do a slow crumple. He drew her into his shoulder, caressing her arm as she cried. "Get it out, honey. Get it all out."

"I feel so *terrible!*"

"Scared?"

"Terrified!"

"So am I."

Rina raised her head. "You are?"

"It hit close to home." Decker straightened up. "You and Hannah are checking out of this place. Your mom's moving in with us until everyone's back on their feet. She's overjoyed that I asked for her help. I never thought I'd be saying this, but thank God for mothers-in-law."

Rina managed a smile. "Cindy really appreciated being part of the experience, too. She's been a real godsend. If it wasn't for her—"

"Don't even *think* about it," Decker interrupted. "It's too damn frightening."

No one spoke for a moment. The silence became eerie rather than comforting. Decker cleared his throat. "So . . . we have your mom and Cindy watching over you . . . and watching over the baby nurse, too. It's terrible to be suspicious, but after what happened—"

"Definitely. Look, Peter, Georgina said Nora was the *best*. But we both know what that means. If you don't want to use a baby nurse, I can manage—"

"No friggin' way!" He wagged his finger at his wife. "I don't want you out of bed, let alone working, even if you think you can do it. Your mom and Cindy'll be there full time, so you don't have to worry about a thing. I don't want you doing anything until the doctor says you're one hundred percent healed, *understand*?"

"Why not? I'm useless for anything else—" She stopped herself and sighed. "There I go again, feeling *sorry* for myself."

"Darlin', life isn't school. You don't have to get straight A's. Just promise me you'll take care of yourself— physically and emotionally. Do something *nice* for yourself, Rina. Read that book you've been putting off. Drink a cup of hot chocolate, smothered in whipped cream. Hey, I've got a great idea. Why don't we finally use the satin sheets we got for our wedding?"

"I'm saving them."

"For *what*?"

Rina thought about that. What was she saving them for? "You're right, Peter. I'll have my mom put them on the bed."

Decker couldn't believe his ears. She was actually *agreeing* with him. "*Thank* you, Rina." He checked his watch. "Do you know where Cindy is?"

"Jack took her away about a half hour ago." Rina knitted her fingers together. "Peter, who's watching Hannah?"

"All the nurseries are under special watch. Don't be concerned with Hannah's safety. I guarantee you she's fine."

"I didn't have a fever last time the nurse took my temperature." Rina's eyes became wet. "Do you think I could hold her now?"

Decker remembered how uplifting it had been to hold his baby—pure love for something so beautifully innocent. Rina needed that feeling.

"I'll ask the doctor, darlin'." Decker stood. "I'm sure it would do wonders for your spirit."

"It's the only thing I want right now."

"You bet. I'll find Dr. Hendricks."

Rina dried her eyes. "Peter, the missing baby . . . is it your case?"

"I took it on."

"I'm glad you did. It was the right choice."

Decker thought about that. *The right choice.*

It had been his *only* choice.

The interview was set up in an empty labor room. A metal-framed bed with stirrups on the end, I.V. stands posing like stainless stick figures, computer monitors, a nightstand with gizmos for positioning the bed, and a nurse's call button. So cold and impersonal, Marge thought. She wondered if there wasn't something in between birthing via high tech and squatting in the fields.

She pulled up a plastic red chair and motioned Cindy and her grandfather onto the bed. It wasn't going to be easy interviewing Pete's daughter, but compared to the Rodriguez boys, the teenager would be a cakewalk. The brothers were a modern-day James Gang, but in the last analysis, Marge felt they had nothing to do with the kidnapping.

Cindy was upset, poor kid. And she probably felt a little guilty, too. Jack Cohen sat close to her, drawing her near, his arm around her shoulder.

"Are you sure you're okay, honey?" he said to Cindy.

"I'm all right."

"Do you want something to eat or drink?" Marge asked.

"No, I'm okay," Cindy answered.

"I want you to relax," Marge said. "The more you relax, the more you can remember."

"I wish I could remember more! I wished I'd been paying closer attention!"

"Baby, no one could possibly have predicted something

like this," Cohen said. "Just relax and answer the questions to the best of your ability. That's the best way you can help."

Cindy felt her throat clog. "Thanks for coming down, Grandpa."

"What are you thanking me for? I had to come down. Grandma would have killed me if I didn't." To Marge, he said, "Detective?"

"Okay," Marge said. "Cindy, do you remember when you arrived at Nursery J?"

"Around three . . . maybe four in the afternoon."

"Who was there when you arrived?"

"Marie . . . Marie Bellson."

"Anyone else?"

Cindy thought for a moment. "There could have been . . . I don't remember."

"But you remember Marie being in Nursery J?"

"When I arrived, yes."

"Who else do you remember seeing in Nursery J?"

Cindy sighed. "Who didn't I see? Marge, there were people coming in and out of the nursery *all the time*. Some of them were suited up—the fathers, grandparents. They could go near the babies. Others stayed in the peripheries—the supply room or the nurses' office only. People like the janitors or orderlies. They'd restock stuff or sweep the floor or change the garbage and then just leave. There really wasn't a lot of control of who was in and out."

Marge rested her pencil against her pad. "You recall seeing janitors and orderlies in the nursery?"

"Yeah, sure."

"Do you recall seeing anyone who wasn't suited up near the babies?"

Cindy thought a moment. "I don't recall, but I wasn't with the babies most of the time. I was in the back room with Hannah. I couldn't really see what was going on. And with all the noise the babies were making, I couldn't hear too well, either."

"Who else besides janitors and orderlies do you remember wandering in and out?"

"Nurses, mostly . . . of course, there were doctors, too. And lots of *supply* people—salespeople, if you can believe that. They'd bring in all sorts of things—boxes of formula and sugar water, free samples of baby medicine, and lots of diapers. And then there were people from Laundry bringing in blankets for the layettes."

Marge frowned, surprised at how busy a single nursery could be.

Cindy said, "I saw them come and go. But like I said, mostly I was with Hannah. I used to take her layette away from the rest of the babies into this back room. Darlene set me up there, and Marie just kind of let me be through inertia. I liked it in the back because I wasn't in anyone's way." She paused. "I wasn't in Marie's way, specifically. She didn't like me—even after I brought her chocolate-chip cookies."

"You brought her cookies?"

"I thought it would help me get on her good side. Maybe it did. She let me stay."

"But you couldn't see or hear other people in front."

"I could hear snatches, catch glimpses of people. That's all. I should have been keeping an eye on Marie. I knew she was weird."

"Cindy," Jack said, "it was not your place or duty to keep an eye on the staff. You were there, but not in any work capacity whatsoever. You were there only as a favor to your father. So stop yelling at yourself."

Cindy sighed. "I just wish—"

"Uh-uh. I don't want to hear that," Cohen said.

"All I mean, Grandpa, is I feel so sorry for the baby. And for the mother. I got to know all the babies. I look at Hannah, I see them all." The teenager's eyes watered. "This is just so bad."

Jack kissed his granddaughter and looked at Marge. "She's just too good for this world."

"Oh, Grandpa!" Cindy returned her attention to Marge. "I remember Marie and Darlene being in the nursery, of course. Mostly, that's who I remember. And Christine Simms wafting in and out . . . oh—and Lily—that's

Darlene's trainee. I met her a couple of days ago. I don't remember seeing her last night, but who knows? All sorts of people were in and out. Babies going into their mothers' rooms, returning from their mothers' rooms."

"Lots of traffic, huh?" Marge said.

"You wouldn't believe it. There was no way to keep track of everyone without sign-up sheets."

Marge said, "Do you remember anyone who looked like they didn't belong there?"

"Not really. I don't remember seeing anyone not in a uniform or surgical scrubs. Everyone looked like they were *doing a job*. But *I* wasn't paying any attention, Marge."

"She knows that, honey," Cohen intervened.

"You're doing great, Cindy," Marge said. "Let's talk about Marie for a moment. You stated she didn't like you?"

"She didn't. I stayed out of her way."

"But occasionally you saw her."

"Yes, a couple of times."

"Did she appear professional when she worked?"

"Yeah, I suppose." Cindy looked troubled. "Sometimes I'd overhear her talking to other nurses about the mothers. Marie had preferences in her mothers. It bothered me."

Marge said, "Did you ever hear her say anything specific about Lourdes Rodriguez?"

Cindy's eyes widened. "Marge, she *did* talk about Lourdes Rodriguez. She told me she was counseling her."

Marge sat up. "What kind of counseling?"

"Baby counseling. How to bathe the baby, how to diaper the baby . . . basic stuff. Marie adopted this superior attitude when she lectured. That bothered me, too."

"Superior attitude?" Marge asked.

"Yeah, like 'They'd be lost without me.' That kind of thing. Darlene told me Marie liked doing that kind of stuff—teaching mothers how to care for their babies. If the mother didn't need her, she didn't like that."

"Marie told you that she didn't like the independent mothers?" Marge said.

"No, that was just my impression after listening to Darlene."

Jack said, "Honey, just stick to what *you* heard from Marie. The rest is what we call hearsay."

Marge smiled. Once a lawyer . . . "So Marie told you she was counseling this baby's mother?"

"Yes—maybe she didn't use the word *counsel*. More like teaching the mother."

"Okay," Marge said. "She seemed to take a special interest in Lourdes Rodriguez. How about this, Cindy? Did you ever see Marie take a special interest in Lourdes's baby?"

Cindy shook her head. "Not that I can remember. She talked more about Lourdes than about the baby. Marie didn't think Lourdes was equipped to handle the baby."

"She *said* that?" Marge asked.

"No, no, no, she didn't say it," Cindy said. "It was just my opinion."

Jack said, "Honey, just stick to what you heard."

"Grandpa, maybe Marge would like to hear my opinions."

Gently, Marge said, "Sure, but maybe a little later."

Cindy nodded. Marge thought she looked wounded. "Did Marie ever mention anything about how Lourdes Rodriguez wasn't fit to be a mother?"

"Truthfully, no. Marie never said that Lourdes wasn't fit. Just that she didn't know much. And that she should appreciate the baby Jesus gave her."

Marge's ears perked up. "Marie spoke about Jesus a lot?"

"Yeah, she liked to pray with her patients. I told Daddy this. We both agreed it was inappropriate."

"Did Marie ever mention she was doing God's work, Cindy?"

The teenager paused. "No . . . no she didn't."

"But she prayed with Lourdes?"

"I don't remember."

"Did Marie ever say anything about how the baby should be taken away from Lourdes because she didn't appreciate what Jesus gave her?"

"No."

"And you never remember seeing Marie being especially attached to Baby Girl Rodriguez?"

"No."

"Did Marie seem unusually attached to *any* baby in particular?"

"Not that I can remember."

"Did Marie ever mention going away very soon?"

"Marge, Marie hardly talked to me unless it was to say *I* was getting *too attached* to Hannah. When Marie was around, I minded my own business. I didn't pay much attention to anyone except Hannah."

"Your dad better be appreciative," Jack said.

"Grandpa, he's very appreciative." Cindy looked at Marge. "I wasn't much help to your case, was I?"

"Of course you've been a help, Cindy. The fact that Marie was talking about the baby's mother . . . hey, that's something we didn't know about. It shows that Marie had prior interest in this particular patient."

"But you're not any closer to finding the baby."

"Things take time, Cindy."

The room was silent. Cindy stood and placed her hands in her pants pockets. "I'm kind of tired. Is there anything else you need me for?"

"No, Cindy, you did great." Marge folded her notebook. "Thanks for your help. Now kick back and go home. Rina and Hannah will be needing you to take care of them."

Cindy sighed. "You know what I'm thinking? Who's taking care of Baby Girl Rodriguez? And who's going to take care of that poor mother?"

Marge looked at her partner's daughter and saw something familiar in her eyes—the fire of determination. Decker's expression to a T. That kind of passion to solve a crime was great for a career detective, but deadly for a nineteen-year-old kid.

"Cindy, you *are* going to go home and forget about this, right?"

"I can't *forget* about something like this, Marge."

"You know what I mean."

"No, I really don't."

"Okay," Marge said. "I'll be blunt. I don't want you going out and looking for the baby on your own."

Once again Cindy's eyes widened. "I hadn't even thought about that."

Her expression seemed genuine. It was then and there that Marge realized she had planted a seed inside Cindy's brain. She stuffed her notebook in her jacket pocket and silently cursed her big mouth.

Decker said, "How'd it go?"

"Your elder daughter's a doll," Marge answered. "But I'm worried she's going to get carried away. You can't very well say to her, don't get involved. She is involved. It's how to turn her off."

"I'll talk to her."

"Let me handle her, Pete. You and I could say the same thing. Coming from me, it'll be different."

"You're right about that," Decker said. "How'd it go with the Rodriguez brothers?"

"They were angry—angry at me, the hospital, authority in general. Real anger. Bottom line is, I don't think they were involved. Back to the obvious—Marie Bellson."

"Search warrant on Bellson's place finally came through," Decker said. "Do you want to come?"

"I'll meet you there in about an hour," Marge said. "I want to stick around here for a while. See what I can pick up." She lifted up Marie's personnel file. "Have you had a chance to go through this?"

"Just had time to skim it. I'm having a copy made for my files." Decker ran his hands through his hair. "From what I've seen, there's nothing much to write home about. Woman worked here for eleven years, had several complaints registered against her. A few noncompliances filed against her by two different doctors; once a patient mentioned she was rude to her. Another patient thought she was cold and uncaring."

"Any complaint dealing with Marie stuffing God down the throat?"

"Cindy told you about Marie praying with the patients."

"That's weird, Pete."

"Yes, it is. I wish to hell I had followed up on it. Maybe she heard Jesus tell her to grab a baby." He slammed his right fist into the waiting left palm. "Damn it, I shouldn't have brushed it aside."

Marge looked at her partner. He was so genuine in his self-flagellation. "Pete, religious people—even fanatics—don't generally go around snatching babies."

Decker knew a lot of religious fanatics—his mother, his wife. And what Marge said was true. Believing wholeheartedly in God—*any* God—had nothing to do with snatching babies. But lots of troubled people *used* God to excuse their impulsive or inappropriate behavior.

"If Marie had complaints about her excess religiosity," Decker continued, "they were probably handled off the record. What exactly did you learn from Cindy?"

Marge filled him in, then asked, "What do you think about Marie counseling Lourdes?"

"Lourdes didn't mention that to you?"

"No. And she didn't mention Marie praying with her. But that doesn't mean anything. She was hysterical when I spoke to her. I'll press her on it, find out exactly what Marie told her."

There was a pause.

"What are you thinking?" Decker asked.

Marge said, "If Marie felt Lourdes wasn't able to handle her child, maybe she snatched the baby out of concern for the kid's safety."

"Did you get the feeling that Lourdes was unusually irresponsible . . . or maybe she had an addiction problem or something like that?"

"No, but our conversation was superficial."

Decker said, "I'm sure Marie has seen hundreds of young teens just like Lourdes Rodriguez. Why'd she choose this baby?"

"Maybe something snapped. Maybe God told her to do it."

"But the profile I'm getting of Marie is not one of a

woman slowly going down the tubes. She wasn't showing any overt signs of cracking up."

"*Overt* signs, Pete."

"Yeah, there could have been some subtle signs that no one picked up. Nobody seemed to know her well."

"Maybe you'll find something at her house."

"Maybe." Decker heard someone call his name. He turned around. "What's up, Sergeant Harlow?"

"Detective Sergeant Decker, we've found something of interest in the parking lot."

"Marie's car?" Marge asked.

Harlow pressed his hands together. "No, Detective Dunn. It's more like fresh blood."

FOURTEEN

TOO MUCH RUSH, TANDY THOUGHT, HAD TO SLOW DOWN. Remember the words of the guru—to build the shape, do fewer reps with heavier weights.

That was the key. You can't lose sight of the key. The shaping, the sculpting. Otherwise, you lose control. Never lose control.

Never, *ever*, lose control.

Fewer reps with heavier weights.

Gotta get the control back.

Don't lose it, Roberts, don't lose it.

Fewer reps, heavier weights.

That would bleed off the excess entropy.

No entropy, only enthalpy.

Controlled energy.

She took a deep breath and let it out slowly, then pulled the pin from the one-twenty weight and slipped it into the one-thirty. Wiping sweat from her face, she felt her cheeks, skin as smooth as fine brandy. When she was modeling, people used to smother her pores with poison. All that base makeup to give her the *appearance* of flawless smooth skin. Why not live right, eat right, exercise right, and have the real thing?

Never lose control.

Otherwise they'd come back.

Only enthalpy.

Controlled energy.

Can't slip up this time, Roberts. Can't slip, can't slip, can't slip.

She clenched her teeth as she slid under the shoulder press, fingers gripped around the handle.

Check the position.

Arms parallel, small of the back secured by a rolled towel, feet planted firmly on the floor.

She felt her heart race.

Inhale, then let it out on the exertion.

One.

The loud, metallic clank of the weights slapping together.

No good. Not *controlled*. *She* needed to lower the weights down. They should never fall by themselves.

Again.

Inhale, exhale.

Two.

Muscles shaking with the effort, perspiration tracking her face, belly, and armpits.

Weights down slowly.

Better, much better.

The control was there.

Bleed it off, girl. Turn the entropy into enthalpy.

Only enthalpy.

Controlled.

You can do it.

Again.

Inhale, exhale.

The bunching of her muscles, the quivering of her limbs. She let go with a roar that would make a lion shrink.

Do it, girl. *Do* it!

Bang! Three!

The clank so loud it hurt her ears.

You're losing it, Tandy. You're losing it, you're losing it—

"You're in early."

Eric's voice.

Thank God. Someone to turn off the demons.

Softly, she said, "I came straight from work. Aren't you proud of me?"

"Atta girl!" Eric cheered. "You're gonna make it!"

Again, inhale. Exhale the roar.

Then she tried to lift the press.

Too much.

Halfway, her arms gave out.

Crash!

She heard it; Eric heard it. They both heard her *failure*! Sweat began to coalesce on her brow. She made herself take a deep breath.

Take a deep breath.

"Why aren't you wearing gloves?" Eric said.

"I didn't bother."

"You have to bother, Tandy," Eric said. "You can't pump with seriousness if you don't have gloves." He held out his hand and helped her off the bench. Stared at her at arm's length. "You look uptight. It's okay, Tandy. You've got the determination, don't worry about the roadblocks. Now go help yourself and get your gloves."

"Eric, I was about to stop anyway."

"Stop?"

"I've been at it for a while."

"But you were trying to do a press. And you didn't do that press. Go back and finish that press. You never, ever, end on failure, you know that!"

"Eric, I've been working all night—"

"So have I, babe. The old lady I've been watching spent hours in the john. Bowel problems." Eric shook his head. "If I'm ever incapacitated when I'm old, do me a favor, Tandy, and pull the plug. Family deserting her like she's the plague. Man, she is *lucky* to have found me."

Lucky as long as the *tips* hold out, Tandy thought. Eric was like the rest of them. Not like her. She worked because she *cared*! It's why she did what she did. She told herself that over and over and over. . . .

"Tandy, you on this planet?"

"You're really terrific, Eric, to help the folks like you do."

"Get top dollar, but I'm dedicated. Whatever you do— even if it's cleaning toilets—you have to be dedicated. That's what's wrong with America. Nobody takes life seriously. It's all one big joke. Lifting isn't a joke, Tandy. Now stop dicking around. Go get your gloves and do that press."

"I'm so tired, Eric. I can't—"

"Tandy, we don't say things like 'I can't' around here. The words 'I can't' don't exist in our vocabulary!"

He had imitated her, using a higher-pitched voice for the words *I can't.*

Making fun of her. Telling her she's bad. She isn't bad. She isn't *bad*, damn it! Working all night saving humanity. Then straight from work to pumping. Too much. Too exhausting. She was going to crack.

She was going to *lose* it!

Unable to move, she watched as Eric stripped off his street clothes until he was down to a G-string, the bulge inside well defined and big.

Eric turned and held her face. "Are you going to *cry*?"

"No . . ."

"Oh, yes, you are."

"No, honestly, I'm okay."

"Okay?" Eric's face became mean. "You're not okay, Tandy. You know what you are? You're *pathetic*!"

And in an instant, she knew she had two choices—the first to remain pathetic like they told her she was.

Or she could get mad.

Kill him, said the low one.

Kill him, said the high one.

A smile appeared across her face. She belted his hand off her face, stinging her own palm in the process. "Do you want to know what *pathetic* is, Eric? Pathetic is you taking only *second* in the Mr. L.A. Dudes at Muscle Beach. Guy who won first made you look like a *shriveled old worm*! So screw you!"

Eric suddenly laughed. "Atta girl! Now *that's* the Tandy I know and love. So fuck you and go get your gloves. I'll do watch for you."

Tandy closed her eyes, felt the wet heat on the palms, the thumping of her heart. She had no choice but to listen. If she didn't, Eric and the others would make her life miserable. Then she'd start to feel out of control.

She knew Eric was only trying to *help* her. Unlike the *others*. The people who gave her life, then made it hell. Couldn't call them parents. They were never parents.

Images popped into her brain—the times before the *control*. Lots of food. Piles of food.

Piles and piles—

"Go get your gloves now!" Eric yelled.

Piles and piles and piles—

"Tandy?" Eric asked. "Tandy, you okay?"

She took in a lungful of air, then screamed as loud as she could, her head throbbing even after the sound had vanished from her throat.

Then she went and got her gloves.

The small fresh red stains made abstract art in a pile of grease. Harlow had cordoned off the area with yellow crime tape. Nothing like an old-timer to do the right thing.

Decker said, "What makes you think these stains have anything to do with Marie Bellson, Bri?"

"I'll tell you the whole story, Sergeant. One of my men comes to me. He's doing the third-floor interviews. He talks to this nurse, gal's name is Janie Hannick. Janie says she knows Marie Bellson but doesn't really know her. My guy asks her what the hell does that mean? Only he doesn't use the profanity, that's my addition."

Decker smiled and told him to go on.

"Janie says she's never worked with Marie—she works in one department, Marie works in another. But for years they've been doing the same shifts, and the same overtime shifts. Soon they notice they're always parking cars at the same time and walking into the hospital at the same time."

Harlow sucked in his belly.

"To make a long story short, as long as Janie and Marie always seem to be together anyway, they decide to walk in and out of the lot together. You know, like protection. 'Cause these underground parking structures are stewpots of crime. So each one waits for the other for about five minutes. If the other doesn't show up, the one who's left goes in solo."

"So it's an informal kind of thing?" Marge asked.

"Seems that way," Harlow said. "Naturally, my guy asks this Janie if she and Marie walked in together last night. She says yes. Lucky break with a capital L. My officer tells me, then I ask Janie where'd she and Marie park their cars. I figure we can maybe pull a tire print or something from the empty space. Boom, I find this!"

"Good work, Brian," Decker said. "Let's get a lab man down and see if they can get a clean sample of blood."

"Gonna be hard," Harlow said. "All sorts of crap on a garage floor—oil and grease with the grime."

"The lab should have cleaning emollients. Hopefully, they'll be able to precipitate something decent. If we can find prior blood workup on Marie Bellson, maybe we can do a rough comparison and see if there's a basis for a match."

Marge said, "We should see if there was blood work done on the baby, too."

Decker made a face. It was a horribly gruesome thought, but Marge was right. "Go ahead. And while the lab is out here, try to pick up a tire print. Marie could be savvy enough to change the plates on her car, maybe even spray-paint it a different color. But most people don't think about tire prints. Also keep an eye out for shoe prints. Lots of grease around here."

Harlow said, "How're you going to find blood work on Bellson?"

"I'll see if she has a private doctor," Decker said.

"Maybe she's been a diligent health professional and has had a yearly checkup."

Marge said, "Maybe she's had surgery done at the hospital. If so, she'd have a chart here."

"Good point," Decker said. "Get someone to check the chart room." He stuck his hands in his pockets. "I'm on my way to Bellson's apartment. Call me through the RTO after you're done with the scene."

"Sure thing." Marge stared at the blood spots. "I don't like this."

"It does get the heart going," Harlow said.

"So does a good cup of morning coffee," Marge said. "And without the bitter aftertaste."

FIFTEEN

THE TEMPERATURE WAS CLIMBING AS DECKER PULLED OUT of the Foothill Substation parking lot. Warrant stowed in his jacket, he turned right onto Osborne, steering the unmarked onto the freeway. Amazing what seventy-two hours indoors could do to the perspective. The streets seemed wider, the buildings appeared taller, and the noise of traffic hurt his ears. But at least he was outdoors, no longer engulfed by the cries of the ill and the smell of death.

Fueled by coffee, he reached into his pocket for the scrap of paper with Marie Bellson's address. She lived about three miles away from his ranch—his and Rina's ranch. After living alone for so long, it was still hard for him to adjust from "mine" to "ours." Not that he was selfish: Rina could have anything she wanted. Decker figured his exclusionary thinking was mere habit. Maybe Hannah would change all that. Something created by their union.

Bellson lived on a windy side street that dead-ended into a wide cul-de-sac. The block was a mixture of old, small one-story ranch-style houses, duplexes, and modern apartment buildings. Marie's complex was at the mouth of the turnabout, three stories done in ecru wood siding pocked by weather. Hunting for a space, Decker managed to squeeze the Plymouth between a white Ford Bronco and a white Volvo sedan. Down the street sat the watch cruiser, Norwegian blond Tim Swanson at the wheel. Decker gave a little wave, and Swanson got out of the black-and-white.

"Sergeant," Swanson said.

"What's shaking, Officer?"

"Nothing." Swanson cocked his thumbs under the belt loops. "Place has been as interesting as a tomb."

"Who's watching Bellson's door?"

"Len Kovacs. Nothing there, either."

"You look bored."

"More like brain-dead, Sergeant. Story of my life. I almost miss the excitement of the riots. I may have been hated, but at least I was *doin'* something." Swanson smiled, then popped a stick of gum in his mouth and offered one to Decker, who politely declined. "We finally located the manager of the building. She'd spent the night at her daughter's and should be here any minute with the key. Save our shoulders some bruises. Unless you want to bust the door down."

"We'll use a key, Tim." Decker slapped the warrant against the palm of his hand and told Swanson that they'd enter together. First they'd check the place out to make sure no one was hiding. Then, *if* Bellson's apartment was empty, Decker would look around by himself—less people, less chance for a screwup.

Bellson lived on the third floor. The elevator traveled like a turtle, smelled of mold, and creaked as it rose. Kovacs was sitting cross-legged on the floor in front of Bellson's door, and he blushed when he saw Decker. He stood and swiped at his pantseat.

"Not used to standing so long." Kovacs shook out his legs. "Guess I'd make a lousy palace guard."

"Anything suspicious at all?" Decker asked.

"Not a thing, Sergeant."

Decker knocked loudly, announced himself, and got no response. He turned to Swanson. "When's this manager supposed to be here?"

"She said around eight. Five minutes maybe."

Decker looked at the space between the door and its frame. Marie had a dead bolt. He couldn't trip the lock with a credit card. Decker jiggled the doorknob. The door was flimsy, and he was impatient. A baby was missing, and so was a nurse—the only thing left behind an empty parking space dotted with blood. One good shove and he'd be inside. But he knew it was more prudent to wait.

Ten minutes later, the manager finally showed up. She seemed to be in her late fifties—scrawny and wrinkled with a bouffant of carrot-colored hair. Her voice was husky, her breath charged with cigarette smoke.

"Renee Fulbright." She offered a bony hand, nails buffed and covered with pumpkin polish. "What happened to Marie?"

Decker said, "Who said anything happened to her?"

Renee pulled out a massive ring and began to sort through keys. "It's gotta be serious. Otherwise, why would the police—ah, here it is. Apartment three-twelve. Marie's been a model tenant, by the way. Never missed a month." She slipped the key into the lock, then turned the handle and opened the door. "Don't go messin' up the carpet . . . if you can avoid it, I mean. I just had it cleaned."

Decker wiped his feet on the burlap mat. "I'll take off my shoes as soon as I'm convinced the place is secured."

"The cooperative type, huh?" Renee gave him a slow smile. "You know, I got this thing for redheads."

Decker said, "My new infant daughter's a redhead. Bet you'd really like her."

The smile disappeared. "That was subtle."

Decker laughed. "You don't have to stick around, Ms. Fulbright. But I'll need the key until I'm done."

Renee sighed, then slipped the key off the ring. "I'm in number one-oh-one. Just drop it in the mailbox."

"Got it." Decker stepped over the threshold and called out the word "Police." After no one answered, he did a quick once-over of the living room. First the closets—clothes, utility, water heater—nothing. Then he started going through the kitchen as Swanson and Kovacs did quick checks on the bedrooms and bathrooms.

It was unremarkable—small counters, white stove and refrigerator, a corkboard hanging on the wall, a calendar thumbtacked to the board. Decker pulled out the thumbtack and leafed through the yearly log. None of the date boxes had the words "baby snatching" written in them. He smiled to himself. Bellson was going to make it hard. He'd look over the calendar thoroughly when he had more time.

Swanson came out of one of the bedrooms. "Guess what I found, Sergeant?"

Without turning around, Decker said, "A cat."

Swanson didn't answer right away. "How'd you know?"

"Litter box and food bowl in the kitchen." Decker faced Swanson, who was holding a gray kitten with black stripes. He chucked the animal's chin. "Cute little bugger. That what they call a tiger cat?"

"I'm not up on my cats," Swanson said.

"Just his pussies," Kovacs said.

The uniforms broke into laughter.

Decker said, "Was the cat locked in the room?"

"Yeah, the door was closed, come to think of it," Swanson said.

"Either of you find anything else that moved?"

Kovacs shook his head.

"Looks like the place is empty. You two can report back to your regular duty."

"What do we do about this?" Kovacs held up the cat.

"Just leave it here. I'll take care of it."

Swanson lowered the animal onto the floor. The kitten immediately made a mad dash for its divided food dish. There was water in one compartment, but the food side was empty. It meowed plaintively.

"I think it's hungry," Swanson said.

"Appears to be the case," Decker said.

"You need to feed the kitty," Kovacs said, then laughed at his own joke.

Decker slipped on gloves, then opened several cabinet doors until he found a box of cat food. "See you, fellas."

After the uniforms left, Decker poured the food into the bowl and watched the kitten stuff its face. Then he took out his notebook.

His overall impression was that the apartment had been expecting its tenant to return home. The cat, of course, suggested that. If Marie hadn't returned home soon, the poor animal might have starved. Ironstone dishes were stacked neatly in the drainer; two hardback library books were lying on the dinette table. Decker read the titles:

Being Single in the Nineties: A New, Revitalized Look at the Feminist Movement.

Adult Daughters, Child Mothers: When Nurturant Roles Are Reversed.

Seemed like Marie was doing some soul-searching.

Taped to the refrigerator was a reminder note—*3 P.M. with Paula.* He found today's date in Bellson's calendar—*PD at 3* marked in red.

Three P.M. was a ways off. If Marie didn't show up, most likely Paula D. would call her up and ask what happened. He wondered if Marie had an answering machine. Scanning the living room, Decker located the phone attached to a machine. A red zero showed on the message window.

No one had called last night while Marie was working.

Or someone had called and the messages had been listened to and rewound.

Decker tapped the Play button, and the machine began to spit back prior messages. There was one from a woman whose voice was raspy and old and hurried—as if she was calling on the sly. Another from a woman named Dotty who left no phone number, and a third from Paula, who left her phone number. Decker copied it down, then depressed the digits into the keypad. Two rings, then Paula's message machine took over. Decker hung up. He'd call back later.

He had no idea when those calls were made. Marie's machine didn't have a built-in clock. Yesterday, Marie had showed up at work in the late morning and worked until she disappeared. If those calls were made when Marie was at the hospital, it meant someone else had rewound Marie's messages. Otherwise, the message dot would have been blinking.

He wrote his observation in his notes and started to take in the living room. Feminine taste from the soft pink plush carpeting to the rows of cherubic figurines that lined a curio cabinet. The walls were white tinged with pink and decorated with posters of cats doing cutie-poo things like wearing top hats, and impressionist prints. A bowl of potpourri sat atop a nineteen-inch TV. The couch was a broadcloth of pale blue and pink waves, spruced up with needlepoint throw pillows. End tables flanked the sofa, and a coffee table was in front.

The coffee table held one book—a King James Bible.

Across from the coffee table was a white rocker, an afghan neatly draped over the back. A matching ottoman rested at the chair's feet.

Having finished dining, the cat jumped onto the ottoman, then leapt onto the chair. It proceeded to claw the afghan until the blanket fell forward, burying the kitten under a knitted patchwork. The cat wriggled out to freedom, then nested in the soft folds of the cloth. It closed its eyes.

"At least one of us is getting some sleep," Decker muttered.

Bellson's bookshelves were nearly empty, except for a

dozen thumbed paperbacks and academic nursing and medical texts. The cabinets below were filled with odds and ends—board games, a picnic basket, Duraflame logs, a couple of cameras. Photographic equipment but no photo albums.

Decker thought everyone had photos. Where were Marie's? He went back to his work.

Seemed like Bellson didn't have a lot of young children as visitors. The light-colored furniture wouldn't last a week around sticky handprints. The carpeting wasn't made for spills and dirty shoes. Lots of breakable things sitting on open shelves as well as uncovered wall sockets. The worst offenders were the magazines on the coffee table. Toddlers just loved ripping the covers to shreds.

He moved on to the bedrooms.

The sleeping quarters held a double bed, sheets folded army-corners tight. Her duvet was a down-filled patchwork of pink, rose, and white. On the left nightstand was a phone; the right was topped with a clock radio. The alarm had been set for 10:00 A.M. There was a television guide stuffed into one of the stand's drawers along with a book rating feature movies shown on TV. The other stand gave space to another King James Bible.

Decker thumbed through it. Lots of underlined passages, but no specific theme he could detect.

Marie the nurse.

Marie the Bible reader.

And that was about all he knew of her. Nothing else was illuminating the woman.

He went over to the closets.

Marie's apparel was neatly stowed in a white lacquer dresser and a wall closet. After he'd sorted through dozens of pieces of apparel, it was clear that there were no secret baby clothes and/or blankets squirreled away. If Marie had been planning on bringing an infant home, she'd done an inadequate job of stocking her place with baby supplies.

As intimate and feminine as the bedroom was, it was as generic as a movie set except for the Bible.

Decker waded through the bathroom connecting the two

bedrooms. It was papered in vining pink roses on a white background with color-coordinated towels and washcloths. Another bowl of potpourri rested on the white linoleum counters. The medicine cabinet held OTC drugs as well as some prescription meds—erythromycin, Gantrisin, Lomotil, Estranol. Decker wrote down the names and would check their functions later. Under the sink was spare toilet paper, facial tissues, and two shampoo bottles.

Exploring the last bedroom—which had been converted to an office—Decker found much of the same. A small secretary's desk topped with a white leather blotter, bronze penholder, a crystal clock, and yet a third bowl of potpourri. The woman liked sweet smells, but he hadn't seen perfume on her dressers. He wondered if that meant anything, then remembered a lot of nurses didn't wear perfume. Scents were often displeasing to sick people.

He started going through the desk drawers.

The supply drawer in the middle contained small items, nothing of any significance. The left drawer held her personal stationery—at the top was *Marie Bellson RN* done in a florid scrawl. Matching envelopes printed with a return address, as well as smaller note cards also in the same matching calligraphy. The right side of the desk was a bank of files—car, insurance, taxes, bills, bank statements, tax-deductible receipts.

Decker picked out the bank statements. After an hour of perusing deposit and withdrawal slips, he surmised she had one checking account, her balance hovering around three hundred dollars. She also had a savings account with approximately three thousand dollars as of three days ago. He gathered her statements and called the bank, only to discover that the account was still active, and no transaction had taken place within the last week.

Didn't look like she cut out of town with her money.

Decker thought a moment. Nothing he'd discovered about Marie revealed a woman planning a kidnapping. And if she took the baby, she had left the hospital with nothing more than the clothes on her back. Her apartment was *neat*.

If she had come home and frantically packed, *something* would have appeared out of order.

It was time to start pulling up cushions and crawling under the bed. Decker had thoroughly combed the living room for the second time when Bellson's phone rang. He stopped and waited for the machine to kick in. It was Paula.

Decker interrupted her message. The woman immediately asked who this was, suspicion in her voice.

"Detective Sergeant Peter Decker of the Los Angeles Police. I was going to call you anyway. I understand you have a three o'clock appointment with Ms. Bellson."

There was a pause on the other end.

"Paula?"

"How do you know who I am?"

"I could say it was fancy police work, but the truth is, you said your name at the beginning of the message."

"How do I know you are who you say you are?"

"Call Foothill Substation and verify my badge number. For now, do me a favor and talk to me. Was your appointment for today?"

Again the pause. "Yes."

"Why were you calling Marie, Paula? To confirm the time and place?"

"I don't feel comfortable—"

"You called Marie yesterday as well."

"How did you . . . what's this all about?"

"Do you remember around what time you called?"

Silence on the other end. Decker said, "Please help me out."

Slowly, Paula answered, "I guess it was around four. She wasn't in, and I realized she was probably at work. So I called today just to make sure . . . what was your name again?"

Decker massaged his temples. Four o'clock. Marie was working by then. *Someone* had come into the apartment, listened to the messages, and rewound them. "Paula, Marie is missing—"

"What do you mean, *missing*?"

"Just that. She disappeared last night at work. Do you have *any* idea where she might have gone?"

"No, I . . . *who* are you?"

Decker repeated his name and his badge number. "No idea where she is?"

"No." Another pause. "If she left suddenly, I'm sure she had a good reason. Why are you bothering to look for a grown wo—*omigod*! It's that *baby* on TV, right? I mean, why else would you be looking for a grown woman. Right? Right? *Right?*"

"The kidnapping happened during Marie's shift."

"Kidnapping!" Paula shrieked. "My God, I didn't even think of Marie's hospital. If Marie's missing, that has to mean the same person who kidnapped the baby kidnapped poor Marie. Why else would Marie be missing! She would have *died* fighting to save any of her babies! She's the most dedicated nurse I know. Omigod, omigod—"

"Paula, I need to talk to you. I have to finish up some work here. I could meet you in an hour, hour and a half. Let's say around eleven."

"I'm working now." Another pause. "Do you think Marie's okay? I mean, you don't think she's . . . *omigod!*"

"I can meet you at work. Is that all right?"

"Of course. I'll take a break. Whatever you say."

"Where do you work?"

"St. Jerome's in San Fernando. Do you know where that is?"

"You're a nurse, too?"

"Yes. I met Marie at Sun Valley Pres. She trained me. Only I switched to pediatrics. I just love the kids."

"I'll see you at eleven, Paula. I'll have you paged when I get there, so you don't have to interrupt your work to wait for me. Don't worry if I'm a little late. I'll be there. What's your last name?"

"Delfern. Paula Delfern. I'm on Pediatrics, Four West."

"Thank you, Miss Delfern, I'll see you in an hour."

"Sure. *Anything* to help." A final pause. "*What* did you say your name was again?"

* * *

Marge walked into Bellson's apartment, Cindy a few paces behind her. Decker glared at his daughter, then at Marge.

"What's she doing here?"

"She followed me."

"Daddy, just let me explain—"

"It better be good."

"First off, don't get mad at Marge. I got down on my hands and knees and *begged* her. I was pathetic, so she took pity on me."

Marge said, "I figured it was better keeping her in view than casting her free to do something stupid."

Decker said, "Cindy, go home and *sleep*."

"Dad, how can I *possibly* sleep with that *baby* missing? I sat with Lourdes Rodriguez for a half hour just holding her hand and watching her cry." Her voice cracked. "It was so *sad*."

Decker turned to Marge, "What was she doing with Lourdes?"

"I walked into the room and found her there."

"Cindy—"

"Daddy, she *needed* someone. Someone who wasn't a cop or a reporter or a lawyer or a hospital administrator who was trying to get her to sign away her rights."

"I don't believe this." Decker rubbed his eyes on his forearms.

Cindy said, "How about if I just . . . *observe?*"

"Observe *what?*" Decker checked his watch. "Oh, hell. Just sit down and don't touch a thing. And stop smiling. I'm going to deal with you later."

Cindy tried to sport a grave look as she sat on the white ottoman. She noticed the kitten and ran a finger across its head. "Who's this little guy?"

"Probably Marie's cat. We found it locked in the bedroom waiting for food."

"Poor thing," Cindy cooed. "Can we keep it?"

"I suppose we can give it some foster care," Decker said. "It can live in the stable with the other strays." To Marge, he said, "Unless Bellson's answering machine has a malfunction, I think someone was here last night, retrieved the messages, then rewound them."

"Could have been Marie."

"Could have been."

"What does that mean?"

"I'm not sure, because other than that, nothing appears out of order. I was about to leave the apartment, then lo and behold I find a couple of keys taped under her desk. This one"—Decker held up a key with his gloved hands—"belongs to a storage bin over her parking space. Only took Detective Snail a half hour to find it."

Marge smiled. "What's in the bin?"

"Lots of old college texts—history, anthro, poli sci, as well as a bunch of sixties radical books."

"Radical?"

"Eldridge Cleaver, Malcolm X, Abbie Hoffman—"

"Who's Abbie Hoffman?"

"A guy who couldn't spell America."

"So Marie has done some transforming," Marge said. "Somewhere along the line she became a born-again."

"You can trace the transition. There were also a lot of texts on comparative religion as well as texts on Eastern philosophies."

Marge said, "From gurus to Jesus."

Decker said, "All religions are similar, once you get past the idiosyncrasies."

"What about the other key?" Marge asked.

Decker shrugged. "I don't know. It looks like it belongs to a lockbox. I've been searching for about twenty minutes and can't find a damn thing. I'm supposed to interview a Paula Delfern. She's a nurse at St. Jerome's who was supposed to meet Marie at three this afternoon. I don't know what the relationship is. I said I'd be there at eleven."

"You're late," Marge said.

"I'm well aware of that, Margie. This Paula may be a good information source for us about Marie."

"Do you want me to continue the search or interview Paula Delfern?"

"You do the interview," Decker said. "I know what I've

already gone through. This key has to belong to *something!*"

"I'll help you, Daddy," Cindy said.

"You, young lady, will sit there and not say another word," Decker said.

"He's cute when he's tough, isn't he?" Marge said.

Decker was about to reply but laughed instead. He reached inside his pocket, took out another pair of gloves, and tossed them to Cindy. "Put these on. As long as you're here, I don't want you accidentally touching the wrong thing, messin' up my evidence."

Cindy grinned and put on the gloves. "Evidence for what?"

Damned if Decker knew. And damned if he was going to admit that to Cindy. "Find any blood work on Marie, Marge?"

"Yes, but it isn't specific. Marie's A-positive and has a normal clotting time. Same as the blood found in the parking lot. But A-positive is a common blood type."

"Yeah, isn't it about forty percent of the population?"

"Something like that."

"Couldn't they come up with any of the specific blood factors?"

"Nothing else is written in Marie's chart."

"What was Marie hospitalized for?"

"A D and C three years ago."

"A D and C? Did she have a miscarriage?"

"Chart didn't say anything about that," Marge said. "Just that she was admitted for a D and C. I wrote down her doctor's name—a Stanley Meecham. Why is that name familiar?"

"Darcy case couple of years back," said Decker. "Remember the bees?"

"Oh yes, the bees."

And a triple murder, Decker thought. He said, "Meecham was Linda Darcy's doc. He was treating her for infertility. I wonder if Marie was having the same problem."

"If so, we've got a potential motive for the kidnapping."

"Woman cracks because she can't have kids?" Decker said.

"Why not?" Marge said.

Why not? Decker repeated in his mind. Look at poor Rina. A hysterectomy had plunged her into a deep depression. And this was a woman who already had three healthy children.

"Why not indeed," Decker said out loud. "If she was having fertility problems, does that mean there was a guy in her life?"

Marge shrugged. "I'll ask Paula."

Decker said, "Why else does a doc do a D and C?"

Cindy said, "Grandma had one when she was getting irregular periods due to menopause."

"Really?" Decker said.

"Marie's a little young for menopause," Marge said.

"It's been known to happen," Decker said. "Could also be a reason for a sudden snap. Marie sees her last chance for a kid slipping away, so she takes one." He stared at the key in his hands. "I'm going to keep looking for the box. You do your number on this Paula Delfern. See what the story is between those two."

"Got it."

"I also put a call in to Marie Bellson's bank, telling them to call us if Marie or *anybody* shows up at any of the branches wanting to withdraw money from Marie's account. So if someone's patched through to you from American International, you'll know what that's about."

"Will do." Marge put her sunglasses back on her nose, then took a tissue and spread it over her right palm. "Let me see that key."

Decker dropped it in the pink Kleenex.

Marge said, "Wrong shape for a safe-deposit box."

"Yep."

"Post office or mailbox?"

"Could be. Looks more like a strongbox key to me."

"Me, too," Marge said. "I'm just thinking that whoever rewound the messages might have taken the box."

"Thought crossed my mind." Decker bagged the key. "I'll give the place another going-over."

"Call when you're done. We'll compare notes." Marge winked at Cindy. "Look after him, kid."

Decker waited for Marge to leave, then said, "Did Rina leave the hospital all right?"

Cindy nodded. "Her parents picked her up right on time. She's very proud of what you're doing, Dad. She's worried about Caitlin, too."

"Caitlin?"

"The baby's name. Lourdes told me."

Caitlin, Decker thought. So the little thing has an official name. "Cindy, the only reason I'm not chopping your head off is because I'm indebted to you—"

"No, you're not."

"Yes, I am, and so is Rina. We both have you to thank for Hannah's safety. *But* . . . as your *father* . . . I'm furious at you."

"It's only because I *care*! Dad, I've got *eyes*. Let me help you look for this box. I won't get in your way after this. I promise."

Decker hesitated. It was unprofessional, but at the moment another pair of peepers just might do the trick. Hell with regulations. Look how regulations had helped Caitlin Rodriguez last night.

"All right," Decker said. "Start with the kitchen. Be slow and methodical. I've already gone over everything twice . . . but maybe I missed something."

"Thanks, Dad."

"S'right." Decker felt a sudden burst of warmth in his heart. "I love you, princess."

Cindy smiled. "I love you, too."

SIXTEEN

SITTING IN THE HOSPITAL CAFETERIA, MARGE PONDERED why all institutional coffee tasted like swill. Lips puckering as she sipped, she noticed that Paula Delfern wasn't making much headway with her java, either. The nurse was gazing into the white ceramic cup as if reading tea leaves, fingers gripped around the mug. She appeared to be in her midtwenties with a creamy complexion and tawny-colored hair cut to the shoulders. Her dark eyes were set into a moon-shaped face. Her features were small but broad—a wide nose, a wide smile. With makeup, she could be pretty. Scrubbed-faced as she was now, she looked the part of a healthy farm girl. Marge took out her notebook.

Paula said, "I really don't know how I can help. I mean, Marie and I are friends. But thinking about that, I really don't know much about *her*. When we used to talk a lot, I was the one having the problems. We talked about me."

"What kind of problems?" Marge asked.

"Is that relevant?"

Marge leaned in. "You never know what's going to help us find her or the baby."

Paula shuddered at the word *baby*. "Gosh, that's just *terrible*!"

"How'd you meet Marie?"

"She trained me at Sun Valley Pres. I was an OB/neonate

nurse for a year before I switched to Peds. Like I told your partner, I love the kids. And so did Marie. I couldn't imagine Marie ever hurting a kid. She just couldn't!"

"Who said she's hurting a kid?"

"Well, she wouldn't do that to a mother. I know Marie, and she likes the new moms, too."

"How did you and Marie become good friends?" Marge said. "From what I hear, Marie isn't sociable."

"No, she's not sociable, but that doesn't mean she isn't nice. Parties just aren't her thing. What we used to do is just sit and talk after shift, you know? She'd make a cup of coffee. . . ." Paula appeared lost in thought. "We'd just talk. I was going through a lot of problems with my ex-boyfriend . . . *commitment* problems. So what else is new, right?"

Marge nodded understandingly, although commitment was the last thing she wanted out of life. Pete seemed happy remarried. But Pete seemed happy before. "So you and Marie talked about your boyfriend?"

"Yes. Marie was very helpful. Not that we didn't disagree about things. We had some pretty intense discussions about God."

"God?"

"Yeah, Marie was into Jesus. She especially liked the parable about the prodigal son."

"The sinner repenting."

"Yep. She used to say everyone has skeletons in their closet."

"Marie mention hers?"

"Not really. Marie really didn't talk much about her personal life. Too busy talking about my problems." Paula's focus fell back to the mug. "Marie could be understanding even if . . ." She wiped her eyes with her napkin. "Excuse me, this is hard."

"Take your time."

"I got pregnant by my ex-boyfriend. . . ." She sniffed, and her voice became small. "He wasn't my ex back then. That's when the commitment issue really came out, you know?"

Marge nodded.

"He didn't want marriage." She sniffed again. "He didn't want a baby. He said he was too young, although he was in his last year of medical school. He could have . . . anyway, when I told him I was going to keep the baby, he had a fit. He told me don't expect help from him . . . he was just too young to be tied down. Then two months later . . . he . . . he got engaged to a classmate." She started to cry. "It's not that he didn't want *commitment*, he just didn't want *me*."

She buried her face in her napkin. Marge waited for the weeping to stop, wondering if Paula's story was relevant. Finally, the nurse dried her eyes.

"Marie was very helpful."

"A shoulder to cry on?"

"Yes, and more. She became close to me. She even invited me to stay with her, saying I'd need help when I got bigger—farther along in my pregnancy. I'm from Des Moines, and I don't really get along well with my folks. To show up back home pregnant and unmarried . . . I'd never hear the end of it. I felt so *alone*. Marie was just *great*! No one could have been as kind as she was to me. She was one of the few people I know who practiced what they preached."

"Did you move in with her?"

She shook her head. "It turned out it wasn't necessary. I miscarried at four months." She smiled through wet eyes. "My ex-boyfriend sent me flowers in the hospital. Can you imagine?"

"Nice guy."

"A very expensive lesson in life, I suppose." She sighed. "At least I felt better losing the baby from miscarriage than from abortion. Truthfully, I was going to get an abortion. But Marie talked me out of it."

"Marie was against your abortion or any abortion?"

"It wasn't black and white, Detective. But she did have feelings about the subject. She asked me if I could live with my decision—terminating my own child's life. It made me evaluate who I was."

"Did Marie belong to a specific religion?"

"She just considered herself a decent Christian woman. But that wasn't the reason for her views. I think she had lost a baby a long time ago . . . when she was very young. I don't know whether it was a stillborn or the baby died at birth. Whatever it was, it was a tragedy. She said it changed her life."

Marge was scribbling furiously. "How so?"

"I don't know. She never got any more specific."

"How old was she when she lost her baby?"

"She just said she was very young."

It was Marge's turn to hesitate. *Very young.* Marie's chart claimed she'd had a D and C a couple of years back. Had Marie had another miscarriage or stillborn? No, it couldn't be a stillborn. Someone would have recalled Marie pregnant. So maybe it was a miscarriage. Maybe *this* was the tragedy that Marie was referring to. She could have told Paula it had been many years ago when in fact it hadn't been. And she might have embellished the severity of it to make Paula feel better.

"Do you know if Marie was married at the time of her tragedy?"

"I'm sorry, but I don't know. Marie didn't get into specifics, and back then, her problems weren't utmost on my mind."

"But she told you she had actually *lost* a baby."

"Yes."

"Not just miscarried."

"She used the term *lost.*"

"Paula, did Marie seem unusually preoccupied with babies lately?"

"I can't answer that honestly. Because lately, I haven't seen much of Marie." Paula sighed again. "I found another boyfriend. A good guy, also with commitment problems." She laughed nervously. "But at least he's up front about it. We've been going together almost four months. Now that things are going okay for me, Marie's sort of dropped out of the picture. I call and invite her out. But as soon as she finds out Joe's gonna be there, she backs off. Joe's a fun-loving guy, and Marie is . . ."

"She doesn't approve of Joe?"

"No, it's not like that. Marie isn't judgmental. She just does better one-on-one. This was the first time I'd seen her in months. I was planning to take her out to dinner for her birthday. Just the two of us. Now I find out . . . this is so horrible. I feel guilty. Maybe she was sending me signals I didn't pick up on."

"Like what?"

"I don't know," Paula said. "Like I said, I obviously didn't pick up on them."

"When was the last time you talked to Marie?"

"A week ago. When we made plans."

"And how'd she sound?"

"Fine."

"Did she say anything unusual to you regarding babies or mothers?"

"No."

"Did she mention her prior tragedy at all?"

"No."

"Did she mention your miscarriage at all?"

"No."

"Do you know of any men past or present in Marie's life?"

"No."

"But she told you she lost a baby."

"Yes."

"She never said *when* this happened?"

"Just that she was young."

"And she never mentioned the father?"

"No."

"Did she ever talk about having another baby, Paula?"

"No. And she only talked about her tragedy *after* I lost the baby. To be empathetic, I think."

"Paula, when you were close to Marie, did you know or meet any of Marie's other friends?"

"I don't think Marie had very many friends."

"Well, when you used to visit her, did she ever get any phone calls?"

"From the hospital."

"How about personal phone calls?"

"No . . . wait, her mom called several times. Marie told me her mom lives in a nursing home in Arcadia. She's kind of nuts, and every so often she escapes and calls Marie on a pay phone. Marie used to visit her twice a week. I'm sure she still does."

Marge paused and looked through her notes. There it was. Pete had played Marie's messages for her. In them had been a gravelly voice on the run. She looked up from her notebook. "Do you know the name of the nursing home?"

"No, I don't know. I'm sorry. I'm terrible with names."

"But it's in Arcadia."

"It was as of six, maybe seven, months ago."

"The only calls you ever heard Marie receive were from her mom?"

"She's the only one I remember calling Marie's house."

"Did you ever hear her talk about Dotty?"

"Dotty?"

"Yesterday someone named Dotty called her house."

"Dotty . . . could you mean Dody?"

"Could be. Who's Dody?"

"Secretary from Sun Valley Pres's pension-plan department. Business. Every so often she used to call me to verify wages and deductions and stuff like that. She's a fixture at Sun Valley."

"Was she a friend of Marie's?"

"Not that I know."

"So you don't know anyone Marie might be friendly with outside the hospital other than her mom?"

"She's nice to the incoming nurses. Really sweet. Maybe she had another special friend. Someone she took under her wing. Like me. I really don't know."

"Anybody specific you have in mind?"

"No. No one."

"Did Marie ever offer to take care of your baby after it arrived?"

Paula scrunched up her eyes in concentration. "Well, she did say I could stay with her. Like I said, she was nice. But she didn't get any more specific than that."

"Did you ever have the feeling that she wanted to raise your baby as her own?"

"No, Detective. She just really wanted to *help* me. *Helping* people. That was Marie's thing. She *cared*."

"You're describing her as such a giving person. Yet you can't remember any other friends she had."

"I know it sounds crazy, but I can't."

"Never got a picture postcard from someone on vacation?"

"Wait, wait, wait!" Paula's eyes lit up. "She received a Christmas card. She stood it up on her coffee table, half-open. I noticed it because it was the only Christmas card she had on display. She said it was from an old friend but never said more than that. Gosh, amazing what suddenly hits you. When you said postcard, I remembered *Christmas* card."

"Do you know who sent the card?"

"You mean the name? Gosh, I'm just *terrible* at names."

"Was it a man or a woman?"

"A woman. I just can't remember. . . ."

"Think, Paula. *Think!*"

"It wasn't a weird name." She closed her eyes. "I'm sorry. It was a while ago."

"The card was signed with a first and last name?"

"Yes, it was . . . I think."

"And no names come to mind."

"No. Just that it wasn't an unusual name."

"Thanks for your time." Marge folded her notebook, wondering if Decker'd come across any Christmas cards. "If you think of that name or anything else—"

"I'll call. Do you have a card?"

Marge handed her a business card. "You can ring me or my partner, Detective Sergeant Peter Decker. I wrote his name next to mine. You can ask for either one."

"Good thing you wrote it down." Paula pocketed the card. "Like I told you, I'm terrible with names."

"We should all be named John Doe, huh?"

"It would help. Or at least Bob—"

Paula stopped talking. Marge asked, "What is it?"

"The last name was Robert. . . . It was Susan Robert . . . something like that."

"Susan Robert?"

"Something like that, but not exactly."

"Okay, that's a real good start."

"But it wasn't Susan. More like Susanna, but that wasn't it either."

"Cynthia?" Marge suggested. "Sara?"

"Uh-uh."

"Cecilia? Sandra? Serita?"

"Sondra," Paula stated. "The name on the card was Sondra Robert."

"You're sure?"

"Pretty sure, I think." Paula beamed. "Guess I'm not so terrible with names after all." She paused. "It's Detective Dunn, right?"

Marge stood and smiled. "Right."

Decker studied the face of the Christmas card—a snow-covered pastoral scene with smoke rising from the country house's chimney. Inside were the words: *Over the River and through the Woods. A Merry Christmas and a Happy New Year.* The signature was large and full of flare. *Sondra Roberts.* No love or sincerely or best wishes or fondly. Just a signature. To Marge, he said, "And Paula said this was the only Christmas card Bellson had on display?"

"The only one she remembered seeing." Marge sat down on Marie's wave-patterned couch. "Where'd you finally find it?"

"In her stationery drawer under her personalized paper—the only personal item I found."

"We never did find any lockbox," Cindy added. "Or wall safe or floor safe or hidden door."

"She must have some photo albums somewhere," Marge said. "Everyone has photo albums."

"Unless you're trying to forget your past," Decker mentioned.

"The prodigal daughter," Marge said. "Then why keep the old books?"

"Maybe Marie didn't want to bury her past entirely. Books are less threatening reminders than snapshots."

Marge raised her brow. "Or maybe the someone who rewound her messages could have taken her personal photographs. Come to think of it, he or she could have taken the lockbox, too. All personal effects that might have linked the person with Marie."

Cindy said, "Then why wouldn't the person take the key to the box?"

Decker stared at his daughter.

Cindy shrugged. "Sorry, I'm just a little bored . . . don't mind me."

Decker zeroed in on her. "All right, Cynthia. If the person was going to take the lockbox, why wouldn't he or she take the key?"

"Because the person knew where the box was but didn't know where the key was."

"The girl's a natural," Marge said.

"That's my daughter," Decker said. "So we're working on the assumption that this key fits a box, and the box was taken, but *not* by Marie. Otherwise, she would have taken the key." Decker thought a moment. "To know about the existence of such a box . . . it would have been someone close to Marie."

"I'll call Paula and ask her if she knew about a box," Marge suggested.

"Good." Decker turned to his daughter. "Thanks for the help, princess. Now will you go home and get some sleep?"

"Yes, I will go home and I will take a nap. I'm very tired."

"Hallelujah," Decker said. "Exhaustion has finally prevailed."

"What first, Rabbi?" Marge asked. "Start scanning the phone books for Sondra Roberts?"

Decker said, "Also the hospitals, the health-employment

agencies, and the vocational-training centers. Dollars to doughnuts, this gal's a nurse."

"Start with Sun Valley Pres?"

"Yep," Decker said. "Do your recall any nurses there named Sondra Roberts?"

"No."

"Neither do I, but that doesn't mean a thing." Decker shrugged. "All right, we'll locate this Sondra Roberts. Why? To find out more about Marie *and* to make sure that Marie isn't holed up with her. Now what about Marie's mom?"

"Paula speaks the truth. She is indeed in an old-age home in Arcadia. The director and staff have been put on alert that Marie is missing. They'll monitor calls to find out if Marie is trying to make contact with her mom. They'll also call if Marie shows up."

"Talk to the mother at all, Marge?"

"No, she was eating lunch. I have an appointment with her at three."

Decker said, "Marie was reading a library book about nurturant role reversals of mother/daughter."

"Well, Paula said her mother was constantly escaping to make calls. Looks like the old lady may have seen the other side."

Decker said, "Marie taking care of a senile mother. Then she goes to work and takes care of people." He tapped his foot. "Seems to me the last thing she'd want is an infant to care for."

"I was thinking the same thing. Maybe Marie was just as much a victim as the baby."

"A possibility," Decker said. "Did you happen to find out if Marie has *any* other family?"

"As far as the staff knows, it's just mother and daughter. But there may be a maiden aunt or cousin locked away in the basement."

"Shades of Rochester's crazed wife," Cindy said.

Marge and Decker stared at her.

"Jane Eyre?" Cindy said. "Charlotte Brontë? Forget it." Decker shook his head and flipped the Christmas card

around to the back side. "This isn't a commercial card, Marge. It's for charity. I was looking for the price, and instead I found an artist credit and statement of nonprofit from the maker. Beth Dillon—member eight years of Overeaters Anonymous."

"So we may be looking for a fat nurse," Marge said.

"Maybe a former fat nurse," Cindy suggested. "Maybe she lost weight when she joined the organization."

"Atta way, Cynthia!" Marge said. "I see in my crystal ball a second generation of Decker detectives."

Decker threw her a dirty look. Then his radio went off. He used Marie's phone to call the station house. A moment later, Detective Mike Hollander came on the line.

"Morning, Rabbi. Looks like some congratulations are in order."

"Thanks, Mike."

"Rina doing okay?"

"Better. Tell everyone at the station house that Rina really appreciated the flowers. And thanks for the roses, Mike. Two dozen and long-stemmed—very nice. Must mean you're a good friend."

"At least a good friend of Rina's."

Decker laughed. "What's up?"

"Just got off the phone with the fire department up in the National Forest Service—Angeles Crest. Had a bit of a bonfire down there. Looks like a car fell down the mountainside and exploded into flames. Potentially dangerous situation. Luckily, they got to it before the winds kicked up. They're still doing some mop-up, but they've recovered the frame of the car."

"Don't tell me," Decker said. "They've got a red Honda with Marie Bellson's license plates."

"Plates were removed, but yes, the frame appears to be a Honda. Fire department said color is hard to ascertain, but a few spots appeared to have some red paint chips."

Decker felt his heartbeat quicken as he related the story to Marge. To Hollander, he said, "Maybe Marie Bellson's hiding in the mountains with the baby."

"Well, Rabbi, there seems to be an adult body in the driver's seat—it's been burned to a crisp."

Decker felt his throat go dry. "And the baby?"

"Can't tell yet, Pete. It's still a mess down there."

"Oh, shit!" Decker turned to Marge and gave her a one-sentence synopsis. "They don't know if the baby's in the wreck or not."

"My God!" Cindy shrieked. Marge took her hand.

Decker felt like punching a wall. *Please, let Caitlin Rodriguez be okay.* "You want to give me directions, Mike?"

"Got them right here, Pete. By the way, do you remember the name of that woman dentist who identifies bodies by the teeth? We worked with her on the Lindsey Bates case."

"Annie Hennon."

"Dr. Hennon," Hollander said. "That's right. Her number should be in the department's file under experts, right?"

"Should be."

"She was good-looking, wasn't she?"

"Yes, she was."

"Then let me call her, explain the urgency of the situation." Hollander paused. "After all, I'm the one with the directions."

SEVENTEEN

STANDING ON THE EDGE OF A THOUSAND-FOOT DROP, Decker studied the distant canyons of Angeles Crest. The flora that carpeted the jagged slopes of rock had turned wheat-colored from unrelenting summer sun. The turquoise sky hosted tufts of cotton clouds that partially shaded the mountains, turning them deep ambers and greens. Where the sun shone unmolested, the landscape was a glittering meld of emeralds and golds. Crows cawed and circled; ebony wings floating upon the hot breeze. Upon these hills, high drama was wind rustling leaves, the dive of a hawk, or the scurry of a lizard.

Decker mopped his brow and rolled up his shirtsleeves.

Today, unfortunately, the wilderness drama was taking a backseat to the human kind. At the bottom of the slopes sat a cauldron of smoldering residue belching smoke and soot. Scattered in the gray fog were fire trucks looking like Tonka toys. The fire fighters' voices echoed throughout the canyons. Decker could make out sentences a quarter-mile up. Not that the boys were saying much at this point, mostly doing paperwork—writing out reports. The fire had been put out, but there was still lots of cleanup. He'd meet with the fire captain as soon as the M.E. and the photographer arrived. Sheriff's deputies had begun cordoning off the area.

The hardest part was keeping his mind off Caitlin Rodriguez, and on the job. If he didn't, a little baby would remain an open file—something gnawing at his gut every time Hannah reached a birthday.

Concentrate, Deck.

He looked over the ledge and tried to reconstruct the scene prior to the drop. He figured the car must have plunged off about five yards from where he stood. It was the sharpest kink of the road's curve, although the turn wasn't a hairpin. It could have been easily negotiated if the driver had been sober and the car had been going at a prudent speed. Tire tracks had carved their impressions in the plants. Some of the shrubbery had been ripped, pulled from the roots—probably entangled in the car's fender and dragged along for the ride.

Decker thought. *If* arson was involved, then it made sense to think of the car as being *pushed* off. But why here? His eyes dipped down below. The drop was vertical, and the spot was isolated—a narrow paved road framed by mountain and sheer falls. No ranger stations or campsites in view. And this particular turn had a slight shoulder. There was enough space for the car to sit while being prepped to explode.

The Santa Ana winds were hot and dry and stirred up the stench of smoke and gasoline. Decker knew his nostrils were too inundated to differentiate which smells were coming from where. He walked over to the tire tracks, picked some random leaves in the area, and put them in a plastic bag. Then he took out a roll of yellow crime-scene tape and began to isolate the area, watching where he stepped. After the area seemed secured, he loaded his camera with film, taking closeups of the crushed plants and tire impressions. When he was done, he checked his watch—a little before one.

The sun was at its strongest, cooking his nose medium well. He cursed his ruddy coloring, then cursed his stupidity for not using sunblock. His mind was just too preoccupied to remember. His shirt was a sodden lump, his feet swollen in his oxfords. What he wouldn't have given for a T-shirt and a pair of rubber-soled sandals.

Take in the details.

The access road to the mouth of the canyon was on the other side of the mountain—a winding adobe-colored stretch cut into the hillside. To get there, he'd have to go back down the mountain, then up on the other side. Too bad the place lacked a skytram.

He caught his name over the static of the car radio, reached through the window, and picked up the mike. Marge was patched through.

"What's going on over there?" she asked.

"I haven't gone down to the actual scene. I think I found the spot where the car fell—or was pushed—over." He explained the details. "Are you coming down?"

"Don't have time. I've got to interview Mama Bellson."

"Oh, that's right. In the meantime, send me a uniform to watch over the area while I go down to the actual scene."

"No deputies around?"

"They're securing the area below."

"I'll call someone for you," Marge said. "I've been going through phone books and directory assistance—no Sondra Roberts. I haven't had a chance to check out the personnel files of hospitals and health-care agencies in a big way, but I'm working on it."

"What about Overeaters Anonymous?"

"Got calls in to the regional chapters. Usually, members are anonymous. But I think we can get some information with a baby's life at stake. There are two of them. I'll keep trying until interview time. Hollander, Fordebrand, and MacPherson are checking the tips that have come pouring in from the TV broadcast this morning. Lines haven't stopped ringing at the station house. I've had to use my radio to get through."

"Good to see people concerned."

"Lourdes Rodriguez is thinking of making a personal plea on the five o'clock news. What do you think, Pete?"

"Good idea if it's necessary." Decker's stomach churned.

"We still don't know if the baby was inside the car. The fire fighters haven't begun to pry the car open yet."

"That poor little girl—both of them. What an ugly mess!"

"If the baby isn't in the wreckage, I'll stop by the hospital and update Lourdes. We both met Marie—maybe if we knock our heads together, we can remember something vital."

"Keep me posted." Marge cut the line.

Decker rehooked the mike and leaned against the unmarked. In the distance, he heard the purr of a motor. He glanced at his watch again. In the past forty minutes, not a single car had gone by. Chances that anyone had seen what had happened to the car would be slim.

The purring grew in volume, and a few moments later a red four-by-four screeched as it emerged from the bend. The top was off, and a woman with short blond hair was at the wheel. Decker flagged her down, and the Jeep stopped in the middle of the roadway.

The woman stuck her head out and smiled. "How's it shakin', handsome?"

"Can't complain. I thought I'd leave the unmarked here, and we'd go down together. I'm just waiting for somebody to come here to watch over the area while I'm gone. Shouldn't be more than five, ten minutes. Photographer and M.E. should be coming momentarily."

"What's in this area?"

"Looks like the spot where the car jumped."

"Mind if I have a peek?"

"Not at all. Just pull up behind the Plymouth, but don't go over the cliff."

"Aw gee, Pete. And here I was, thinking of doing some bungee jumping." She parked the Jeep, slid out of the seat, and gave Decker a big hug. "God, you're all wet!"

"Forgot my beach towel." Decker smiled and held her at arm's length. "How're you doing, Annie? You look great."

And she did. She'd cut her hair short and dyed it white-blond. But with her fair skin and green eyes, she had pulled it off without looking silly or, worse, as if she were desperately clinging to youth. Not that age hadn't presented itself in four years—the crow's-feet around the eyes, the wrinkles at the mouth. But her overall expression looked happier, more confident, than when he had last worked with her. She wore a thin white cotton blouse tucked into khaki pants. Her feet were bereft of socks, housed solely in sneakers. Around her neck was a camera; on her head was a sun hat. She looked ready for a safari.

She pinched his cheek. "I *feel* great. You don't look so bad yourself, kiddo. Although your nose could do with a little schmear of something."

Decker laughed.

"I see you've got a ring on your finger," Annie said.

"So do you," Decker said.

"Don't compare. Mine's a lot nicer."

"It's quite a rock."

"He's a wastrel, Pete. When he's not racing cars, he putters around the family wineries in Napa."

Decker eyed the stone. "He must be doing all right."

"Family is *loaded* with a capital *L*. First time I ever met them was over dinner last Christmas. It was a very traditional, formal affair with a zillion relatives flown in for the occasion. The table was set for royalty—imported antique china and crystal, and a bank vault's worth of silver in the form of eating utensils. I was so afraid of using the wrong fork, I lost ten pounds that weekend."

"You mean you didn't snarf it through your nose?"

"Glazed ham and mucous, yum, yum."

Decker groaned.

Annie said, "So it looks like you took the plunge into matrimony?"

"Guess so."

"You *guess*?"

Decker chuckled. "Yes, I got married a little over a year ago."

Annie regarded his face. "You don't seemed thrilled."

"I'm thrilled with the marriage. But it's been a stressful couple of days." Decker rubbed his nose again. "My wife just had a baby."

"That's *wonderful*!" Annie paused. "Or is it?"

"No, it is wonderful!" Decker looked at the sky. "How much detail did Detective Hollander give you?"

"That the victim might be a missing nurse."

"He didn't mention any baby?"

Annie paused. "Is this the nurse that's been on the TV news? The one accused of kidnapping a newborn?"

"Yes."

"Oh, my God, so you think that there may be a baby in the wreck?" Annie turned white. "It's not *your*—"

"No, no, no," Decker interrupted. "No, mine's safe at home with Mama. But it happened at the hospital where Rina was staying. The missing nurse was one of my newborn daughter's nurses."

"Oh, *shit*!" Annie covered her face with her hands. "I'm so sorry. You must be freaked!"

"It's a little disconcerting."

"You never were a big one for emoting, were you, Pete?"

"I'm calm for your sake, Annie."

"What a prince."

Decker shook his head. "Wait, there's more. In addition to looking at the victim's teeth, you have the lovely chore of seeing if there are any baby bones."

Annie looked pained. "They never tell you about this in school, do they?"

"Maybe your wastrel fiancé has the right idea."

"Could be so, could be so." Annie sighed. "Anything interesting where the car went off?"

"From your perspective, I don't think so. But I haven't combed the area yet."

Annie walked along the edge of the yellow tape. She stopped, bent down, and stared at the depressions in the shrubs. "As long as I'm in the field, I like to get a feeling for the crime."

"I can understand that." Decker heard another car down the mountain—a sheriff's car. It slowed, then stopped in the roadway. Decker instructed the deputy—a young woman named Picks—to pull up behind the unmarked after he and Dr. Hennon pulled the Jeep out.

" 'Preciate the sheriff's cooperation on this one," Decker said.

"Anything to find that poor little baby," Picks said. "News cameras are on their way. Will that screw your investigation up?"

"I'll talk to them," Decker said.

Annie primped her hair. "Am I presentable?"

"How about you let me be the media star?"

"Hog."

"I'm going to try to persuade them to hold off for a while. Soon as this hits the news, we'll have dozens of gawkers in the area. That'll screw everything up." To Picks, Decker said, "I should be back here to grid-search for evidence within a couple of hours. Make sure no one mucks up the scene."

"Got it."

Decker turned to Annie. "Let's move it, Doctor."

In the charred crater that was once a glen, the temperature seemed ten degrees hotter. The smoke and ashes swirled with each blow of the wind, filling the air with soot that clogged Decker's lungs and burned his eyes. He felt as if he were viewing a grainy black-and-white movie.

"Wonder how chimney sweeps do it," Annie said. "And I had the good sense to wear a white blouse." She shrugged. "At least it's washable—easier to clean than my lungs. Where should I start?"

"First, we've got to get you a body to examine." Decker watched as the jaws of life carefully stretched brittle metal, trying to pry apart the driver's door. "I'd like to maintain the position of the body as much as possible. But they may have to cut part of it away to get it out. Charming, huh?"

"Are we talking body or bod*ies*?"

"I hope to God it's singular. Should know more once the package is opened." Decker caught a wave of a hand out of the corner of his eye. "C'mon. Let's go talk to the fire captain."

They walked a few yards into the hub of activity. Deputies patrolling the area, fire fighters still wearing their yellow slickers, helmets, and boots, conferred. Decker wondered how they didn't melt in the heat. Captain Donnell had taken off his helmet but still wore the protective gear. He was in his fifties, his face beefy and ruddy. He had hooded eyes, a bulbous nose, and thick lips. His smile was open and friendly.

Decker said, "Captain Donnell, Dr. Hennon."

Captain Donnell shook Annie's hand. "Call me Liam."

"And you call me Annie." She shrugged. "Now we're all friends. Isn't that nice?"

Donnell smiled. "We should have a body out for you in a jiffy, Annie. Have you been with the Coroner's Office a long time?"

Decker said, "She's not from the Coroner's Office. She's a forensic odontologist."

"Just think of me as your tooth woman, Liam." Annie turned to Decker. "And for your information, I do have an official appointment with the M.E.'s Office. Unpaid, to be sure, but that's because I'm so altruistic."

Decker smiled. "M.E. should be coming soon, Liam."

Donnell said, "Maybe we'll even have a body for him . . . her . . . whoever."

Decker's toe fell on a mound of ashes. "With the heat and winds, this canyon is a pit of kindling. How'd you boys contain the fire so rapidly?"

Donnell said, "We had copters in the area because of the Santa Anas. This is prime season for arsonists because, like you said, with the heat and wind they don't have to work as hard. One of our men spotted the flames before it went out of control. Got to it right away, and *look* at the damage it did. Gone on longer, we would have had a real disaster."

"Did your copter see the car fall off the mountain?"

"Nope. Just the fire. At the time, he didn't really know the origin. It looked to him like a fireball—could have been the impact of explosion. But he couldn't be sure what caused it. He tried to go down for a closer look, but it was too black." He turned to Annie. "Ever been in the eye of a firestorm?"

"Never had the pleasure."

"The door to hell, I call it. An uncontrolled fire creates its own windstorm. It sucks the oxygen from the air, turns it black and gritty. No visibility. You're not just battling the heat and smoke, you're battling searing winds that rip the flesh off the face."

"Sounds like fun," Annie said.

"It isn't for the fainthearted."

Decker said, "Do you think the car was bombed from the inside?"

"Nah," Donnell said. "Frame's smashed and toasted but intact. Bomb would have exploded it to smithereens. What we got was probably a simple case of arson. Someone dousing the car with gasoline and then pushing it over the cliff."

No one spoke for a moment as they watched the car being pried open. A few minutes later, the machinery backed away from the scene.

"Looks like they got it open," Donnell said. "You two can go in and—uh-oh! Here come the news people."

Decker saw a TV van pull up. He jogged over to the group and asked who was in charge. A coiffed blonde in a tailored white suit and heels came out, a young kid daubing makeup on the blonde's cheeks. The newscaster broke from her assistant, took out a notebook, and offered Decker a hand. "Alyssa Morland, feature reporter for Primetime News. Are you in charge?"

"Something like that," Decker said. "Look, I'll be happy to talk to you, but I've got one request. And that is, don't report this until the eleven o'clock news."

"What?"

"We're doing a search here, for a baby, an infant—"

"I'm well aware of that. Why do you want us to hold off reporting? I'd think you'd welcome any knowledge the public might have of this case."

"It brings on the hordes of lookie-looers."

"Can't the police keep them at bay? That's their job."

"We'd rather use the police officers to look for the baby. And if the crowd breaks through and mucks up the works . . ."

The newscaster made a face. "I had my choice of assignments. You mean I shlepped out here for *nothing*? In a *white* suit of all things. God damn those production assistants! I *told* them to scope it out beforehand!"

Decker tried a disarming smile. "I'll make it up to you for eleven o'clock."

The reporter swore. "Well, I'm not about to screw up a search for a baby."

"Bad publicity for the station," Decker said.

Alyssa glared at him. "For your information, I don't want it on my conscience. Yes, even we newspeople have little Jiminy Crickets telling us right from wrong. So when can I do my story?"

"How about in a couple of hours?"

"Fair enough. I'll take some scene footage in the meantime." Alyssa blew air on her forehead. "You are going to give me an exclusive, aren't you?"

"Yes, you scratch my back, Alyssa, I'll scratch yours."

"Medical examiner just phoned," Annie said. "Traffic accident is clogging the freeways. He said to start without him. Just tread lightly." She offered Decker her arm. "Shall we?"

A few feet later, Annie said, "You think Liam was trying to impress me with his door-to-hell firestorm thing?"

"Were you impressed?"

"Slightly."

"Then it worked."

Annie laughed. "Wonder how many times he's used that as a pickup line. 'Ever been in the eye of a firestorm?' I mean, who can answer 'yes' to that? Got to hand it to him. It's an original."

They stopped in front of the blackened remains of the car. By this time, more deputies had come on the scene. The police photographer was snapping pictures, poking his head inside the auto frame. When he reemerged, his face had darkened from ash. "Got a piece of advice for you, Rabbi. Don't breathe too deeply."

Decker nodded and peered inside the car. In the driver's

seat was a scorched skeleton. The skull was skewed to the left, wedged between the wheel of the car and the bony thorax, the facial bones smashed, the occiput crushed from the impact of the roof of the car. Bits of brain had been exposed and had turned to cinders. The left arm, hanging limply at the side of the rib cage, still retained some flesh. The right was just a humerus; the ulna and radius had detached, both lying on the car floor. The pelvis was intact and attached to the femurs. Both sets of tibiae and fibulae were splintered and crushed. Where the tiny bones of the feet should have rested sat piles of dusty powder.

The driver was wearing a seat belt.

Decker wondered if the model had air bags. Not that it would have helped much. Air bags were for front-end collisions, offering little protection against a ton of metal crashing down on the head. Heart ramming against his chest, he put on his gloves and stuck his head inside the vehicle.

It reeked from smoke and gasoline and made him cough violently. He pulled his head out and covered his nose and mouth with a handkerchief. Inside the car again, his eyes burned, but as far as he could tell, he didn't see any smaller skeleton in the front seat. The backseat was a jumble of metal filled with soot and ashes. He sifted through the debris, felt his lungs fill up with dirt. Quickly, he surfaced for fresh air and took in a mouthful of smoky dust instead. He coughed and spat on the ground. Annie hit his back.

"Are you okay?"

"Other than breathing poison, I suppose I'll live." He coughed again. "Thought I gave up shit when I quit smoking."

"What's the verdict?"

"Backseat's a mess. So far I didn't find any buried baby bones. I'm going in again."

"Hold your breath," Annie said.

Decker nodded and went inside for a third look. He quickly sorted through the ashes, stirring up black dust, feeling for something hard and bony. He repeated the procedure a couple more times. "I hope I don't eat my words, but I don't think the baby was here."

"Thank God!" Annie said.

"You want to take a look at the skull?"

Annie slipped on latex gloves. "I am now an official forensic odontologist." In an Austrian accent, she said, "Give me room, please."

Decker backed away. About ten minutes later, Annie stood up and coughed.

"You lasted longer than I did," Decker said.

"Good pair of lungs." She looked down at her chest. "Wish it were so." She raised her brow. "I can't tell anything definitive right now. Be able to tell you a heck of a lot more once the skull is removed from the body."

"You're frowning. What is it?"

"There isn't a lot of definition. The anterior maxilla and mandible are smashed to bits. No teeth or bony structure from roughly canine to canine—just a big gaping hole."

"The face probably got smashed when it hit the steering wheel."

"It would take more than a steering wheel to do that kind of damage. The bone looks pulverized. Could be bits of the front teeth are mixed with all the cinders."

Decker took out his notebook. "What about the back teeth?"

"I can't look at them because of the way the skull is situated. You're going to have to detach the head from the spine."

"Let's do it this way," Decker said. "Let me bag all the debris in the car, and I'll sift through it later. As soon as I've got the car clear of whatever evidence there might be, I'll remove the body . . . at least the skull."

"Fine."

"From a quick glance, can you tell if the skeleton is male or female?"

"No guarantee, but from the spread of the pelvis it looks like a woman—a big woman."

Marie Bellson was tall, Decker thought.

He pulled out several plastic bags. "Wish me luck."

"Good luck."

Shoveling piles of ashes into bags, Decker realized it was not only dirty work, it was *tedious* work. He had to move slowly to minimize stirring up the dust. After he removed most of the cinders from the front seat, he moved on to the backseat. Halfway into the cleanup job, a glint caught his eye but was buried under dust before he could retrieve it. Carefully, he slid his hand in the direction of the sparkle and let ashes rain through his fingertips. A minute later, a lump of what looked like gold rested on his glove. He surfaced for air. Annie smiled at him.

"Ever think of doing a remake of the Jolson story, Pete? You look the part."

Decker wiped grime from his forehead. "I've got a lousy voice. Look what I found." He dropped the metal into Annie's gloved hand. "I thought it might be a gold filling or something."

"Way too big. It's jewelry."

"Could it have been a gold cross?"

"You mean like a big crucifix? Sure, could have been."

"I was thinking more like a pin."

"Too heavy for a pin." She hefted the piece of gold. "Probably a ring." She studied the object again. "The metal melted around most of it, but there's a stone inside. Looks intact at first glance."

"What kind of stone?"

"A dark stone . . . cabochon cut, maybe a sapphire." Again she felt the nugget. "Wouldn't say for certain, but with this weight and the cut of the stone, I'd say this was once something like a class ring. Did Marie Bellson wear a class ring?"

Decker said, "I'll find out."

EIGHTEEN

A SHOWER, A SHAVE, A SANDWICH, A HALF-HOUR CATNAP, and the joy of seeing Rina holding Hannah to her breast. With a lightweight quilt across her lap, Rina was nestled in a rocking chair next to the living-room picture window, feet tapping rhythmically against the floor as Hannah drank herself silly. The baby was wrapped in a blue blanket that provided a shield against the soft, cool breeze of the air conditioner.

Decker pulled up a chair next to his wife and looked out the window. The citrus boughs were heavy with fruit, some of which had already fallen to the ground. Time to do a little harvesting. It was going to be a banner year for juices. His eyes went back to his infant daughter.

"She's got an appetite like her old man," Decker said.

"We're very hungry, Daddy." Rina's eyes drank in her baby. "It's so wonderful to hold her. It makes me feel useful."

"Of course you're useful."

Rina didn't answer.

"How're you feeling, honey?" Decker asked.

"When I'm occupied—which is ninety percent of the time—I'm fine." Rina's eyes moistened. "The other ten percent comes and goes in waves—the self-pity, the anger, the depression. Then I spend another ten percent feeling guilty for not feeling grateful." She paused. "I'm over a hundred percent, aren't I?"

Decker laughed. "Didn't you used to be a math teacher?"

"And a bookkeeper. No wonder the company went under." Rina took her finger and inserted it into Hannah's mouth, causing the infant to break suction. "Well, we drained that one." She shifted Hannah to her other breast. "Can't look lopsided, can we?"

She looked at Peter.

"Why am I talking in the first person plural? *I* can't look lopsided."

"You talk that way because you're bonding with your baby."

Rina's smile was wide. "I'll say. This has to be the prettiest baby in the world."

"No argument from this side."

Decker kissed his wife's cheek, eyes traveling around what was once his living room. The buckskin chairs were draped with baby blankets, infant T-shirts, and opened packages of diapers. A cradle and a carriage sat side by side on his Navaho rug. At least the fireplace hadn't been converted into a larder for Pablum.

"Place is a bit of a mess," Rina said.

"It's fine."

"We need another room."

"When Cindy moves out, we'll have another room."

"Be nice to have a guest room."

"Who wants guests?"

Rina slugged him in his good shoulder—the one without the bullet wound.

"I thought you wanted to move, anyway," Decker said.

"I thought you *didn't* want to move."

"I never said that. I just said I didn't want to move into something inferior. All the houses we looked at were twice the price and half the size."

"So let's just stay here and add another room. If you'd just let me get a few bids from a couple of contractors—"

"I can build it at half the cost."

"Peter, when are you going to have time to add a room?"

"Let's drop the subject. It's not the right time to talk about it." Decker waited for a comeback. When Rina didn't answer, he said, "Our energy should be directed toward getting you on your feet again. Not dissipated by construction."

"Agreed."

Decker was amazed—consent with no argument. She must be *really* tired. He turned to kiss her and caught her staring at him. "What?"

"As exhausted as *I* feel," Rina said, "I think I feel worse for you."

"Me? Nonsense. I'm just doing my job."

"I'm very proud of you."

"Thanks." He touched his infant daughter's tiny ear. She stopped suckling. "Sorry. Don't let me interrupt your meal."

"Just a pause to catch her breath."

"How's the baby nurse working out?"

"Nora? She's terrific. Between her and Mama, I feel like a hothouse flower. They're cooking up a storm right now for the *shalom nikevah* Sunday morning."

"Oh yeah, I forgot about that. How many people did you invite?"

"About a hundred."

"Rina, don't you think it might be wise to put off the celebration for a couple of weeks?"

"It's too late now. I'm not going to uninvite everybody. Besides, I'm not doing any work. All I have to do is show up and smile. Even I can do that. Mama's handling everything. The boys are great. The nurse is wonderful—"

"That's good."

"And then there's Cindy. I think Hannah remembers her—or at least recognizes her smell. She never fusses when Cindy holds her," Rina muttered. "All that early bonding that *I* couldn't do."

"She isn't fussing now."

"No, she isn't. And I am very grateful to Cindy. I don't mean to act so babyish. Sometimes I just can't help myself."

"Blame it on the hormones. Do you know where Cindy is? I need to talk to her about Marie Bellson."

"She's sleeping."

"I don't want to wake her. . . ."

"Knock softly on her door. I *know* she'd want to help."

"Yeah, I'm afraid of that." Decker stood and kissed his wife on the lips. "I love you."

"I love you, too."

Gently, he kissed Hannah on the top of her downy head. Again, she stopped nursing, eyes looking up in wonderment. Decker said, "I'm your old man, with an emphasis on the *old*. Do me a favor and go easy on me, kid."

Cindy's eyes snapped opened when she heard the rapping at her door. "Yes?"

"It's Dad."

"Oh . . . wait a sec."

"I can come back."

"No, just wait a sec . . . please."

She had fallen asleep with her clothes on and felt as wrinkled as an old paper bag. She sat up cross-legged and rubbed her eyes. The room held several abortive attempts at a decorative theme. There was a fold-out couch and desk that suggested a former guest room or an office. There was also the full-sized crib—a portent of the baby's room to be. Finally, there was her furniture, a bed, dresser, nightstand, and a wall covered with college banners—Dad and Rina's stab at converting the place into her summer room. The result was an odd mixture—the ghosts of rooms past, present, and future.

Cindy told her father to come in. Dad opened the door and walked across the threshold. "Sorry to wake you."

"I was up. What's going on in the investigation?"

"We don't know anything definite, but it looks like the baby wasn't in the car wreck."

Cindy slapped her hand to her chest. "Thank goodness!"

Decker sat on the corner of her bed. "Yeah, as long as you heard about the car crash, I thought you'd want some follow-up."

"Thanks for telling me."

"You're welcome." Decker pulled out his notebook. "I'd like to ask you a few questions, then you can go back to sleep."

"Ask away. I want to help."

"Describe Marie Bellson for me."

"Didn't you meet her, Daddy?"

"I want your description, princess. Tell me about her."

"Well, physically, she's tall and thin. Her face is long, with lots of little wrinkles. Like sun wrinkles. Only she wasn't tan."

Decker nodded. He had noticed the same thing. "Go on."

"A normal-size nose. She has this stern expression in her eyes, if you'll allow me a bit of editorializing."

Decker smiled. "Did Marie wear any makeup?"

Cindy closed her eyes a moment. "Maybe a spot of blush and lipstick."

"Any other ornamentation?"

"Like nail polish?"

"Did she wear nail polish?"

"I don't think so." Cindy shook her head. "No, I believe her nails were short and unpolished. Utilitarian, no-nonsense hands—except for the ring."

Bingo! Decker said, "She wore rings?"

"A ring—singular. On her left hand, I think. She used to play with it when she got nervous or agitated. That's my interpretation. I don't *know* for sure if she was nervous or agitated."

"Play with it?"

"Slip it on and off her finger. She had bony fingers."

"What did the ring look like?"

Cindy hesitated a moment. "It was like an old-fashioned school ring."

"A class ring?"

"Exactly. A big, heavy gold thing. I think it had a stone in it."

"Do you remember what kind of stone?"

"The round kind. Not a cut stone but smooth. There's a word for it."

"Cabochon."

"That's it." Cindy stared at her father. "Did you find the ring with the wreckage, Daddy?"

"We found a big gold lump that could have been jewelry—maybe a ring. Nothing conclusive, unfortunately, the gold was melted. But your observation was an interesting one. Thanks."

"You're welcome. Is there anything else I can do to help?"

"No, there really isn't."

"Did Marge find out who this Sondra Roberts is?"

"Not yet."

"Did she try Overeaters Anonymous?"

"She's waiting for a call back from them."

"Did you try Alcoholic Anonymous, also?"

"What?"

"For Sondra Roberts? Did you try AA?"

"Why should we try AA?"

"Because people with addictive personalities sometimes have more than one addiction. One Twelve-Step program is like another. Sometimes addicts join more than one program."

Decker paused. "Where'd you come up with that?"

"Psych one-oh-three." She grinned at him. "All that money you're pouring into my education. Maybe you can actually cash in on something."

Decker rolled his eyes. "Tell me about Psych one-oh-three."

"You mean the addictive-personality part, Daddy. The theory is, addiction hides some other personal pain. Symptom substitution. That's why addicts often substitute one addiction for another—alcoholism for drug addiction or sex addiction or overeating. Which means if Sondra Roberts was a compulsive eater, she might have substituted eating for alcohol. Or alcohol for sex or something else. She could be a member of a host of Twelve-Step programs."

Cindy uncrossed her legs and stretched.

"Probably be easiest to start with AA, since they're the largest. I can call them up if you want."

Decker smoothed his mustache. "I'll have Marge do it."

"I can do it."

"I can't authorize you to work in an official capacity, Cynthia. Nor do I want to. Let Marge handle it."

"If I want to do some snooping on my own—"

"*No*, Cynthia! No! No! No!"

"Daddy, I've reached my majority. I can do what I want."

"Cindy, I've just spent over an hour sifting through debris and trying to identify a body that was charred to dust. The wreck wasn't an *accident*. Do you *understand* what I'm saying?"

Cindy cast her eyes on her lap. "You don't want me to get hurt. And I understand your concern. I just want to help, that's all. I saw the baby in the layette, Dad. I can't just sit passively and pretend I didn't."

"Leave it up to the police, Cindy. That's not a request, that's an order!"

Cindy sighed, then threw up her hands. "I'll listen to you, because I can see you're completely stressed out."

"*Thank* you, Cindy."

"You're *welcome*, Father."

Decker regarded his daughter, then reached over and gave her a big hug. He decided to trust her. He had always trusted her, and she had never given him cause to doubt his trust. He just hoped he wasn't making a grave mistake this time around.

It took Decker almost twenty minutes to get through hospital security. A little late for the extra muscle and beef, but he supposed the administration would like the way it played on TV. All those armed guards looking very serious and official. As if the babysnatcher had had to break through a fortress. If only they had been a little more careful beforehand.

Security was equally as heavy around Lourdes Rodriguez's room. Decker couldn't figure out the reason for that, unless someone got word that the asshole who snatched the baby was coming back for the mother. That'd be a new one. Probably it was the hospital's way of minimizing the press passing through her room. A distraught mother wasn't the kind of PR the hospital had in mind.

A burly, bald guard blocked the entrance to Lourdes's room. Decker was about to show him I.D. when he was intercepted by Georgina, Rina's labor nurse.

"Is this man giving you a hard time, Detective?" Georgina turned to the hospital guard before Decker could answer. "You'd better not be giving him any trouble. He's already had enough for the year." She returned her focus to Decker, her eyes filled with concern. "How is Rina? That poor child. I'm so sorry, Detective. Sorry for your wife, sorry you had to experience such dreadful tragedies—both personally and professionally."

"Thanks, Georgina." Decker looked down. "Rina talks about you in superlatives. And we're very pleased with the baby nurse you recommended."

"Nora's working out?"

"Very well."

"Thank goodness. One less thing to worry about. I just wish I could have done more for you two. Then this terrible thing came up." She shuddered involuntarily. "I'm walking around in a daze. So is most of the staff." She waved in the direction of Lourdes's room. "That poor little girl in there. I just wish . . ." Georgina's eyes became moist.

Decker patted her shoulder, and the labor nurse turned it into a genuine hug. A good, caring woman, Decker thought. Georgina was a hard worker and a dedicated nurse—like thousands of others in thousands of other hospitals. It was important for him to bear that in mind as he explored the lives of a few bad apples.

"Georgina, I want to apologize for giving you such a hard time."

"Don't you dare. I thought you comported yourself decently."

Decker smiled. "That's nice for you to say. I think I acted like a jerk."

"Of course you didn't. If you need anything at all, please

call." Georgina straightened her uniform. "I have to be getting back to work. Keep morale up here."

"Not an easy task."

"Simple compared to yours, Detective. Take care of yourself and your beautiful family."

"Same, Georgina. Thanks for everything."

The labor nurse gave him a slight wave, and she was off, marching down the hall in a military cadence—a kind and caring woman.

Lourdes was awake and dry-eyed, her attention given over to a young, heavyset Hispanic male. He had a bronze complexion, his cheeks full and smooth. His dark eyes were round and shaded by long lashes, his lips red and wet and topped with a wispy mustache. A chunk of dark whiskers grew from the depression between his lower lip and chin. Beyond that, he had no facial hair. He looked massive compared to tiny Lourdes huddled in her blanket, her face resting against her knees. The teenager was gaunt, her reedy appearance emphasized by long, dark, unwashed hair falling down her face.

The stocky boy looked up at Decker and yelled, "I already told you, man, we ain't signing any of your shitty papers. Go leave us alone!"

Decker's eyes went from the boy to Lourdes. Frozen in her position, she hadn't reacted to the boy's outburst. He closed the door behind him and leaned against the wall.

"I'm from the police."

The boy blinked long lashes and lowered his voice. "You look like a lawyer—one of *their* lawyers. I thought you was trying to get us to sign one of their fucking settlements. I'm no genius, man, but I'm not stupid."

Slowly, Lourdes turned to Decker. "Did you find my baby?"

When Decker shook his head, the young girl covered her face with her hands. Her shoulders heaved, but no sound came out. The heavyset boy threw a thick arm around her shoulder.

"Now see what you *did*, man?"

"Would you rather I not keep in contact with you?"

He bit his wet, thick bottom lip. "You dissing me, man?"

"No, I'm not dissing anyone. I'm just trying to keep you two informed."

The boy's eyes turned steely. "Yeah, well, then just what's goin' down, man? Heat doing *anything* else besides beatin' up minorities?"

Lourdes rebuked her friend sharply in Spanish. He fired back a retort. She snapped at his sarcasm. Before the boy could lob back an answer, Decker broke in.

"Look, people, first of all, I'm here to help, not to create problems. Second, if you want to dis *me*, you're going to have to switch to another language. I speak Spanish." He turned to the boy. "You're Matthew Lopez? The child's father?"

The boy nodded.

"Detective Sergeant Decker." He stuck out his hand. "I'm very sorry. I'm doing all I can. I wish I could do more."

Lopez looked at Decker's hand, then took it. Lourdes stared at him. "You're Cindy's father?"

"Yes."

"Matty, he's the policeman who had a baby ... same time I had Caitlin." Again she cried mutely into her hands. Lopez glanced at Lourdes but didn't offer any comfort. Instead, his eyes were fixed on Decker.

"You just had a baby?"

"My wife did."

"You're *old*, man."

"Don't rub it in, Matty."

"Your wife is young?"

"Younger than I am. Not as young as Lourdes."

"You're as old as *my* old man! Probably like my old man, too. Three sets of kids from three different wives, not to mention the other bitches along the way."

Decker patted Matty's shoulder, then turned to Lourdes, who had stopped crying. "Can I get you something to drink? Something to eat?"

The girl shook her head.

"Did you find the bitch nurse who took my kid?" Matty asked.

"We might have."

Lourdes's eyes snapped wide open. "Where is she?"

"It's complicated, Lourdes. We think we found Marie Bellson's car."

"You think?"

"The car we found was torched. There was a body inside—"

"Omigod!" Lourdes shrieked.

"We didn't find the baby inside the car, thank God."

"Then where *is* she?"

"We don't know. As of yet, we don't even have a positive I.D. on the body."

"You found Marie, but not my baby. . . ." Lourdes started weeping, this time aloud. "If Caitlin's not with Marie, where *is* she?"

Decker said, "Lourdes, I'm determined to find out what happened to your daughter. Believe me, I couldn't be working any harder if it was my own kid."

Lourdes sobbed bitterly.

"You're upsetting her, man!"

Decker silenced Matty with a glare and waited for the young girl to cry it out. Time was going to move very slowly for her. Lourdes dried her eyes on the backs of her hands. "Why did they take *my* baby?"

"I don't know."

"I was thinking that maybe some stupid gringo took my baby. All these stupid old gringos want to adopt babies cause they can't have their own. But they want *white* babies. Caitlin was Hispanic."

"The gringos can't find white babies, they settle on Hispanic babies," Lopez said. "Besides, you're not real dark."

"I'm not a gringo."

"You could pass for a gringo."

"So maybe a gringo took my baby," Lourdes said. "What do you think?"

"I wouldn't even hazard a guess, Lourdes, until I have

more information. As soon as I find out anything, I'll tell you."

Lourdes said, "Cindy was very nice to me. She told me she was going to try to find Marie herself."

Decker paused, wondering *what* Cindy had in mind. "Well, it looks like we may have found Marie. Now we have to find your baby. I'm going to do everything I possibly can."

"Yeah, you'll work *real* hard until the TV cameras go away."

"Matty, stop it!"

"Mr. Lopez, you can be as skeptical as you want," Decker said. "Tell you the truth, if I were in your position, I'd probably be ripping out some walls. Not that I'm telling you to do it, just that I think you people are handling this well. Especially considering how young you are."

Lopez made a half-smile, then a half-frown. "I got my own method of ripping up walls, man. Wanna hear?"

"Shoot."

"Lourdes and I are going to make a *statement* to the press. We're going to talk about how bad the hospital is and how the hospital's trying to make like it's not their fault. How they're trying to buy us off if we sign away our rights. We're *American* citizens, man! We have rights just like all you rich white gringo assholes! Unless we see some real . . . some real . . . you know . . ."

"Some answers?"

"Yeah, that's it. Unless we get some answers . . . and some . . ."

"Compensation?"

"Exactly, Mr. Policeman. We want compensation! And unless we get something big, we're going to tell every fucking paper and reporter how bad they treated us. Like we was a bunch of dumb wetbacks."

"*You're* going to make a statement, Matty?"

"Yeah, I am. *You* got a problem with that?"

Decker rubbed his burnt nose. "You might think of hiring a lawyer to represent you."

"Right, man. And just give away like thirty, forty percent of the settlement. They're all rip-off artists."

"I'd still consider hiring a lawyer."

"Yeah, that's cause you're the lawman. They don't fuck with the lawman. But they see me, they see some stupid *choelo*. They rip me off right and left."

"I don't care about money," Lourdes whispered. "All I want is my baby." She looked at Lopez. "Our baby!"

"Yeah, *chica*, I want our baby, too. But we might as well play the system for all the trouble they gave us. We deserve something for all the pain, *querida*."

Lourdes sighed. "Maybe we *should* get a lawyer. That's what Mama says."

"Your mother? You look for advice from your mother?"

"Matty—"

"I know what I'm doing, man."

"Lourdes," Decker said, "you met with Marie Bellson several times, didn't you."

"Yes."

"Describe her to me."

"Describe her? Like what she looked like? What she wore?"

"Yeah, that kind of thing."

Lourdes fluttered her eyelids. "She was a tall, skinny white woman. She wore white pants and a uniform shirt. Sometimes she'd have a mask around her neck."

"Did she wear anything on her shirt?"

"Like a scarf?"

"I was thinking more like a name tag."

Lourdes paused. "Yeah, she did. Marie Bellson, Charge Nurse. And she wore a little gold cross. She was religious. Once we even prayed together. I'm not real religious, but I didn't mind."

Decker took out his notebook. "Did she wear any other jewelry besides the gold cross?"

"She wore a ring. A big ugly gold thing with a blue stone. Only ring she wore. It was ugly. She was always pulling it on and off."

"You're sure?" Decker asked.

"Positive. I wondered why she wore it. If she was going to bother wearing a ring, she should wear something pretty. I was gonna tell her that. Then I thought it was none of my business. I just wanted to take my baby and go home." Her eyes became wet. "That's all I want still."

"I'm sorry, Lourdes."

She just shook her head. "Anything else? I'm tired. I want to rest before my family shows up. They was real mad at your questions, you know. Like they had something to do with it."

"We have to question everyone," Decker said. "It's part of the job. Lourdes, you said that Marie wore only a big gold ugly ring with a blue stone. Do you remember her wearing any other type of jewelry?"

Lourdes closed her eyes. "Her ears were pierced. She wore gold studs, I think. Maybe they weren't gold. But they were studs."

"Necklaces?"

Lourdes shook her head. "I can't remember."

"Marie was nice to you, Lourdes?"

"Yes, she was nice. I liked her. I still can't believe she would do such a shitty thing to me. Now you tell me you think she's dead." She bit her thumbnail. "I'm scared."

Decker patted her hand. "Honey, can you think of *anything* that might be important to this case? Maybe someone said something about Caitlin that you thought was a funny thing to say."

"Only *Marie*." Lourdes insisted. "She kept saying I should appreciate Caitlin. She was a gift from Jesus. If I wanted to put her up for adoption, she said she'd help me. But when I told her I really wanted to keep her, Marie was superhelpful. She showed me how to hold her, feed her, diaper her, even how to bathe her. Then my *mother* would come and tell me something different. *She* didn't like Marie at all."

Decker thought a moment. "Your mother and Marie didn't get along."

"No big deal." Lopez grinned. "Her mother hates everybody."

Decker tossed him a dirty look. Lourdes said, "He's right, Detective. Mom's a real pain in the ass."

"Did your mother want you to put Caitlin up for adoption, Lourdes?"

"She'd *kill* me if I put Caitlin up for adoption. My mom . . . she's gonna take care of Caitlin so I can finish high school. Mom can be a pain, but she's okay."

Matty rolled his eyes. Lourdes fell silent for a moment.

"When they told me Caitlin and Marie was missin', I was shocked, man. I couldn't believe Marie . . ." She brushed tears from her eyes. "Now you think Marie is dead? What about *my baby*?"

"I'm busting my chops to find her, Lourdes." Decker stood and took out a business card from his pocket. "In the meantime, rest up as best you can. And call me if you think of *anything*."

She took the card and placed it on her bedstand.

Decker said, "Take care of her, Mr. Lopez."

"Oh, I will. I always do. She's my girl. And the baby's my kid, too, you know." Lopez paused. "You really think we should get a lawyer . . . for the statement?"

Decker said, "Yes, I do."

"You know anyone, man?"

Decker extracted a pen from his pocket and wrote on the back of his business card. "Call this number. It's the local chapter of the American Bar Association. Maybe they can help you . . . give you a referral."

"How will I know these people aren't rip-off artists?"

"You interview them, ask them intelligent questions. Even then it's no guarantee. But unless you want to go through piles of legal mumbo jumbo, you're going to have to trust someone eventually."

"Yeah, you're probably right," Lopez said. "You don't have a lawyer you like?"

"Nope."

"C'mon, man! You gotta know someone."

"Not really. I'll keep in touch."

Decker closed the door and slowly walked down the corridor now populated with uniforms of various colors—

doctors, nurses, orderlies, security guards. Busy, busy, busy, in stark contrast to last night.

He felt a little guilty for sidestepping Matty Lopez's request for help. But he was not about to tell Matty that *he* was a lawyer. Way the kid was talking, Decker wouldn't have been a bit surprised if the boy had offered *him* the case.

Now *that* would be sorely tempting.

Suing those bastards at the hospital for allowing something like this to happen. Getting out all his frustration of the past three days. Not to mention filling his pockets with some cold cash. Lopez was right. Contingency cases like these, lawyers often walk away with a chunk of the settlement. With punitive damages thrown in, the case could net upward of a couple of mil. Forty percent of that would certainly be enough to add a room, plus.

Decker laughed to himself.

Nice to dream.

NINETEEN

THE GOLDEN VALLEY HOME FOR THE AGED IN ARCADIA was a sprawling one-story structure of gleaming white stucco that sat in a quiet strip of rural tract. The front held a U-shaped driveway outlined by hedges of boxwood and yew that surrounded a lawn of yellow marigolds. Behind the building were acres of brush and wild specimen trees of oak, maple, sycamore, and eucalyptus. Marge noticed a creek bed meandering through the back woods, but at this time of year it was not much more than a dried depression of rocks and dust.

The afternoon was hot, wisps of clouds drifting through the sky causing the sun to play peekaboo. The results were bursts of bright rays, then muted sunbeams, as if someone were playing with a light switch. Not much noise pollution in the sticks—ambient sounds were provided by birds and insects.

As Marge opened one of the front double glass doors, Nature's songs receded, taken over by electronic talk and canned laughter. To the right was a lobby with a mounted TV. A lone pink sofa was the resting spot for a lady with an afghan on her lap. To her right was a walker. There was one set of table and chairs, all the seats empty. Around the boob tube was a semicircle of occupied wheelchairs, backs facing Marge. She couldn't see any bodies, only the tops of the heads. Some were bald, some were crowned with white filaments. The chairs were emitting sounds of their own—a heated conversation about last night's dinner, a few phlegmy guffaws of laughter, and one deep snore.

If one took into account the wheelchairs, there was actually more furniture in the lobby than a first glance would concede. It was just the mobile kind of seating. Made for easy access back and forth.

She walked up to a front desk that was manned by a blocky young man—a tackle bag in a spanking-white uniform. He had a broad face, his skin oily and slightly mottled by old acne scars. His eyes were deep blue—intense and alert. His hair was light brown and thin and brushed against wide shoulders. Above his uniform pocket was the nametag L. MCKAY, RN, ADMINISTRATION. L. looked at Marge and smiled with big white teeth.

"May I help you?"

The voice was resonant and deep. Sound waves probably tumbled inside his bull-like neck. Marge displayed her badge. "I'm here to see Lita Bellson."

L. studied the badge, then Marge. "We've been expecting

you. Welcome. Strict orders have come down from the top to be looking for Marie. She hasn't called or visited since I've been here."

That made sense in light of what had been discovered in the canyons. Marge said, "I'd like to talk to Mrs. Bellson anyway."

"You bet, Detective. I'll take you to her."

L. stood.

Too cooperative, Marge thought. Too smooth. She studied him as they walked. In reality, he wasn't tall—just cubic. He led her past the lobby down a long, wide corridor. Off the hallway were the rooms; almost all had the doors open. To Marge's surprise, the rooms seemed well lit and well ventilated. She heard some moaning and coughing that made her feel uncomfortable, but she also heard a lot of pleasant conversation.

Several wheelchairs dotted the pathway—small, shrunken people smiling as she approached them. L. said hello to each of the people by name and gently squeezed their hands as he addressed them. The old folks responded with big smiles, some dentured, some toothless. Marge said hello, too. One of the women asked L. if she was new. L. responded that Marge was just passing through.

The hallway eventually emptied into a big dining hall, the walls papered with a floral miniprint. The tables and chairs were pink and white rattan, set with linen napkins and silverware.

"You've never been to a retirement home, have you?"

"Pardon?"

"Way you're staring at everything. What did you expect? A house of horrors?"

Marge smiled. "You hear stories."

"Truthfully, this is one of the best. Hate to say it, but it can afford to be the best because it's private. Most of these folks have amassed a sizable savings."

"Probably all gone by the time they leave," Marge said.

"It's gone at the time they're accepted in the home. The board of directors looks over the financial status of each applicant. We have a waiting list like you wouldn't believe.

The board goes on to determine the assets versus the liability. If they think the patient is a good risk, the home accepts the person's entire worth in exchange for perennial board and care. Most of the time the board comes out the winner monetarily. But sometimes we get a few foolers—folks that hang on and on and on."

L. smiled.

"I like them. Gives the old board what-for—always evaluating everything in dollars and cents." He gently tugged on Marge's arm. "This way."

"So you're a nurse?" Marge asked.

"An RN with a year to go for my master's," L. said. "Guess I should introduce myself. Lawrence McKay. Call me Leek."

"Leek?"

"As in the vegetable, as opposed to a drippy faucet. You ever talk to Lita Bellson before? She's quite a character. We call her Harriet Houdini."

"Escapes a lot to make phone calls?"

Leek stopped walking. "You've done your homework." He resumed his pace. "Lita is amazing. If I were the betting kind, I'd bet that the board is going to lose money on Lita. She's gonna hang on for a long time despite the fact that she's eighty and has got everything medically wrong with her."

"She's eighty?"

"Yep. I'm betting she'll last another ten years. Too mean to die."

"Wa ... is Marie her only child?"

"Don't know for sure. I think so. I've never seen anyone else visit her except Marie."

"Marie seem like a devoted daughter?"

McKay shrugged. "She visits. That says something."

He made a sharp turn into one of the rooms. Marge followed. It was a semiprivate that looked more like a hospital ward than a bedroom. It was filled with medical equipment and pharmaceuticals. At least the window was large and framed with pretty lace curtains. The shade was pulled down. In the bed closest to the window lay a woman sleeping with her glasses on. She had Coke-bottle lenses that made her eyelashes look like feather fans, white hair, and a tiny face. Leek went over to the woman and removed her spectacles.

"They're like babies. One minute they're sitting up smiling, the next minute they're sound asleep." He smiled. " 'Course, you can't treat them like babies, even the ones who lost it up here." He pointed to his temple. "Gotta treat everyone with respect, that's my motto."

Marge studied Leek's face. He seemed genuine enough, but there was something rehearsed about his speech. Maybe it was just a cop's cynicism.

McKay said, "Lita isn't in her bed. She must be in one of the dining rooms."

"You have other dining rooms?"

"Yeah, the communal one is for people that don't need help feeding themselves. We have smaller rooms that are under supervision." The nurse checked his watch. "Too early for dinner. Maybe she went in to get a snack. It's Jell-O and ice-cream time. Come."

McKay led her to a solarium filled with tables and chairs. The floor was white linoleum; the two walls of windows were shaded by bright blue miniblinds that let in the light but blocked out most of the glare. The air conditioner was acting more like a fan than an instrument of cooling, just blowing around tepid air. Someone must have set the thermostat at a high temperature. The walls that weren't windows were plastered white and hung with lots of children's art. Sweet, colorful stick drawings made with crayons and markers. Most of the pictures were children's views of the home. The old people were drawn almost indistinguishable from the young; the only difference was that their bodies were smaller and their hair was white.

"Like our artwork?" McKay asked.

"Cute."

"Courtesy of the great-grandchildren. We give them art supplies when they come to visit. Kids get so bored here . . . nothing for them to do, so they start acting up. We can't allow that, because we've got some real sick people here.

We have plans in the future for a playroom. Whether it'll come to pass . . ."

"Are the kids squeamish about seeing such infirm people?"

"Not at all. If you and I see some drooling old gnome hold out his hand, our natural instinct is to turn away. Kids go right to them. The old folks eat it up. Nothing makes a crotchety octogenarian smile like the face of a two-year-old. You want to meet Lita, she's the loudmouth arguing with the group in the right-hand corner."

Marge turned. The woman was in a wheelchair, with hair so pink and threadlike it looked like cotton candy. She had on big glasses, and dangling earrings hung from long, droopy lobes. Her body seemed emaciated, tented in a multicolored Mexican serape. Her face was folds of saggy, wrinkled skin, and she had tiny hairs growing out of her chin.

McKay walked over to her and shouted, "Lita, you have company."

Lita looked up and scowled. "I haven't finished my ice cream." She stared across the room, thick glasses eventually landing on Marge. "You the police?"

Marge nodded.

"Do you mind if I finish my ice cream?" she yelled.

"No," Marge yelled back.

McKay said, "Lita, why don't you turn up your hearing aid?"

"Then I hear Maude's bitching."

"It will make the interview easier."

"Aw, shit!" Lita adjusted some dial. Then she spoke in a lower voice. "God, doesn't that woman ever shut up? We all got aches and pains. Wouldn't be stuck in this stinkhole if we didn't have aches and pains. Y'hear me bitchin' all the time?"

"Never," McKay said. " 'Course, I'm deaf. . . ."

"Oh, shut up! What the hell! Just wheel me over to the lady. I'll finish my ice cream with her. Can you get me another one, Leek? They were real miserly with the grub today."

"Lita . . ."

"C'mon, Leek. Do an old lady a favor."

"I guess I'll do it this time."

"At's my boy. Give me sugar, gorgeous."

The nurse kissed the top of her pink hair, then wheeled her into a corner and motioned Marge over.

"I'll let you two ladies talk."

Lita took off her glasses and stared at Marge. Her eyes were clouded by cataracts, but the color that was visible was deep green flecked with chocolate shavings. Lita said, "You want some ice cream, honey?"

"Thanks, but I think I'll pass," Marge said.

"It's real good. Spumoni."

"No, thank you. I'm really fine."

Lita moved in closer and whispered, "Ask him for some anyway. I'll eat it."

Marge looked up at Leek. "Can I have some ice cream?"

McKay nodded his head. "Sure, Detective. I'll be back."

"Don't you just love him?" Lita laughed, then dropped her voice to a whisper. "We're in cahoots together."

"What do you mean?"

Lita moved toward Marge until they were almost nose-to-nose, the old woman smelling as stale as mothballs. "Home thinks they own me lock, stock, and barrel, the dumb clucks. I have a *secret* account that even *Marie* doesn't know about. Turned out to be a pretty good investment. Leek set it all up."

Marge's ears perked. "Leek set *what* up?"

"The partnership or somethin' or other. He's made me a good little nest egg. Soon I'm gonna retire to Hawaii. Whadaya think about that?"

Retire from what? Marge thought. "Lita, how much of a nest egg are we talking about?"

"Why? You wanna go in?"

"No, I just want to make sure you're protected. That Leek isn't doing something funny."

Lita exploded into laughter, spittle flying out of her mouth. "*Leek?* Leek don't need money. He's a zillionaire. He just works here for fun."

Marge paused. Either Leek had her completely snowed, or the woman was in fantasyland. "You say he works here for fun?"

"Yep. He works here 'cause he loves us. He loves me. Everyone who works here loves me."

Marge gave her a weak smile. "How much did you give him, Lita?"

"I don't know. 'Bout a hundred bucks. 'Course, it's worth a lot more than that now. It's worth a fortune from what Leek's told me. He says soon it's Hawaii time. This place is okay, but *c'mon*. How long can I look at these walls without falling off my rocker? Or wheelchair. Leek said he'd even come and take care of me, that gorgeous hunk of manhood. Whadaya think about that?"

Marge took out her notebook and smiled again. If Leek was scamming her, Marge would find out. But there was something unreal about Lita's confession. Maybe it was the ease with which she had revealed her secret. She'd opened up only minutes after meeting Marge. Most likely, she'd mentioned it to others as well. The whole thing was probably wishful thinking.

"Mind if we talk a little about Marie?"

"Where is my daughter, anyway?"

"We're not sure, Mrs. Bellson."

"Call me Lita! I hate anything with a Mrs. in front of it."

"Okay, Lita." Marge took out a notebook. "Do you consider yourself close to Marie?"

"Close?"

"Yes, close."

"You don't know Marie at all, do ya?"

"No, I don't."

" 'Cause if you did, you'd know one thing right away. I was a real shitty mother to Marie. I mean *real* shitty. I left her father when Marie was just a babe in arms. It was only me and her. I was older when I had Marie. My parents were so disgusted with me by that time—disgusted I divorced my first husband, Henry, and disgusted that an unmarried woman of my age was pregnant. I took the father's name just to match Marie, but I never married the jerk. He wanted to, I didn't. Case closed. A stubborn lot, us Whitson gals. Mules—every one of us."

"You were estranged from your parents?"

"Estranged? More like we hated each other. S'right. It never bothered me much. But it bothered the hell out of Marie. Guess she wanted grandparents like all the other little girls in school. Guess she would have liked a daddy, too. Too bad. I tried my best, but I had a life to live. Sorry, but I just wasn't the martyr type." Lita frowned. "Where the hell's my ice cream? What are they doing, milking the cows?"

"I'm sure it will be here soon." Marge brushed hair out of her eyes. "What kind of child was Marie?"

"A Whitson—meaning stubborn and wild. Whitson females are only made out of one mold."

"That's funny. People who know Marie haven't described her as wild."

"That's 'cause they didn't know her in her younger days. The girl was a jalapeño pepper—full of heat and fire. Now all the fire's for nursing and God. She's about as interesting as a bowl of oatmeal."

Marge thought about a different Marie—the radical one buried in a storage bin over her parking space.

"But not so when Marie was young?"

"Not so at all."

"She got pregnant very young, didn't she?"

"You might say that."

"Was she married?"

"Never married any of them."

"Any of them?"

"Nope, not a one."

Marge paused. "How many pregnancies are we talking about?"

Lita narrowed her eyes. "I don't know if Marie would want us talking about her personal life."

"It could be very important, Mrs. Bellson."

"Lita!"

"Lita, sorry."

"You really think my daughter's missing?"

"Yes."

Lita shrugged. "That would be too bad. Not that Marie and I get along so great. But she is my own flesh and blood. I'd feel bad if something happened to her."

Marge didn't answer.

"What were we talking about? Where's my damn ice cream? What're they doing? Growing the cherries?"

"How many times was Marie pregnant?"

"Oh, three or four that I know about. She aborted them all."

Marge kept her expression impassive. Marie had made quite a transformation. From radical politics and free sex to nursing and God. She said, "Marie had three or four abortions?"

Lita smacked her lips. "Yep. Cost me a *pretty penny*! Abortion was expensive in those days. But by that time, my old man had kicked and left me some money. Guess he was feeling remorseful for never talking to me. So Pop made up by filling my pocketbook in his will. I was spending an awful lot on myself. I really didn't mind spending a little on Marie."

"Did Marie ever lose a baby?"

"Lose—like in a stillborn?"

"Or a late miscarriage."

"Not that I know of. Far as I know, she never got that far in any of her pregnancies. She'd come to me and say, 'Ma, I'm in trouble—again.' I'd give her cash, and that's the last I heard about any of them."

"She mentioned to a friend that she lost a baby when she was young. Maybe it was after Marie left the house. Around nineteen or twenty?"

"Around twenty . . ." Lita scrunched up her nose as she thought. Then she glared at the tabletop. "This is just ridiculous. Where's my ice cream? What are they doing? Shelling the nuts?"

"Here comes Leek."

"Well, it's about time!" Lita grabbed the bowl out of McKay's hands. "Took you long enough."

"Spumoni's a hot item, Lita." The nurse set a bowl of ice

cream in front of Marge. "Here's your ice cream, Detective."

"I changed my mind." Marge pushed the bowl in front of Lita. "Is it okay if I give it to her?"

McKay gave her an admonishing look. "Boy, Lita, you really fooled me with that one."

Again the old woman broke into howls of laughter.

"Now if you'll excuse me, I have work to do." McKay waved good-bye.

"Ain't he gorgeous?"

Marge smiled.

"He's going to take me to Hawaii."

"Yes, you mentioned that, Lita."

"I'm supposed to give all my money to the home, you know."

"I know."

"No one knows about my secret money. Not even Marie."

"I understand."

"Hawaii was actually Leek's idea. He wants to settle there for a while. Just him and me. Like honeymooners."

Marge waited a beat, then said, "Lita, let's go on with Marie for just a moment more."

"You're missing out on this ice cream."

"Enjoy, Lita. So you don't know if Marie ever lost an infant when she was around twenty?"

"Nope. I never remember seeing Marie actually pregnant. She'd always scoop 'em out before she got big. Least that's what she claimed she did. Maybe she was just taking my money and having a good time. I wouldn't have been surprised. Hell, that's what I would've done."

"Would it have been possible for Marie to have lost a baby and you not know about it?"

"Sure. By the time Marie was twenty, she was on her own, living up North. Following in the footsteps of *all* those crazy sixties hippies. Miss Flower Child complete with tie-dyed T-shirt and love beads, always living in one commune or another, fucking her brains out. Those were her words, not mine. She'd come home from Berkeley, I'd ask her what she learned. She told me she learned how to fuck her brains out. I told her she didn't need college to learn how to do that."

"So she could have lost a baby and you wouldn't have known."

"Yep." Lita licked her cream-soaked lips. "I think she woulda told me about it, though. She sure as hell told me about everything else—all the drugs, all the sex and the orgies. She screwed everyone and everything—alone, in groups, guys, girls, students, professors, anything that breathed. She went from one commune to another. And when she couldn't find peace in sex, she went from one *god* to another. Then she found Jesus, left Berkeley, and became a nurse."

Lita stopped talking and appeared to be lost in thought.

"Wanna know the truth, Detective? Marie did better than I did. She's adding to this world; all I ever did was take, take, take. Not that it was my fault, nobody ever gave me anything. So I just took it. Deep down in my heart, I'm really proud of my daughter. I tell her that, too. I tell her I was a shitty mother and that I'm proud she overcame my deficiencies to make something more of herself than just a libertine woman."

"What did Marie say when you told her that?"

"Just smiled. She doesn't say too much. Too busy reading me the Bible. I don't mind. I can use all the help I can get."

Marge was writing so fast her hand started to cramp. She took a deep breath and said, "Did Marie seem preoccupied with children lately?"

Lita shook her head. "Nope."

"Did she mention anything about her past abortions by any chance? Any guilt, maybe?"

"Nope."

"Do you recall if she had any guilt?"

"Girl never seemed guilty to me. But I'm not one to look for guilt. I never feel guilty about anything. Life's too short for guilt."

Marge nodded, thinking how blatantly self-centered the

old lady was. Conversation revolved around me, me, me. She probably *was* a shitty mother. No wonder Marie was reading a book about parent-child role reversals.

But what, if anything, did that have to do with Marie taking a baby? Perhaps Marie was capable of feeling a loss and guilt. Perhaps she felt her abortions were past sins, and even Jesus' forgiveness wasn't enough. Maybe she decided to atone in a very harmful way. From what Lita had described, Marie had been self-destructive before. Why not now?

But *why* now? What exploded this potential time bomb?

"Do you know if Marie was seeing a gynecologist lately?"

"I wouldn't know."

Marge asked, "Had Marie been feeling well lately?"

Lita shrugged. "She seemed fine to me."

As if the old woman would notice. "Do you know if she'd been seeing any doctors lately?"

"Nope."

As long as they were on the subject of doctors, Marge had found herself a perfect opportunity to slip the question in. "Do you know the name of Marie's dentist?"

"Her dentist? Why would *I* know Marie's dentist?"

"Maybe she took you to him."

"I don't have any teeth."

"For dentures."

Lita furrowed her brow. "She did take me to a dentist once. 'Bout five years ago."

"Do you remember his name?"

"Nope. Just remember his breath smelling like coffee. I think he worked in Glendale."

"You're sure?"

"Nope. Not sure of anything."

"Lita, would you know any of Marie's friends?"

"Not a one."

"She never mentioned any friends to you?"

"I said no."

"How about Paula Delfern?"

"Never heard of the girl."

"How about Sondra Roberts?"

"Sondra?"

Marge said, "*You* know her?"

"She's a friend of Marie's?"

"I don't know, I'm asking you," Marge said.

"Well, if she is, that's news to me."

"How do you know Sondra?"

"She used to work here. I think she quit a while back in a huff. Some sort of problem about her license . . . that was the rumor."

"What kind of problem?"

"I don't know. Then she quit, and that was the end of her."

Until now, Marge thought. If the employee quit under clouded circumstances, the home would want to keep good records to protect itself legally. Disgruntled employees are often suit-happy. The records would probably be old, but it would be a start. Not that Marge would know exactly what to do with Sondra, even if she found her. There was no indication that she was relevant to this case.

"So you didn't know that Marie and Sondra were friends?"

"News to me. I know that girl had the hots for Leek."

"She was Leek's girlfriend?"

"Unrequited love, Detective. Girl was nice enough, pretty face, too. But downright fat."

Fat . . . Overeaters Anonymous. All made sense. Marge was hoping for that tiny off-chance that maybe Marie stashed the baby with a friend before she did her kamikaze over the cliff. *If* Marie was the one who actually took the baby.

"Well, Lita, you've been a big help."

"I have?"

"Yeah, giving me your insight into your daughter." Marge stood. "Can I talk to you again if I need to?"

" 'Course." Lita finished her ice cream off by scraping the bowl with her spoon and started on Marge's bowl. "You can come anytime. Just bring some ice cream with you . . .

or pudding. The four-packs. Get chocolate or butterscotch." The old lady flashed a toothless grin. "Or both."

"You got it, Lita."

Marge turned to walk away.

"Oh, Detective."

"Yes?"

"One thing."

"What?"

"About Sondra Roberts. That was her official nametag name. Most of us here called her Tandy."

TWENTY

LEEK HAD GONE ON BREAK BY THE TIME MARGE COMPLETED the interview. In his place at the front desk was a middle-aged black woman in a white uniform. Her name was Sarah, and she had worked at the home for four years.

"Sondra Roberts . . ." the woman said to herself. "You mean Tandy, don't you? Sure I remember Tandy. A nice girl, but kind of sad." Sarah shook her head. "She was very heavy and shy. She also had a terrible crush on Leek. Needless to say, the feeling wasn't reciprocated."

"That's what Lita Bellson told me."

"Lita told you that?" Sarah laughed. "Gracious, they are observant—see and hear it all."

"I heard Tandy quit because of problems with her license."

"Really?"

"You heard different?"

"I thought it was just cutbacks. They let go of a dozen people at once. Had us all a little worried. Excuse me." Sarah picked up the phone. "Golden Valley . . . yes, Mrs. Louden, how are you?"

Marge waited until Sarah was done with the phone call, then said, "I'd like to talk to someone in the personnel department. Can you ring anyone up for me?"

"Certainly." Sarah punched in numbers on the intercom system. "Grace will come get you in a moment."

"Thanks."

"You're welcome, Detective."

"Do you like working here, Sarah?"

"It's one of the best."

"Seems like an upbeat place."

"Compared to others, Detective, it's Disneyland."

"Other nurses feel the same way?"

"I think so."

"How about Leek?"

"He doesn't complain."

"Lita told me he had independent wealth."

Sarah let out a deep chuckle. "Detective, if you had independent wealth, would you be working at a place like this . . . even if it was one of the best?"

Marge smiled. "Wonder where Lita came up with that one?"

"Lita's prone to fantasy, Detective. Not just Lita, most of them. And why *not*! At their age, they don't like their lives, they just make up new ones. Like kids telling stories. Ah, here's Grace. Grace, Detective Dunn."

Grace held out a tiny hand. Marge took it and observed that the tiny hand was attached to a tiny body—tiny in absolute terms, not just in relationship to Marge's five feet ten inches. The tiny woman spoke in a whisper.

"Pleased to meet you, Detective. How can I be of help?"

"I'd like to look at a file—a past employee."

"Tandy Roberts," Sarah said. "You remember Tandy, Grace?"

"Certainly I remember Tandy. She worked here about a year, I believe."

"Do you know why she quit?" Marge asked.

"I thought she was laid off," Grace said. "Budget cuts."

"She didn't quit?"

"No, I do believe she was laid off." Grace smiled at Marge. "I'm sorry, Detective, but if you don't have the proper forms, I can't let you see the files without permission from the higher-ups. Invasion of privacy, you see."

"We're talking about a former employee."

"Still, she's entitled—"

"The life of an infant may be hanging on this."

The tiny woman's eyes widened. "Well, I could call the administration office and see—"

"And how long will it take them to get back to you? Grace, we're looking for a helpless two-day-old infant."

"What does Tandy have to do with the missing infant?"

"Maybe nothing. But we're exploring every possible avenue."

"Detective, if you'd just let me make a call."

Marge checked her watch. Four on the dot. Administration probably shut down at four-thirty, five. Unless Grace got through to the boss and was granted permission immediately, it was going to drag out for another day.

"Grace, how about if you go on a five-minute break and talk to Sarah while I wander around and get lost in the back offices."

"Detective, this is highly irregular."

"And so is a kidnapped infant. I was the one who had to interview the mother. Her *first* baby, Grace."

The tiny woman said nothing. Marge could see her wrestling with her conscience. Finally, Grace's eyes traveled to the wall clock. "I suppose I could use a cup of coffee. Five minutes. Files of former nurses are on the right side, tagged with a blue dot . . . for your information only."

"Thank you."

"Lord, I hope I'm doing the right thing."

"Oh, you are," said Marge, giving her absolution.

Before the woman had a chance to change her mind,

Marge was in the back offices. The door to the Personnel Office was open and marked. A desk blocked the entry to the room, which was lined with banks of files. Marge skipped around the desk and dug in. Grace's tip on the former nurses' files was an enormous time-saver because there was a slew of color coding, the largest section belonging to the orange-dot category—the patients. Quickly, Marge started flipping through the *R* section of the blue files. There was only one Roberts, and the first name wasn't Sondra or Tandy.

Marge cursed and began at the beginning of the *R* section, figuring the folder had been misfiled. After her third time through the *R*'s and finding nothing, Marge started on the other colors. It was a lost cause, something that couldn't be done in fifteen minutes, let alone five. A moment later, Grace walked through the doors.

"I'm sorry, Detective, but I'm going to have to ask you to leave."

"Grace, I need your help."

"Detective—"

"I couldn't find Sondra Roberts's file under the blue dots. Can you look elsewhere for me . . . just to let me know it's here?"

"Of course it's here."

"Then find it for me. You do that, I'll play by your rules."

Grace sighed. "Have a seat."

"Thank you very much." Marge sat down at the desk and watched the tiny woman tiptoe over to the blue-dot section. Marge had told her the file wasn't there but didn't feel insulted by the rechecking. Best thing to do was let Grace discover the absence with her own eyes. A minute later, the tiny woman quietly shut the file drawer, a disturbed expression on her face. She started in on a bank of red-dotted files.

"These are our current employees. Maybe someone neglected to pull her file." A sigh. "That someone would be me, of course."

"Mistakes happen."

"I've worked here for fifteen years. I should know better."

Marge didn't answer. A minute later, Grace closed the red-dotted drawers.

"It's not there, is it?" said Marge.

"I just don't understand. Maybe I filed it in the nonmedical employees' file."

"Who specifically is contained in the blue-dotted folders?"

"Former *nurses* only. We keep the nurses separate so we can get to the registry if we need help on a temporary basis. Wait a moment. I'll try looking up . . ."

After twenty minutes, Grace had flipped through every color of the rainbow. She leaned against the wall and folded her arms in exasperation. "It has to be *here*. It's simply lost in the shuffle."

"Maybe someone took it."

"I just don't know. . . ."

Leek stuck his head in the door. "Sarah told me you were still here, Detective. I'll keep an eye out for Marie." He paused. "Everything okay, Grace? You look upset."

"Leek, do you remember Tandy Roberts?" Grace asked.

The color drained from Leek's face. "Sure, I remember her."

"Her file's gone."

Marge said, "What do you know about it, Leek?"

Leek pointed to himself. "Me?"

"Yes, you, Mr. Innocent. You look like you drank chalk. Want to tell me about it?"

"There's nothing to tell." Leek looked at his feet, then at the ceiling. "I know Tandy. I see her all the time."

Marge stood. "Where?"

"At Silver's Gym. I got her into it . . . working out." McKay turned his attention to Grace. "You wouldn't recognize her, Grace. She's about a third her former weight. She looks terrific. And her confidence is amazing."

"You don't say. She was such a mouse."

"Not anymore."

Marge cleared her throat. Leek and Grace stopped talking. "This Tandy," Marge said. "She lifts weights?"

"Not weight lifting, *bodybuilding*." McKay looked at his feet. "Why are you looking for Tandy?"

"Why do you ask?" Marge said. "Are you planning to call her up after I leave?"

Again McKay blanched. "Not if you don't want me to."

"I don't want you to."

"Why are you looking for her?"

"She was friends with Marie," Marge said. "We're looking for Marie."

McKay said nothing.

"Did you know she was friends with Marie, Leek?"

"Sure."

"Were they good friends?"

McKay rubbed his hands together, then turned his head. "That's the phone. I really need to go back to the desk. People call and can't get through, they start worrying about their aged parents. You know how it is."

"Go answer the phone," Marge said.

Grace said, "Do you still need Tandy's file, Detective?"

"Yes, I'd like to see it."

"I'll go through all the folders. It will take me a few days, but I'll do it. If it's here, I'll find it."

Marge gave her a business card. "If you find the file, give me a call."

"I certainly will." Again Grace shook her head. "I don't know how that happened."

Marge said good-bye, leaving Grace alone to admonish herself for her carelessness, and went back to the front desk. Leek was on the phone and seemed to be doing home business, not sneaking in a phone call to Tandy. After he hung up, he faced Marge.

"Okay, so what do you want from me?"

"Why'd you turn white when I mentioned Tandy?"

McKay dropped his head in his hands. "It's sort of embarrassing. . . ."

Marge said, "Tandy had a schoolgirl crush on you."

"So you know." McKay grimaced. "Not that Tandy wasn't a nice kid, but she wasn't exactly my type."

Marge took out her notepad. "She was fat."

"Not that I have anything against fat people, but . . ."

"But you do."

"Yeah, okay, so I'm a confessed narcissist. I'm into my body, and I can't stand to see anyone let themselves go to seed. There's simply no excuse for it."

Marge's expression was deadpan.

"All right, all right. So not everyone is as disciplined as me. I can't help it, okay? Just the way I am."

"All right. I won't be judgmental. Tell me about Tandy and bodybuilding."

"She showed up one day at Silver's. She told me she was determined to take off the weight and wanted me to help her. It was clear to me . . . at least at *that* time . . . she had no real interest in building. She just wanted an excuse to be with me. It was very embarrassing, but I just couldn't be an asshole. So I went along with her charade, and we worked out a beginning program for her. Also a diet—a strict diet. I figured she wouldn't last more than a week."

He let out a soft chuckle.

"Last laugh's on me. Man, she took to building like a fish to water. As soon as she started looking great, she wasn't interested in me anymore." He looked down at his lap. "She told me she was once a model. I can believe it. She's gorgeous. It's hard for me to think of her as she was. I can't tell you how different she is. See, not only was she fat, she was weird. Now she's just your typical gorgeous-chick egotist."

Marge looked up from her pad. "Weird in what way?"

"She'd mumble to herself a lot."

"Mumble?"

"Yeah, like mutter to herself. That's not so weird, I guess. Lots of people mutter to themselves. It calms you down. Only with Tandy, it had the opposite effect. She seemed really upset whenever she muttered to herself."

McKay paused.

"I don't know if the muttering got her upset or she was

upset and that started her muttering. What's the dif? It's history now."

· The phone rang. McKay excused himself and picked it up.

"Golden Valley, this is Leek McKay. How can I help you? . . . Well, hello, Mrs. Graham. Mom's doing great today."

Marge waited until Leek finished his conversation, thinking about Tandy's muttering. Marge muttered to herself but not frequently. For McKay to mention it, Tandy must have been doing quite a bit of mumbling. McKay hung up the phone.

Marge said, "You knew Marie and Tandy were friends?"

"Sure."

"Then why wasn't Lita aware of her own daughter's friendship with Tandy?"

"Lita's only aware of Lita."

"How close were they—Tandy and Marie?"

"They were friends." McKay paused. "I think Marie was trying to help Tandy find work after she quit."

"I thought Tandy was laid off."

Leek hesitated. "Actually, Tandy was officially laid off, that's correct."

"What do you mean by officially?"

"Tandy was going to quit, but they laid her off before she turned in her papers. I told her that was really better. She could collect unemployment until she found other work."

"So Marie was helping her find a job?"

"I think so . . . for a while. I remember Marie coming down to Silver's to watch Tandy work out. I think it annoyed Tandy having Marie hanging around. It annoys most builders to have an audience that doesn't understand. There's lots of grunting and swearing and muttering—"

"Does Tandy still mutter?"

"Yeah, but not like she used to. Anyway, to the average eye, it's sort of weird. Having friends there breaks the concentration. Hold on, it's the phone again."

Marge nodded, and McKay picked up the receiver. She

thought about what the male nurse had said. Marie seemed to have had a passion for taking in lost girls who eventually ditched her once they felt emotionally strong. And Marie also liked the parable of the prodigal son. Marge wondered if Marie imagined herself on a cross.

McKay set the receiver in the phone's cradle. "Sorry. Anything else?"

"Leek, did Tandy reject Marie after she got into working out?"

"I really don't know, but I'll tell you this. When you're really into building, your social life drops to nil. Building is an all-consuming activity. From what you eat, to how often you sleep, to how you move. It's a demon, Detective . . . takes over your life."

"Did Marie ever ask you about Tandy after Tandy left here?"

McKay stopped and thought a moment. "I really don't remember. Maybe once or twice. And I don't know what Tandy's relationship to Marie is now. I see Tandy all the time, but we don't talk much. Tandy's changed so much. I can't tell you how wimpy she was."

"When she wasn't talking to herself."

McKay smiled. "It wasn't all that bad. Just that she seemed so upset. I felt sorry for her." He shook his head. "She's completely blown me off. Our conversations are professional—muscle groups and diets. Nothing personal."

"I'm going to try to catch Tandy at Silver's, Leek. *Don't* call her. I don't want to scare her. I don't want her to think she's in trouble, because she isn't. I'm just asking her questions in regard to Marie Bellson."

"Because of the missing baby." McKay hesitated. "Personally, I just can't picture Marie Bellson kidnapping a baby. Then again, I would have *never* thought Tandy had it in her to be a committed builder. Shows you what my thoughts are worth."

Probably more than you're letting on, Mr. Leek McKay, RN, Marge thought. She stared at him. His words seemed straightforward, his manner honest enough, but *something* was hinky. She broke her gaze, then gave him a Mona Lisa smile. Let him squirm. Never know what people'll do when they squirm.

TWENTY-ONE

MARGE BIT INTO HER HOT DOG, MUSTARD SQUEEZING OUT the other end. She wiped her yellow-stained fingertips with a napkin and said to Decker, "Lita thought Marie's dentist was in Glendale. She didn't get more specific than that. Lots of dentists in Glendale?"

"A fair amount." Decker sipped lukewarm coffee from a paper cup. "But if he exists, we'll track him down."

"I hope Lita's memory is intact. The woman is given over to fantasy."

"If I don't find him in Glendale, I'll look into the neighboring communities, I also have an after-hours appointment with Stan Meecham, Marie's gynecologist. See what the reason was for her D and C."

"Twenty bucks says Meecham was treating her for an abortion."

Decker looked up from his java. Marge filled him in on the details of her conversation with Lita Bellson.

"Three or four abortions?" Decker said.

"That Lita knows about."

"But they were all when Marie was very young."

"That's true. According to Lita, Marie found Jesus and

changed her life. But I'm skeptical. She could be leading a double life."

"And indications of that?"

"Other than the book collection, not really. But what if Marie was wrestling against impulses, Pete? What if impulses won out?"

"So because she was sexually deprived, she took a baby?"

Marge didn't respond. She was lost in thought.

Decker said, "On a more mundane note, did you get a chance to ask Ms. Delfern about Marie's hidden key?"

"As I was leaving I asked her about the box. You know ... trying to be casual. She said she didn't know a thing about the key or a locked box," Marge answered. "When they socialized, it was primarily after work—at a restaurant or at Paula's place."

"What about the nurse who was Bellson's walking partner?"

"Janie Hannick," Marge said. "They were just that— walking partners. Not social friends."

Decker took out his notebook and began jotting down some notes.

Marge said, "Try this on, Pete. Remember Marie had a D and C? Suppose the D and C triggered memories of all her abortions? Maybe something snapped inside her. All these babies she felt she killed."

"Wasn't the D and C over two years ago?"

"Maybe she cracked slowly and no one picked up on it," Marge suggested. "Jesus' help could only do so much. Looks like we're working with two nutcases, Tandy and Marie."

"Being religious doesn't make you nuts, Marge."

Marge looked at Decker. "No, I didn't mean to imply it did. But don't you think there are some weirdos out there who use religion to hide other problems?"

Decker didn't answer, thinking about Cindy's description of symptom substitution. "Why do you say Tandy's nuts?"

Marge gave him a brief description of Sondra Roberts.

Afterward, Decker said, "She talked to herself, or did she talk to someone who wasn't there?"

"McKay just said talked to herself."

"Let's check this girl out."

"My very thoughts," Marge answered. "I called Silver's fifteen minutes ago. She's not in. I'll keep at it."

Decker said, "Go over this Leek guy for me again—his so-called investment sideline?"

"Figured the best way to handle it is for someone to check into his finances. His scamming may not be relevant to Caitlin Rodriguez, but what he's doing is probably illegal . . . *if* it's true. Like I said before, Lita has an active imagination."

"All right. We can't have him screwing the old folks. I'll see if Hollander can't do a little side work. But this is not top priority right now. The baby is."

"Agreed." Marge finished off her wiener. "You find anything interesting on Marie's calender?"

"Nothing marked Baby Kidnapping Day. I'm still working my way through April."

Marge licked her fingers, then excused herself and bought another hot dog, this one with sauerkraut and onions. She sat down at the bench chair and placed her meal on the plastic picnic table. Slowly, she unwrapped her wiener, liberating a puff of steam. Decker patted the aroma away from his nose.

"Am I making you hungry?" Marge asked.

"Yes, you sadist."

"Go on, Pete. I won't tell."

"You're telling me to cheat?" Decker laughed. "You are a bad one, Dunn. Leading people off the straight and narrow."

"And doing it while I stuff my face with nitrites. What would the builders at Silver's Gym say about that?"

Marge happily chewed her wiener.

"You know, Pete, there is the real possibility that Leek disregarded my warning and called her up anyway."

"But you made it clear to him that Tandy isn't wanted for anything."

"I did, but I think cops make Leek nervous."

"Maybe Tandy and Leek are scamming together. You said she left under unclear circumstances."

"Unclear is right. Without her records, I really don't know whether she was laid off or fired or quit." This time, Marge finished chewing before she spoke. "I'm gonna get a drink. You want a warm-up on your coffee?"

"Please. And as long as you're up, see if they have a bag of potato chips. Something kosher. You know the ropes by now."

"You're really hungry."

"I had a sandwich about an hour ago. It wasn't enough."

"Stay put. I'll be right back." Marge returned five minutes later with a Coke, a cup of coffee, a bag of potato chips, a salted pretzel with mustard, and a pickle. "Here you go. But don't take your blood pressure for at least twenty-four hours."

Decker took a chunk out of the pickle. "Thanks, kiddo."

"Oooh, my mouth puckers just watching you." Marge drank her Coke. "Will Meecham be able to tell you what he was treating Marie for? Isn't that against the law?"

"I'm not sure if it's privileged information. Stan's an okay guy. I think he'll help me out. He may even have the name of Marie's dentist, come to think of it. Marie's health insurance is provided by the hospital, but it doesn't provide dental insurance. Maybe Stan gave her a recommendation. I'll call the office."

Marge crunched down on a piece of ice. "What did the coroner come up with?"

"No baby bones."

"You're sure?"

"Reasonably. We combed the car trunk and immediate area and didn't find anything. Captain's currently conducting a full-scale search for the baby—Rangers, sheriffs, LAPD. Never seen so much cooperation between the different agencies. We've got an army's worth of manpower on one spot. Not to mention the newspeople. Got them to hold off reporting until nightfall."

"How'd you do that?"

"My charm." Decker smiled. "And no one wants responsibility for lousing up the investigation of a kidnapped baby. If Caitlin Rodriguez is in Angeles Crest, we'll find her."

Decker stopped chewing and exhaled forcefully.

"I keep thinking about Caitlin. If Marie's dead, where is that poor little infant? Is she safe? Is she hungry? Is she dirty? Drives me *nuts*! Then I start thinking about Rina and Hannah and how I should be home with them, making sure they're safe."

"Rina wants you here. You're doing the right thing, Pete."

"I sure as hell hope so."

"You are," Marge said, "What'd the coroner say about the body?"

"Female . . . a large female." Decker polished off the pickle and started on the potato chips. "From the vertebrae, the doc figured her to be around five-ten. Marie was tall." He stopped talking a moment. "I wouldn't have guessed her as your height, but she was taller than Cindy, and Cindy's five-seven."

"You seem doubtful."

Decker shrugged and resumed his eating. "As soon as we find Bellson's dental X rays, Hennon's ready to do the comparison. When I left, she was still in the lab sifting through debris. She told me there wasn't a lot of frontal bone mass—the face was smashed pretty badly. Hennon figures some of the tooth structure might have fallen out among the ashes."

"What about the back teeth?"

"Some of them are still intact. Hennon thinks she'll have enough material to work with once she gets the X rays."

Marge said, "Did you ask Hennon about Marie's gold stud earrings?"

"She couldn't tell if the body wore earrings or not—too burned. As far as the gold goes, it would be in small amounts, would have melted in the heat. We'll look for gold when we sift through debris." Decker finished his potato chips and drained his coffee. "I'd better get back to the lab and start my prospecting."

"I'm off to Silver's then."

"Want my pretzel?"

Marge stared at the twisted strands of bread, then wrapped it in a napkin. "Maybe I'll be in the mood later."

As Decker stood, a four-by-four pulled up in the fast-food stand's parking lot. Annie Hennon bounced out of the driver's side. Her hands were white, but her face and neck were gray from ash and soot. She strolled over to the table, whistling "Working in a Coal Mine," then sat down.

"And Loretta Lynn thinks she's the only one who ever got her hands dirty."

"Your hands are clean," Marge stated.

"That's only because I'm smart enough to wear gloves." Annie examined her nails. "I could really use a decent manicure." She blew on her cuticles and rubbed them against her blouse. "I suppose you want to know why I'm here."

"Can't be for the hot dogs." Marge made a fist and hit her stomach. "Stuff repeats on you."

"It's the sauerkraut, Marge."

"Good going down, though."

"You want a hot dog, Annie?" Decker offered.

"Always the gentleman," Annie said. "No, Pete, I don't want a hot dog. I want to give you Hennon's pearls of wisdom."

Decker unfolded the flap on his notebook. "Shoot."

Annie pressed her palms together. "First we must recite the Om. Ommmmmmmmmm . . . Gosh, I feel so much better now." She grew serious. "It's about the ring. Or what we think was Marie's class ring. I've been doing a little fooling around while what was left of our victim's jaw was being bleached. I weighed the glob of gold, taking into account the stone. Then I went over to Krechers in Pasadena. Have you ever heard of Krechers?"

"It's a jewelry store, isn't it?" Marge said.

"Close. It's a big-mama place where people buy stones and wax figures and instruments to *make* jewelry. They have all kinds of wax molds and impressions—earrings, pendants, plaques, figurines—but mostly rings. Lots of rings. I looked through the catalogs and bought five or six wax impressions for different class rings. I also bought gold equal in weight to the glob of gold we found at the smoke scene. My idea was to try to recreate Marie's I.D. ring. It's easier to look at a reconstructed model than a chunk of gold. Are you with me so far?"

Decker and Marge nodded.

"All right, so here's the deal. I cast about four or five different rings from different impressions. Cost me some bucks in gold, and I haven't even asked the department for reimbursement. How's that for being a dedicated scientist?"

"You're A-one, Annie," Marge said.

"A peach." Hennon dumped several rings on the table. "These are the rings I've come up with. Standard class rings minus the stone. The jeweler sets the rock afterward."

Marge picked one up. "You do nice work."

"Thanks. I've made some jewelry before, but never have done it for this purpose. It's kind of exciting to do something new. I can understand why you guys like detection."

Decker hefted another ring. "They're not as heavy as the glob was."

"Some of it may be stone. But basically, it's the same weight, just different distribution. A small glob feels heavier than a finished ring."

Annie took out a bag and carefully placed a half-dozen plaster models of breadsticks on the table. "Take a look at these."

Decker separated them and stared at the shapes carefully. "They're fingers."

"What an eye," Annie said. "I made a plaster cast of the fingers of our victim. Not an easy trick, because the bones were brittle." She studied one of them. "They're missing a few anatomical bumps. The alginate picks up the details, but unfortunately the plaster doesn't." She waved her hand in the air. "Irrelevant, but it bothers me. What is important is, I got the right dimensions. So what do you see?"

Decker picked up a ring and placed it on the plaster finger. The edge of the gold caught on the second knuckle and scraped it going down. He tried several rings on several plaster fingers.

"So what's your verdict, Pete?" Annie asked.

"The rings you made are too small for these fingers."

"What a brain," Annie said. "Didn't you say Bellson used to play with the ring, Pete?"

"My daughter said it." Decker paused. "So did Lourdes Rodriguez, come to think of it."

"She wouldn't have been able to slip the ring off her finger if it was a basic class ring. Too tight." Annie picked up another ring. "Now using the weight of gold we found, this is what the ring would have had to look like in order to fit over any of those fingers."

The piece wasn't too thin for an ordinary ring, but thinner than any class ring Decker had ever seen. Most class rings were engraved at the sides. A ring of these dimensions wouldn't have allowed for more than a little etching. Annie slid the ring over the plaster fingers.

"See how well it fits now."

"The ring looks way too big actually," Marge said.

Annie said, "Take into consideration the flesh on the bones, Marge."

Decker studied the thin ring, then passed it to Marge. "Doesn't look like any class ring I've ever seen."

"Me neither," said Annie. "The band's way too thin for the kind of carving and monogramming they usually do. Plus, with this much gold used for the circumference, there's not a lot of gold left to support the stone."

"How about a pinkie ring?" Marge suggested.

"I didn't bother bringing the pinkies," Annie said. "But you're right. This could have been the victim's pinkie ring. Except that the band would be *so* thick, it would practically take up all the space between the hand and second knuckle. A nurse wearing something uncomfortable like that? I didn't see it. But it could be an ill-fitting pinkie ring."

"You think the ring doesn't belong to the body you found," Decker said.

"That's my off-the-record observation," Annie said. "It's

inconclusive. I was just fooling around in case it took you a while to find the radiographs. Might set your thinking in a different direction."

"I'll say." Marge licked her lips. "So if the ring belonged to Marie . . . and the ring doesn't match the bones . . . whose bones were in Marie's car?"

Decker ran his hand over his face. "Good question."

Annie gave a wry smile. "Good question indeed."

TWENTY-TWO

EXPECTING TURMOIL, DECKER WAS SURPRISED TO FIND THE house in solid working order. The living room had been cleared of blankets and diapers, and the dining-room table had been set for dinner with *real* dishes. Something aromatic was brewing in the kitchen. Decker followed his nose and opened the oven. Two roasting pans held stuffed Cornish game hens that were browning nicely. He poured himself a glass of milk.

In Jewish law, the mixing of meat and dairy was prohibited, but one could drink a glass of milk *before* eating flesh. He thought about the reasoning behind the seemingly antiquated law. In Hebraic times, pagan tribes would eat suckling calves because they were the tenderest. And, as an added bonus, the cooks would boil the calves in the milk from the engorged udders of the nursing mother. Generally, he gave little thought to the law other than a twinge of annoyance at having to give up cheeseburgers. But now that Hannah was born—and seeing Rina nurse her—he recognized the kindness behind the prohibition.

He took a deep breath, enjoying the quiet until he realized that the house was *too* quiet.

He drew back the curtain from his kitchen window. Underneath the veranda, his mother-in-law and the baby nurse were having a coffee klatch outside. Actually, it was more like an iced-tea klatch, judging by the amber-filled pitcher and two frosted tumblers. He wondered where Rina and Cindy were, but was hesitant to go outside. The women would probably consider him an intrusion. His eyes swept over his back acreage. The land was dry and dusty. The horses needed to be checked. He finished his milk, took a deep breath, then went out the back door. The women looked up and bid him welcome. Everyone was in a good mood. That was novel.

"Ladies." Decker kissed his mother-in-law's cheek and took a seat. "Where are my other pretty ladies?"

"Ginny and the baby are napping. Cindy and *Opah* went to pick up the boys. They take Ginger with them so she won't bark and wake up anyone. Cindy figures maybe she's bored and wants a ride. You have a wonderful daughter, Akiva."

"Thank you, I have two wonderful daughters."

Magda laughed and slapped his shoulder playfully. "Oh, that's what I meant. You want some iced tea, Akiva? I have extra glass."

"Love some, Magda." Decker held out his hand to the nurse. "I'm Peter Decker. You must be Nora. Georgina speaks very highly of you."

The nurse took his hand. She was black and had coiffed gray hair that matched her eyes. Her hands were strong and calloused. "Georgina's a good friend. Nice to finally see you in person. You've got a beautiful baby, Sergeant."

"Thank you."

"The missus been telling me about what you're doing for that little lost baby." Nora shook her head. "I saw a picture of her on TV, I just wanted to cry."

"It's a tough one." Decker took his glass of tea and downed half in one swig. "But that's what the police are for."

"Everything's okay here, Akiva," Magda said. "You want to work, you can go back to work. We take care of everything."

It was a genuine offer of help. Why did Decker take the comment as if she meant he wasn't needed? He finished his tea and placed the tumbler on the table. "Thanks, that was good. I have some calls to make. Figured I could easily make them from here."

"You just go on and make your calls," Nora said. "Maggie and I will take care of everything."

Maggie?

Decker said, "Great. I'll just check on the horses, then do my work."

"I just fill up the water basins, Akiva," Magda said. "I hope that's okay."

Decker couldn't believe his ears. His perfectly preened mother-in-law actually stepping into the stables, picking up a garden hose, and watering the horses for him. He let out a small laugh. "Thank you, Magda. That was very considerate of you."

"I'm hot and thirsty, maybe they hot and thirsty, too. I would feed them, but I don't see no horse-food bag."

"You have to pitch them hay. You can leave that to me."

Magda smiled and nodded. There was a moment of awkward silence. Decker knew he had overstayed his welcome. He said, "I'll be in the living room if anyone needs me."

The women said good-bye in unison. They didn't resume their conversation until he was back in the kitchen. Peering out the back window, Decker saw their mouths moving, their hands gesticulating, as they picked up where they had left off.

He parked himself on the living-room couch and opened a Glendale phone book to dentists. Of course Stan Meecham's office *hadn't* given Marie Bellson a dental referral, so that put Decker back to square one. He hoped Lita's information was accurate.

To Decker's surprise, the dental listings took up a full page—front and back—of the local directory. Some were general practitioners, but there were a lot of specialists, at least a dozen who listed themselves as experts in cosmetic dentistry. Guess the moneyed liked their smiles nice and white.

He picked up the phone, made the first call, then scratched the first name off the list. He'd finished a half-dozen names by the time Cindy, Stefan, the boys, and Ginger came charging through the house.

Decker shushed them and held the dog by the collar until she settled down. "Your mom and the baby are sleeping."

The boys dropped their voices to a whisper. Decker hugged them both. Cindy sank into one of Decker's buckskin chairs and plopped her feet upon the ottoman. "Good night."

"Tired?"

"Just resting."

"What are you doing here?" Sammy asked. "Cindy told us you were out looking for the weird nurse and the baby."

"I'm working at home, making some calls. How was school?"

"School was school," Sammy said. "*Eema* okay?"

"She's fine. Just resting."

"Can we go riding?" Jake asked.

"I have no objection," Decker said. "Just don't overwork the animals. It's still hot outside."

"Can you come with us?" Jake asked.

Decker felt his heart sink. "Maybe a little later. I've really got work to do."

"You haven't found the baby, Dad?" Sammy asked.

"No."

Jake said, "You want to go riding with me, Sammy?"

"I've got a lot of homework."

Decker watched his stepson's frustration grow. "Jake, give me about an hour, and I'll take you out, okay? It'll be cooler, and I'll be more settled. In the meantime, grab a snack and do your homework."

The boy's blue eyes sparkled. "Thanks, Dad!"

"I'll go, too," Sammy announced.

"Who needs you if Dad's coming?" Jacob said.

Sammy punched Jake in the shoulder. Jake hit him back. Sammy gave him a kick in the thigh. The boys continued to karate-chop their way to the kitchen as Decker told them to keep it down. Ginger jumped on the couch. Decker pushed her off.

"You know better than that."

The dog cocked her head, then slunk off and curled up on the Navaho rug in the middle of the room. Stefan rubbed his stomach. "Something smells good."

"Cornish hen," Decker said. "Magda's out back."

Stefan paused. "Maybe I take a little nap. You have a lounge chair outside?"

"Several."

"I go take a nap outside." Stefan looked at Decker. "You need nap more than I do, Akiva."

"I'm fine, Stefan."

Stefan's expression was dubious, but he didn't argue. He said good-bye and slowly shuffled out of the room. Decker said to Cindy, "Looks like you could use a nap."

"Nah, I don't need any sleep. I take after my father. What are you doing?"

"Looking up dentists. Lita Bellson told us Marie's dentist was in Glendale. We'll need a copy of Marie's X rays if we hope to I.D. the body."

"Can I help?"

"Yeah. Go take a nap."

"I'll call some offices. Cut your work in half."

"Cindy, you're blatantly ignoring me."

"That's what I'm supposed to do. I'm your daughter." She kicked off her shoes. "Besides, you're not going to finish all those names in an hour. Jake'll be disappointed if you don't take him riding."

"That's dirty fighting."

"Give me some names."

"I only have one directory."

"I'll make a copy of the page on the fax machine and

take *M* and below. I'll use the second line to call out. You've run out of excuses."

Decker frowned but tore out the listings. A moment later, Cindy came back with the original. "Should I tell them I'm from the police?"

"Tell them you're working for me." Decker grinned. "You can even say you're my secretary."

Cindy punched him in the shoulder. "Chauvinist."

"You don't like it, quit."

Decker picked up the phone and tried his next listing. After forty-five minutes, Decker bounced up and clapped his hands. "Yes!"

Cindy looked up from the dining-room table. "You found him?"

"Yep. He's making a copy of the radiographs for me. By the time I get down there, they should be ready."

"What about riding with the boys?" Cindy asked.

"Oh, shit!" Decker heard small bleats from the other room. "That was clever, Deck. You just woke up the baby."

"Peter?" Rina shouted from the bedroom.

"Sorry," Decker answered back.

"S'right. We needed to get up anyway."

"Be there in a minute."

"I'm quaking with anticipation." Rina's voice was light. First time he'd heard her cheerful all week. That was good.

"I'll pick up the X rays for you, Daddy. I do know how to drive. You even taught me . . . remember?"

"How could I forget?"

Cindy punched his shoulder again. "Don't think of me as your daughter. Think of me as a cut-rate messenger service." She paused. "No rate, actually. Maybe I should start charging?"

"You charge, you're fired."

"Wait till the labor board hears about you," Cindy said.

Decker exhaled. "All right, Cynthia. I'll let you pick up the X rays. Let me call Dr. Haverson's office and tell them you'll be in. Bring the radiographs here, and don't open them under *any circumstances*."

"Evidence tampering, right?"

"More like common sense."

"I won't open them. I'm not stupid."

"You're not stupid at all. Matter of fact, you're too smart for your own good."

"Atta guy, you know how to say the right thing. Now, what about Sondra Roberts? Did you call AA?"

"Are you checking up on me?"

"Yes."

Decker smiled. "It's not necessary. We found her."

"You *did*?"

"Yes, Cindy, the police can actually function without you."

"Where'd you find her?"

"Long story."

"What's the upshot?"

"You don't give up, do you?"

" 'Course not. Where'd you find her?"

"We found her by luck at Silver's Gym. Marge is there now, doing an interview."

Cindy was silent.

Decker said, "What? You're disappointed because we didn't find her through your tip-off?"

Cindy broke into laughter. "Truthfully, yes."

"Ah, the girl has an ego just like her old man." Decker shook his head. "Anyway, with a little more luck, maybe Sondra—or Tandy, which is her nickname, I guess—can help us find Marie."

Cindy didn't answer right away. "I thought you found Marie at the bottom of the canyon."

Decker scratched his head. "Things are turning out a little more complicated."

"What?" Cindy asked. "That wasn't Marie?"

"I don't know," Decker said. "That's why we need the X rays. So if you'd kindly get moving. . . ."

"Peter?" Rina called out.

"Be right there."

"Take your time," Rina answered. "Did Mama make dinner? I smell something good."

"She sure did, God bless her. Are you hungry?"

"Famished. But it's too early to eat now, isn't it?"

"I'll fix you a snack."

"You're a doll. I'll need a pitcher of water, too. Your daughter has a healthy appetite, *baruch Hashem*."

"You got it." Decker slapped his knees, stood, and picked up the phone. "I'll call the dentist for you. And seriously, thanks for helping me out, princess. It's not my idea of a hoot to go riding right now, but the boys . . . new sister and all. Guess they need me."

Cindy threw her arms around her father's waist and hugged him hard. "Daddy, *everyone* needs you."

"Very funny," Decker said. But he thought, Ain't that the truth.

Marge thought, Baden-Baden had nothing to worry about.

Silver's was not a spa or a health club or even a community-center gym. It was a warehouse, stripped of anything decorative. No piped-in New Age music, no plush carpets underfoot. Instead, the space had cracked-plaster walls and hanging broken mirrors. The acoustic-tiled ceiling showed water spots from prior leakage; the linoleum floor was old and yellowed. There were a few fly fans running at full blast, but the place was still hot. Nothing but *nothing* here suggested anything comfortable and *soft*.

The area was filled chockablock with workout equipment and heavy weights. About two thirds of the stations were in use, and more people were coming through the front door. It looked to be a busy evening.

To say these guys were musclemen or hunks didn't do them justice. They were mutations, like fancy goldfish—this one bred for a long fantail, this one for bubble eyes, this one for a dwarfed body. Instead, it was: This one lifted for elephant neck size, this one for a rhino chest, this one for legs as thick as tree trunks. Bodies blown up like overstretched balloons. As they worked out, blood vessels popped and pulsated under hairless skin; muscle and tendon became anatomically defined. It made Marge hurt to look at them.

What *possessed* men to do this to themselves? Spend hour after hour lifting backbreaking weights? Getting their butts shot up with anabolics that could potentially cause cancer or sterility?

Then again, what possessed women to starve themselves to flagpoles and barf up their meals?

When Marge stood the thoughts side by side, she realized that anorexia wasn't all that different from extreme bodybuilding. Both groups contained people with distorted body images going to extreme measures to "perfect" their bodies.

The perfect body.

Marge regarded her own corpus collosus. She wasn't fat, but she was large—heavy-boned, thick wrists, long limbs, and more than a fair share of muscle mass. And like every woman she had ever met, Marge was dissatisfied with the way genetics had molded her. Big-gal physique would never be featured in *Sports Illustrated*'s swimsuit edition. But Marge could live with the pain. All her parts worked and required little maintenance to run efficiently. Perfecting the body was just too much damn work.

But obviously not too much work for the twenty-five or so men in the room. As Leek had described, the builders grunted and growled, sweat bathing their faces and bodies. Dressed solely in tiny little briefs, they did squats and lifts, leg and bench presses, thousands of sit-ups on slant boards, hundreds of push-ups and pull-ups. They lifted umpteen pounds' worth of freestanding weights atop their heads, muscles bunching, veins bulging, their wet beet-colored faces turning more purple with each second. Then, in a flash, the barbells crashed to the floor, sending vibrations Marge could feel through her spine.

But no one else in the room seemed to notice.

The smell of toil and sweat combined with the heat made the place stifling. She felt deep wet circles soaking the pads under her armpits.

She jumped as metal crashed against metal, sending a ringing into her ears. Weights slamming into each other. A deep shout followed.

"Can someone teach this dickbrain how to use the weights properly!"

No response.

Without reason, Marge suddenly opened her purse and felt for her gun. Not that it would probably do much good against these guys. Their chests were probably steel-lined.

Her eyes surveyed the room. She hadn't noticed any women. But the man she spoke to said Tandy had just started her workout and would probably be here for the next two hours. Maybe there was a separate workout area for women. Briefly, she scanned the room again.

This time her eyes fell upon a figure with a long black braid, shaped like a well-built man. Around five-nine with a broad back, small hips, round, muscular buttocks. The legs were long, with tight thighs and well-defined calves. The arms had biceps and triceps. The back rippled with definition. Then it turned around. It had breasts. It was a woman.

A beautiful woman, with features that could have been on the cover of *Vogue*. An oval face with wide-set eyes, smooth olive cheeks stretched over a sweeping zygomatic arch, thick dark lips. She wet them with her tongue, then picked up a weight and did a set of arm curls. With each lift of the dumbbell, her biceps became increasingly more contracted and defined. Marge started toward her, dodging sweat-soaked beefcake. The woman's back was turned when Marge arrived.

"Tandy Roberts?"

There was no response. The woman picked up another free weight, sat on the corner of the bench, and began another set of curls.

Marge said, "Excuse me, do you know where I can find Tandy Roberts?"

The woman spoke without looking up. "Bug off. I'm busy."

Such naked aggression. The girl must be on steroids. Marge reached inside her purse and pulled out her shield and I.D. "Police. Are your Sondra Roberts?"

The woman stopped and studied the badge. "Why didn't you say so in the first place?"

"I asked you a simple question, Ms. Roberts. I didn't expect hostility. You got something on your mind?"

Tandy finished her curls, then set the weight down. Picking up a rag, she wiped sweat off her forehead. "You don't understand buffing. It's a consuming process, one that requires continuation once you start. Interruption throws off your timing. Mind waiting until I'm done?"

Marge paused. Tandy was still sullen but more respectful. Not nervous, though. Good eye contact.

"Tandy, I need your help now."

Tandy wet her lips. "My help? For what?"

Once again a loud clank boomed from one of the weight machines.

Tandy said, "Idiot! You're not supposed to let the weights fall like that. It shows a lack of control."

"Anywhere we can talk where it's a bit quieter?"

"There's a juice bar across the street." She stood. "C'mon. Can you give me a hint what this is all about?"

"Marie Bellson."

"Marie?"

"Yeah, I understand you were pretty good friends with her."

"Once."

Marge followed the girl toward the exit. As they were about to leave, a pile of chuck steak shouted, "Hey, Tandy, you couldn't possibly be done yet."

She tossed Steaks a smile and said, "In the words of the inimitable Arnold, 'I'll be back.' "

"Not good, Roberts . . . to stop and start."

"Tell that to the cops, Eric."

"Cops?"

Another voice said, "Will you two shut the fuck up?"

Eric said. "Fuck off."

Tandy held the door open for Marge. "Classy place, huh?"

"You people aren't long on patience."

"It's part of the mind-set," Tandy said. "You've got to

approach lifting like the enemy. The swearing and all that kind of jazz is needed to psych yourself up. Lifting is really hard work."

"Why do you do it?"

The question seemed to throw her. She thought a moment before responding. "Each person has their own personal reasons."

"What were yours?"

"What does this have to do with Marie?"

"Nothing."

"So my personal reasons are my personal reasons."

"Fair enough."

They crossed the street and walked into the juice bar in silence. The place was small, holding a horseshoe-shaped counter and about twenty empty stools. Behind the counter were baskets of fresh fruit, a couple of citrus juicers, several presses, and three juice dispensers bubbling up lemonade, orange juice, and some kind of green citrus drink. A young woman in a leotard and leg tights came out from the back and smiled when she saw her customer.

"Hey, Tandy."

"Hey, Kathy."

"Usual?"

"Not yet. Haven't finished my workout yet. Get my friend a special—"

"An orange juice is fine," Marge said.

"You're missing out on something wonderful."

"I'm not hungry," Marge said. "I just ate two hot dogs with sauerkraut."

Tandy frowned. "Each his own, I suppose. When I was having eating problems, nobody could tell me the gospel, either."

"Eating problems?"

Tandy sighed. "Do you want to talk about Marie, or do you want to talk about me?" She paused. "What's with Marie, anyway?"

"Did you happen to catch any TV news today?"

"Nope. Don't watch the news. It's a downer. Don't watch any TV if I can help it."

"So you didn't see the missing infant on this morning's broadcast."

Tandy wet her lips. "No."

Kathy, the bartender, placed a beer mug filled with orange juice on the counter. Marge picked up the stein and sipped, waiting for Tandy to speak, throwing the ball in her court. She picked it up nicely.

"What about this missing infant?"

"Marie was the baby's nurse. Marie seems to be missing, too."

"Marie's missing?"

"That's what I said. How well did you know her?"

Tandy paused. "Pretty well, I suppose."

Again Marge waited, expecting to hear Tandy ask questions. She didn't. Nor did she clarify her friendship with Marie. "Do you want to elaborate?"

"We were good friends for about a year . . . maybe two years. What exactly do you mean, Marie is *missing*?"

"One minute she was on shift, the next minute she and the baby were gone."

"You think Marie kidnapped one of her babies?"

"*Her* babies?"

"Excuse me, *a* baby. She always referred to the infants under her care as *her* babies."

"Interesting." Marge paused, thinking that if Marie thought of the infants as *her* babies, she could rationalize taking one of them. "Hypothetically, Tandy, if Marie were to take one of her babies, where would she and the baby go?"

Tandy's face registered confusion. "I haven't the faintest idea. I haven't talked to Marie in a couple of years. The Marie I knew wouldn't ever kidnap a baby even if she wanted to. So if she did, she must have changed pretty drastically."

"What do you mean by 'even if she wanted to'?"

She paused. "I don't know why I said that."

"Of course you do. So why don't you explain yourself."

"Okay, maybe I do. But I don't think Marie would actually kidnap a baby, okay?"

"Okay." Marge took another sip of her juice. "So why would Marie even *want* to kidnap a baby . . . even if she wouldn't?"

Tandy didn't speak.

"Ms. Roberts?"

"It's just . . ." Tandy sighed. "Marie's very dedicated. Sometimes it hurt her to send a baby into a home with two strikes against it, know what I mean?"

"No, I don't know what you mean."

"You know . . . send the baby to a broken home, to a teenaged mom who maybe would neglect her or maybe even abuse her. Maybe the mom is even a drug user. Marie used to feel it was condemning a kid to a life of misery. She takes her work to heart."

Marge nodded, wondering why Tandy chose to sex the anonymous baby as a female.

Tandy blurted, "Marie lost a baby when she was young. I don't think she ever got over it."

"Really?"

Tandy nodded.

"She told you that?" Marge said. "You two must have been pretty close then."

"Yeah, we were. Funny how things change."

"Why do you think she told you that, Tandy?"

"I guess to draw us closer. And it did. That and our professions. I'm a nurse, too. I don't work full time, just float around. I have some money saved from when I used to model. Not enough to live on for the rest of my life, but enough to dip into."

"You used to work at the Golden Valley Home for the Aged."

"Ah, so that's where you got my name. From Lita."

Marge smiled cryptically. She wanted to leave Leek's name out until she had a chance to fully investigate him. "Why did you say that Marie's loss of a child brought you two together?"

"What is this? True-confessions time?"

Marge waited.

Tandy sighed. "I lost a child when I was young, too. It's

a unique experience, one that you can only share with someone who's gone through it. Our losses drew us together."

Marge tried to appear casual as she wrote in her notebook. Just coincidence? Marge didn't believe in coincidences.

"It was a long time ago." Tandy's eyes seemed far away. "I was very, very young . . . and stupid. I used to be a model. A scumbag in the industry got me pregnant. He offered me five grand to have an abortion because he didn't want his boyfriend knowing he was bi, can you believe that? I refused the money. I should have taken it, 'cause I miscarried in my sixth month. Bret gave me a couple of g's anyway not to blow his cover. I had lousy taste in men. If you knew my dad . . . doesn't Freud say we go for our fathers?"

"Sounds like Freud," Marge said.

Tandy bit her lip. "I was in a bad way for a while, but I pulled out of it."

"How old were you when you lost the baby?"

"Fif . . . no, sixteen actually. I was sixteen by the time I miscarried." She picked up Marge's orange juice and took a sip. "What does that have to do with Marie?"

"Do you know how old Marie was when she lost her baby?"

"I dunno, older than I was. Around twenty maybe. She said it turned her life around, forced her to look inward. She found Jesus and became a caring person. That's why she went into nursing."

"Did losing a baby turn your life around?"

"Why are you always coming back to me?"

"Just trying to get some parallel that might make me understand Marie better."

"How will talking about me make you understand Marie?"

"Can you just indulge me, Tandy?"

Tandy flipped her braid over her shoulder. "*Buffing* turned my life around. First time I've ever felt in *control*."

Marge was silent, thinking how Tandy emphasized the word *control*.

Control over *what*?

She said, "Why did you become a nurse, Tandy?"

"I wish I could say it was for some Florence Nightingale reason, but the truth was, I needed a job." Tandy laughed bitterly. "Can't exactly model if you weigh three hundred pounds, can you?"

Marge tried to look surprised. "You?"

Tandy's smile was genuine. "Hard to believe, huh?"

"Impossible."

"It's the truth. Anyway, I became a nurse 'cause I needed a job. No one would hire me as a secretary 'cause I was too fat. But no one cares what you look like in an old-age home. I started out changing bedpans, went to school at night, and became an L.V.N."

"That's turning your life around," Marge said.

Tandy smiled. "More like crawling out of the gutter. I was a five-hundred-dollar-an-hour model in New York when I was *fifteen*! When I got pregnant, it all disappeared. I did lose the weight . . . I could have gone back, but I was so disgusted by the way they treated me—my mother, my agent, the industry. I dropped into this blue funk, and my mind started going nuts. I ate myself to nearly three hundred pounds." She drummed her fingers on the table and gave Marge a painful smile. "It's all for the best."

Marge smiled back. "And you met Marie at Golden Valley?"

"Yep."

"I hear she was helping you find a better job."

"You do your homework, don't you?"

Same phrase Leek had used. Marge wondered if Leek hadn't called her. If so, Tandy hadn't bolted—a good sign for her. She said, "Just that Marie seemed close to you. And now she and this baby are missing. The mother is absolutely distraught."

Tandy bit her lip. "I'm sure. But like I said, I haven't spoken to Marie in ages."

"Why's that?"

"Marie doesn't understand building, and building is my life."

"Prevents the mind from going nuts," Marge said.

Tandy's features froze—a death mask of tranquillity. "Yes, exactly, Detective. Anything else?"

"Let's go back to Marie. Did she help you find another job after you left Golden Valley?"

"No, not really. Well, she could have found me stuff, but it was all full time and I wanted part time. No prob, though. It's easy to pick up part-time work as a nurse. Someone is always looking for temps. We're much cheaper than hiring staff—no benefits or union stuff. I'm strictly fill-in."

"You get called a lot?"

"All the time. I can pick and choose. I like that."

"Where do you work?"

"Anywhere from a private home to a hospital."

"Give me an example. Like yesterday, for instance. Where did you work? Or did you work?"

"Yesterday? I floated at Tujunga Memorial—late shift. Why? Are you going to check up on me?"

Marge laughed. "You watch too many cop movies."

Tandy's eyes blazed clear and purposeful. "Don't watch TV, don't watch movies. I wish I could help you with this missing baby, but I can't."

"Did Marie ever talk about any relative or friend of hers?"

"Just her mom. Marie didn't talk much about herself. Too busy listening to my problems."

That was consistent with Paula's statement. Marge said, "Did she ever go visit anyone out of the city?"

"Not that I know of."

"Did she ever leave the city for any reasons? Vacations? Weekends?"

Tandy drummed her fingers against the counter again, then folded her hands. "We went camping a couple of times."

Marge paused. "Whose idea was that?"

"Marie's. She loved to camp. She said she could really talk to God in nature. I think she used to go off by herself on weekends and camp. She certainly was good at it. Camping wasn't for me."

"What do you mean she was *good* at camping?"

"Just that she seemed at home in the wilderness. She knew different plants and what you could eat and all that kind of thing. Kind of a survivalist but without the guns. She could use a knife, though. She used to cut her own timber for the campfires. Me? I prefer running water and salad bars, thank you very much."

Tandy threw back her hair.

"Anything else? I'd really like to get back to work."

Scribbling hurriedly, Marge finished up, flipped the top cover of her notebook closed, and laid a couple of bucks on the table. "That's it for now."

From inside her Honda, Marge watched Tandy return to Silver's. She picked up the mike, called DMV, and got the make and license of her car—a black 1988 Audi. It took Marge only a few minutes to find it, resting in the back parking lot. Settling her Honda a few rows down from the Audi, Marge waited. After about ten minutes, she shifted in her seat.

If Tandy Roberts was guilty of something, she wasn't making any sudden moves.

Marge picked up her mike and placed a call to Tujunga Memorial. As expected, the Personnel Office was closed for the day. She called the station and checked for messages. No trace of the baby. Pete had a seven o'clock with Dr. Stan Meecham. He also planned to meet Annie Hennon at the station house's lab around eight. Seems he had found Bellson's dentist and X rays. Could she make it?

Marge checked her watch—quarter after seven. Twenty minutes had passed. It appeared that Tandy was going to finish up her building routine. That being the case, she probably wouldn't be leaving for a while. Reluctantly, Marge convinced herself she had better things to do with her time than sit on her butt chasing an intuition.

She'd make the meeting with Decker and Hennon.

TWENTY-THREE

A SCHEDULED MEETING BROUGHT OUT THE NESTING IN-
stinct in Meecham. When Decker first met the obstetrician,
he had showed up at Meecham's private office. The place
had been a mess. This time Meecham had taken care to
empty his ashtrays and garbage and neatly stack his charts
on his desk. Decker knew the doc must be close to retiring,
but he carried his age well. Still trim with a head full of
white hair, he had shaved his snowy mustache, and his face
was weathered from the sun. His nose was thin and veined.
Apparently, he hadn't given up the hooch. He wore a
starched white coat over a maroon shirt and navy tie and
held out his hand to Decker.

"So we meet again under lousy circumstances," Meecham said.

Decker took the proffered hand. "Thanks for making
time for me, Dr. Meecham."

"Stan, please." The obstetrician sat at his desk and
pointed to a chair on the opposite side. "We're old buddies
by now."

"You ever hear from the Darcy family?" Decker asked.

"From the aunt."

"How's the little girl doing—Katie?"

"What a memory. She's doing remarkably well. More

218

than you can say for Marie Bellson. You being here. You haven't located Marie yet."

"No, not officially."

"Not officially . . . that sounds ominous." Meecham took out a pack of cigarettes. "You smoke, don't you?"

"Used to."

"Oh, God, we lost another good man to *health*."

Decker laughed. "How do you justify it, Doc?"

"Years of specialized training." Mcccham lit his smoke and blew out nicotined air. "Do you want to know the truth, Sergeant? I've seen every sort of inequity that disease can bring. Young, strapping women reduced to skin and bones, their bodies ravaged and disfigured by neoplasm. It hurts, let me tell you. Some people see that kind of thing, they take it as a warning to take better care of themselves. Me? I take it as a sign to have some fun. Maybe it's stupid. But my kids are grown, I've got trust funds for the grandchildren, and a good life-insurance policy for my wife. I say, the hell with it."

Meecham took a deep drag of his cigarette.

"Look at poor Marie. I saw her just a month ago, and she was doing so much better. Nothing to suggest she'd make the morning news in such an odious way. Now you tell me you haven't officially found her. Which means what? You've unofficially found her?"

"Wc found her car and a burned body inside—"

"Oh, *shit*!" Meecham rested his face in his hands. "Life's a goddamn ill wind that blows nobody good." He looked up. "So that's why you called the office and asked for her dentist. You're going to make the I.D. through dental radiographs."

"Exactly. We've sent for them. I'm due to meet the forensic odontologist in about forty minutes."

"If you want a backup, I'll take a look at her hips. Lord knows I took enough radiographs of the region."

"You did a D and C on her about two, three years back?"

"Sure did."

Decker looked Meecham in the eye. "It was an abortion, wasn't it, Doc?"

Meecham threw his body back in his chair. "Where'd you get *that* idea? No, it wasn't a termination of a pregnancy. It was a dilation and curettage, plain and simple. Well, not so plain and simple, actually. Nothing with Marie was plain and simple. She had a lot of medical problems."

"What kind of problems?"

"Well, I suppose if she's deceased, I don't have to worry about confidentiality, do I?"

Decker shrugged noncommittally.

Meecham shook his head. "Aw God, the whole thing just makes me sick! Poor Marie. She's been battling endometriosis for years. Cramping, irregular bleeding, and fibroids to boot. Her plumbing was a mess."

"Were her problems caused by abortions in her youth?"

"You do your research."

"Part of the job."

Decker waited for Meecham to continue. He was slow to respond.

"Were her conditions caused by prior abortions?"

Meecham took another drag on his cigarette. "Could have been if the procedures were botched. Or her problems could have been just bad genetics. From my perspective, I didn't care what *caused* her problems. I was only interested in *treating* them. And how are her medical problems relevant to her and a missing baby?"

"Did Marie seem more depressed than usual? Say in the last six months?"

"Ah, I see where you're going. You think her problems may have driven her over the edge?"

"I'm asking *you*. Was she depressed over her problems?"

"Of course, she was depressed. She was only forty and had begun to go through menopause."

Menopause! Suddenly, Decker remembered Cindy's mentioning menopause as a reason for doing a D and C way back when. Taking out his notepad, he said, "You want to tell me about it?"

"I suppose since she's dead . . . I still feel funny talking about her to a noncolleague—no offense."

"None taken."

"Menopause can be quite an ordeal. Besides all the hormonal disturbances that wreak havoc on the system, there's the emotional component. That time of life is hard for most women. At forty, cessation of menses is a bitter pill to swallow. It can do strange things to your mind."

"Did Marie talk as if strange things were going through her head?"

"She never said she was planning on kidnapping a baby, if that's what you mean."

"I wasn't referring to anything specific. I was referring more to her attitude."

"Well, she was in hormonal flux. But she was bright enough to recognize it for what it was. We were trying a number of different therapies to help stabilize her mood swings."

"Were they successful?"

"Yes, I'd like to think so. She said she was doing fine at work. Being home alone at night was hard for her. Depression was most likely to hit her then. I'm sure you know this, but her mother's in a rest home. Marie doesn't seem to have other family."

"What about friends?"

"I'm sure she has friends, but who wants to talk about early-onset menopause with friends? I suggested she get a dog or a cat . . . something alive and unquestioningly loyal. And you know what, Sergeant? She *listened*! She said it helped her!"

Decker thought about the little kitten locked in Marie's bedroom. Her legacy. It had found a home in the stallion's stall. He supposed it would need shots and made a mental note to take it to the vet. Meecham stubbed out his cigarette.

"Anyway, the long and the short of it was," the doctor went on, "she was a woman who suddenly saw the last vestiges of her youth snatched away. Forty ain't that old in life. That kind of thing is bound to have an impact on the emotional makeup."

"Certainly puts a whole new slant on the case," Decker

said. "Everyone we've talked to said Marie hadn't appeared any different than usual."

"Like I told you, Marie said she was functioning well at work."

"Or maybe not," Decker said.

"I just can't see her kidnapping a baby, Sergeant. Yes, I know what hormones gone awry can do to an otherwise intelligent being. But I can't see Marie harming a little baby."

"Who said she harmed anyone?"

"Or kidnapping a baby, don't get technical." Meecham took out another cigarette. "You told me you found Marie's body. I'm no police professional, but that indicates foul play to me. Someone must have forced Marie to take that kid."

"Possibly," Decker said.

"You never told me about the baby."

"We haven't found the baby."

"See, that just reinforces my theory. Marie's dead; the baby's not there. Someone must have killed Marie and made off with the kid."

"If the body is Marie's, yes, it looks that way."

"What do you mean, 'If the body . . .'?"

"We haven't positively identified the body yet."

Meecham's eyes hardened. "You let me talk about one of my patients as if she were dead, and now you tell me she may be alive?"

"Doc, I never told you we positively identified—"

"Sergeant, how could you *do* that? Do you realize I just broke confidentiality!"

"Dr. Meecham, I'm looking for a three-day-old infant, and I'm going to use every avenue available to me to get information. If I misled you, I'm sorry. But at this point in the investigation, when we have diddlysquat to go on, any kind of data is valuable. While it is true that I'm trying to find Marie, my heart goes out to the infant. What did *she* ever do to deserve this shit?"

Meecham sighed and rubbed his eyes. Decker leaned over the desk and patted his shoulder. "Thanks."

"S'right."

"Try not to beat your chest so hard, Stan. You helped. You didn't harm. Isn't that what your profession is all about?"

Meecham broke his cigarette in half and shook his head. "I heard that somewhere in my training."

Placing the sets of radiographs side by side on the monitor, Annie Hennon studied the illuminated negatives. At that point, Decker realized you didn't have to be an expert to tell what *didn't* match. But he said nothing, watching Annie talk teeth into a Dictaphone, waiting patiently for her to make a diagnosis. Marge was quiet as well. Twenty minutes passed before Annie spoke.

"It's not the same person." Her eyes were still on the X rays. "Not by a long shot. The body's teeth are bigger, more dense in the enamel and dentin, longer rooted. They don't match the radiographs of Marie's teeth. So we've either got two different people, or the dentist gave you the wrong set of pictures. Did the dentist or an assistant give the envelope to you?"

"My daughter picked up the envelope," Decker said. "She told me the dentist put the X rays directly into her hands. The envelope was sealed when she delivered it to me."

"Well, that pretty much rules out an office error." Annie put her hands on her hips. "So if this isn't Marie, you've got to assume she's still alive, right?"

"She may or may not be," Marge said. "The only thing we know for certain now is, she's not the body in the car."

"Who are we looking for?" Decker asked.

Annie flipped off the monitor's light switch. "A big-boned female. Around five-ten, according to the length of the femurs. The anthropologist said the marks on the long bones reflected quite a bit of pull, meaning *weight*. She was probably heavy as well as tall. And she was probably black."

"Black?" Marge asked.

"Yep." Annie sat down. "Betcha the anthropologist says the same thing. Of course, he'd be basing his findings on other things. I'm basing mine on the teeth. Different ethnic groups generally conform to certain tooth alignments—not foolproof, but after a while you detect patterns. I'd be even more surefooted if I had the front part of the face." She rocked her wrist back and forth. "But with a little imagination, I can extrapolate. I bet I'd find a bignathic configuration that can be typical of blacks."

"Black," Marge said. "Nobody we've talked to mentioned that Marie was friendly with a black." She paused. "Then again, you've got to ask the right questions."

Annie stood. "This confirms what I suspected once I found the discrepancy between the finger and ring size. And it complicates the case, doesn't it?"

Marge said, "Just one more factor."

"You've been great, Annie," Decker said. "We'll need your report to file into evidence."

"I'll write up my notes from my Dictaphone and fax them to you. Is tomorrow afternoon okay?"

"Fine," Marge said.

"You two want to take in a couple of drinks before calling it an evening?" Annie asked.

"I've got to get home," Decker said.

"Ah, the new baby," Annie said. "Have fun doing the burp, Pete."

Decker laughed and stood. "I'll walk you to your car."

"I'll bag and label evidence," Marge said. "Meet you in the squad room. We can play postmortem there."

"Got it."

Decker opened the door to the lab for Hennon, both of them walking down the empty basement corridor, footsteps reverberating against the tile. At this time of the evening, the upstairs was still busy, but the lab personnel had gone home. They took the elevator up to the first floor, Decker steering Annie clear of the activity in the lobby by going through the back entrance adjacent to Booking. The evening was balmy, set under a charcoal canopy spangled with stars. It was the kind of night that invited a romantic stroll with arms wrapped around one another's waists. Decker wished he were home with Rina.

He and Annie ambled through the parking lot in silence, both of them enjoying the air. Annie got out the keys to her four-by-four but hesitated before unlocking the door.

"What kind of postmortem are you talking about?"

Decker smiled. "She means we're going to swap our daily interviews."

"You don't interrogate your suspects together?"

"No, generally we do our interviews separately."

"How come they always work in twosomes on TV?"

"They don't have the budgetary constraints we do."

"And they couldn't do good cop, bad cop with only one person."

"There you go."

"Do you and Marge have a good cop, bad cop routine?"

"Mostly it's just cop." Decker held out his hand. "Thanks again for your help."

Annie took it and squeezed. "Pleasure is mine, big guy."

"Have fun with your wastrel."

"Thanks." Annie unlocked the car. "With a little bit of luck, I'll learn to be dissolute."

When Decker returned to the detectives' squad room, Marge had checked the X rays into the evidence room and was filling out paperwork at her desk. During daylight hours, the place looked anything but high tech. But with all the activity going on, there wasn't much time or space to take in visuals. In the dim loneliness of night, the squad room was downright depressing. The summer stuffiness certainly didn't bring any excess cheer, the hot air an unwelcome guest that refused to depart despite open windows and fans.

Marge said, "I made a pot of fresh decaf. You can pour."

"Usual?"

"Two teaspoons of sugar instead of one tonight. I'm living dangerously."

Decker smiled and filled Marge's seashell mug with java, lacing it with whitener and sugar. He poured a black cup for himself, took the two mugs over to Marge's desk, and pulled up a seat.

"Thanks." Marge sipped her coffee. "Here's the evidence check receipt. Keep the original in your file since you're the primary investigator. You know, we should make a copy of the victim's teeth so we can have them in our files for immediate access."

"Good idea."

"I'll do that tomorrow." Marge crossed a *T*, then signed her name. "Your John Hancock?"

Decker scanned the report, then signed his name at the bottom. "You want to go first?"

"Nah, you can go ahead."

Decker drank half his coffee, then recapped his conversation with Dr. Meecham. Marge related her talk with Tandy Roberts. By the time they were both done, Decker's brain was a swirling cesspool of unrelated facts. Time to strain the garbage.

"Menopause at forty." Marge shook her head. "Man, that would be hard for *me* to handle. And I'm not exactly the maternal type. But to have all my options taken away from me so suddenly . . ."

Decker was quiet.

"What it is, Pete?"

"What you just said, Marge. Marie had her options taken away." Decker paused. "That's what happened to Rina. Her choice was taken away. And she has healthy children. I could imagine what this would do to a woman who didn't have children. Of course, all this motivation crap still isn't going to tell us who was burned in Marie's Honda."

"You know, Pete, maybe we should get hold of a division that has one of those computer-enhancement programs . . . send them the dimensions of the skull and the facts we know from the body. Ask the programmer artist to put a face on top of the bones."

"That would take two, three weeks minimum. But we can use all the help we can get. Morrison would probably cough up expenses for a kidnapped baby. Last I heard, Toronto has a top-notch division for that kind of thing. Maybe there's a place closer to home."

"I'll look into it."

"In the meantime, let's go back to some old-fashioned brainstorming. Question number one."

"Who's our body?" Marge said. "Like I said before, neither Tandy nor Paula mentioned Marie having a black friend. Should I go back and ask them about it?"

"You think Paula's straight up?"

"She seems on the level . . . unlike Sondra-Tandy Roberts."

Decker said, "Call Paula. See if she knows anyone. As far as Miss Autoconversationalist goes, the less Tandy knows, the better. You know, Marge, ever since Annie brought up the ring not fitting, I've been assuming that the body wasn't Marie's."

"Me too."

"So I've been thinking, who could it be? Irrespective of race, my guess is that this was someone from the hospital. Or at least someone who was in the hospital last night."

"Why's that?" Marge asked.

"The blood in Marie's parking space."

"You're saying if it wasn't Marie's, it had to have belonged to the body. Lab should be able to check that out."

"Yeah, we'll call them in the morning."

Marge said, "So how are you playing the scene out?"

"Couple ways." Decker finished his coffee. "Scene number one, Marie freaked out and took the baby. Then a big black female saw her making off with the kid and tried to stop her. Marie killed her and covered her tracks by burning the body in her car . . . hoping we'd think it was her."

"And then we'd stop looking for her."

"Yeah."

"Pretty naive, don't you think? She was a health professional. She must know we have ways of identifying bodies."

"The body was torched; the facial bones were smashed. Maybe she thought she destroyed enough, and we wouldn't be able to I.D. the body."

"She left in the back teeth."

"It's hard to destroy them unless you yank the jaw out of

the mouth. Marie was panicked. She had murdered this woman, had kidnapped a baby. She did whatever she could to cover her tracks. It just wasn't enough. So . . ." Decker paused to collect his thoughts. "So what I want to do is go back through our hospital notes and see who was working at Sun Valley Pres last night."

"I thought we had them all accounted for."

"Maybe there was a slipup."

Marge said, "Maybe this black woman was a floater and not on the hospital's payroll."

"Yeah, Darlene mentioned floaters and temporaries. Hollander's going over the duty roster from the night. We'll talk to him and tell him to look for any names we don't already have on our list."

"Pete, you might want to ask Cindy about this woman. She was around the nursery more than any of us."

Decker inwardly groaned. "I'm trying to wean her away from police work." He made a face. "It isn't working."

"Of course it isn't going to work. She sees her father all excited about his cases. Kids pick up on what you do, not what you say."

"Thank you for that psychological gem, Detective Dunn."

"Don't get cranky, Pete. It shows your age. Talk to Cindy."

"I will, don't worry." Decker exhaled and wished he still smoked. "I'll do anything to find the baby."

Marge finished her coffee. "You want to know what I'm thinking? If Marie isn't dead, she and the baby must be somewhere. I'm betting they're out camping, probably right under our noses."

"Camping?"

"Tandy said Marie was an experienced camper. Which means she could afford to lay low for a long time, long enough until we give up our search."

"Marie was a *camper*?"

"According to Tandy, she used to go to the woods and talk to God." Marge shook her head. "Getting weirder by the moment."

"Not so weird," Decker said. "My father-in-law talks to

God, too. He claims God answers him back. What's weird is, I actually believe him."

Marge stared at her partner. Decker smiled. "What I don't buy is Marie as a camper."

"Why not?"

"I went through her house and items meticulously, Marge. Nothing, but nothing, gave me any indication that this woman was athletic, let alone a survivalist camper."

Marge said, "She could have dashed home and taken her equipment."

"There were no empty spaces found in any of her closets—places where she'd store tents, sleeping bags, Sterno, cooking implements. Camping equipment takes up room. Just ask Rina. All my gear's been moved to the garage. And there was no gear in Marie's storage bin over her parking space. Only books by old radicals."

"Yeah, I found a copy of a speech by a Jerry Rubin. Doesn't he play guitar for the Grateful Dead?"

"That's Jerry Garcia." Decker tapped his foot. "Margie, I went through Marie's clothing piece by piece. No rugged pairs of jeans, no hiking boots, no jackets, no heavy socks. Do you want to know what I found? A lot of potpourri and pink cutie-lacy things that have never been worn. I found nothing but *nothing* to suggest that this woman could possibly be an outdoorsperson."

Neither of them spoke for a moment.

Decker finally said, "Given Tandy's history of talking to herself, I'm more likely to believe that Tandy was the one who camped and talked to God—or to herself. So you have to ask yourself *why* would Tandy say that *Marie* was a camper?"

Marge thought a moment, then said, "Maybe she wants us to believe that Marie is hiding in the mountains."

Decker said, "You want to hear something interesting? When you interviewed Tandy Roberts, the news agencies hadn't reported the manhunt. Remember, I asked the networks specifically to hold off announcing it until the eleven o'clock news because I didn't want spectators ruining our grid search, especially in daylight hours."

Marge thought a moment, then said, "Yeah, you're right."

Decker took their coffee mugs over to the urn and refilled them. He handed the seashell back to Marge. "So my question is this: Why would Tandy Roberts want us to believe that Marie was still in the mountains, if she couldn't have *known* we were searching there?"

"A news leak."

"Possibly, but more likely . . ."

"She knows something," Marge said.

"She knows something," Decker said. "She's trying to keep us buried in Angeles Crest when maybe we should start looking elsewhere."

"In what capacity do you think she's involved?"

"Maybe only tangentially. Marie ran to her in a panic—Tandy's an old friend. Maybe she's stashed Marie and the baby somewhere."

"Or possibly the two of them were in it together," Marge said. "Remember, Tandy lost a baby when she was young, too."

Decker nodded. "Two women still grieving over their loss. Each one working up the other."

"Tandy claims she hasn't seen Marie in a couple of years."

"We can start by checking out Tandy's phone calls," Decker said. "See if there has been contact between her and Bellson."

"Should I keep a tail on her?"

"Someone should. She hasn't bolted, but as we get closer, she may suspect someone's sniffing her butt. Also, let's check to see if she was where she said she was last night."

"First thing tomorrow, I'll call up Tujunga Memorial." Marge stared at her tepid coffee. A white skin had formed on top. She swirled the cup and watched it make designs. "You said you had a couple of ways to play this out. What's your other idea?"

"Lots of variation on this theme, but here goes. The black woman saw someone taking the baby. She interfered and was killed. Marie walked in on the action, and the third party—the one who killed the black woman—forced Marie at gunpoint to take the baby and help dispose of the body. For Marie to kidnap a baby and murder and dispose of a body seems like a lot of work for one person."

"So in this scenario, you're saying Marie was just as much a victim as the body we found."

Decker stood up and began fishing around in his pants pockets.

"What is it?"

"I took . . ." Decker found the bag he was looking for. He remembered changing his clothes and was glad he was smart enough to check his pockets before putting the suit in the cleaner's pile. "I took some leaf samples." He unbagged them, then sniffed them, backing away from the odor. He handed it to Marge. "What does your nose say?"

Marge smelled the foliage. "Gasoline."

"Yeah. I couldn't smell anything out there but smoke. But here . . . know what this means?"

"Car didn't accidently fall over the cliff."

"Yep. It was doused before it was pushed over but wasn't lit. Otherwise, I would have found scorched leaves."

"Also, it's pretty hard to push over a car once it's on fire."

Decker broke into laughter. "I *knew* there was a reason I kept you as my partner." He hit his head. "Anyone home? Anyway, someone was counting on impact to explode the car and get the fire started."

"Someone wasn't too bright. Not all cars explode." Marge paused. "Maybe the someone *realized* the car wasn't going to explode and threw the match at the car at the bottom of the ravine."

"Possibly."

"Pete, if this person killed the black woman, why wouldn't this person also kill Marie?"

"Who said this person hasn't killed Marie?"

TWENTY-FOUR

BEFORE KILLING THE MOTOR, DECKER TURNED ON THE dome light of the Plymouth and made a to-do list for the next morning. After having written down all minutiae that came to mind, he finally allowed himself to turn off the work meter. Decompression was a hard state of mind.

He shut off the engine, got out of the car, and walked out into perfumed darkness, the scent of citrus drifting through the air. Crickets were doing an abstract choral number; a nightingale, nested in a twenty-foot sycamore, was singing arias from *The Magic Flute*. The house was as still as stone when he opened the door. It took a few moments before he realized that a cot had been set up in the living room. A nightgowned figure rotated on a mattress too small for its girth, then sat up. In the moonlight, Decker made out Nora, the baby nurse. A few seconds later, Ginger's hulking shadow came into view. She recognized her boss, jumped on Decker's chest, and licked his face.

"How's it going, girl?" he whispered.

The dog licked his face again, her tail swinging like a feathered window wiper.

"Hello?" the nurse whispered.

"It's just me, Nora," Decker said softly. "Sorry to wake you."

"That's okay, Sergeant."

"Is everyone asleep?"

"We played taps 'bout ten o'clock. Your big girl was so exhausted, she nodded off in front of the TV. I practically had to carry her into bed."

Decker smiled and scratched Ginger's scruff. "The baby's with Rina?"

"Yes, she is. You need to have a long talk with your wife, Sergeant. She isn't going to heal if she keeps on overdoing it."

Decker placed his briefcase on the dining-room table and sat down. "What's she doing specifically?"

"Walking around when she should be in bed. Getting up for the baby. Why bother paying my wages, if she's going to get up and feed the baby herself, tiring her poor body out? The child lets out a whimper, she whisks it out of the crib. She's not only tiring herself, she's not giving Hannah a chance to develop her sleep. She's going to be a wreck if she keeps it up. Her mama's worried sick about her, but there's no talking to her when she gets an idea in her head."

"*I'll* talk to her," Decker said.

"Well, don't wake her now," Nora said. "She and the baby just dropped back to sleep."

Decker nodded, looking around the shadowy room. He wasn't consciously thinking about work, but his brain was still sparking enough to prevent sleep. He longed to crawl into bed with the newspaper, a little Letterman, and a tall glass of iced tea. With Rina sleeping, watching TV in bed was out of the question. But he supposed he could park himself in the kitchen for a while without disturbing anyone. As soon as he got to his feet, Ginger dashed away, then returned just as fast, carrying a leash in her mouth.

Decker looked at the animal. "Trying to tell me something, girl?"

Nora said, "Poor thing. Everyone's forgotten about her."

The dog cocked her head, leather strops hanging on her muzzle.

Decker sighed. "All right. A quick walk."

At the word *walk*, the dog began a frenzied circle dance.

Decker secured the leash to the animal's collar. "We'll come in through the back door, Nora. Sorry to wake you."

"No problem, Sergeant." She paused. "Any luck with your search?"

"It's coming."

"Well, that's wonderful."

Decker didn't answer. Instead, he gave her a sick smile, then realized it was too dark for her to see it. He and Ginger went out to the backyard first, to check on the horses. They were all in repose, but lifted their heads as he entered the barn. A mare let out a soft whinny. He shushed her, then filled the water basins. Giving them a quick wave, he bade them good night and was about to leave when he noticed a ball of fluff sharing a corner with a divided feed bowl of cat food and water.

Decker bent down and stroked the kitten's back with a finger. It lifted its tiger-striped head and let out a soft purr. Ginger stuck her muzzle in the kitten's face, and it responded by licking the dog's nose.

"How you doin', sport? Looks like someone set you up with dinner."

The kitten opened its eyes a little wider. Ginger stuck her snout in the cat food and began crunching away at it. Although the cat didn't voice a protest, Decker gently pulled the dog away from the cat's sustenance.

"Wondering where your boss is, little guy? We're kind of wondering the same thing."

The animal lowered its head. Decker ran his palms over the kitten's eyelids. "Go to sleep. We'll talk in the morning."

The kitten seemed more than happy to cooperate.

He took Ginger through the citrus grove, the setter prancing in the dirt when she wasn't sniffing tree trunks. Decker picked some melon-sized pink grapefruits—great for tomorrow's breakfast. He also pocketed a half-dozen tangerines. Releasing Ginger from her leash, he watched her scamper through the trees, then he sat down under the leafy branches of an avocado tree, his back against the thick gnarled trunk. Pulling out a tangerine, he peeled it, fastballing chunks of rind through the trees, each throw a little farther than the last. Scattering peel was his idea of a natural compost pile.

He popped half the tangerine in his mouth, the fruit swollen with sweet juice. The dog returned to his side and sniffed his hands. Giving her a tangerine wedge, Decker listened to the nighttime lullaby and decided life was good. He slumped against the tree and closed his eyes just for a moment. The next time he opened them, Nora was shaking his shoulder and Ginger was licking his face.

"Are you okay, Sergeant?"

"I'm up, I'm up."

"I didn't mean to wake you—"

"I'm up." He stood, hit his head on a branch, then cursed. "I'm up."

"My Lord, are you okay?"

"I'll survive." He rubbed his head. "I fell asleep out here. Can't believe I did that. What time is it?"

"Little after two," Nora said. "I heard Rina get up and went in to check on her, and you weren't there. . . ." She tightened the folds of her robe against her body. "I got worried."

"I'm fine." He stretched his creaky bones. "It's time to make my entrance. I'll go in and talk to Rina. Go see my baby, too. C'mon, Ginger. Time to return to civilization."

Rina said, "And how's our midnight camper this evening?"

Decker towel-dried his hair. The shower had revived him instead of making him sleepier. He hung the towel on the back of the door and slipped under the sheets. "I didn't want to wake you."

"Peter, there's consideration and then there's common sense." Rina released the baby from her breast and wiped her mouth. "You've been going practically nonstop for the past few days. You need your sleep."

"You and me both, kiddo." Decker leaned over for a better view of his little daughter, then extended his hands. "May I?"

"She needs to be burped."

"I'll burp her." He stood, threw a cloth diaper over his shoulder, and placed his infant daughter on his chest. Gently, he tapped her back. She molded against him, her tiny body as soft as eiderdown. A moment later, Hannah let out a deep, resonant belch. It always cracked him up to hear sailor sounds coming from a tiny little body.

"We did it, Mommy," Decker said.

Rina's smile was wan. Decker sat down on the bed and cradled the infant in his arms.

"Darlin', are you resting enough?"

"Matter of fact, I've done nothing but rest—"

"Not according to Nora."

"Oh, *Nora*—"

"I thought you said she was terrific."

"She's good. Trouble is she's *too* good. If it were up to her, I wouldn't do a thing except vegetate."

"Is Nora nursing the baby?"

"Peter—"

"Rina, you've got to rest if you're going to heal."

"I'm resting so much, my backside's numb. I can't get uninterrupted sleep anyway, because I'm nursing. What is the big deal if I want Hannah to sleep in our room?"

"Because when Hannah sleeps in our room, she becomes our responsibility. We hired a baby nurse to give you a little slack during these first few weeks—"

"I don't need *slack*, okay? It's good for me to feel useful, okay? Hannah brings me so much joy. What's wrong with a little *joy*?"

"Of course you should have joy. I just want you to heal up. . . ."

"Peter, I'm resting so much I'm nothing but a big, inert lump."

"Rina—"

"*Look* at me, Peter! I'm as big as a cow on top, I still look like I'm five months pregnant, and I don't have a uterus! I don't want to rest and think about myself, okay?"

She burst into tears. The baby immediately began to cry.

"Oh, great!" Rina sobbed. "Now look what I've done! I'm no use to anybody anymore!"

Torn between wanting to comfort his wife or his child, Decker chose the kid. He started walking around the room with his daughter, holding her tightly, cooing in her ear, trying to toss Rina reassuring smiles as he paced. He supposed he was partially successful, because Rina stopped crying. She wiped her eyes on a blanket and stared at him, looking forlorn and waifish. The woman was *drained*!

Decker kissed his daughter's cheek, feeling the tiny body get heavier and heavier. He felt soft breath on his hand, smelled the perfume that only newborns could produce. His thoughts turned to another infant ripped away from her mother. As fury welled up inside his breast, he told himself to breathe deeply, not wanting to inject his poison into his daughter. The bedroom had turned very quiet.

Finally, Decker whispered, "I think she's asleep. I'm going to tell Nora to set up the portable crib tonight. If you don't want sleep, that's your business. But I do. I'll be right back."

Rina nodded, a chastened look on her face.

Decker sighed, then walked into the living room. "Nora, you want to set up the Portacrib in here?"

The baby nurse looked stunned. "How'd you do it?"

"Spouse's magic."

Nora smiled. "You seem to work magic with all your women. Hannah looks happy being with her papa."

"Not half as happy as I am. I know I'm prejudiced, but she really is gorgeous. An exceptionally beautiful baby. And intelligent. I can see it in her eyes."

"Her eyes are closed, Sergeant."

"Her intelligence is so remarkable, it shines through the eyelids."

The nurse burst into laughter and began unfolding the Portacrib. "I'll take her whenever you're ready."

"Just another moment." Decker kissed a silken cheek. "God, she feels good. Why do babies feel so good?"

"The Lord made them that way so we'd take care of them. Can you imagine waking up at all hours of the night to take care of a thing that smelled and felt like beef jerky?"

Decker laughed.

"You need your sleep, Sergeant."

"Yeah, I suppose I do." Reluctantly, Decker yielded his daughter to the nurse.

Nora cradled the baby in her arms, then placed her in the crib, tucking her in tightly with a pink blanket. She checked her watch. "She's sound asleep, probably won't be needing another feeding until three, maybe even four, hours from now. I suggest you catch your sleep while you can."

"Thanks, Nora."

"Night, Sergeant."

Decker lingered a moment over the Portacrib, staring at the small face, the tiny hands clenched in fists. He patted the curled fingers, feeling bones so thin and fragile. He thought, Even the bad guys start out this way. How we muck up our lives. He blew Hannah a kiss, then went back to the bedroom. Rina had wrapped herself under the blanket.

"Can I talk to you for a moment?" Decker asked.

"Talk."

Rina's voice came out muffled.

Decker ran his hand over sheeted curves. "First off, I want to say that I love you. Second, I want to say that I think you're coping really well."

"That's a *laugh*!"

"I don't think a man could manage a tenth as well as you're doing."

"That's being patronizing!"

When the frustration mounts, what better to do than laugh. Decker let out a soft chuckle.

"Great! Now you're laughing at me! You think I'm being childish, don't you!"

"No, Rina, I don't think you're being childish." Decker pulled down the blanket, exposing his wife's face. "I think you've been through a terrible ordeal, and I'm amazed that you're functioning as well as you are. Look at you, sweetheart. You're taking care of an infant, you're spending time with the boys—"

"I was falling asleep in their faces."

"Honey, they're so happy just to see you ... talking. They know what you've gone through. You're doing terrific. Just give yourself *time*."

Rina snaked under the covers and curled her body, bringing her knees to her chest. "I feel ugly and useless." She pulled the blanket off her face. "But at least I make beautiful babies."

"Because *you're* beautiful. And you've got an entire family that *needs* you. I *need* you, okay?"

"That's all good and fine, except you just don't understand, Peter."

Decker sighed. "Explain to me what I don't understand."

"What's the use? You won't understand anyway."

Decker bit his lip. "Give it a whirl. Please?"

Rina turned to face him. "Well, imagine if you were suddenly castrated—"

"Darlin', that's not the same thing—"

"See, I *told* you you wouldn't understand."

Again Decker bit his lip. "Sorry. Go on."

A moment of silence passed.

"Okay, so maybe you're right." Again she looked at him. "It's not exactly the same thing. Because men's images of themselves are usually confined to that one location. With women, it's the whole body. Not only have I been rendered useless *locally*, making me feel I've lost my purpose as a woman—"

"Rina—"

"Will you just *hear* me out?"

"Go on."

"Thank you!" She cleared her throat. "Not only have I lost the seat of my womanhood, but right now, as of this moment, my whole body is about as sensual as an overstuffed pillow. I've got rolls and lumps and mammoth-sized hips and breasts the size of watermelons!"

Decker muttered out loud, "So what's wrong with that?"

Rina laughed, then began to cry.

"Honey, it's all in your *mind*."

"The reading on the scale is not in my mind, Peter!"

"Why the hell are you weighing yourself when you've just delivered days ago?"

"I always weigh myself. That's what women do."

"You're setting yourself up. Of course you've got a little extra weight. You've just had a baby, for Christ's sake!"

"Will you stop scolding me!" Rina yelled.

Decker didn't answer, reminding himself to unclench his jaw and breathe normally. He had popped an Advil fifteen minutes ago when he had felt a headache coming on. Maybe he should have taken two. Finally, he said softly, "I know you won't believe this, darlin'. But really, you are still very sexy to me!"

"It's not enough to be sexy to you, Peter," Rina whispered. "I want to feel sexy, period! Feel like a woman again. I want to *look* like a woman again. Not some useless piece of breeding stock. That's why I want to be with Hannah. At least when I'm with her, I see what my body produced." She smiled softly. "She was worth every lump and bump. I just wish I . . ." Tears formed in her eyes. "What's the use?"

Decker digested all her words. "You think about your appearance a lot?"

"Not a lot. Just when I feel useless *and* look like a cow." Rina paused. "That's not totally true. I do think about how I look. Every woman does. Just because I have a ring on my finger doesn't mean I don't take pride in my appearance. Don't you?"

Decker said, "Truthfully, I don't give it a whole lot of thought. Just as long as I'm clean . . . maybe I should. Do you have any complaints?"

"No, Peter, I don't. And that's the problem—the unfairness of it all. Men appraise, and women are appraised."

Decker slipped under the covers and wiped a tear off his wife's face. "One of the nicest things about my position at the department is, I don't have a lot of people standing over my shoulder . . . checking me out. Sure, I have bosses, but I've got a lot of independence. I'd hate to have people judging me all the time. I guess in a way, you have fifty percent of the adult population always judging you, although I dare say your ratings are always superior. Even so, that's pressure that most men don't think about."

"And it's out of our control. We can't help what we look like ... how we age ... if we get a hysterectomy ..."

Decker cuddled his wife. "All I can say is I love *you*, not your uterus, and I think you're beautiful. And by beautiful, I mean the inside kind as well as outside. I was attracted to the outside beauty, no question about it. But I fell in love with the inside beauty. And I'll think you're beautiful even when you're old and wrinkled." He paused. "Because however old you are, I'll be twelve years older."

Rina slugged his good shoulder.

"So for the past three years, you've looked like my daughter. How about you giving me a break and start looking like what you are. My second and younger—much, much *younger*—wife."

Rina was quiet for a minute. Then she said, "We'd better get some sleep."

"You mean you don't want to engage in mad, passionate sex?"

Rina broke into laughter.

"Just trying to make you feel good about yourself."

Rina shook her head, then kissed his lips. "I love you. Thanks for talking to me."

"Honey, it's my pleasure."

Rina flopped down on the bed. "I'm exhausted. Good night."

"Good night." Decker fluffed up his pillow. Infinitely better than a tree trunk.

TWENTY-FIVE

SLEEPING THROUGH THE SIX O'CLOCK FEEDING, DECKER thought, Some mother I'd make. But by seven-thirty, he had showered, shaved, dressed, and felt almost human again. Rina had fallen back asleep, so Decker took his *tallit* and *tefillin* out of the bedroom, opting to say his morning prayers in the living room. Standing over Hannah's crib, watching her snooze, he had a lot to be thankful for and felt God should know about it. He had just about finished winding the leather straps of his phylacteries over the boxes when Hannah began to stir, cheeks flushed and a look of displeasure stamped across the tiny features. Within seconds the unhappy physiognomy was howling in protest. Decker took off his prayer shawl and stowed it in the velvet bag, then picked up his daughter.

"Do we have something to say?"

Hannah turned her face toward the sound of his voice, eyes slowly opening.

"Good morning. Did you have a nice nap?"

The baby didn't answer and continued to focus through sleepy eyes. Decker felt something on his arm and looked at his jacket sleeve. A damp spot had darkened the material from gray to black. "I'll make a deal with you, Hannah Rosie. I'll change your diaper if you don't give me any surprises."

The baby continued to stare.

"Yeah, as if you give a hoot. Your clothes don't have to be dry-cleaned." He gently placed her in the Portacrib and changed her soaked diaper, tickling her tummy when he was done. "Feeling better?"

The baby let out a sudden howl. Quickly, Decker swooped her up. "We certainly do have opinions."

Nora walked in. "Tell me the truth, Sergeant. Did you wake her up?"

"Absolutely not. She woke up of her own accord. I just changed her diaper and was slow to pick her up. That didn't set well with her."

Nora held out her hands. "Go get some breakfast."

"Boys get off to school okay?"

"Sure did. Your big girl made them breakfast and left with them in the car 'bout half an hour ago. There's a box of cornflakes on the counter, milk's in the fridge."

"Thanks."

The front door opened, and Cindy waltzed through. She threw her arms around her father's neck and kissed his cheek. "Good morning, Paterfamilias. May I offer you some victuals for your daytime fare?" She noticed Nora holding Hannah. "Well, look who's up?" She plucked the baby from the nurse's arms and started walking toward the kitchen. "How's the sanest person in the family? Would you like your sugar water?"

Decker's eyes went from Cindy to Nora. "She's in a good mood."

Nora laughed and began cleaning the living room. "Between your wife and Cindy, I don't have to do a thing. Easiest money I ever made."

"Don't complain."

"Who's complaining?" The nurse laughed again.

Decker followed his daughter into the kitchen, took out a knife, and halved one of the grapefruits he'd picked last night. It was pink and juicy. "You're certainly chipper this morning."

"I got sleep." Cindy poured bottled drinking water into a

four-ounce bottle and added a teaspoon of sugar. "When I'm rested, I'm invincible."

"How's your memory, Superwoman?"

"Uh-oh." Cindy sat down and began to feed the baby. "Something's on the sergeant's mind."

Decker was silent. Cindy said, "Really, Daddy. Do you need to ask me something?"

"When you were in the nursery, Cindy, do you remember any black women hanging around Marie Bellson?"

"Black women?"

"Or just maybe a specific black woman. Don't confine yourself to nurses. She could be a doctor, an orderly, a janitor, an administrator, a medical-supplies salesperson—just as long as she's big and black."

"Why?"

"I'll tell you in a moment, after you've answered the question. But take your time. Think sequentially, Cindy—take it day by day."

Cindy was quiet as Hannah happily downed her sugar water. "You may be asking the wrong person. I tried to avoid Marie as much as possible."

Decker cut wedges of his grapefruit. "Do you remember *any* black women loitering around the nurseries, period?"

Cindy thought for a long time. "I think I remember a black cleaning woman."

"You know, I remember one, too," Decker said. "I'm going to have to go over my notes inch by inch."

"And of course, there was Lily. But she belonged there." Decker looked up from his grapefruit. "Who's Lily?"

"One of the neonate nurses."

"What?"

"What's wrong, Daddy?"

"This Lily is black?"

"Last time I saw her she was."

"Don't be cute. Do you know her last name?"

"No, but Darlene would. I think Lily was one of her trainees."

"Why the hell don't I remember the name?" Decker dashed out of the kitchen and opened his briefcase, quickly sorting through his notes. Cindy followed, babe in arms, and took a seat at the dining-room table.

"What is it, Daddy?"

"Just a sec, okay?"

"What are you looking for? Maybe I can help."

"It's not what I'm ... just hold on, please." Decker sat down and began to examine his notes more carefully. "I don't have any Lily written down for Nursery J. Just a Christine Simms."

"What about Christine? She isn't black."

"I know that. Do you remember seeing Christine the night Caitlin Rodriguez was taken?"

Cindy furrowed her brow in concentration. "Yes ... yes, definitely."

"How about this Lily person?"

Again Cindy thought a while. "I don't remember if I met her the night of the kidnapping or the night before. But like I said, Darlene would know if Lily was on duty."

"According to my notes, Darlene didn't mention Lily, and I asked her all about the people under her care."

"Then probably Lily wasn't on that night. All that hospital time blurs for me, Daddy."

"But even if Lily wasn't on *official* duty, she could have been hanging around Nursery J and you wouldn't have thought a thing about it."

"No, not at all. But I don't know why she'd hang around the nurseries if she wasn't on duty ... unless you think she was involved."

Decker didn't answer.

Quietly, Cindy asked, "Daddy, why'd you specifically ask about a big black woman?"

Decker ran his hand down his face. "The bones in the Honda don't belong to Marie, honey. They belong to a big and heavy woman who's probably black. Was Lily big and heavy?"

Cindy nodded gravely, then her eyes began to water. Decker felt like a jerk. He should have been more subtle in his questioning, remembering Cindy was his *daughter*, not just another witness. But once he got into the swing of questioning, it was hard to turn off the cop mode.

"She seemed like a nice person," Cindy said. "Lily, I mean. She was young . . . not much older than I am."

"Princess, we haven't even identified the body yet. This Lily could be safe and sound, at home watching TV and munching Cheetos as we speak. I shouldn't be exposing you to this kind of garbage."

"No, it's really . . ." Cindy forced herself to smile at Hannah. "Do you actually think Marie Bellson *killed* Lily?"

"I won't even begin to speculate before we have an I.D. on the bones. Right now I'm thinking about Darlene. I don't know if she was holding out on me or if she just made an honest mistake."

"Or like I said, maybe Lily wasn't on duty, Daddy."

"Maybe." Decker put down his briefcase and went back into the kitchen. He stared at the grapefruit resting on the counter. His stomach was a knot, but he had to eat if he was going to be productive. He put up a pot of coffee, poured himself a bowl of cereal, scrambled some eggs, and forced breakfast down his gullet. Going through his notes one more time, he couldn't understand how this Lily person was overlooked. About ten minutes later, Cindy came in with Hannah and sat beside him. Decker took his daughter's hand.

"Are you okay, Cindy?"

"Fine."

"Honey, I want you to forget about the case, all right?"

"No, it's not all right. If you need my help, you *have* to ask me. You owe it to Caitlin Rodriguez."

Decker stood. "I'd better get to work."

"You're brushing me off."

"No, honestly, I want to get to the hospital and talk to Darlene . . . if she's even there. I've got to check out Lily. I've got a load of details to work out if I'm ever going to make headway on this case."

"Speaking of specific details, did you ever find a box to fit the key we found in Marie Bellson's apartment?"

Decker shook his head. "Not yet."

"What happened with Tandy Roberts yesterday?"

"Cindy, please."

"I'm curious."

Hannah began swallowing air bubbles. Decker said, "I think she needs to be burped. Give her to me. I'll do it."

Cindy handed him a diaper. "Cover your jacket."

Decker threw the diaper over his shoulder and began walking with his daughter. As he patted her back, her eyes widened, her expression seemingly remorseful for her gluttony. Her stomach was sloshing liquid.

Decker said, "You've got good head control, Hannah Rosie."

"I told you she was precocious."

"Takes after Sis." Decker smiled.

Cindy smiled back, then looked at the ceiling. "So what's with Tandy?"

"Why do you keep asking about her?"

"Because she was a friend of Marie's. I'm wondering who the heck could be Marie's friend?"

"Paula was Marie's friend."

"Is it the same situation as Paula? Was Marie Tandy's training nurse?"

Decker didn't answer. He heard Cindy sigh, then said, "I know you're your own person, Cynthia, but I see *my* obsessive streak in you. It's bad enough when cases eat me up. Why should they eat you up, too? Especially when you're not even getting paid."

"So you do it for the money, Dad?"

"It puts bread on the table."

"You do it because you *like* it. Be honest. If it was just money, you'd have been a senior partner in Grandpa's firm by now."

"Yes, I like what I do. But I've been trained and you haven't, and therein lies the rub."

"How can I be trained if no one will train me?"

"This isn't an apprentice job, Cynthia. If you want to be a cop, apply to the Academy." Decker paused. "God, what am I *saying*! You don't want to be a *cop*, for godsakes! You're way too smart for that."

"Implying that you're a cop because you're dumb?"

"Princess, I applied because I didn't know any better. I was a twenty-year-old kid with no guidance who had just gotten out of the army. I was at loose ends, and someone suggested being a cop. Like a dunce, I signed up. Just like with the army. They said sign up, I signed up. You know what, Cindy? I was *dumb*!"

"So why did you come back to it even after you passed the bar?"

"Because being an estate lawyer was worse than being a cop. I did it to please your mother, who wanted me to be just like Grandpa. I should have signed up for the D.A.'s Office." Decker paused. "Not that I'm complaining . . ."

"I think your work is exciting."

"Mostly, my job is paperwork and legwork, but yes, it can be exciting. And it can also be dangerous." He started to pat the bullet scar on his shoulder, but stopped himself. Last thing he wanted to do was to traumatize his daughter any further. "You've conveniently left out dangerous, Cynthia."

"What am I doing that's dangerous? Asking a few questions?"

"Cindy, someone presoaked a body and Marie's Honda with gasoline and pushed them both off a hundred-foot drop." Decker suddenly lost patience. "We're talking *desperate* people. Stop arguing with me and just stay put."

"Can you at least tell me if Tandy's a nurse? Last question, I promise."

Decker bit his lip. "Yes, Tandy might be a nurse."

Hannah let out a big burp.

"Atta girl, Han, you take after your old man."

Cindy said, "I never remember you belching."

"You never saw me in my rowdier days after a couple of six-packs."

"You were once rowdy?"

"Before your time. 'Bout a century ago."

Cindy smiled. "I'll take the baby."

Decker gave his little daughter to his big one and studied them both with pride. Two girls with two boys in the middle. A beautiful and bountiful family. All he had to do was make sure no harm befell any of them for the rest of their lives.

"So what did Marge think of Tandy?" Cindy asked.

"You promised last question. Now, forget about the case. Leave it up to the police." He kissed her cheek. "I'm going to say good-bye to Rina. No more talk about joining the Academy, okay?"

"I wasn't intending to drop out of college, Daddy."

"Thank God one of us can think!" He kissed his daughters, pinched both of their cheeks. "Bye."

"Bye." Cindy sat back in the chair, waiting for her father to leave. Having studied him as he talked, she had recognized that look in his eyes—trying to be casual, but he had been concerned. She knew why. Her questions were good ones, but he didn't want her to know that. Tandy was involved. Since old Dad wasn't about to help her out, Cindy decided to check out Ms. Roberts by her own lonesome.

She rocked Hannah in her arms until her father called out another bye. She answered him, breathing a sigh of relief when the door closed. In the distance, she heard the motor to the unmarked kick in, then recede in Dopplerian fashion.

They'd located Tandy at a gym, but Cindy didn't remember the name of the place.

How in the world would she ever be an ace detective if she couldn't remember simple things like names of places? She sighed. Holding Hannah firmly in the crook of her right arm, she pulled out a phone book with the left hand. Under the Yellow Pages, she found two columns' worth of listings under "Gyms." She studied each name carefully, stopping when she hit the name Silver's.

That was it.

Security was still tight and visible, but the extreme tension brought on by yesterday's crisis had dissipated. Within a few months, Decker predicted Sun Valley Pres would return to its normal lackadaisical self, more concerned with budgetary issues than with medical problems. The administrative offices didn't open before nine, leaving Decker with forty-five minutes to track down Darlene Jamison and the duty roster the night of Caitlin Rodriguez's kidnapping.

Although he had no problem getting through the front door of the hospital, the nurseries were still under microscopic scrutiny. Even after he showed his I.D., he was met with suspicion by TECHWATCH's body for hire. Finally, the guard let him pass through the maternity halls. All the nurseries had guards posted outside the entrance doors. Once again Decker showed his badge to the sentry outside Nursery J and was allowed to step inside the glass station. A blond nurse turned around. She was young, slim, with a round face and saucer blue eyes, but the ingenue effect was ruined by a face weathered with stress. Her name tag said C. Simms, RN. Decker showed her his I.D.

"Can I speak to you for a moment, Christine?"

Christine smiled wearily. "Have a seat. I have to check the lines on the premies. That can't wait, Sergeant. But it shouldn't take too long."

"Is Darlene Jamison on duty this morning?"

Christine looked pained. "Darlene's on temporary leave of absence. I suppose it was inevitable, but I feel bad for her." She looked down. "Susan Altman is with the babies in the back. If you need anything, page her. But please don't cross the yellow line—contamination."

"Is Darlene at home?" Decker called out.

"Probably," Christine answered.

"Do you have her phone number on hand?"

Christine didn't answer as the door closed behind her. Decker opened his briefcase and checked his notes. He found Darlene's number and used the wall phone to get the hospital operator and an outside connection. Darlene's machine kicked in after two rings, and Decker left his message slowly, giving the woman time to interrupt the call and come on the line.

She never did. Either she wasn't home, or she was avoiding him.

He stuck his hands in his pockets, then noticed the door to the nurses' area. Much to his surprise, it was open, so he went inside. The glass room held three identical-size desks that were typical institutional issues—sturdy and ugly. Two of the desks held nameplates—*Marie Bellson, RN,* and *Darlene Jamison, RN.* Staring at the letters so intensely, Decker found the names undulating like waves of heat. Like the ghosts they were. How many victims did the case really have?

Marie's desk had been gone through meticulously the day of the kidnapping. Decker's notes contained the items reported—nothing significant. But since Darlene was not an immediate suspect, her desk had remained a private affair. Decker scanned the charts resting on top, then began to sort them. He took a quick peek over his shoulder, then quietly he opened the drawers, looking for personal items: a desk calendar or Rolodex or diary or letters—anything revealing. But as with Marie's desk, Darlene's drawers seemed to be repositories for medical charts and patient information. At a glance, nothing seemed out of the ordinary.

"Detective, that's private!"

Decker turned around, smiled at Christine, and closed the file drawer. "I was just passing time."

Christine raised her eyes. "You were snooping. Do you have a warrant to snoop?"

Decker grinned boyishly. "If I had a warrant, I wouldn't need to snoop."

"How can I help you?" Christine sat down. "Better still, how can I help the baby? We all feel so responsible. I keep going over that horrible night, asking myself what *I* could have done differently."

"Did you come up with anything?"

"Maybe I should have checked in more often. We were so short-staffed."

"Who else was on duty in Nursery J, Christine?"

Christine stared at him. "I'm sorry. Everything's a blur. Maybe you can check the duty roster."

"I have."

"So why do you need me?"

"To see if your account agrees with what's on the roster," Decker said. "I'm sorry to take up your time, but it's important."

"I understand completely. For J, on duty officially? I think it was just Marie, Darlene, and me. I was actually assigned to three nurseries. I was moving back and forth between them. No backup. Budget cuts, they tell us. . . ."

Her voice trailed off.

"What about Lily?" Decker said.

"Lily Booker?"

"Wasn't she one of Darlene's trainees?"

"Yes, she was, but I don't think Lily was on that night." Christine paused. "Don't hold me to this, but she may have been crossed off the roster at the last minute. Another reason we were so short-staffed."

Decker glanced at his nails and said, "Refresh my memory, Chris. Isn't your nursing roster written in pen?"

"The official assignments are written on paper, then transferred to the plastic board that hangs from the wall in the front nursing station. We use a grease pen on the board, because assignments change at any given time. If the roster was written in pen, it would be a big mess."

"Just like our station house's scoreboard."

Christine smiled. "Yeah, that's what we call it, too."

Decker tried to be casual. "So by 'crossed off,' do you mean you remember seeing Lily Booker's name on the plastic board, and then it was erased?"

"I guess that's what I meant. Why?"

"When is Lily due back on duty?"

"I really don't know," Christine shrugged. "She wasn't written into today's roster. Why all these questions about Lily? Was she involved?"

"Do you have her phone number?"

"No. But she should be in the medical directory."

"Even if she's just a trainee?"

"Oh, that's right. She's too new. But Darlene would probably have it. I'll get you Darlene's number."

"I just called her house. Either she isn't home or she isn't answering her phone—at least for me. She may be mad at me."

"More like scared."

"That could be. Can you do me a favor and call her? See if she picks up the machine for you?"

Immediately, Christine picked up the phone and punched in some numbers. After a moment, she said, "Hi, Darlene, it's Christine, are you there?" Pause. "Darlene, hi, are you there? Can you pick up the . . . Hi. Yeah, everything's fine over here. Detective Decker is here . . . Darlene, he's looking for Caitlin Rodriguez. He *needs* to talk to you. We've got to *help!*" There was a pause. "Hold on." She handed him the receiver. "Anything else?"

"No, Chris, you've been an enormous help."

"Then I'll get back to work."

Decker mouthed her a thank-you and spoke into the receiver. "Darlene, I need to ask you a few questions. Was Lily Booker on duty the night Caitlin Rodriguez was kidnapped?"

There was a long pause over the line. "What does Lily have to do with this?"

Darlene's voice sounded frightened. Decker felt his stomach sink. "Can you just answer the question?"

There was another long moment of silence. "She called in sick."

"At the last moment?"

"Yes, at the last moment. How did you know? Have you talked to Lily recently?"

Her voice had become anxious. Decker said, "No, I haven't talked to her. Have you?"

"No." Darlene quickly added, "But I haven't talked to too many people since I was relieved of my duties."

"Darlene, did you take Lily's sick call?"

"No, Detective." Another hesitation. "Marie did."

"Marie did?"

Again the pause. "Yes."

"Darlene, you seem to be unsure of yourself. Should we talk in person?"

This time Darlene started to cry. "Yes, Sergeant, I think we really should."

TWENTY-SIX

FIRST THE LOW ONE WENT AWAY.

That was good except the low one wasn't the real bad one.

It was the high one that wreaked the most havoc.

And so hard to listen to. So sure of herself when calm, and shrill when she wasn't.

But even the high one was fading—a peep now and then, but she could shut her up.

Turn her off.

Things returning to normal.

She could turn her off, because she had the control.

Control.

Better than drugs.

Better than food.

Control.

She had the control.

"Where are you?" Decker asked. "You sound like you're on a portable phone."

"I think the technically correct word is 'cellular,' " Marge said. "And in answer to your question, I'm outside Tandy Roberts's condo in Marc's Beemer. Let me give you the phone number."

"Wait a sec." Placing the mike in his lap, Decker reached

over into the backseat of the unmarked and fished out a pen and his notebook from his briefcase. "Shoot."

Marge dictated the number. "These gadgets are real neat. You know, you don't even have to dial one before the area code."

"Let's hear it for technology," Decker said. "Just hope you don't get brain cancer."

"Perish the thought."

"What's Tandy up to now?"

"I came up to her place about a half hour ago. Kind of acting like Columbo—'Uh, just one more thing, ma'am.' I was looking for the baby. Obviously, I didn't find her."

"Anything suspicious?"

"No telltale signs like a playpen in the living room."

"Could you check the other rooms?"

"Superficially only. Nothing out of the ordinary."

"What was the 'one more thing' you asked her about?"

"If she remembered specifically where she and Marie camped."

"Did she remember?"

"With unusual clarity. Now I'm not an expert camper. Take me into the wilderness, and all mountains look the same. But Tandy described the flora and the fauna in detail. You're right, Pete. *She*'s the camper. *She* knows all about the Angeles Crest region."

"Meaning she'd know where to shove a car off the mountainside."

"My very thought," Marge said. "Man, I'd sure like to pop her trunk and find out if it reeks of gasoline. I'm sure she had the car cleaned, but lots of times people forget about trunks."

"Be hard to convince a judge to give us a warrant." Decker thought a moment. "Tell you what, though. I'll call Mike and ask him to run a credit check to find out what kind of plastic she owns. Let's see if she recently charged a major gasoline purchase on any of her cards. Did you have a chance to call Tujunga Memorial? See if Tandy was working there the night of the kidnapping?"

"Offices hadn't opened yet. I'll call in about ten minutes.

Ye olde cellular does have its merits. So you think our body's this Lily Booker?"

"Unfortunately, it's possible. I just came back from Lily's apartment. Found out the address from Darlene Jamison. No one was home, but I did find the manager, and she opened the door for me. There was mail on the floor, old messages on her phone machine, wilted salad in the refrigerator. Whole place seemed a little stale. It doesn't look good."

Marge was quiet.

"She was a young kid," Decker went on. "Twenty-two. Didn't even own a car yet. She had a bicycle in the living room, and the manager told me she went to work by bus. Now it looks like I'm going to have to locate a set of parents and ask them for her dental X rays. God, I *hate* this part of the job. You know, you should really make the call, Marge. Cut your teeth for homicide."

"I'm on a stakeout."

"All you need is a phone, Detective."

"But having them call me back would be a bitch. This is not the type of call you can do from a cellular phone."

"All right. *I'll* do it."

"Look, if you really want me—"

"Nah, it's all right," Decker said.

"You happen to check in with Lourdes while you were at the hospital?"

"She and Matty are gone. When I asked the desk for a forwarding address, they informed me that all further contact with them must be conducted through their lawyer. Looks like they took my advice."

"Did they set themselves up with someone good?"

"I've got a name and a number. That's all I know about him."

"Poor little girl . . . girls, actually—both Lourdes and the baby."

"It's a real tragedy," Decker said. "I'm off to see Nurse Jamison. I'll check in with you in about an hour. Oh, and one more thing, Dunn. Who the hell is Marc?"

* * *

It was one thing to be on unfamiliar ground. It was quite another to be on alien soil. Garbed in bicycle shorts, a green muscle shirt, and sneakers, Cindy had dressed the part, but her body didn't fill out her clothes the way the others did. She took a quick peek in a cracked wall mirror. Besides her having been cursed with pale, freckled skin, her arms and legs had absolutely no shape or definition.

It was only nine in the morning, and yet the place was hot and smelled of sweat. About half the machines were taken; those remaining idle beckoned her forward with a malevolent finger. She didn't know what to do with her gym bag, she didn't know where to begin on the machines, and no one had given her so much as a glance, let alone a smile. It was moments like these that let her know how truly stupid her ideas usually were.

She found an unoccupied bench, dropped her bag at her feet, and sat down. Rather than looking stupid, trying to fake out that she knew what she was doing, she felt it was probably better to observe a while. Then, afterward, maybe she'd try to imitate.

She chuckled to herself.

As if imitation were possible. These guys were lifting Mack trucks. Staring at the grunting masses, bodies sculpted and defined, she could almost discern the striae in the voluntary muscle and the vessels that fed them. It was weird—like looking at three-dimensional pictures from *Gray's Anatomy*. She found it interesting, but not at all sexy. The muscles seemed too waxen to be real. Probably because all the guys were hairless. Still, it was fascinating to watch the human body being stretched to the limit. Like observing a freak science experiment. So entranced by the motion, Cindy didn't even notice the blocky body looming over her until he cleared his throat.

His bronze skin was shiny with oil. He had blond hair past his shoulders and wore a headband to keep the tresses out of his eyes. He looked like the cartoon character He-Man. His smile was nice, though. He sat beside her.

"Are you looking for someone?"

Cindy stared at her feet. "Not really. I thought . . . you

know." She looked up. "That maybe it was about time I started to do something with myself."

His eyes slowly scanned her body, and he nodded. He was agreeing that she was a wreck. It made her feel terrible.

"I don't know what I'm doing," Cindy admitted.

"That's obvious."

"Thanks."

He stuck out his hand. "Eric."

She took it. "Cindy."

"So what brought you here, Cindy?" Eric said. "Why not a health club?"

"I'm interested in building my body, not in getting picked up." She smiled. "No offense."

Eric smiled again. His teeth were too white to be real. "None taken. That's the correct attitude. So much of what we do is attitude. The other part is hard work."

"So I've been told."

"By who?"

Cindy paused for just a second before she thought of a response. "By friends."

"Who are your friends?"

"You don't know them. They live in New York."

"You're from New York?"

"No, I just go to school there. Columbia."

"Columbia, huh? That's cool. There's nothing wrong with brains and brawn."

Cindy laughed. "So where do I begin?"

"What are you interested in?"

Cindy paused. "My arms, I guess."

"You guess?"

"My whole upper body maybe."

"Maybe?"

"I don't know really."

"Well, you'd better figure out what you're after, or you'll never last."

Cindy bit her lip, trying not to get sucked in by the dare. "Any girls around here?"

"Why? You a les?"

"No, I'm not a *les*. And even if I was, it would be none of your damn business."

Eric smiled. "Hey, now you're getting good!"

Cindy stared at him. "Good at *what*?"

"Getting mean. You've got to get mean, or you'll never last."

"I'm supposed to be mean?"

"Yep."

"How mean?"

"As mean as you can. You've got to look at the weights as enemies to conquer and *control*. Without that attitude, you won't last. Believe me, I've seen chicks come and go in this place. The kind of girls who bitch and moan every time they break a nail? We don't put up with that kind of 'tude around here. That was the first thing I noticed about you. You have short nails. It tells you a lot about a person."

Cindy sneaked a look at her hands. She had tried growing her nails, polishing them. It was fun but too much work. "Are you a teacher here?"

"Two days a week."

"What does it cost to join?"

"Fifty a month to use the equipment. But the boss always gives newcomers a month free. If you last a month, you'll probably last, period."

"Are there any girls around here?" Cindy asked again.

"We've a few dedicated chicks."

"No offense, but maybe I'd be more comfortable if there were some girls around."

"No one will hit on you here, Cindy. We're all friends, but that's all. Friends in work. Guaranteed."

"Still . . . when do they come around?"

Eric frowned at her. "We've got about six serious chicks. They pop in and out all during the day and night. We're open twenty-four hours, in case you've got a bad case of insomnia."

"That's convenient."

"Yes, it really is. Anyway, do you want a little help starting up? First lesson is on the house."

"Right now?"

"Right now."

Cindy stood. Why not? "Sure."

Eric said, "First, I've got to take your measurements." "Why?"

"Because how are you going to know if you're improving if you don't have a baseline?"

"True."

"Yeah, true." Eric pulled out a tape measure and stretched it across her back. "Now lift up your arms."

Cindy obeyed.

Slipping his arms around her body, Eric placed his hands over her breasts. Quickly, she spun around and stepped backward. "What the *hell* are you doing?"

Eric growled at her. "I was *trying* to measure you—"

"You were feeling me up!"

"I was feeling you, but not up—"

"That's bullshit!"

"Hey!" Eric grabbed her right hand. "It's muscle, Cindy. That's all it is! Just fat and muscle." He wrapped her fingers around his arm. "Muscle." He placed her hand over his chest. "Muscle." Around his leg. "Muscle. Over his groin. "Muscle. That's all we humans are. Fucking bone, muscle, and fat. The idea here is to get more muscle than fat. I can't tell a fucking thing about your chest if I can't feel your tits, see what the condition of your underlying muscle is. From the quick feel I got, it looks like you've got some decent pecs under all that mammary fat."

He released her hand. Cindy stared at him but said nothing.

Quietly, Eric said, "I probably should have warned you. I'm used to people who know the routine. You want to try again?"

"I would really feel more comfortable if this was being done by a girl."

"Get used to guys, Cindy. 'Bout ninety-eight percent of our clientele is guys. And just for your info, 'bout a third of them are gay. They don't give a shit what's between your legs. Like I said, to a dedicated builder, it's all muscle."

"Are you gay?" Cindy asked.

"No," Eric answered. "But I'll say yes if it'll make you feel better. Will you relax?"

"It's difficult."

"Just go with the flow. Lift your arms up."

Cindy wondered if Marge had ever been in a situation like this. Of all the dumb things she'd ever tried to pull off, this had to be one of the dumbest. But she was here already. She lifted her arms.

Again Eric snaked his massive limbs around her body. Each arm must have weighed fifty pounds. Again she felt his hands on her breasts and involuntarily flinched.

"Just take it easy," Eric said, "you're doing fine."

After a moment, it was clear to Cindy that old Eric was telling the truth. He was feeling her breasts, but it wasn't sexual.

"See . . . right there," Eric stated. "That's where the fat of your tits ends and where your underlying pecs are. Did you ever do lifting before, Cindy?"

"No."

"You've got good raw material." He let go of her breasts, then measured across her bust. It took him twenty minutes to finish charting her body, recording the inches of her waist and hips and thighs. When he was done, he said, "Good raw material. I'd like to take you through the first month myself. You want to set up some dates?"

"Can I call you on it?"

Eric gave her a disgusted look. "Are you committed or what?"

"How should *I* know?" Cindy placed her hands on her hips and stared at the entrance. Just then a woman walked through the door. She was absolutely gorgeous—perfect skin, sleek black hair, and black eyes as luminous as obsidian. She was wearing a black lace body stocking, filling it out in all the right places. She turned to Eric and said, "Can you turn me into her?"

Eric let out a deep laugh. "Tandy's certainly an example of everything that can go right."

"Tandy?"

"That's her name. She was over two-fifty when she first walked through the door."

Cindy's eyes widened. "What?"

"No lie. I'll introduce you."

Cindy watched Eric duck-waddle to Tandy. He threw his arm around her lithe shoulder, leading her over to Cindy. He said, "Hey, Roberts, come and meet the new kid on the block."

Cindy suddenly felt her heart race. This was the whole reason she was here, and now that she was face-to-face with Tandy, she had no idea what to do. She looked up at Eric as if he had the answer. All he had was a goofy grin on his face. With deliberate motion, Tandy sidled up to him and placed her hand on his shoulder. Her fingers were long and delicate, but the nails were clipped short. She didn't just rest her hand on his muscle, she kneaded it. Then she offered her hand to Cindy.

"Tandy Roberts."

"Cindy." Her answer had an odd rhythm because she didn't state her last name. Just in case Marge had given her Dad's business card. She felt her face go hot.

"Your hands are sweaty," Tandy said.

"I'm nervous."

Tandy laughed. "Why?"

"I don't know. Don't you get nervous when you're in a strange environment?"

"I used to. . . ." Tandy's dark eyes peered into Cindy's. "But I don't anymore."

"It's great to have that kind of self-confidence."

"I owe it all to building. It's given me control over my life." Tandy turned to Eric. "Did you work out a routine for her yet?"

"I've just finished measuring her. She's got potential. Lots of raw material."

"Potential, huh?" Tandy's smile was secretive as she walked over to the weight rack. "So let's start with something a little bit more challenging."

Lifting a fifteen-pound weight from the rack, Tandy sat on the bench. She supported her right arm by resting the elbow on top of her left hand. She extended her right arm downward until it was straight, then slowly brought the weight up to her shoulder by bending at the elbow. "That's called a curl . . . an arm curl. See?"

Cindy nodded, watching Tandy's bicep bunch as she curled the weight again.

"Do you want to try it?" Tandy asked.

"Sure."

"Come sit. Remember to keep you feet planted firmly on the ground. Don't use your back when you lift. And breathe normally."

"You're *not* giving her a fifteen-pounder," Eric said.

"You said she had potential."

"Stop teasing her, Roberts. Give her a three-kilo. If that's too easy, give her a five."

"I'll try the fifteen," Cindy said.

"It's too heavy for you," Eric stated. "You might hurt yourself, and that would be really *dumb*."

Cindy thought a moment. If she didn't try it, she knew she'd lose Tandy's dare and respect. The idea was to get close enough to talk to her—woman-to-woman. She said, "I'll be careful. And if I fail, big deal. I don't mind looking like an idiot."

Eric said, "Tandy's just being evil."

Tandy laughed. But Cindy knew where the truth lay. "You said the idea was to get mean." She glared at Tandy. "Give it here."

With a slight smirk, Tandy handed it over to her. Then she added, "Really. Watch your back."

The weight was heavy, Cindy thought, but didn't seem unmanageable.

"Breathe out first," Eric said.

"What?"

"Exhale, Cindy." Tandy blew out air forcefully. "Then inhale. While you're lifting, you exhale again. You always exhale on the exertion, okay? Like this."

Cindy watched the perfect breasts heave as Tandy demonstrated the curl. Eric was hypnotized, and Cindy understood why. The woman was exotic, as captivating as a black widow. When she was done, she handed the weight to Cindy.

"Your turn."

Cindy shrugged. "Here goes nothing."

Slowly, she brought the weight upward, her muscles feeling a sizable tug as the dumbbell neared her shoulder. Carefully, she brought the weight back down, then curled it two more times. By the time she was done, she was surprised how sweaty she had become. She was also shocked by how *good* she felt, despite the strain in her arm. "I think that's it, guys." She placed the weight on the floor and massaged her overworked arm. Looking at Tandy and Eric, she thought they seemed stunned.

"What's wrong?"

"Nothing." Eric smiled. "See, Roberts, I told you she had good raw material."

"I did well?"

Eric's smile formed to a grin. "Don't let it go to your brain, Cindy. Even though you have the potential, you're still a sack of fat."

"Nothing like a backhanded compliment to massage the ego." Cindy's eyes fell on Tandy, and she remembered why she was here. Her heart began to hammer in her chest. "Would you mind working with me? Even if it's just for today. I told Eric that I'd really prefer working with a woman. I guess I'm a little shy."

"That's not good," Eric chastised.

"One thing at a time, okay, Eric?"

He-Man smiled. "Up to you, Fat Sack."

"Oh, go stuff it!"

"Now, *that's* more like it!" Eric stated. "Got to get mean, Cindy. Only way to reach your full potential. Lifting is not a game. It's a commitment, and it's not for wimps."

"I'll keep that in mind, Eric." Cindy laughed. "Do you mind helping me out, Tandy?"

Tandy looked down, then up. "Hey, it'd be my pleasure. I'm impressed."

Cindy studied Tandy's face. She really did look impressed. Impressed and mean.

TWENTY-SEVEN

MARGE TOSSED THE MAGAZINE IN THE PASSENGER SEAT OF the Beemer and was ready to start the car. But Tandy wasn't walking toward her Audi. Instead, she was chatting animatedly with a redhead, the two women crossing the street in the direction of the juice bar. Quickly, Marge picked up her binoculars and began focusing on the moving figures. Then her hands began to shake. In shock, she lowered the glasses to her lap and tried to unscramble her thoughts.

If Marge *didn't* intercede, Pete would strangle her as well as Cindy. But if she *did* intercede, it would blow the tail, putting Tandy wise to their suspicions. But Tandy was being watched as a suspect in a kidnapping/murder; she could be dangerous. How could Marge, in good conscience, allow Cindy to remain in the presence of this woman?

Of course, she and Decker had no *evidence* that pointed to Tandy's involvement. But Roberts was a nutcase. Marge knew that by letting Cindy proceed, she could be endangering the teenager's life.

Marge swore out loud. Decker's kid must have gotten a taste of excitement, and the adrenaline had kicked in. Teenagers—pains in the butt. The shy ones got eaten alive, and the bold ones believed they were immortal. Pete wouldn't be the only one who'd have a few choice words to say to Cindy. What to do! What to do!

The girls had gone inside the juice bar. Marge could either put a stop to it now or wait. Again Marge cursed, trying to be rational and careful at the same time. After a minute of conflict, pros and cons competing for brain space, Marge finally decided to cool her heels. She could see the entrance to the bar as well as the Audi. Tandy couldn't escape without Marge detecting her getaway.

Let the ladies have their chat. Afterward, when they went their separate ways, when Marge was calm, she would have a long, long talk with Cindy.

But the decision gnawed at her gut. What if Tandy went crazy?

Marge could see the screaming headlines: MASS MURDER IN JUICE BAR: PEOPLE DIE AS COP LOOKS ON. Subtitle: *Victim daughter of cop's partner.*

Forced to resign in humiliation, Marge would spend the rest of her life as a security guard in a mall—guarding *teenagers*!

She shook exaggeration from her thoughts. Passing seconds seemed like hours. Eyes darting back and forth, Marge felt the tension of every muscle in her body. She thought, Why should Pete have the honor of killing Cindy? The pleasure should be exclusively hers.

Darlene Jamison lived on the ground floor of a two-story beige stucco apartment. Each unit had an individual entrance, and Darlene's was located on the left side. Decker knocked on the door and waited. He had to knock again before Darlene answered the door. The petite woman was swallowed up by a tentlike algae-green smock that approximated the color of the place's swimming pool. Her hair was tied back, her round face mottled and doughy. She stepped backward, allowing him to come inside the small living room.

"I'm on the phone. Take a seat. I'll be off in a minute."

The nurse disappeared behind a closed door, and Decker walked around the generic apartment living room—shagged brown carpet and white walls. A six-foot sofa provided the seating for the area. It was upholstered in brown-and-white-striped fabric and had brown Naugahyde strips around the couch's sides for decoration. Facing the sofa, against the wall, was a sixteen-inch color TV on a metal stand.

The back end of the living room bled into a dining area filled with a Formica-topped round table and four chairs. To the right was the kitchen stocked with a freestanding stove and fridge, but it did have a built-in dishwasher. A home-made installation job, judging from the carpentry that surrounded it. On the wall were samplers, one of which read *Busy Hands Are Happy Hands* in ornate embroidery scroll. He didn't have time to read the others, because Darlene had returned. She sat down on the sofa and clutched her hands.

"Have a seat."

"Thank you." Decker sat down on the opposite end of the couch and pulled out his notebook. "I just finished speaking to Lily Booker's mother. I'm not in a very good mood. Let's both try to be as cooperative as possible."

"Lily's mother?" Darlene sounded hopeful. "So Lily *is* with her mother!"

"No, Darlene," Decker said. "Lily is not with her mother. There's a possibility that Lily might be the body we found in Marie's burned-out Honda. I had to ask Mrs. Booker for her daughter's dental X rays to see if they match the teeth of the body." He shuddered, rehearing the woman's sobs, then looked at Darlene. She seemed stunned, her eyes watering.

"I can't believe . . . are you saying . . . are you *sure*?"

"I'm not sure of anything yet." Decker's eyes went to the blank page of his notebook. He wrote down Darlene's name and the time and date. "When was Lily Booker supposed to show up for work?"

Darlene didn't answer, her eyes moist and glazed. The mottled face had turned ashen. She looked ill.

"Darlene, do you need a drink of water?"

Slowly, Darlene shook her head. "What about the baby?"

"We're still searching."

Darlene gazed at the wall. "If what you say is true, then I'm responsible. . . ."

"Responsible for what?"

Again Darlene was silent. Decker said, "Darlene, when was Lily supposed to show up for work? I'm trying to get a time frame. I need your help."

Finally, Darlene whispered, "Lily showed up for work around eleven."

Decker jerked his head upward. "Come again?"

"Lily's shift started at eleven. . . ."

"She showed up for work?"

"Yes."

"Then why did you tell me she called in *sick*?"

"Could you stop yelling?"

"Just *answer* the question, Darlene. On the phone this morning, you told me that Lily Booker called in sick."

"I was protecting her. . . ."

"From *what*?"

"I didn't want her to get into trouble for leaving early. Especially since Marie told me she had been called away for a family crisis. I didn't think it was fair to involve—"

"Wait, wait, wait!" Decker realized he *was* shouting and lowered his voice. "I'm confused. Start from the beginning."

"Oh, *Sergeant*!" Darlene burst into tears. "I really *messed* up this time!" She buried her face in her hands and sobbed openly.

Decker leaned back on the sofa and ran his hand over his face. He waited until the weeping subsided, then said, "Darlene, *when* did Lily show up for work?"

Darlene dried her eyes with a tissue. "At the beginning of her shift. She showed up at eleven."

"So Lily came to work."

"Yes."

"And you didn't tell anyone who questioned you about that, did you? Because you were protecting her."

"Yes. I didn't see the point of getting her involved if she wasn't even there."

"But she was there, Darlene. She may have been involved. Or she may have been a victim. Either way, you should have let us know everything. We could have been looking for her. We *should* have been looking for her!"

Darlene's face crumpled. "Yes, I know." The sobs came back. "I'm *sorry* I messed up! You maybe could have found her. And I didn't tell you, so you didn't even know. In my own way, *I'm* responsible for that girl's death!"

Darlene rushed out of the living room and slammed the door to the bedroom. Decker followed, afraid of what the nurse might be contemplating. He found her on her bed, weeping into her eyelet-trimmed pillow. Chewing on his mustache, he wondered how Rina was doing. She seemed okay when he left this morning, but she was so fragile right now. Just like this sobbing woman. Decker's focus fell upon Darlene. He felt her pain. She was trying to protect her trainee and she fucked up.

"Darlene, everyone makes mistakes. To equate your mistake with murder is absurd. Let's work together. Let's find the bastard or bastards who might have hurt Lily or the baby. I want to get them before they can hurt again. But I need your help."

Darlene cried out, "I don't deserve to be a nurse! Nurses *help* people, not put them in danger!"

"You help people. You're going to help me. Now I want you to focus in on that horrible day. I need a time frame if I'm going to figure out what happened. Stop your crying and *concentrate*!"

Still sniffling, Darlene sat up, eyes crimson and swollen. "We should go back and talk in the living room."

"Yes, that would be a good idea."

The two returned to the living room. After Decker reorganized his thoughts, he asked, "When did Marie tell you that Lily had left the hospital due to a crisis in the family?"

"I've got to think about it." After a long period of silence, Darlene said, "When I met her in the hall . . . the last time. She said she was going back to Nursery J 'cause Lily had to leave. Must have been 'bout an hour or so before we . . . we discovered the missing baby."

"So that would make it what time?"

"Around midnight, twelve-thirty that morning," Darlene mumbled. "I think. I remember Lily hadn't been on shift all that long, maybe an hour. But I talked to her several times before she left. That's why I didn't ... I saw no reason to penalize her for a family crisis. I was wrong, Sergeant! Not that it does Lily any good, but I was ..."

The tears started coming. Decker broke in, "Did Marie seem upset when she told you about Lily's crisis?"

Darlene nodded and wiped her eyes with a crumpled tissue. "But I just figured it was because without Lily, we were real short-staffed—working with a skeleton crew."

An apt choice of words, Decker thought. His face must have registered cynicism.

"I know, Sergeant. Your wife and baby were there. You must be very upset to hear insider stuff like this. I wish I could say it was a freak thing, but it isn't. We often have to do double or triple our load because some cheapskate administrator would rather have new office furniture than hire needed staff." The nurse put her hand to her mouth. "I suppose you're not interested in hospital politics."

"I am, but not right now," Decker said. "So tell me about Marie. She was upset?"

"Yes. She told me to float in nurseries A through F, and she'd take care of nurseries G through L. She told me to check in with her in about an hour."

"And you didn't see her after that?"

"No."

"Did she have blood on her uniform?"

Darlene's eyes widened. "No, I don't think so."

"Did she seem messy or disheveled?"

"I don't remember real clearly. Just that she was in a hurry. She was walking fast, mumbling about Lily as she walked. I figured she was jogging 'cause of the workload."

"If Marie was headed back to Nursery J, who'd been watching the babies in Nursery J?"

"Probably no one, with Lily gone." Darlene looked down. "Dear Lord, what I'm telling you. Opening myself up to a dandy lawsuit ... not to mention the hospital. I'll probably never work in the city again."

"I'm not going to sue anyone. Lourdes Rodriguez is another story. So the babies were left alone?"

"They may have been. Chris and a few temps were helping me. Marie had a few temps as well. Maybe one of the temps was watching the nursery."

"Either way, that's understaffed to me."

"That's true. If it's any consolation, Sergeant, I assure you that's not our standard procedure."

Decker didn't answer.

"I know. I must seem like a negligent person. I also should have told you about Lily. It just never dawned on me that Lily could be involved. You must think I'm the stupidest person on earth." Her cheeks became wet. "Another road to hell paved with good intentions."

"I've had a few of them myself, Darlene."

Darlene wiped her face. "That was a nice thing to say."

"We're all too human." Decker tapped his pencil on his notebook. "Do you know a nurse named Tandy Roberts?"

"*Tandy?* Is *Tandy* involved?"

"You *know* Tandy?"

"Not well, but I knew her. She used to be very close to Marie. They had some kind of falling out. Poor Marie. She felt very hurt, though she didn't say much. But I could tell."

"Did you happen to see Tandy at the hospital the night of the kidnapping?"

"No. Why?"

"I don't know. I'm grasping at straws now. It's hard for me to imagine Marie murdering Lily . . . if the body is Lily . . . and kidnapping a baby all by herself. I'm assuming she had help. And this Tandy Roberts was at one time a close friend of Marie's."

"I haven't seen Tandy in a couple of years."

"You're sure she wasn't at the hospital that night?"

"I'm not *positive*. But Tandy'd be a hard woman to miss."

"Did she ever work at the hospital?"

"Marie got her a part-time job at Sun Valley, but Tandy only lasted a couple of months. I thought she was a dull girl, but Marie was wild about her. Like I said, Marie always took pity on the underdog. But she really took a shine to Tandy. Like she was her own kid or something."

Her own kid—a weird choice of words. Decker did some quick calculations. Roberts was around twenty-five, and Marie was forty. He frowned. Marie's friend Paula had said that Marie had been around twenty when she had "lost" her baby. But maybe Paula was wrong. Maybe Marie'd had a baby at fifteen and had given her up for adoption. Maybe Tandy was *that* baby—the "lost" baby.

A big leap with a few holes. Surely, Lita Bellson would have noticed Marie's pregnancy. When Marie was fifteen, she was still living with Lita. And the old woman distinctly told Marge that Marie never had babies, only abortions.

But perhaps the old woman was senile.

Worry about that one later on.

Decker said, "When I asked administration about Tandy, they told me she wasn't on the hospital's work roster. Wouldn't she have been on it if she worked for the hospital in the past?"

"She was pulled from the roster because she had some trouble with her license. Marie told me she got that fixed up, though."

"What kind of trouble?"

"Marie told me it was some clerical error, but I think she was covering for her. I don't think she was licensed as an RN."

"Tandy wasn't a nurse?"

"No, she was an LVN—a Licensed Vocational Nurse—but not an RN—a Registered Nurse."

"What's the practical difference?"

"RNs have more training, higher status, and make more money. I never got the feeling that money was Tandy's thing. But she was real interested in status. Being that much overweight, I bet she wanted to be important at *something*. But it doesn't make it right—morally or legally."

Decker nodded in agreement.

"Marie said the rumors were garbage. That Tandy was an

RN. But like I said, she was wild about Tandy. She was always attracted to the downtrodden."

"Downtrodden?"

"Well, Tandy wasn't exactly a basket case, but she was overly shy." Darlene paused, then said, "Once I remember her crying in one of the supply closets. When I asked her what was wrong, she became flustered. Finally, I got her to tell me what was bothering her. She kept saying they were putting her down again."

"Who was putting her down?"

Darlene seemed surprised by the question. "I don't know if she ever said. I just assumed that she meant her parents. 'Cause of the way she was talking. 'They always tell me I'm no good, I'm too fat, I'm a disappointment. . . .' Things like that."

Decker was writing furiously. "What happened after you talked to her?"

"She stopped crying and went back to work."

"So you knew her pretty well."

"Not *very* well, but well enough to notice if Tandy had been in the hospital that night. Someone that heavy . . . the eye just can't help but notice. I would have spotted her on a dime."

"Darlene, suppose I were to tell you that Tandy is now around a hundred and twenty pounds—*Vogue*-model slim and beautiful to boot. What would you say?"

"I'd say you were pulling my leg. That girl was pathetic-looking." She paused. "You are kidding me, aren't you?"

"No, I'm not kidding you. My partner interviewed her. I'm telling you what she told me."

"But the girl musta weighed over three hundred pounds! Her face looked like she was on steroids, she was so swollen up."

Decker said, "Let's suppose someone passed you in the hallway the night of the kidnapping. And all you caught was a glimpse of that person—someone weighing around a hundred twenty pounds. Think you would have recognized Tandy at a hundred and twenty pounds, Darlene?"

The nurse closed her eyes, then reopened them slowly. "I

was very busy that night. Maybe I would have, but maybe I wouldn't have."

Hearing the RTO call out his unit number, Decker picked up the mike of the unmarked. Marge was put through a moment later.

"I got news."

"So do I," Decker said. "Should we meet at the station house, or do you want to grab a cup of coffee somewhere?"

"I can't leave where I am. I'm watching Tandy's Audi."

"Okay, so I'll come to you."

"No, *don't* do that!"

Decker was taken aback by Marge's forceful tone of voice. "What's cooking, Detective Dunn? Why don't you want me crowding your space?"

Marge didn't answer right away. Then she said, "I just don't want the unmarked anywhere in sight. I think this gal is really clever."

"Okay. So should we exchange info over the airwaves? Remember you're on a cellular phone and that's not private like a tactical line."

"We'll keep it short. You go first."

"First just tell me if Tandy Roberts was working at Tujunga Memorial the night of the kidnapping."

"She was, Pete, *but* she was off shift at eleven. So she could have taken a little drive over to Sun Valley Pres."

"Great." Decker recapped his conversation with Darlene Jamison. "It's very possible that Tandy *was* there at Sun Valley Pres, and even people who *knew* her wouldn't have recognized her. She could have been skulking through the halls, still dressed in her uniform, and even if Darlene had caught a glimpse of her, Tandy would have just looked like a thin, anonymous floater."

"So the timing is on our side."

"Now all we need is evidence linking her to the kidnapping or at least to Sun Valley."

"We should go back to Sun Valley and pass around current pictures of Tandy," Marge said. "See if *anyone* remembers seeing the slim version."

"She hasn't officially worked at Sun Valley for a couple of years. She was pulled from the work roster because of licensing problems. Consistent with what Leek told you about her at Golden Valley Home. Seems the girl is passing herself off as an RN."

Marge said, "You mean, '*was* passing herself off.' Past tense. I asked about her license at Tujunga Memorial. They told me she was a licensed RN. Gave me her license number and everything."

Decker thought a moment, then asked, "Is there a Board of Nurses' Examiners in Sacramento?"

"I'm sure there must be," Marge said. "They regulate just about everything except palm readers."

"What about the tarot-card interpreters?"

"They have their own board," Marge said.

Decker smiled. "Call up Sacramento. Find out about Tandy's license from *them*. I'll find out if Mike dug up any interesting gas purchases billed to Tandy." He paused. "So, we have Marie and Lily at the scene, Tandy possibly at the scene. Where's the thread?"

"Tandy and Marie both lost babies. Maybe one took the kid and the other is abetting. Maybe they were in it together."

"Why would Tandy help Marie if Marie took the kid?"

Marge paused. "I don't know."

"So reverse it," Decker said. "Why would Marie help Tandy if Tandy took the kid?"

Marge said, "Didn't Darlene say that Marie treated Tandy like her kid? Maybe she *was* her kid."

"You've seen both women," Decker said. "Do they look alike?"

"No."

Decker said, "Did Lita Bellson mention her daughter giving birth at fifteen? She certainly told you everything else about her daughter."

"No, Lita never said anything like that. But Lita's kind of out of it. Tell you what, Pete. Why don't you pop over to Golden Valley and ask her?"

"I'll do just that."

"In the meantime, I'll keep an eye on Tandy."

"Right."

Marge said, "What's your take on Darlene? Do you think she might be involved?"

"I'm not ruling out anybody, but my instinct tells me she just honestly fucked up."

"Sounds like you feel bad for her."

"Part of me is angry as hell. And the other part says we're all human." Decker didn't speak for a moment. Then he said, "I'm outta here."

"Kiss Hannah for me."

"A big kiss from Auntie Marge, huh?"

"Auntie Marge?"

"The kid doesn't have a lot of extended family," Decker said. "We improvise."

He cut the line. Marge laughed and hung up the phone. Her eyes had never left sight of the entrance to the juice bar. They had been in there for almost an hour. She was getting antsy.

Ten minutes later, the women emerged. Marge breathed a sigh of relief. Tandy headed back to the gym; Cindy appeared to be walking to her car. Marge waited until the doors had closed behind Tandy to sprint over to Decker's daughter, catching her totally off guard. Cindy turned red and looked at her feet.

"I'm in trouble, aren't I?"

"Be thankful it's me and not Daddy."

"Yeah, I was thinking the same thing." Cindy followed Marge over to the Beemer. "Nice car. Is it yours?"

"Just get inside and don't ask questions."

Quietly, Cindy slipped into the passenger's seat.

TWENTY-EIGHT

THE HOUSE WAS CEMETERY QUIET AS DECKER CAME through the door. Figuring someone had to be asleep, he tiptoed through the kitchen and went out the back door. Once again Nora, the nurse, and Magda had set up camp around the patio table, chatting happily as they sipped iced tea and munched grapes. Hannah was snoozing in her new cradle—a gift from his brother, Randy—and Ginger had curled up under the tabletop. The setter didn't bother to greet Decker with her usual yipping and yapping, just raised her head and lowered it. For some reason, that bothered him. He took it as a neurotic sign that he was being displaced.

"How's everyone?"

Nora said, "I'm glad you had that little talk with your wife. She's been resting all morning. It's what she needs to make her heal."

"Good to hear."

"Do you want some iced tea, Akiva?" Magda asked.

"Maybe a little later. How's my baby?"

"Sleeping like one," Nora said.

"Isn't she a good girl?" Magda said. "Just the best?"

"No argument from me," Decker said. "Is Cindy around?"

"She went out early in the morning," Magda said. "I

think she go swimming. She has with her a swimming bag."

"Really?" Decker said. "That's great. She must have hooked up with some friends."

The women stopped talking and smiled at him. His presence must be wearing thin. Or maybe it was the other way around. He smiled and said, "I'll just go inside the house. Get myself a snack and check in on Rina."

The women nodded enthusiastically, as if they couldn't wait to get rid of him. He reentered his kitchen, took an apple out of the refrigerator, and ate it before he remembered to wash it. So what's a little weedkiller between friends?

He picked up the phone and dialed Florida. His father's gruff voice came over the answering machine:

Leave a message. Beep.

Decker left his message. He hadn't spoken to his parents since the baby was born; they kept missing each other. But the congratulations card in yesterday's mail along with the lengthy handwritten note told Decker his parents had received the news and were excited. Ordinarily, his mother never wrote more than a couple of perfunctory sentences.

How are you? We're fine. Bye.

Initially, they had been disappointed in his selection of a spouse. Nothing personal against Rina, but like Decker's first wife, she was Jewish. His parents, being good Baptists, didn't cotton to her rejection of the Savior. And when he announced he was joining his wife's faith, he knew his mother would be heartbroken.

He had made the move after much deliberation. Accepting Judaism had taken him full circle, back to the faith of his biological parents. Even though Decker considered his adoptive parents his only parents, he knew his renunciation of Christianity was tantamount to renunciation of his parents in his mother's eyes. For a while, the relationship with his parents was sticky. But things were improving. Mom genuinely liked Rina as a person.

And now the baby . . . their granddaughter.

Time and babies heal all wounds.

Not really hungry, Decker decided to peek in on Rina.

He opened the door to the bedroom. She was curled into a ball and wrapped in her blanket, only a tiny area of skin showing from her face. He bent down to kiss her cheek, and she opened her eyes.

"Nora says you've been resting. That's good, darlin'. The only way to heal."

"You mean it's good for *her*," she squeaked out.

"Rina, if you don't like Nora, I'll fire her right now."

No response.

"Honey, do you want me to get rid of her? We certainly don't need another interfering nurse around here."

Rina pulled the blanket off her face and turned to him. "What do you mean, 'another interfering nurse'? Who was the first one?"

Decker winced. "No one. I'm just babbling."

"You were referring to your case, weren't you?"

"I suppose it's all blurring. Is Nora preventing you from taking care of Hannah?"

"No, not at all." Rina fell back on her pillow. "I suppose she feels she's doing the right thing by helping me rest. She just makes me feel *useless*!"

"You're not useless."

"Useless and uterusless." She let out a bitter laugh. "That's me!"

Decker said, "Rina, I love you and need you and want you and find you sexy, and I'll keep saying those words over and over until you *believe* me!"

"I believe you." She sighed. "I just want my baby, and I'm too tired to care for her. I'm cranky."

"You can be cranky."

Rina tried to smile. Instead, the mouth turned down into a look of despair, and she started crying. Decker bit his mustache. All this outpouring of emotion was wearing him down. Rina's catharsis was so honestly expressed—but that didn't make it any easier to deal with. He felt like galloping his stallion around the corral, building up a sweat until his muscles ached with that satisfied throb of physical work. But instead, he lay down next to his wife and held her in his arms, trying to sympathize with her plight without being consumed by it.

"I love you, baby," Decker said.

"I love you, too." Rina sniffed. "I feel so much *better* when you're here."

Decker thought about that one as she sobbed in his arms. He supposed crying was a definite improvement over catatonic depression. "I'm glad, Rina. Just give me a few more days on this case, and I promise, I'll take a few weeks off. I'll do everything I can for you. We'll work through this together."

"I *hate* when I drag you down like this."

"You're not dragging me down. I'll finish this case, and then I'm all yours."

Rina broke away, propped up her pillows, then laid her head down and folded the sheets across her lap. "Thanks for being so wonderful."

"Any time." Decker glanced at her nightstand, and picked up a handwritten note.

Palm Springs—April.

"What's this?"

Rina read the slip. "Oh. Abba and Eema Lazarus called to congratulate us."

Decker smiled weakly. Abba and Eema Lazarus—the parents of her late husband.

The boys' grandparents.

"That's nice. So what does their call have to do with Palm Springs?"

"They invited us to go with them to Palm Springs for *Pesach.*"

Decker frowned. "Palm Springs for Passover? Correct me if I'm wrong, but isn't the saying 'Next year in Jerusalem'?"

"One desert's the same as the next."

"I think you're missing a crucial point."

Rina smiled. "Jerusalem is lovely, but Palm Springs is a little closer."

"What's in Palm Springs besides golf?"

"Sonny Bono."

"Rina—"

"They have this huge Kosher for Passover tour. I've spoken to people who have been there. They take over a resort hotel and turn it into a Club Med for the Orthodox. The hotel has a pool, spas, tennis courts, a health club. The tour provides activities—Israeli dancing, cooking, wine tasting, a bingo contest—"

"My heart can't take the excitement."

"No, Peter, it's not chasing felons, but I bet your body could use a real rest. Anyway, I didn't refuse them outright. It's up to you."

"Up to *me*?" He paused. "Do you actually *want* to go?"

"My first instinct was to say no. But then I thought, Rina, what's wrong with lying around the pool all day? If we stay home for the holidays, we'd just wind up working around the house."

Decker was silent.

"You don't want to go, we won't go," Rina said. "They're just trying to be nice. This is the honeymoon the Lazaruses *wanted* us to have. They felt terrible about last year. Calling us to come for the holidays, then making you work."

"It wasn't their fault a kid decided to run away with a psycho."

"But you wound up spending all your vacation time looking for him. They felt lousy about it. They want us to have some fun. Remember fun?"

"Describe it to me."

Rina touched his cheek. "I think it involves lots of time in bed—sleeping or otherwise."

"It's coming back . . . *slowly.*"

Rina punched his good shoulder.

Decker smiled. "They know I won't come to Brooklyn. They want to see the boys, don't they?"

"I'm sure that's a big part of it. You can understand that. And even if Channaleh isn't technically their own, they feel like she is. *Eema*'s already booked us two rooms—one for us and one for the children."

"Nothing like pressure."

"I never committed. Don't go if you don't want to. Life's too short for doing things you don't want to do."

"Who else is going?"

"Just *Eema* and *Abba*. It'll be just the seven of us."

"What about your parents?"

"They're going to Israel to be with my brother."

"What about your former sisters-in-law and their families?"

"*Eema* and *Abba* spend plenty of time with them. They just want it to be the seven of us."

Decker rubbed his eyes. "Would it make you happy to go?"

"Spending some time *alone* with you would really make me very happy. And it's free."

"That's not the issue."

"It's a legitimate issue if you saw how much these things cost. They wouldn't take our money anyway. They want it to be *their* treat. But it's totally up to you, Peter. I mean it."

Decker bit his mustache. The poor people had lost their only son from illness. Now, more than ever, he could feel their heartbreak. It seemed so cruel to deny them their grandsons, too. And it would please Rina and wouldn't involve going to Brooklyn. Plus, to be honest, the idea of having nothing to do for a week except make love and lie around the pool did sound pretty damn good. A free family vacation with built-in baby-sitters and kosher food provided to boot. Rina wouldn't have to drag along pots and pans and kosher food packed in an ice chest. And if he said yes, he'd look like a prince in Rina's eyes.

"If it's just them . . ." Decker massaged his temples. "Sure, we can go."

Rina's smile was wide and happy, and for a moment Decker saw her old self. He knew it would take time for her to get over her trauma, and he hoped his agreeable attitude was helping her along.

Rina gave him a big kiss on the cheek. "You really are a nice person. Just the best!"

"No prob, darlin'. It's worth it to see you smile."

* * *

Marge said, "Just answer me one question, Cindy. What in the world could have possibly gone through that *brain* of yours?"

"I got some very important information, Marge."

Calm, Marge told herself. Just remain calm. First thank God she's not your daughter, then treat her like any other dingbat witness. "And what is that information, Cynthia?"

"I know why Tandy might have taken the baby . . . if she did take the baby. I mean, I don't *know* that she took the baby. But I have a motive if she did."

"She lost a baby when she was fifteen," Marge said.

Cindy stared at her, disappointment clouding the sunshine of her eyes. "How did you *know*?"

"Because I *interviewed* her, Cindy. That's what the *police* do. And they don't even have to pose as bodybuilders to do it. I don't have to tell you how dangerous and stupid your little stunt was. Your dad and I aren't TV detectives with cute little mannerisms who wrap things up in an hour minus twenty minutes for commercials. We get things done by putting in long hours and trying out different tactics that often lead nowhere. It's hard, it's tiring, and it's *frustrating*! What we don't need is someone blowing all of our careful planning by being *stupid*!"

The girl looked as if she was going to cry. Marge softened her tone. "Did you have a good workout at least?"

Cindy didn't answer.

"Look," Marge said, "no harm done." *She hoped.* "What'd you two talk about in the juice bar? You were in there for almost an hour."

"Nothing much." Cindy sighed. "What are you doing here?"

"What do you think? I'm keeping an eye on Tandy."

"You're watching her car?"

"Yes. Promise me you'll back off for good, okay?"

"I was supposed to return to the gym tomorrow—"

"Cindy!"

"They have this whole routine worked out for me. They say I have lots of talent."

Marge stared at her. "Cynthia Decker, if I find you

within a mile of this place, I'll arrest you and throw you in the clinker with all sorts of unsavory women."

Cindy smiled. "I'll stay out of your face, Marge."

"You'll stay out of our *business*!" Marge took a deep breath. "Now . . . what did you two talk about?"

"Just talked—about school, about guys, about our families. Don't worry, I didn't tell her my father's a cop. I'm not stupid, only adventurous."

"No, Cynthia, it's stupidity!"

Cindy smiled sadly. "And here I thought I discovered something really important. I was going to lay a real insight on you."

"So I beat you to the punch. How did losing the baby come up in conversation?"

"She talked about her modeling career. How one of the directors made her pregnant."

"How long was she a model?"

"Since she was five. A kid's model at first for clothing catalogs. Then she graduated into haute couture and the catwalk. She told me how brutal the whole thing was. How mean everyone was to newcomers, how she had to *starve* herself to stay thin. She was bulimic. Even when she was pregnant, she used to starve herself, didn't start showing until she was in her sixth month. She wound up losing the baby shortly afterward. Afterward, she was five-nine, ninety-five pounds."

"*Jesus.*"

"Yeah, a real skeleton. Even her *agent* told her to gain a few pounds back. Which she did. She worked for a few more years. Then she said she got pregnant again and lost that baby—"

"Wait a minute, Cindy." Marge pulled out her notebook and began to scribble furiously. "She got pregnant again?"

"Yeah. This time when she was eighteen. She was still living in New York." Cindy's eyes lit up. "You didn't know that one, did you?"

"No."

"See. I found something—"

"Just cool the pats on the back for the time being, okay? Did she lose that baby, too?"

"Yes, but earlier than the first one. In the fourth month, I think."

"Did it send her into a depression or anything?"

"Well, it made an impact on her. And on her professional life. Because the second time around, she refused to starve herself. She felt the starvation was the reason she lost the first baby. She said people told her over and over it was her fault she lost the first baby."

"Which people?"

Cindy shrugged. "She just said people. Probably her mom. So the second time she got pregnant, she ate. And ate and ate and ate and ate. It was the first time in years that she could eat normally. When she lost the second baby, she had put on fifty pounds. But she didn't care. By that time, she was so disgusted with the business and her mother for pushing her, she left New York and came out here."

"She's originally from New York?"

"No, from Berkeley. Her parents were divorced when she was a kid. Her mother took her to Manhattan to model shortly after her parents split. She used to live with her father during the summers, but when she got real busy with her career, she stopped visiting him. She said she was glad. She *hates* both her parents, I can tell you that much."

"Sounds like a lovely girl."

"She's had it rough, I guess. A bitch stage mom—real pushy—and a philandering father. We talked about divorce for a while. How hard it can be on the kids."

Cindy started biting her nails.

"It's hard under the best of circumstances. My parents really tried to shield me, but their hostility toward one another was palpable whenever my dad picked me up for weekends. It got easier after my mom remarried; they became a little more civil. But I don't think there's ever going to be any love lost between them. It hurts. . . ." She shrugged. "But you move on. You get past it. You realize that your parents can make mistakes and still be good people. I don't think Tandy ever got past that. She still talks about her parents' divorce as if it happened last year instead of years ago."

"Did she talk about her parents' faults specifically?"

"Yes. She kept repeating that her mother was a stage-mom bitch and her father was a pathetic Lothario who couldn't keep his pants zipped. She was happy to stop seeing him in the summers because he was getting real desperate as he aged—the students getting younger and him getting older."

"He was a college professor?"

"Yep. English literature, I think. Geoffrey Roberts. Geoffrey with a *G*. Tandy said even the spelling of his name was affected. He didn't have a drop of English blood in him. He was Hispanic. His parents were refugees from Cuba. That's why Tandy's so dark. Her mom's the prototypical WASP, and her dad was a WASP wannabe. So he changed his surname to Roberts and got educated. Must have been a smart fellow. From what Tandy said, he just really got carried away with this professor/student thing."

Cindy noticed she was biting her nails and folded them in her lap.

"There are a couple of those at Columbia. We snicker at them behind their backs. I know it isn't nice, but it's such a cliché, Marge. It must be really *embarrassing* to see your father making a fool out of himself. At least my dad was always a *dad*. Even after he got divorced, he didn't go through that juvenile stage. You know, picking up younger women and flirting with your friends. At least if he did, I never saw it. Dad's always been a good guy. And my mom is a good woman, too."

Cindy laughed.

"But God, they were just *terrible* together."

Marge patted Cindy's hand. "You're a good kid. I'm sorry if I came down hard on you."

"I'm sorry if I screwed up your investigation."

"You didn't screw anything up, Cindy. You almost did, but you didn't."

"I won't butt in again, I promise. To tell you the truth, Tandy gives me the willies. There's something off about her. Between her parents' divorce and the babies she lost, I think it affected her brain. She kept talking about how bad she was and how good she is now that she works out. I think it's the only thing that keeps her sane. She said it brought meaning back into her life, gave her control over her eating and over all the bad thoughts."

"Bad thoughts?" Marge repeated.

"Her words verbatim." Cindy stopped talking for a moment. "You know, as strange as this may be, I can kind of understand the way she feels just from today. In some perverse way, challenging your body like that really makes you feel superhuman. Right now, I'm sore as hell, but while I was doing it, Tandy and Eric rooting me on, I felt really special. Like I was Amazon Woman. It does give you a sense of control, although it's all illusion."

Cindy smiled sadly.

"Then again, I suppose we all have our little illusions to help us get through life. Can I go now?"

Marge patted the teenager's back. "You can go now."

TWENTY-NINE

Bʏ THE TIME DECKER FINISHED LUNCH, RINA WAS HAPPILY cuddling Hannah. Her spirits were high, and together they had decided to cut short the baby nurse's stay, agreeing that Nora should work over the weekend and help get the kids off to school the following Monday. By then, Rina insisted she'd be able to handle Hannah but would allow her mother to drop by daily to make sure she wasn't overworked. Curtailing Nora's stay made Rina much more willing to rest now—while she still had a chance.

It was half past the noon hour when Decker called the station house. Mike Hollander brought him up-to-date. Sondra Roberts owned a Visa and a MasterCard, her latest debits including a twenty-five-dollar accessory purchase at a discount dress store and ten bucks' worth of gasoline at a station in North Hollywood. The gas was bought at 2:52 P.M. yesterday. Her last gas purchase before that one was a week ago—again a ten-dollar charge at a place in Tujunga.

"Ten bucks' worth of gas is enough to douse a car," Decker said to Hollander.

"I guess. I'm just thinking if she was smart enough to torch a car, she probably paid cash for the gas—wouldn't leave a paper trail."

"True, but call around anyway. See if anyone remembers filling her tank. According to Marge, Tandy's a stunning-looking girl." Decker gave Mike a description. "Talk to the young guys. See if you can't jog someone's memory."

"I'll give it a whirl. You know, Rabbi, it could be she siphoned off gas from her *own* car's tank, and that's why she had to have a refill yesterday."

Decker pondered his words. "Man, that would require a pretty cool head."

"We've got a murder and a kidnapping with no leads," Hollander said. "We're working with a cool-headed person. I got a spare afternoon. Nothing pressing other than forms to fill out. Want me to watch her?"

"Marge is tailing her now, but I'm sure she wouldn't mind a break."

"I'll give her a call—"

"Wait a minute, she's not using one of our cars." Decker gave him the cellular phone number. "She traded cars with her latest social interest."

"What's she driving?"

"A Beemer. Don't say anything important over the phone. Cellular transmission isn't limited access like our tactical lines. Did Lily Booker's dental X rays come in yet?"

"Nope. Want me to call her parents again?"

"No, they'll cooperate, sooner or later. It's the denial. Let's give them another day."

"Ain't it the shits being a parent?" Hollander paused. "Oops. Sorry."

"Nothing to be sorry about," Decker said. "It's tough."

"Where are you off to, Rabbi?"

"To visit Lita Bellson. I'm not even sure what I expect to accomplish. At the present time, Marie's our only link to the missing baby. For all I know, they both might be dead."

"And this Roberts lady?"

"She's a link to Marie," Decker said. "Speaking of links to Marie, did you get hold of Paula Delfern?"

"Yep. She hasn't heard from Marie, either. She gave me her work number and told me to call her as soon as I had any information. I checked out the number, and it was her work number—some doctor's office. The night of the kidnapping, she was moonlighting at St. Joe's just like she said. Her nursing license seems kosher, her yellow sheet's clean. But if she's a link, I can keep on her."

"You mean a tail? No, I don't have any reason to justify that yet. Just check in on her from time to time. Tandy's the one with some hanky-panky in her life. I've got to find out about this license thing. And what—if *anything*—it has to do with Marie."

"You're investigating Tandy just because she was a friend of Marie's?"

"Initially, yes. But she's turned out to be a nutcase. I don't have anything specific on her, but she's worth watching at this point." Decker ran his hand through his hair. "How's the search going? How much manpower's still out there?"

"About fifty percent of what we had. But that's still a lot of feet."

"But for how long?"

"You know the situation, Rabbi."

And Decker did. He swore to himself. The case was taking on a chill. "I've got another call on the line, Mike. I'll check in later."

"Maybe I'll have better news," Hollander said.

"At this point, I'll just take news." Decker depressed the line to liberate his second call. Marge's voice came over the wire.

"Got a callback from the Board of Nurses' Examiners, Pete. About Tandy's license: It's not Tandy's. The number she's using actually belongs to one Lawrence McKay—aka *Leek*, the scamster of Golden Valley Home."

"Tandy's using *Leek*'s license number?"

"Appears that way."

"How can she do that?"

"I don't know."

"Don't these agencies cross-check for things like that?"

"I'm sure they're supposed to, but you know bureaucracy."

"Does Leek know she's using his number?"

"Beats me."

"What's Leek using for his license?"

"Someone should ask him these very questions, Pete. Since I'm stuck here at the parking lot at Silver's, keeping watch over a black Audi, I suggest you take a trip to Golden Valley Home real soon."

"I'm leaving right now. I spoke to Hollander. One of his cases was postponed. He said he could relieve you for a couple of hours. How about we meet at my house at about"—he looked at his watch—"how does two, two-thirty sound?"

"What's wrong with the station house?"

"I'd like to check in on Rina . . . and the baby."

"Proud papa, huh?"

"More like neurotic papa."

Marge had described Golden Valley as a step up from the usual retirement home, and Decker agreed with her assessment. It was bright and clean, and the staff seemed professional. But all that could be facade. Lawrence McKay worked there, and McKay was a man with something to hide. His yellow sheet had come up empty, but that didn't mean the man was clean. All criminals have blank records until they get caught.

McKay was still out on lunch break when Decker arrived. He was due back in fifteen minutes, so Decker decided to make use of the time and have a talk with Lita Bellson. He didn't expect a breakthrough, but anything was worth a try.

Lita was in the solarium, sun shaded by tinted windows. The back of her wheelchair was tilted downward, and her foot rest was raised. Her head was to the side, and she appeared to be asleep. As Decker moved closer, he saw her eyes were closed and her mouth was emitting soft snores. He pulled up a chair beside her, and a moment later a young black nurse named Tonya came by to offer him coffee. He accepted, and when she returned with a steaming cup, the aroma aroused Sleeping Beauty.

"Coffee?" Lita muttered. "Did somebody make coffee?" Her eyes snapped open to reveal startling green eyes flecked with brown. She stared at Decker. "Who are you? More important, where'd you get the coffee?"

"I'm Detective Sergeant Decker, and a nurse brought me the coffee."

"Can I have it?"

Nurse Tonya clucked her tongue. "Lita, you know you can't have coffee."

"Why the hell not?"

"Because, Lita, the caffeine's bad for your heart, and the acid upsets your stomach."

"Girlie, my stomach is just fine, no thanks to you."

"Lita, now don't you start getting nasty—"

Decker said, "Why don't you just take this away? It seems to be creating a problem."

"What doesn't cause a problem with this one?" Tonya took the coffee cup and left.

"Bitch," Lita muttered, watching the young nurse go. "I don't suppose you'd sneak me a cup."

"I follow orders, Lita."

"So I order you to get me a cup." She wheezed a spasm of laughter. "Who did you say you were?"

"Sergeant Decker of the Los Angeles Police. My partner, Detective Dunn, came out yesterday to talk to you. She asked you questions about Marie."

Lita looked blank.

"Detective Dunn's a tall blond woman with brown eyes. She asked you all about Marie, her history, her friends. . . ."

Lita waited a moment, then said, "I haven't seen Marie for a while. Where is she?"

Decker paused. He was sure Marge had informed Lita of her daughter's disappearance. "I don't know. She seems to have . . . gone somewhere."

"Really?"

"Yes, really. Lita, do you remember talking to Detective Dunn at all?"

"Sorta."

"What do you remember?"

She didn't answer, and Decker didn't push it. Start from scratch—taking into consideration that the woman might have Alzheimers. It made all her answers suspect. "Any idea where Marie might have gone, Lita?"

"Nope."

"Did Marie have a favorite place to go to think when she needed some time alone?"

"Marie lived alone. Check her condo."

"We did. She isn't there."

Lita frowned. "Doesn't make sense that she'd just up and disappear. Marie turned out to be the stable, dependable one. Just like my first husband, Henry, except Marie wasn't his. Funny how things like that work out. Marie became a nurse. Said Jesus told her to become a nurse."

"Did Marie often talk to Jesus?"

"You mean was she crazy? The answer is no. But she was always a little fanatical in her beliefs."

The old woman was silent for a moment.

"First it was drugs was God. Then it was gurus was God. She wound up with Jesus. Better him than a cow. So you can't find Marie, huh?"

The old lady didn't seem concerned. Decker asked, "Has she ever done this before. Just disappeared?"

"Not that I can remember." Lita burped. "But I don't remember so good anymore. Least that's what they tell me."

"Lita, could Marie have gone camping?"

"Camping?"

"You know . . . go out to the woods, pitch a tent . . . sleep in the wilds?"

"Are we talking about the same Marie?" Lita scratched her nose. "Nah, I've never known her to camp." The old woman furrowed her brows. She looked like a wizened gnome. "It has been a while since she's visited me. 'Course, all the days seem to run together when you're stuck under one roof. What's she up to?"

"Marie?"

"Yeah, Marie. What kind of trouble did she get herself into?"

"What makes you think she's in trouble?"

"She used to come to me when she was in trouble. Used to do that all the time when she was a teenager. 'Ma, I'm in trouble. Give me money.' Long as she was okay, she didn't want anything from me. 'Course, I was a shitty mother. I didn't want much to do with her, either. Two stubborn bodies under one roof. It wasn't good. Neither one of us would give in."

Talking about the past, the old woman seemed on surer footing.

"I remember once Marie wanted a dog. I said no, but that didn't stop her. Marie got herself a dog. Took care of her, too. I was surprised. But that was Marie. Fanatically loyal, and loyal to the point of fanatical."

"To people?"

"People, ideas. She believed in free love to the point of fanatical. It was the times—late sixties and early seventies. The sexual revolution. Kids were wild, especially up north—land of the flower child. People living on the street in Haight-Ashbury, screwing everything in sight." Lita shook her head. "Miserable time to be a mother."

There was regret in Lita's voice. Not at having to rear a

child during turbulent times, but because she hadn't been young herself back then. Decker asked, "Did Marie ever get pregnant?"

Lita burst into laughter. "More times than a rabbit."

"What happened to the babies?"

"She didn't have babies, she had abortions."

"She never carried any of her pregnancies to term?"

"Not so far as I know. When she was away at the university, I don't know what she did. My daughter just couldn't keep her legs together." Lita laughed. "Wonder where she learned that from."

Decker didn't touch that one.

Lita said, "She did it to spite me. You know, give me a taste of my own medicine. She wasted her time. I don't regret my life. Got some nice memories. In fact, that's all I got right now."

"She lived with you when she was in her early teens, didn't she, Lita?"

"Yep."

"And she didn't have a child when she was around fifteen?"

Lita stared at him. "Of course not. I'd have known about it if she did." She paused, her eyes far away. "Might have been nice to have a grandchild . . . someone else to visit me."

"She didn't have a baby and give it away for adoption?"

"Why're you asking me these silly questions? As long as Marie lived with me, she didn't have a baby. Just abortions. Must have had three before she left for Berkeley. I don't know what was so hard that she couldn't get the pill right. I suppose Jesus did what the pill couldn't do. Gave her self-respect. Other gods couldn't do that. She went through lots of gods—blue gods, hermaphrodite gods, gods with eight arms, fat gods. She finally settled on Jesus. Probably 'cause he was wiry and cute."

Decker forced himself to remain impassive.

Lita shrugged. "I mean that. Look at all the cute boys in the sixties. All of them thin, wearing raggedy clothes and beards. All of them wanted to be Jesus—from Jim

Morrison down to Charlie Manson. That's kids for you."
She closed her eyes and leaned her head the other way.
"You got some Milk Duds or anything like that?"

"Sorry, no."

"I'm tired. Come back tomorrow, and we'll talk some
more." A small bony hand touched Decker's arm. "Do me
a favor, handsome. When you come back, bring me a four-
pack of butterscotch pudding?"

"You bet, Lita."

"You're a peach." Lita turned her head and dozed off to
another lifetime.

Decker waited a few moments before leaving. Though
Lita's memory wasn't on the firmest ground, she sounded
convincing when she talked about her daughter's past.
Decker believed that if Marie, while living with her mother,
had had a baby, Lita would have known about it. Unless either she or Tandy were lying about their ages, Marie
couldn't be Tandy's biological mother.

So just why was Marie so strongly attached to Tandy?
So much so that Darlene Jamison said Marie treated Tandy
like her own kid. Lita's words ran in his ears.

Fanatically loyal.

Maybe Marie had made up her mind to mother Tandy.
Then Tandy rejected her, and she cracked.

Grasping at straws.

Decker checked his watch and stood: McKay should be
back by now. But when he went to the front desk, the re-
ceptionist informed him that Leek had just left a moment
ago. He wasn't feeling well.

The nurse was still explaining McKay's symptoms, but
Decker didn't wait to hear the full medical report. He
dashed out the front door and spied a navy Cressida pulling
out of its parking space. Sprinting, Decker jumped on the
hood just as the car slipped from Reverse to Drive. Immediately, the driver slammed on the brakes, almost throwing
Decker to the ground. But he managed to hold on. The motor fell dead; the driver's door opened and slammed shut.
The man who emerged was medium height but as solid as

a concrete divider. He had thin chestnut hair and coarse-looking skin, which at this moment was beet red.

"Are you out of your fucking *mind*!" he screamed. "What the hell are you doing? Trying to get yourself *killed*?"

Decker scrambled down from the hood of the Cressida and dusted off his pants. "Nah, not at all. Just trying to catch you before you left, Leek."

"You scared the shit out of me. Who the hell are you?"

"I think you know," Decker said. "I think that's why you made a mad dash out of here."

"I left because I'm sick, mister."

"It's Sergeant, Leek."

McKay became quiet, his eyes guarded. "So that's what they teach you in the Academy? How to scare innocent citizens?"

"Nah, I learned that on the streets." Decker pulled out his shield and showed it to him. "I need a few minutes of your time."

"There's a thing called the phone."

"Sometimes people get squirrelly about answering it." Decker pocketed his I.D. "Man, you left in a hurry."

"I'm sick as a dog. Anything illegal about that?"

Decker said, "Cut the crap. I need to speak with you. Anyplace is okay, including a parking lot. But you may want to choose a place that offers a little more privacy. We may get into some personal stuff."

McKay covered his face, then dropped his hands to his side. "Can't it wait until tomorrow? I really don't feel well."

"A baby's missing, Mr. McKay."

"I swear to God I don't know a *thing* about that. I haven't seen Marie Bellson at the home in over a week. I told your partner I'd call if I heard from Marie. I haven't. I'm useless for information, Sergeant. You've got to believe me."

"What about Tandy Roberts?"

"Your partner told me to stay away from her. I've been staying away."

Decker thought about that. If McKay had warned Tandy she might be in trouble and she was guilty of something, would she still be hanging around, working out at Silver's?

"Listen, if you're as virginal as you say you are, you're going to want to help, right?"

"I really don't feel well, Sergeant." Abruptly, McKay's face whitened. "Really. I'm sick to my stomach. . . ." He seemed to teeter on his feet. "I'm real dizzy."

Suddenly, he lurched forward. Decker got him before he hit the ground, but not without feeling a sharp pull in his bad shoulder. He bit back pain that shot through his arm and steadied the weight lifter until he was stable on his feet. McKay leaned against the Cressida and tried to breathe rhythmically. His face was ashen, his lips devoid of color. He looked genuinely sick, but at this point Decker didn't care.

"You shouldn't be driving, Leek." Decker shook his head. "Not safe for you or other motorists. Tell you what I'm going to do for you. It's an off-hour right now for lunch. Let's find a quiet place where you can sit and catch your breath. And to show you what a sport cops can be, I'll buy you some herbal tea."

THIRTY

SINCE DECKER WAS FEELING BENEVOLENT, HE LET MCKAY pick the place. The muscleman directed him to a health-

food grocery with NATURE'S WHOLESOME GOODNESS stenciled
on the front window. The interior reminded Decker of a
general store of yore—bins of whole grains, dried fruits,
and unprocessed sugar and flour. It also had a good-sized
produce section, many of the fruits and vegetables un-
trimmed or uncut. The lettuce looked freshly yanked from
a garden, clumps of dirt still clinging to the large green
leaves. The only nod to modern times was a back-wall
dairy case. On the opposite side of the entrance stood a
bakery—sweet smells emanating from the back. In front of
the bread counter were a few sets of tables and chairs. Mc-
Kay took a seat and lowered his head in his hands.

Decker sat beside him. "Place smells good, Leek, but it's
not very private."

McKay looked at Decker, then covered his face again.

"Place have waitresses?" Decker asked.

"You order at the counter," McKay mumbled.

"What's your pleasure, Lawrence?"

"How about some solitude and a bed?"

"How about some peppermint tea?"

McKay dropped his hands to his lap and smiled sickly.
"Chamomile."

Decker stood and came back a minute later, carrying two
cups of tea and a cinnamon bun. He sat back down. "I
brought you some munch food. It smelled good."

"You eat it." McKay took the tea. "I'm sick to my stomach. I woke up feeling that way. Thought I could beat it. I
was wrong."

"So your illness has nothing to do with my visit?"

"Your visit isn't a boon to my health. What do you guys
want from me?"

"How about we start with your investment-counseling
sideline. Did you promise all the old ladies trips to Hawaii?
Or did you individualize, with a different scam for each
one?"

McKay stared at Decker, a gray pallor washing over his
cheeks. Decker reached into his pockets and took out a
small tape recorder. "Sometimes I use a notebook. But
sometimes I use this. Do you mind?"

The bodybuilder's eyes drifted to the cassette player. "Do I need a lawyer?"

"That's up to you."

"Are you charging me with anything?"

"Not yet. But if you say something incriminating, I can use it against you."

Again McKay was quiet.

"Up to you, Leek. Call your lawyer if it'll make you feel better. We can make the questioning as formal as you want."

Leek sipped tea. "If I call some lawyer, it becomes like a serious thing, huh?"

"You break the law, it's serious," Decker said.

"I'll talk to you if you use a notebook instead of that thing. It makes me nervous."

Decker looked at the recorder, then placed it in his pocket. He pulled out his notebook and wrote down the date, time, and place of the interview.

"So talk to me, Mr. McKay. Tell me about your investment strategy. I'm always interested in tips from the experts."

McKay said nothing.

Decker said, "Just get the first sentence out. It's easier after that."

McKay sighed. Softly, he said, "If you're looking to find big time on me, forget it."

"What's big time, Leek?"

"Not me, that's for sure. All I ever did was penny-ante stuff—nickels and dimes."

"Lita was talking more like hundreds."

"Lita talks too much, period! Doesn't make a difference to her—nickels versus hundreds. She'd have never seen the money anyway. It'd just line the pockets of the board of directors at the home."

"Embezzling is illegal, Leek."

"I didn't *embezzle* anything, Sergeant. If some of the folks asked me to hold some pocket change for them, how's that embezzling?"

"Okay. Then show me the paperwork, Leek. All the accounts you've opened for your old folks. All the transactions you made in *their* names."

The nurse closed his eyes and didn't answer.

"Not to mention that as a contingency for staying in the home, occupants are required to sign documents surrendering all their assets."

McKay's eyes snapped open. "And you think that's fair?"

"I think some homes do take advantage of the fact that no one wants the burden of caring for the aged. But they work within legal bounds. If I don't like their rules, I don't have to choose them. But they're a far cry from people who use charm to cheat the elderly out of their savings."

"Cheat the elderly?" McKay whispered fiercely. "Let me ask you something, Sergeant Self-righteous. Do you deal with the *elderly* on a day-to-day basis? Do you act like a *jackass* just to get them to smile? Do you sneak them extra food or even sometimes buy them candy out of your measly salary, because food's the only thing these people got now? Do you wipe their spittle? Change their diapers? Bathe their decrepit bodies after they've vomited over themselves?"

"I've been vomited on by drunks, Leek. I've been cursed at, spit at, punched, clawed, and I've even been shot. It's part of my job."

"Yeah, it's my *job*," McKay retorted. "But there're a lot of ways for nurses to make a living. I do it 'cause the elderly are the garbage of society. I do it 'cause I took care of my own grandparents and understand the pain. So maybe I do pocket a twenty now and then. I know a ton of private nurses who've built nest eggs by kypping a little here and there over the years. Think the folks don't know about it? Sure they do. But they don't *care*! Long as *someone*'s caring for them. What I get from them is nothing more than a tip for my services."

"It's illegal, Leek."

"So *arrest* me! Then you go to the home and tell them you locked up Leek McKay and see what the old folks say."

Decker sipped his tea and waited.

"Good old Lita." McKay shook his head. "Can't keep her mouth shut. I should have come down on her, but I didn't want to screw her out of her only fantasy."

"You're a regular white knight."

Again the bodybuilder started to say something, but stopped. "What's the use? I'm just wasting my breath."

"Who else knows about your extracurricular investment activities besides the folks you take tips from?"

"No one. Well, that's not true. You do."

"What about Tandy Roberts?"

"What about Tandy?" McKay shrugged.

"How long has she known about it?"

The nurse was silent.

"Protecting her?" Decker said. "Or is she protecting you?"

A spark passed through McKay's ailing, dull eyes. Decker studied his face closely.

"You knew Tandy had a terrible crush on you. As long as you played interested in her, you knew she wouldn't drop your secret. Unfortunately, you had to do more than just *play* interested in her."

The nurse whitened.

Decker said, "How long were you two lovers?"

"God, do we really have to get into this?"

"How long?"

"About a year." McKay bit back a gag. "It was disgusting. Like going to bed with a hog."

Decker said, "When did it stop? Or did it?"

"Nah, it's all over. It stopped when she started buffing out. Actually, it stopped before that. Too bad. I wouldn't mind now."

Decker looked up from his notebook. "What do you mean, stopped before she started buffing out?"

McKay hesitated. "It's not important. The main thing is, her interest in me stopped. She doesn't care about me or what I do—legal or otherwise. I'm irrelevant to her now that she looks good and acts normal. Just my luck."

"Leek, why did you stop sleeping with her?"

"You mean why did *she* stop sleeping with *me*. She initiated everything. For your information, it has nothing to do with my extracurricular activities."

"Tell me about it anyway."

The nurse sighed. "Can you get me another tea first?"

Decker bought him another tea, noticing Leek had also finished the cinnamon bun. "Are you hungry?"

"How about a whole-wheat roll and some jam, if you don't mind."

Decker said, "Talking's good for your complexion, Leek. You look a whole lot better."

"I hate to say this, but I feel a whole lot better."

Decker bought him a roll. "Confession's good for the soul. Tell me why you and Tandy stopped your affair."

"She stopped it when it was clear to her that no matter *what* the circumstances were, I wasn't going to *marry* her."

"What the circumstances were . . ." Decker repeated. "Meaning you knocked her up?"

McKay slapped some strawberry jam onto his wheat roll and took a big bite. "I don't know how it happened. I was careful. I mean real, real *careful*! Nothing without a rubber—two rubbers. It was the last thing on earth I wanted. We didn't even *do* it that much. And half of the times when we did do it, I couldn't even come. I don't know *how* she became pregnant."

"All it takes is one time."

"Yep."

"What happened to the baby?"

"I don't know. I assumed she got an abortion. I gave her money. I don't ever remember seeing her pregnant. But she was so fat, she could have been and I wouldn't have noticed. If she did have the baby, she must have given it up for adoption. I know she doesn't have kids now."

Decker tapped his pencil against his notebook. "Let me ask you this, Leek. She stopped sleeping with you after you made it clear you wouldn't marry her even if she had the baby, right?"

"Right."

"So what did she say? I don't want to sleep with you anymore?"

"It wasn't that honest a thing. She just started avoiding me . . . stopped inviting me over to her apartment. That's where we did it. I certainly wasn't going to have her over to my place."

"And weren't you worried?"

"Worried? Are you kidding, I was *relieved*!"

Decker said, "You weren't concerned that she'd reveal your investment scheme when you turned her down matrimonially?"

McKay stopped eating. Once again, his complexion took on a sickly shade of pewter.

Decker said, "As a matter of fact, Leek, I see Tandy getting very angry and threatening to *expose* you—which she obviously didn't do. Now I *have* to ask myself why."

"Maybe she felt loyal to me," the nurse whispered. "Old feelings die hard."

"Maybe you offered her another incentive to keep her mouth shut. Like you knew she was in trouble because she was misrepresenting herself as an RN when she was only an LVN."

"Shit—"

"Or maybe Tandy wasn't even an LVN," Decker said. "Maybe she faked *everything*. Maybe the home found out about it and was going to fire her. But you talked them into laying her off. And then you stole Tandy's records so no one would ever be able to trace her problems back to the home."

McKay covered his face.

"But you know hell hath no fury like a woman scorned," Decker said. "Burying her problems still wasn't enough for her. So you made her a final offer that would help her tremendously in her career as a 'nurse.' "

"I think I'm going to be sick," McKay said. "Excuse me."

Decker watched McKay race to the back of the grocery store. He followed him to the outside of the bathroom, hearing the nurse retch. After a minute or so, McKay stepped out of the men's room, his eyes slits oozing tears at the corners.

"You don't look well," Decker said.

"Can you take me back to my car now?"

"Let's sit for a moment longer. Give you a chance to catch your breath." Decker led him back to the bakery and sat him on a chair. "How long have you been letting Tandy use your license number?"

McKay looked defeated. He whispered, " 'Bout a year and a half."

"Why didn't Tandy just make up a license number?"

"Because they're specifically coded. If she accidentally used someone else's by mistake and that someone caught on and exposed her, she'd be in trouble. Why take chances?"

"Don't employers check the numbers on nurses' applications with the board?"

"They're supposed to, but they usually don't unless there's a reason to do it. I never complained, so the number was clean. And just for your information, Tandy *is* an LVN. It's pretty hard faking nursing without *any* training."

"Are you kidding?" Decker said. "People have faked being doctors, even *surgeons*. That's a hell of a lot trickier than being a nurse. I can't understand how an institution wouldn't at least cross-reference the license number with the Board of Examiners."

"Why bother unless the nurse was problematic? So far as I know, Tandy never created any problems."

"So far as you know," Decker said.

McKay sighed. "So far as I know."

Marge was sitting on the living-room sofa, reading the morning paper, when Decker walked into his house. She lowered the newsprint to her lap.

"The baby nurse has informed me that Rina and Hannah went down for a nap about . . ." Marge checked her watch. "About an hour ago. What is it, three? You're late."

"Good interviewing takes time. Where is Nora?"

"In the kitchen preparing tonight's dinner—eggplant Parmesan, garlic bread, salad, and baked apples with raisins and sour cream for dessert. Makes my mouth water just repeating the menu."

"Would you like to join us for dinner?"

"Nah, that's okay. I'm sure you'd like a little privacy."

"Privacy?" Decker let out an incredulous laugh. "Under one roof, I've got a wife, two daughters, two sons, a baby nurse, a mother-in-law, a father-in-law, a dog, and a new kitten. To me, privacy is a word in the dictionary. You're welcome to stay if the mood hits."

"You've twisted my arm."

"I take it Hollander found you without a hitch?"

"Smooth as silk."

"Where is Ms. Roberts at the moment?" Decker asked.

"She left directly from the gym to Tujunga Memorial—presumably she's working the three-to-eleven shift. Don't worry, Mike's playacting the janitor at the hospital. He's keeping watch on her in case she decides to filch something—human or otherwise."

"Good."

"So what did Leek McKay have to say for himself?"

Decker sat on a buckskin chair. Ginger, who had been in the kitchen, made her entrance, prancing over to Decker, then sitting at his feet. He petted the setter's gleaming fur. "Good to see you still remember me."

The sarcasm went unnoticed by the animal.

He said, "Well, he admitted embezzling petty cash from the old folks. He also admitted looking the other way when Tandy started using his license number."

"What about lifting Tandy's employment records from Golden Valley?"

"He claims he doesn't have them. He doesn't know what happened to them. I told him that wasn't what I asked. I asked him if he filched them. He hemmed and hawed, and the upshot is, he thinks Tandy lifted the records herself."

"How?"

"Leek didn't want to go into detail. Lord only knows why. He wasn't shy about confessing his other crimes. As far as involvement in the kidnapping goes, I don't have any evidence that points in his direction."

"But we've got him for embezzlement."

"Yes, we do. But now that we've got him, I'm not quite sure what I want to do with him."

"What do you mean?"

"His arrest record is clean. Which means if the case goes to court, his lawyer'll plead *nolo contendere*. Which means he'll probably be sentenced to probation. First thing he'll have to do is pay back the money he took from the old folks. Unfortunately, it won't go to them, it'll go to the home. He'll probably have to do some community service as well—which in a way, he does anyway. He arranges entertainment for the elderly at the home; he's in charge of the home's Halloween party, Christmas party, Easter party—"

"Pete, you are *not* going to let him get away with embezzlement?"

"I'm just saying if he's sentenced, he'll undoubtedly lose his license. Which means the home'll lose a nurse the old folks are crazy about."

"Decker, the sleaze can't break the law."

"I'm not suggesting for a moment that we let old Leek get off scot-free. But not everything has to bollix up in the courts."

"Pete—"

"McKay and I took a nice little drive over to the home after confession time was over. I set him up with one of the home's management and told him to spill out his dirty deeds. Then I left. I'm waiting to hear back from them. If they decide not to bring charges against him, what case do I have?"

"You can press them to charge McKay."

"If it's necessary."

"I don't believe I'm hearing this!"

"I also told McKay to place a call to the Board of Nurses' Examiners. Tell the board that he suspects Tandy Roberts of using his license number—"

"But he *knew* she was doing it."

"So he suddenly got an attack of conscience. Let's concentrate on what we know. Leek gave Tandy his license number as a way to guarantee her silence. She knew about his embezzling . . . discovered it by talking to the old folks. At first, Tandy used the information to blackmail him into an affair. Eventually, he got her pregnant."

"*He* got her pregnant, too?" Marge shook her head. "That's three pregnancies. Girl's a fertile Myrtle."

"Three pregnancies?" Decker said. "When was number two?"

"When she was eighteen, still living in New York."

"How'd you find *that* out?"

Not wanting to rat on Cindy, Marge smiled mysteriously. "We all have our sources."

"Margie . . ."

"It's not important how I found out. What is important is we now know this girl, Tandy Roberts, supposedly lost three babies in a relatively short period of time."

Decker said, "Lost them? Leek said she aborted."

"Lost? Aborted? Who knows?" Marge shrugged. "Tandy sounds unstable to begin with. First starving herself, then eating her way to obesity. And she used to talk to herself. If we throw in all these lost or aborted babies, it adds up to one psychologically compromised girl."

"You interviewed her, Margie. Did she seem really crazy?"

Marge tapped her foot. "Actually, she seemed very sane. A typical self-obsessed California girl."

"So where does that leave us?"

"We have a motive," Marge said. "Tandy doesn't have children and neither does Marie Bellson, who was going through menopause. They were once great friends. Maybe they became great friends again with a common goal. They both cracked at the same time, each one working up the other one until they both went nuts and did the ultimate grievous sin. Isn't there a psychological term for that—two nuts working each other up?"

"Yeah, two nuts working each other up."

Marge gave Decker a sour look. "I'm sure they're in cahoots together. I just *feel* it."

"Their bond to each other being they both lost babies."

"Yep," Marge said. "We've got to start looking into Tandy's background. She was born in Berkeley, moved to Manhattan when she was a kid, had a lot of connections in the fashion industry. . . ." She paused, then said, "I'll do a complete background on her. In the meantime, what are you going to do about Leek? You can't let this little piece of *navel lint* get away with stealing."

"I'm going to let the home decide how they want to handle it. If they want to prosecute, I'll testify to back them up. But if they want to handle it more discreetly, I've got better things to do than come down on a nurse who changes bedpans for the elderly. It's in the home's hands."

"I don't understand you!" Marge was frustrated.

"Drop it, Marge!"

They both were quiet for a moment. Then Decker said, "Okay, so you'll do a thorough background check on Tandy. See if we can dig up more links between her and Marie. But we'd better move quickly. The feds were called in this morning."

"You're kidding!"

"Wish I was. They just can't wait to play big shot."

"Bastards!" Marge tossed the newspaper off her lap and began to pace. "How about this for a link, Pete? What if Marie was Tandy's mom and gave her up for adoption?"

"The timing doesn't work, Marge. Marie was still living at home with her mother, and Lita's *sure* her daughter never became pregnant as a teenager."

"And you trust Lita's memory?"

"No, not entirely. But she seemed cogent."

The front door opened. Ginger stood and wagged her tail, jumping on Cindy as she came through the door. With Cindy was a girl around the same age, both of them slightly sunburned and with wet heads.

Cindy kissed her father's cheek. "You remember Lisa Goldberg, don't you, Dad?"

"Hi, Lisa," Decker said. "How are you doing?"

"Not bad." Lisa smiled and shrugged shyly.

"We went swimming," Cindy explained. "I just came back to change. We're having a one-year mini–high school reunion. A bunch of us are going to dinner and the movies tonight. I should be home at one, maybe two at the latest."

"Take the car phone," Decker said.

"My *lifeline* to the outside world."

"Don't be fresh."

"I know it's because you care." Cindy sneaked a look to Marge, who winked. "See you all later."

As Cindy left, she mouthed a thank-you to Marge. Decker caught it. "What's that all about?"

"I'll tell you later."

"No, tell me now. What are you and Cindy planning be-hind my—" Decker interrupted himself. "I just thought of something. About two years ago, when Tandy was pregnant with Leek's baby, she was still very good friends with Ma-rie, right?"

"I think so," Marge said. "Why?"

Decker smiled slyly. "You and my daughter can keep secrets—so can I." He picked up the phone and, as soon as the line connected, asked for Dr. Meecham, telling the re-ceptionist his call was an emergency. Meecham picked up the call within minutes.

"What's up, Sergeant?"

"I'm about to ask you to compromise your ethics again."

"Sergeant—"

"It's less painful if you remember a baby's life may be at stake. Listen, let's just play it theoretical. . . ."

"Sergeant, I thought you said this was an emergency. C'mon! I'm a busy man!"

"A missing infant is an emergency."

"Get on with it, Sergeant."

Decker knew he was putting Meecham in a precarious position and felt bad about it. But not too bad.

"Suppose I assume that about maybe two years ago, your patient, Marie Bellson, brought you a young, distressed obese woman who had a problem."

Meecham paused. "Go on."

"Let's just suppose that this young obese woman was in the family way and came to you for a possible termination of pregnancy."

"I don't think that's a good supposition at all, Sergeant."

Decker waited a beat. "Okay, perhaps this girl may have had her pregnancy terminated by someone else. Maybe he even did a botched job, and Marie brought the girl in to you to fix up someone else's butchery."

"Interesting theory. Unfortunately, it's fiction."

Decker tried to organize his thoughts. "Okay, suppose this obese woman miscarried—"

"I don't like that supposition, either."

Decker thought. Tandy didn't miscarry; she didn't abort. That left just one more option. "Perhaps you became this imaginary young woman's obstetrician and delivered her child at term."

"Perhaps I didn't."

"Maybe someone else did?"

"No."

Confused, Decker was silent. Then he said, "Thanks for your forbearance, Doc."

"I'm sorry I couldn't help you with your dilemma. Now I really must go." Meecham paused a moment. "On a conversational note, Sergeant, did I tell you I attended a very interesting lecture last month as part of my continuing education? It was on *Pseudocyesis*."

"Pseudo—what?" Decker took out his notebook. "How do you spell that?"

"Look it up, Sergeant," Meecham said.

And with Meecham's parting line, Decker was on the receiving end of a dial tone.

THIRTY-ONE

"**P**SEUDOCARP, PSEUDOCARPOUS, PSEUDOCLASSIC, PSEUDO-morph, pseudonym . . ." Decker bit his lower lip. "Pseud-onymous, pseudopod, pshaw, psi . . . what is this *bullshit* Stan's giving me? How can I look it up if I can't find or spell it?" He picked up another dictionary and flung it open, flipping through the pages until he came to the *P*'s. "Pseudocyesis . . . Do you think *cyesis* is with an *s* or a *c*?"

Cindy and her friend Lisa came into the living room. "It's with a *c*, Dad."

Decker looked up. "You know what pseudocyesis means?"

"It's false pregnancy."

Decker put down the dictionary. "Where'd you learn about that?"

Cindy said, "English history. Queen Mary Tudor, better known as Bloody Mary, had a false pregnancy. She was married to Philip the Second of Spain, who was much younger than she was. A couple of months later the State announced that the queen was with child, to the cheers of her good countrymen. After a full ten months of so-called pregnancy, Mary gave birth to a lot of bloat and gas. Philip was not pleased. He left England for his beloved Spain and never returned."

Decker shook his head. "Just shows the difference between a high school and college education."

"And here you were, wondering about the high price of my tuition," Cindy said.

Decker thought about that: fifteen grand a year to learn about Bloody Mary's psychological problems.

Marge said, "By false pregnancy, do you mean the woman fakes being pregnant? Or does she honestly *think* she's pregnant?"

Cindy shrugged. "I don't know. I learned about it in history, not in psychology." She turned to Lisa. "You're pre-med."

"I'm still mastering the Krebs cycle, Cin," Lisa answered. "You need a medical textbook. Or just call up any ob gyn. They should have the information you're looking for."

"Who had a false pregnancy?" Cindy's eyes brightened mischievously. "Is it our friend?"

"Don't you just love how kids butt into conversations?" Decker said. "Good-bye, Cindy. Have a pleasant evening."

"I didn't *butt in*. You *engaged* me."

"Cindy . . ." Marge said.

"Don't worry, Marge, I remember my *promise*."

"What promise?" Decker asked.

"I promised Marge I wouldn't interfere with your investigation."

"When was this?"

"Now who's butting into whose conversation?"

Lisa said, "I'll wait outside for you, Cin."

"Good idea." After Lisa closed the front door, Cindy said, "You know, Dad, you have a double standard. . . ."

"Cut it, Cynthia. You and Marge are keeping something from me. I want to know what it is *right now*!"

Cindy ran her toe along the seam of the Navaho rug. "I paid a visit to Silver's Gym. . . ."

"You *what*!" Decker homed in on Marge. "And you *let* her?"

"I saw her coming out, not going in."

"But you didn't *tell* me."

Marge shrugged. "No, I didn't, Pete."

"How could you do that!" He glared at Cindy. "And how could *you* do that! Between the two of you, I don't know who I'm more pissed off at."

"Why don't you save your anger for assholes like Leek McKay?" Marge said.

Decker remembered Rina was sleeping and lowered his voice. "What exactly are you saying, Marge? You're keeping secrets about my daughter from me because you're pissed at the way I handled Leek McKay? That makes a lot of sense."

"It's not that," Marge retorted. "You're frustrated, and you're taking it out on the *wrong* people—"

"Hell, yeah, I'm frustrated. Especially when my partner colludes behind my back—"

"I wasn't colluding—"

"The hell—"

"I'll see you guys later," Cindy said.

"Don't you move a muscle, young lady," Decker said. "I'm not done with you."

"Daddy, Marge dressed me down enough for the both of you. Believe me, I'm very sorry I butted into your affairs. It was dumb but I did it because I cared. I cared about the baby, I cared about Lourdes Rodriguez, I cared because it could have been Hannah. I almost blew Marge's tail on Tandy, and I feel very foolish about it. I didn't ask Marge to keep it a secret, but she did. And I appreciate that—her trust in me. I was going to tell you. I was just trying to find the right time."

Cindy sank into one of the buckskin chairs. "Stop growling at me, Daddy. I'm just as worn out as you are."

Decker folded his arms across his chest and tapped his foot. Finally, he blew out air. "What did you possibly hope to accomplish by going to Silver's?"

"In my naïveté, I thought *maybe* I could get Tandy to talk to me. And she *did* talk to me. She talked a lot. Unfortunately, she didn't talk about Marie Bellson or Caitlin Rodriguez. But she did say she lost two babies in New York."

With clenched teeth, Decker said to Marge, "So *that's* where you picked up Tandy's second pregnancy."

"We all have our friendlies." Marge's smile was tight. "So what do we have? Two pregnancies in New York and a false one that Meecham was referring to."

"Maybe all of them were false," Decker said. "The woman has been described to us as a fruitcake. Who knows what the hell we're dealing with?" To Cindy, he said, "What else did you and *Tandy* talk about?"

"Divorce—her parents' divorce," Cindy corrected herself. "She was really bitter over it, still grieving over the ordeal like it happened yesterday."

"When did it happen?" Decker asked.

"When she was young. I think around five."

Decker paused. "Tandy's twenty-five . . . the divorce would have been around . . . what? About twenty years ago?"

"I guess."

"Marie Bellson would have been around twenty back then," Decker said. "Cindy, did Tandy say where she was from?"

"*Oh, no!*" Marge exclaimed. "I must be the world's biggest *moron*! Marie Bellson went to *school* in Berkeley." She faced Cindy. "Didn't you tell me Tandy's father was a *prof* at Berkeley?"

"Yeah . . ."

"A prof who couldn't keep his *pants* on?"

"Yeah."

"Pete, Lita Bellson said her daughter screwed everything in sight, including professors. Betcha Professor Roberts was one of her past amours."

"The connection between Tandy and Marie," Cindy said.

"I told you the girl was a natural," Marge said.

Decker tossed her a dirty look, which Marge returned in kind. Cindy felt uncomfortable, knowing she was the reason behind the tension in the room.

She cleared her throat and said, "Once Tandy started on her parents, it was hard to get her to stop. She *hates* them. Just puts them down mercilessly. She kept repeating how horrible they were to her, always screaming at her, telling her how bad she was for getting pregnant."

"Who's 'they'?" Decker asked. "Wasn't she living only with her mother?"

Cindy just shrugged. Marge said, "Pete, you know we have Tandy and Marie living in the *same* neighborhood when two traumatic things happened in both their lives."

"What's that?" Cindy put her hand over her mouth. "Or aren't I allowed to ask?"

Decker felt a wave of resignation wash over his body. "Tandy's parents got divorced, and Marie supposedly lost a baby around the same time. Not to change the subject, Cynthia, but I think your friend's waiting for you."

"Omigod, I forgot about Lisa!" Cindy kissed her father. "I'm very sorry, Daddy."

"It's all right." He gave his daughter a bear hug. "It's only because I love you so damn much."

"I know."

"Are you going to keep your promise?"

"I swear."

"Good," Decker said. "Now go have some fun."

"Sure. Bye."

"Cindy, I may have a couple of questions later on for you, okay?"

Cindy grinned. "You call the shots, Father." She bounced out the door but remembered to close it quietly.

Decker glared at Marge, who returned his angry stare. She said, "If you want me to apologize for not telling you about Cindy, forget it. She's an adult, Pete. I treat her like an adult. It wasn't my place to fink on her."

"You don't understand, Marge," Decker said. "It isn't your fault, because you've never had kids. But your kid is your kid no matter how old she is. And the worrying never stops. Remember how angry you were at your father for not telling you he had surgery for cancer?"

"Sure, I was angry. But it was his choice. He chose not to tell me; he suffered the consequences. If Cindy chooses not to tell you, she'll suffer the consequences."

"You don't understand."

"So if I'm so dense, why don't we stop plowing old ground and get on with the case?"

Decker sat on the sofa. "Fine. Get on with the case."

Marge clasped her hands. A fog of hostility sat between them, but she knew they'd get over it. Just as soon as they concentrated on the case. It was bugging the shit out of both of them. "We have Marie and Tandy in Berkeley. And Marie screwing everyone, conceivably—no pun intended—even Tandy's father."

Decker pulled out his notebook. "Conceivably."

Marge smiled. "We have two traumatic incidents happening to both of them at the same time. So how do we connect the two?"

"Start with the obvious." Decker tried to control the tartness of his voice. Man, he was *pissed*. "Tandy's father was a lech, Marie was a wild chick. They had an affair."

"The affair led to Tandy's parents getting divorced and possibly to Marie Bellson's pregnancy," Marge stated formally.

"I like it."

Stiffly, Marge gave a little smile. "Thank you."

"You're welcome." Decker suddenly bit back a laugh. "All right. Let's assume Tandy's all pissed off at her parents' divorce. And assume that Tandy knew that her father's affair with Marie was what led to the divorce."

"Then Tandy would be pissed off at *Marie*," Marge said. "Not acting like Marie was her best friend."

"Maybe she was acting all this time, Marge. Maybe Tandy had planned from the start to get Marie."

"Pete, the trauma happened twenty years ago. Unless Tandy's the original *demon child*, I can't picture a five-year-old hatching a two-decade plot. Then we'd have to assume she knew at five that she was going to purposely become a nurse, meet Marie, become her best friend, then pin a kidnapping and murder on her."

"You're right. It's absurd."

"At least you're capable of giving me *some* credit."

"I give you *credit*, Dunn. But you've got to see it from

my perspective. You and my daughter—two women out of the four I trust implicitly—are keeping *secrets* from me."

"Rina's the third—who's the fourth?"

"My mother. Now what the hell difference does *that* make? Do you see my point, or don't you?"

"I see your point. Can we move on now, please?"

"You brought it up. Why do women bring up things, then drop them when they hear what they don't want to hear?"

"Pete—"

"Okay, okay, I'll cool it." Decker smoothed his mustache. "Even if Marie and Tandy's father had an affair, what does that have to do with the price of eggs in Outer Mongolia?"

Marge said, "Let's suppose this. Suppose Tandy's father—"

"Guy have a first name?"

"Geoffrey spelled G-e-o-f-f-r-e-y."

"Veddy English."

"He's Cuban," Marge said.

"How'd you find that out?"

"Cindy."

"My daughter has become a wealth of information." Decker paused. "You think it's a coincidence that the kidnapped baby was a Latina?"

"That's an interesting observation."

"I don't know how it fits, but it's interesting. So how did Cuban parents come to give their son a name like Geoffrey?"

"Caitlin isn't exactly a Hispanic name. Immigrants adopt Anglo names to acculturate." Marge flipped the pages of her notebook. "Actually, I think Tandy told Cindy her *father* had changed his name."

"Geoffrey Roberts," Decker said. "A prof. Think he still lives in Berkeley?"

"We could find out."

"Let's do that," Decker said. "Where were we?"

"Still assuming that Marie Bellson and Geoffrey Roberts had an affair."

"Okay. Now how about this? Suppose little Tandy, at the age of five, was made aware of this affair by Mom's yelling."

"Lots of yelling."

"*Especially* if we assume that Geoffrey Roberts knocked up Marie. A lot of women can tolerate indiscretion. But getting the other woman pregnant?"

"Fireworks," Marge said.

"Yep. I can picture the irate wife screaming it for all the world to hear. 'You f-ing bastard, you not only slept with the little tramp, you got her pregnant.' That kind of thing."

"Sounds good."

"So let's assume that Tandy, even at five, knew that a Bellson, and/or Marie Bellson's *pregnancy*, was the reason behind her parents' divorce. It traumatized her, but maybe she was able to hide it. Kids can hide their pain well. Suppose she could deal with her past by ignoring it. Putting it out of her mind. Then, lo and behold, at fifteen, *she* got pregnant. And all the old traumatic feelings began to resurface."

" 'A stage-mom bitch,' " Marge read from her notes. "That's how Tandy described her mother to Cindy. You know, maybe Tandy's pregnancy brought out old feelings for Mom as well as for daughter. The pregnancy ruined Mom's life once, now another pregnancy was ruining it again. Especially if stage-mom bitch had a lot invested in Tandy's modeling career. Can't you picture Mom screaming at her, 'You've just *ruined your entire life*,' etc?"

Decker paused a moment. *She seemed so upset when she talked to herself.* "Tandy talking to herself? Or was she actually talking to someone else who was yelling at her?"

"She was hearing voices?"

Decker said, "Could be."

Marge said, "Well then, suppose the voice also told her about another pregnancy that once ruined her entire life— Bellson getting pregnant by Pop. Too much trauma for her to deal with. She quit modeling, moved out West, and began to eat her anxiety away. Soon she had ballooned to three hundred pounds."

Decker said, "Wow!"

"Food is love," Marge said. "Then she met Marie. And . . ."

"And what?"

"And I don't know. I'm asking you."

"I don't know, either," Decker said. "They became best friends? Like you said before, it doesn't make sense. Tandy should have *hated* Marie."

"Unless *demon child* suddenly reappeared as demon young adult. And the woman began to have demented conversations with herself. Saying things like, I'm going to find and screw Marie Bellson if it's the last thing I do."

Decker said, "So you're assuming Tandy recognized Marie Bellson as the evil woman who caused her parents' divorce twenty years ago. Marge, Tandy was only *five*."

"Maybe Tandy didn't recognize her face, but she recognized the name. Maybe Mom never let her forget it."

Decker held up a finger. "You know, it could be it was the other way around. Maybe *Marie* recognized *Tandy*. She was the adult twenty years ago. Certainly, she'd have recognized Tandy's name if she had an affair with her father."

Marge nodded. "Then Marie saw this young, obese schizo woman who was once the cute little daughter of a man she'd loved. It tugged on her heartstrings. Bellson took Tandy in as if she were her own—making up for the past, so to speak."

"*Especially* if we assume the kid Marie lost—or aborted—was Geoffrey Roberts's child," Decker said.

"Maybe they both recognized each other, but neither one said anything. Both keeping the skeletons inside the closet. Marie out of guilt, Tandy out of crazed hatred."

"Then what happened?" Decker said.

"Tandy had a false pregnancy," Marge went on. "She longed for a baby. But being more than a little nuts, she took one from *Marie's* nursery. Because she knew Marie wouldn't fink on her *out of guilt*."

Decker said, "Sounds good except *Tandy's still here acting normal*. Where are Marie and the baby?"

Both of them were silent.

"Our theories hinge on a link between Marie and Geoffrey Roberts," Decker continued. "Marie's gone, but maybe Geoff's still around. Let's make a few calls to Berkeley. Let our fingers do the walking. Cheaper than a trip up north. The department would approve."

Marge nodded. "You know, Pete, if Tandy is really a certified psycho, we'll never get a conviction even if she did murder Lily."

"A conviction isn't what concerns me at the moment. If the voice told her to kidnap and kill once, it can tell her to kill again."

"The baby?"

"The baby."

THIRTY-TWO

IT WAS COOL.

She was in control.

She was in control.

Police can't get her.

She was saved.

Jesus saved her.

Jesus loved her.

Jesus loved everyone.

He loved good and bad. Friend and foe.

Even Auntie.

Even the *voices*!
Jesus loved *her*, 'cause she had the control.

Marge hung up the phone and called out, "Got us a minor problem, Rabbi."

Decker emerged from the kitchen, cradling Hannah with one hand, shaking a bottle of sugar water with the other. "What now?"

"According to Berkeley's payroll department, the last paycheck made out to Geoffrey Roberts was over two years ago. The secretary gave me Roberts's last-known home address and telephone number. Guess what?"

"It's out-of-date."

"No current address in the Bay Area, no forwarding address, either. I called the squad room and asked MacPherson to see if he could get Geoffrey Roberts on-line with the computer. I've also called Santa Cruz and Davis, thinking maybe he switched to another UC campus in northern California. So far, nothing."

Decker sat down on his sofa and offered a sugar-coated nipple to Hannah. She accepted it eagerly. "When's MacPherson due to call back?"

"Any minute."

The phone rang.

"How's that for predicting the future?" Marge picked up the receiver, listened, and laughed. "It's one of your sons."

Taking the phone with his free hand, Decker winked. "So much for your powers of the supernatural." Into the receiver, he said, "Yo. Hey, Sam, what's up ... what time will you be done? Sure I can pick you guys up. No prob. She's fine. Hannah's fine, too. How was schoo— Okay, I understand. We'll talk later. Love you both."

Decker hung up. Marge kicked off her shoes and placed her bare feet on the ottoman. "Did I tell you that Morrison scheduled a meeting with the feds and us tomorrow morning at ten?"

Decker was silent. Then he said, "Well, we're going nowhere. All we have at this point is a couple of lame theories."

"I think of them as inventive," Marge said.

Decker smiled at his little daughter. "At least we've got theories. With no way to verify them unless we find Professor Geoff."

The phone rang again. Marge picked it up. It was Paul MacPherson.

"I got Geoffrey Roberts on the monitor—his Social Security number, his tax I.D. . . . all that stuff. Unfortunately, I don't think it's gonna do you any good."

"Why's that, Paul?"

"Last known address on his tax statement was the one you gave me in Berkeley, Marge. It appears that Mr. Roberts hasn't filed taxes since he left the bastion of radicalism."

Marge swore under her breath and recapped the message to Decker. Into the phone, she said, "He must be living on some income. Some pension or something. Even if he's just living off the interest from his savings, you've got to pay taxes on them. Banks send statements on interest-bearing accounts to the IRS."

"Well, the computer doesn't have anything listed," MacPherson said.

"Did the guy die?" Decker suggested. Marge relayed the question to MacPherson.

"Tell the Rabbi I'm one step ahead of him. I can't find a death certificate. What you got is a phantom."

"Thanks for trying, Paul." Marge cut the line. "He says we've got a phantom."

"Maybe Tandy knows where he is."

"Should we ask her?"

"*No.*" Decker was emphatic. "If she's nuts, she might bolt or do worse. I don't want to spook her. We'll tell our suspicions to the feds and let them decide if they want to question her. We've still got a couple of hours to handle the case the way *we* want to do it."

Marge said, "From the summary Cindy gave me of her conversation with Tandy, it sounded like Tandy thought her dad was still in Berkeley."

"Marge, *someone* in the English department at Berkeley had to have *known* him."

Rummaging through her notes, Marge found the phone number of Berkeley and asked for the English department. Ten minutes later, after a half-dozen false starts, she was put on hold once again.

"I'm waiting for them to locate a guy named Bert Stine. He used to team-teach with Geoffrey Roberts."

"Good," Decker said. "Did you ever get through to Stan Meecham?"

"Yep. And as you predicted, the doctor wasn't happy to talk to me. But he did explain the condition to me. And after considerable hemming and hawing, he admitted that Marie did bring Tandy to his office. He only admitted that because he said Tandy never returned, so officially he doesn't consider her a patient."

"When did Marie bring her in?"

"Around two years ago . . . in November. Back when she and Marie were as thick as thieves."

"So tell me about pseudocyesis."

"The way he described it, it sounds like an unconscious mental thing. The woman actually convinces herself she's pregnant. She stops menstruating, her breasts and cervix enlarge, she can even experience morning sickness. It's usually found in adolescents, but not exclusively—"

Marge held out the palm of her hand and spoke into the phone.

"Professor Stine? This is Detective Dunn of the Los Angeles Police Depart— No, no one is in trouble. I'm just trying to locate Professor Geoffrey Roberts, and I understand you used to team-teach with him?"

Decker looked at her expectantly. Marge rolled her eyes.

"No, I can assure you he's not in any trouble . . . at least as far as my business is concerned."

Marge gnashed her teeth.

"No, I'm not deliberately *prying* into anyone's affairs. At the moment, I'm just trying to *locate* him. . . . No, I don't *know* if he's missing. . . . No, Professor Stine, we don't think he's dead. At least we haven't found a death certificate for him. Do you happen to know where he went after he retired from Berkeley? . . . Well, then after he *left*. . . ."

Again Marge waited.

"Unfortunately, Professor, the nature of my business with him is official. But believe me, I'm not out to cause him any grief. If you could just help me out. Please, it could be very important. Sure, I'll hold."

Decker said, "He's giving you a hard time?"

"A bit police-shy."

"At least he hasn't slammed the receiver in your ear."

"I take that as a very good sign," Marge said. "Hi, Professor . . . He moved to Los Angeles? Do you know *where* in L.A.? No, no, no, that's okay. That's a start. I take it you haven't heard from Professor Roberts in the last two . . . No, that's okay. If he's currently residing in Los Angeles, we'll find him . . . No, he's not in trouble. I do appreciate your help. Thank you very much. Good-bye."

"He's here?" Decker said.

"Stine wasn't absolutely sure that Roberts moved to L.A., but he sounded reasonably certain." Marge stopped talking, then said, "You know, Pete? To hear Stine talk, his tone of voice, it sounded to me like Roberts left Berkeley under a cloud."

Decker gently placed Hannah over his shoulder. "Tandy's father moves to L.A. and becomes a phantom. Marie is Tandy's friend, and she's suddenly a phantom. And we still don't have a thing on *her*."

"First let's find Geoff," Marge said.

Decker knew she was right. "Okay. If you were an English prof, where would you live in the area?"

"Near a major university," Marge said. "I'll check the phone books around UCLA, USC, Cal State Northridge, Cal State Long Beach, Cal State Fullerton . . . in other words, the whole damn area." She stood and smoothed her gray slacks. "You coming with me to the station house?"

"You go ahead. I have to wait for Hannah to burp, then I have to finish her feeding." He smiled. "I don't *have* to finish feeding her. I *want* to finish feeding her. And if the FBI doesn't like it, tough shit!"

* * *

Frustrated and defeated, Decker slid into bed. It was after midnight Friday morning—the Sabbath about twenty hours away. Now he realized why God made a day of rest. He lay on his back, eyes focused on the ceiling, staring at a cobweb that caught the glint of moonlight. He felt a warm hand touch his arm.

"Is she up?" Rina croaked out.

"Who? Hannah?"

"Yes. Is she up?"

"No, honey. Everyone's asleep. Did I wake you? I'm sorry. I tried to be quiet."

Rina turned and faced him. "You didn't wake me, my breasts did. I just got another milk letdown."

"You want me to nurse to relieve the pressure?"

Rina smiled. Decker could see it even in the dark. He said, "You want to express your milk in a bottle. I'll be happy to feed her so you can sleep."

"S'right. I *love* feeding her," Rina said.

Decker was silent. Rina could tell he was disappointed. The baby was a big source of joy for her. No doubt she created pure love in Peter as well.

Rina said, "I suppose I could use the rest. Hand me a bottle and my breast pump."

Decker got up and gave Rina the nursing accoutrements. "Might as well do something useful."

"You're sounding like me." Rina sighed. "You're upset. Talk, Peter."

Decker was silent.

"Please?"

Decker smiled at her. "Morrison decided to turn the case over to the FBI. It's a kidnapping, it's his prerogative. Officially, I can still work on the case, but when there's more than one agency, we step all over each other's toes. I'll let them handle it. It'll be out of my hands."

"You don't sound relieved."

"What can I do?" He shrugged. "I'll give them my notes and my theories—see if they can shed some light on what's going on."

"I'm sorry, Peter."

"Aw, the heck with it. It's only work." Decker smiled. "Main thing is, we've got a beautiful family."

Rina returned his smile. "I'm looking forward to the *shalom nikevah* brunch for Hannah on Sunday. Everybody I've spoken to sounds so excited."

"Brunch . . . you didn't *cancel* it?"

"No. Why should I? The caterer is handling everything. . . ."

"Rina—"

"Peter, this is my *last* baby! Forever! I've done nothing but grieve. Now I want to *celebrate*! Nothing is going to dissuade me!"

"I'm stuck?"

"You're stuck."

Decker ran his hands over his face. "I think you're crazy for doing this."

"Of course I'm crazy. I'm irrational. I don't care."

Decker laughed. "You're smiling. It's good to see you happy."

Rina stopped filling the bottle with breast milk and put it down on the nightstand. "Happy? Let's not overdo it." She smiled. "What would make *you* happy?"

Decker thought about that one. "I'd really like another week on the case."

"*Talk* to Morrison, Peter. Maybe he'll give you a few more days."

"I would if I had something concrete. I can't even find the guy I'm looking for. Marge and I have tried every phone book in the entire southwest region of the state clear down to Baja California. I can't look up every phone book in the country. I'm so damn frustrated!" Decker blew out air. "Ah, don't worry about me, Rina. I've got a couple days off next week before I start Homicide in Devonshire. I'm not going to waste them brooding."

Both of them heard a little peep from the living room. Decker bounced out of bed. "I'll feed her." He snatched the bottle from Rina's nightstand. "I've got fresh warm milk and everything."

"Bring her in here," Rina said. "We'll talk while you feed her."

"That'll be nice." Decker kissed his wife's cheek. "You can tell me all about the brunch . . . tell me how many rabbis are going to bore us to death."

Rina laughed. "Just Rabbi Schulman . . . and maybe a few others. . . ."

"I *knew* it!"

"Friends of the family. How can I not let them say a few words?"

"Knew it! Knew it! *Knew it!*" Decker left the room and came back with a bundle in his arms. "Somebody's wet and hungry. Feed first, then change?"

"I think that's the order of business."

Decker sat and rocked his daughter in his arms as she devoured the bottle of breast milk. A gift so soft and warm . . . The case would have suddenly seemed meaningless, except there was another bundle out there. . . .

Still, there was no crime in being grateful for what you had.

"So I really have to put up with all these rabbis' enlightening words of wisdom?"

Rina thought a moment. "You may doze off during the speeches, Peter. That's acceptable. But you may not snore. It's déclassé."

Decker grabbed the receiver with shaky, sleep-deprived hands.

Marge said, "Wake-up call."

He looked at the clock. "Do you know what time it is?"

" 'Bout quarter to six."

"Obviously, something's on your mind."

"Obviously."

"Hold on," Decker whispered. "Let me put on a bathrobe and take the call in the other room."

He'd been wondering when the fatigue was going to catch up with him, and now he could stop his ruminations. His eyes were heavy, his stomach a whirlpool of acid. He ached from muscles he never knew he had. He picked up the phone in the kitchen.

Marge said, "Remember when I spoke to Bert Stine, I told you it sounded to me as if Geoffrey Roberts left Berkeley under suspicious conditions?"

"Yeah?"

"So what if Roberts has been using an alias?"

"Roberts doesn't have a record."

"That doesn't mean he didn't do something wrong. It just means he hasn't gotten caught."

"Well, if he's using an alias and has started over with a new Social Security number, profession, etcetera, etcetera, we're not going to find him unless he gets caught for something else."

"Pete, remember I said something about Roberts originally being Cuban?"

"So?"

"I think Cindy mentioned that Roberts changed his name to Anglicize himself. What if he went back to using his original name?"

Decker thought about it. "We can't ask Tandy what the original name was."

"I know. I was thinking more like we should check name changes registered in the courts at Berkeley. Trouble is, the official offices don't open until nine. By that time, the case'll be turned over to the FBI."

"So this is why you called me at quarter to six?"

"Wait, there's more," Marge said. "Couldn't sleep to save my soul, so I decided to pull an all-nighter. Bear with me and my far-fetched assumptions."

"Shoot."

"Let's suppose Roberts did Anglicize his name. I figured he'd stick to a name that sounded like Geoffrey Roberts. So I worked backward. I looked at Hispanic surnames that sounded like Roberts—Roberto, Berto, Humberto, Umberto—"

"Those aren't last names. They're first names."

"I found that out. So I started from scratch, went down the *R*'s in the phone book until I found something that sounded Hispanic *and* sounded like Roberts. The closest name I found was Robles. What do you think?"

Decker shrugged. "Roberts . . . Robles. Could be."

"Well, it's all I have. I started checking out all the Robleses, and I found quite a few possibilities. The one I like best is a Geraldo Robles. Geoffrey Roberts . . . Geraldo Robles. *Guess* where he lives, Pete?"

"In Westwood, right near UCLA."

"Even better. What's the closest place ideologically to Berkeley in L.A.?"

"Venice."

"You've got it. Want to take a morning stroll with me down the boardwalk to visit Mr. Robles?"

"Marge, we're talking a *long* shot. We should at least look up this Mr. Robles on our house computer before we barge in on him."

"Pete, we don't have a lot of time. A baby's at stake. Tandy's a possible nutcase who could blow any moment. The feds are taking over soon. Worse comes to worst, we wake up some poor schmuck and apologize profusely. *I'm* going. Are you with me or not?"

"I'll be waiting outside."

"Me and my Honda will see you soon."

THIRTY-THREE

A T SIX-THIRTY IN THE MORNING, THERE WAS PLENTY OF
street parking in Venice, allowing Marge to bypass the public lots that would soon fill with vehicles driven by the
summer beachgoers. She pulled curbside on Rose Avenue
near Speedway, both she and Decker stretching as they
stepped out of her Honda. It was just a short jaunt to the
boardwalk.

The parkway was lined on the eastern side by old apartment houses, storefront boutiques, stall shops, and cafés.
On the west stood the shoreline receding into an endless
stretch of pewter ocean. Cutting through the strand was an
asphalt bike path that meandered through the golden sheet
of sand like a frayed gray ribbon. Not too many bike riders,
skateboarders, or rollerbladers at this hour. But there were
some joggers in all shapes and ages, as well as a number
of unleashed dogs out for their morning constitutional.

Decker was surprised to find *anyone* awake, a reflection
on his own need for sleep. He expected his mood to be
foul, but there was something rejuvenating about the boardwalk. Maybe it was the freshness of sunrise: The giant star
had just popped over the horizon. Yet the air was still cool,
a salty breeze drifting over the waves. Too bad he couldn't
enjoy the scenery.

The boutiques were closed, but some of the cafés had

opened their doors to the breakfast crowd. Today the patrons were prototypical Venice residents—the elderly, students, old-style hippies and arty types who didn't work nine to five. And then there were the homeless, with their life possessions stuffed into plastic bags. They dined side-by-side at outdoor tables, drinking coffee and eating Danish or croissants as they read or stared at the rhythm of the sea.

Park benches were also hot gathering spots for the homeless. Some ate sandwiches out of paper bags; others spooned directly out of cans. An old, hunched black man, weighted down by a mountaineer's backpack, read the morning paper as the people around him kibitzed with each other. Discussions ranged from jocular ribbing to the inequities of politics. Decker sensed a well-formed camaraderie. And, as he and Marge passed by, not one of them asked for a handout. Perhaps it was the realization that at this time of the morning, the crowd could only be locals—people on fixed incomes or no income at all. Why squeeze blood from a turnip?

Decker studied the faces as he looked for Robles's address. Yes, the men and women looked unkempt, uncared for, but they didn't seem depressed. They may have been down, but they weren't out.

Robles's address put them in front of a square apartment building checkerboarded with patio windows. The building was fronted by a cinder-block wall painted in several shades of beige and brown—different colors used to hide graffiti rather than for decoration. Robles's window was covered with drapery. The front door was flecked with peeling white paint and had no knocker or doorbell. Decker used his knuckles.

Immediately, a baby started to wail. Marge gave him a wide grin. She felt excitement down to her toes. "You say a long shot, do you?"

Decker said, "People named Robles are allowed to have babies, Marge."

"Admit it. Your heart's beating."

Racing actually, Decker thought. As much as he tried to remain detached to avoid disappointment, he couldn't help but hope. He knocked again. Finally, a husky, agitated female voice spoke from behind the door, asking who it was.

"Police, ma'am," Marge said. "We'd like a few minutes of your time."

There was a stretch of silence that went on too long. Decker knocked harder. "Police, ma'am! Open up!"

Marge said, "Should we break down the door?"

"Don't have probable cause."

"But the baby's crying."

"That's what babies do," Decker said. "Where's the back door?"

"I don't think there is a back door."

"Well, then she can't go anywhere." Decker pounded on the door. "Police, ma'am. Open the door right now!"

A moment later, the door opened a crack, a small, useless chain still attached from the door to the jamb. The woman asked, "Just what do you want?"

"To ask you a few questions," Marge said.

"So talk."

"Open the door, ma'am," Decker said.

"If I'm going to open the door, I'll need to see identification."

Marge showed her I.D. through the crack in the door. A moment later, the door closed, then opened all the way.

Decker's mouth dropped open.

He was looking at a computer-aged Marie Bellson. Rationally, he knew Marie's mom was in a rest home, but this woman—this woman who *had* to be in her late fifties—was Marie's older clone. Both had long faces with webbing at the corners of the eyes and mouth. Both had wavy lines across the forehead, only this woman's lines were scored deeper. She was built like Marie—long and lean. Only the eyes were different from Marie's. The nurse's were bright green dotted with brown; this woman's eyes were hazel but muddied like silted water.

Who *was* this woman? Was she related to Marie?

The harried woman held a babe in arms who was beet red and had dark, feathery hair. The infant was screaming as the woman rocked her vigorously. She looked at Decker, then smoothed the white terry robe she wore.

"I know why you're here," she declared. "And I intend to fight this on whatever grounds I have available to me. *Typical* bureaucracy!" She held the infant over her shoulder and patted her back. "The baby is *our* flesh and blood. The county has no right to put her up for adoption when she has living relatives. I don't care *what* Tandy's last wishes were."

Decker closed his mouth. "Can we come in . . . is it Mrs. Robles?"

"Henrietta," the woman stated. "Hetty for short, and it's definitely *Roberts*. I never changed it back to Robles. Just because *he* went through a midlife identity crisis doesn't mean *I* have to."

"You're Tandy's mother?" Marge asked.

The woman narrowed her murky eyes. "Let me see your papers again."

"Can we come in?" Decker asked. "Unless you want to conduct an interview so all your neighbors can hear."

Hetty paused a moment, then stepped aside.

The apartment was furnished simply. A couch, a couple of side chairs, and a coffee table holding art and interior-design magazines. The walls were covered with book-shelves that contained reading matter as well as small abstract sculptures and figurines. Resting against the back wall were a small crib and a stack of unopened paper diapers.

"Please try to keep it quiet," Hetty stated. "*His Majesty* is sleeping, and I'd like to keep it that way. Between the two of them, I barely manage any rest. But I'll survive. I've certainly survived worse."

"May I see the baby?" Decker said.

"I am *not* going to relinquish the child without proper authority!"

"Agreed. Right now, I'd just like to see her face."

Reluctantly, Hetty permitted Decker a peek of the infant's face. He pulled out the hospital's infant picture of

Caitlin Rodriguez. He looked at it a moment, then his eyes went back to the baby.

A wave of overwhelming relief washed through his body. Then his usual stoic professional demeanor was broken by a Cheshire-cat grin. The expression was infectious. Marge let go with a full smile.

Decker showed the picture of Caitlin to Mrs. Roberts. The woman sighed—a long-suffering sigh. Something told Decker she'd used it many times before.

"I intend to fight this with all my resources. I don't particularly relish the idea of a baby at my age, but she's *mine*. Tandy didn't know what she was doing when she signed that will forbidding me guardianship of the baby."

"Will?" Marge said.

"Will, testament, codicil. I don't know the technical legal term for it. But I do know it won't stand up. My daughter wasn't well when she signed her last wishes."

Decker said, "Tandy's not dead."

"I realize the legality involved, but I'm prepared for a long, drawn-out court battle," Hetty asserted.

"Mrs. Roberts," Marge asserted, *"Tandy isn't dead!"*

For the first time, Hetty's face registered confusion rather than anger. "What are you talking about?"

"Your daughter is very much alive," Decker said.

"That's impossible!" Hetty said. "The whore said she died in childbirth."

"The whore?" Marge said.

Decker said, "Mrs. Roberts, who gave you this baby?"

"The whore. She said she was Tandy's labor nurse. Her intentions were to leave the baby with Geoff, but she found me here instead. How's that for poetic justice?"

There was a moment of silence. Decker thought about Hetty's words. Her hatred seemed pure enough, but the speech was written with lots of false notes.

He said, "Does this whore have a name?"

Hetty sneered. "Marie Bellson."

"Marie Bellson gave you this baby, Mrs. Roberts?" Marge asked.

"Better known as the whore. Not *my* name for her. Just

ask anyone who was at Berkeley at that time. *Everyone* called her that. She called *herself* that. Geoff was the only one stupid enough to fall in love with her."

Marge said, "He got her pregnant, didn't he?"

Hetty clenched her hands. "The stupid ass. For her, he destroyed our marriage *and* our daughter. Tandy never forgave him. And for some stupid reason, Tandy never forgave me, either. I was just as much a victim as she was."

"How'd Marie find you?" Decker asked.

"She didn't find *me*." Hetty's eyes deepened in color. "She found *him*. She knew where Geoff lived. Geoff had looked her up when he moved to L.A. She didn't want anything to do with him. Spurn him once, shame on her. Spurn him twice, shame on *him!*" The woman let out a bitter laugh. "Anyway, the whore found me. I could see the pain in her eyes as she handed me the baby. It was delicious."

Marge and Decker exchanged glances. Decker said, "Marie told you Tandy was dead?"

Hetty nodded. "She told me Tandy bled out during childbirth. I believed her. Why shouldn't I? Tandy was never well—physically or emotionally."

Bled out during childbirth! Rina!

Decker felt his stomach knot. Someone was using his own wife's tragedy to fashion a role for some sick play. "Tandy is very much alive, Mrs. Roberts." He looked at Marge. "We'd better call it in."

Marge said, "Mrs. Roberts, I'm going to use your phone." To Decker, she said, "I'll call Pacific, get them to call DPSS for the kid. Should I contact Lourdes Rodriguez?"

"Let Social Services do it. I don't want to foul up procedure at this point," Decker said. "Someone has to pick up Tandy."

"I'll call Hollander."

"Fine." Decker said to Hetty, "We're calling the proper agencies. Someone is going to take the baby from you."

"I'll fight it."

"Mrs. Roberts, I have a strong reason to believe that this isn't your grandchild. I have reason to believe this baby was kidnapped from Sun Valley Presbyterian maternity ward a few days ago."

"Of course she was kidnapped," Hetty said. "The whore admitted she'd taken the baby. Otherwise, the county was going to put her up for adoption. She was trying to cut through the legal red tape. For Geoff's sake, not mine. I suppose she felt she owed him one for aborting his seed twenty years ago."

"She *aborted* the baby?" Marge asked. "I heard she lost it."

Hetty paused, then said, "Aborted it, lost it, end result was the same, thank God. The whore would have made a lousy mother."

An old voice called out Hetty's name.

"Now doesn't this just end all!" Hetty declared. "*He's* up! I won't get any rest for the remainder of the day. I should throw him out, but I'm too softhearted. That's why I stuck with him as long as I did. I knew the whore wasn't his first foray into adultery, but I had a child to raise. As I said before, Tandy was never well."

"When did she start hearing voices?" Decker asked.

"She was always a little overimaginative, especially after the divorce." Hetty's eyes drifted as she spoke. "It got worse over time. The doctor said puberty exacerbated it."

"You treated her?" Marge said.

"Many times." Hetty spoke softly. "Many, many . . ."

The room was quiet, the stillness broken by an old voice. "Hetty? What's going on?"

Hetty looked at the baby in her arms. "You're not leaving with her?"

"Not yet," Decker said.

"Then could you hold her for me?" Hetty asked.

"I'd be glad to."

The old voice cried out, "I've got to go to the bathroom."

Hetty handed the baby to Decker. "I'm coming, Geoff. And don't worry about your bladder. You're wearing a diaper."

She disappeared behind a closed door.

"Sweet gal," Marge said.

Decker tossed Marge a tired smile, then looked at the baby. In her tiny face, he saw his own daughter—helpless and dependent. Thank God this part was *over*!

"Great work, Detective Dunn. *Really top-notch!*"

Marge dialed the phone. "Yeah, sometimes you get the breaks. How's the kid?"

"Seems to be well cared for." Decker smiled at the infant. "Little girl, you've just made a lot of people very, very happy." He returned his attention to Marge. "Don't get too complacent. Marie Bellson's still missing, and we've still got a homicide on our hands."

"At least it belongs to us and not the feds." Marge spoke into the receiver. "This is Detective Dunn from Foothill Division. I need to talk to someone in Juvey right away. It's an emergency." She looked at Decker. "What do you think about Mama?"

"She looks exactly like Marie," Decker said. "I mean *exactly*."

"Think they're related?"

"Could be. Or maybe old Geoff went for the same type of woman." Decker shook his head. "Can you imagine the interaction that went on in both Tandy's and Marie's minds when they met up? Marie must have known Tandy was her ex-lover's daughter by her name. Maybe Marie felt guilty. She remembered Tandy as this cute little girl, and she turned into an unbalanced adult who was grossly obese and pathetically shy. And then there was Tandy. She must have taken one look at Marie and seen the benevolent young mother she never had. Maybe in the recesses of her warped mind, she thought Marie *was* her mother."

"She got fed up with one mom, tried Marie, then got fed up with her as well." Marge returned her attention to the phone, explaining the situation to the detective on the other end of the line.

The bedroom door opened. Emerging from the hallway was a shriveled man in a wheelchair pushed by Hetty. He was bald and painfully thin, his bony wrist and fingers clinging tightly to the blanket on his lap. His dark eyes were sunken; his skin was bilious and translucent.

Hetty said, "Say hello, Geoff."

"Geraldo," he whispered.

"Geraldo is what your parents called you, sweetheart," Hetty said. "It was your barrio name, Geoffrey. Why you'd want to go back to it is beyond me. But your behavior has always confused me. Look where it got you." She looked at Decker and Marge. "Can you imagine this man was once dubbed the stud of Berkeley's English department?"

"Hetty—"

"Sweetheart, I don't see any of your paramours running to minister to you. Or am I missing something?"

Roberts lowered his chin to his breast.

Hetty said, "When Geoff got sick, who came to help him? Did Beth or Jeanie or Pat or *Marie* come?"

Roberts's mouth began to quiver.

"Who came, sweetheart?" Hetty asked.

"You," Roberts whispered.

"That's right, sweetheart. You called me, because no one else came when you called. But I came, didn't I?"

Roberts's hands began to shake. "Yes."

"Yes, I came. Because I still love you, Geoff. Despite all you put me through, I still love you." Hetty sighed and patted his bony shoulder. "And I'll never leave you the way you left me."

Tears rolled down Roberts's cheeks. "Promise?"

"Promise. Would you like your breakfast now? A bacon omelet?"

"Please." Roberts lifted his sickly face. "And could you turn on the TV for me?"

"Of course, Geoff." Hetty wheeled him into the corner of the room and turned on a small portable TV that rested inside one of the bookshelves. "I'd do anything for you. You know that." She looked over her shoulder to Decker. "Baby's going to need to be fed. You want to do it?"

Decker said, "The baby seems well nourished."

"Of course she is! What do you think I am? A child abuser?"

Decker gave the woman a weak smile. "Let's wait for Social Services before we give her anything to eat."

"Why?" Hetty went inside the kitchen that was an out-pouching off the living room. "Do you think I'm going to poison her?"

A chill ran through Decker's spine. "Just routine procedure."

Hetty frowned and took out a slab of bacon from the refrigerator. "Are you hungry?"

"No, thank you."

"It's your loss." Hetty smiled. "I make a terrific omelet." She began to chop up bacon.

Decker said, "Mrs. Roberts, you've known all along your daughter is still alive. Why'd you lie?"

Hetty didn't answer.

"Mrs. Roberts?" Decker said.

"The whore told me to," Hetty said softly. "To protect Tandy."

"Protect her from what?"

Hetty shook her head. "I need to speak to my lawyer."

"Fair enough," Decker said.

Hetty suddenly turned to him, her eyes ablaze. "What *difference* does it make if Tandy's alive or dead? Tandy could never raise a child."

"This isn't her child."

"I don't *know* that."

Decker said, "Do you know where Marie is?"

"I don't know, and I don't *care*! I took the baby because I thought it was Tandy's. That's the only reason I have this child!" Hetty took out a bowl and began to scramble some eggs. "I was only trying to help my daughter. She can't cope now, she certainly couldn't have coped then. This only justifies what I did ten years ago."

"What did you do?" Decker asked.

Hetty bit her lip and didn't answer.

"You forced her to have abortions, didn't you, Hetty?"

"Just one abortion. The second pregnancy was in her mind."

Sounds familiar, Decker thought.

"Stupid girl. I told her to be careful. Then it happened and she never forgave me for doing the right thing." Hetty stared at the bacon. "She called me an underhanded bitch and a liar. I told her to save her epithets for her father. He was the one who deserved them."

"How'd you get her to do it?" Decker asked. "Did you drug her?"

"She thought she was going in for a routine examination. She never had an exam before, so she didn't ask questions when the doctor put her to sleep. I meant the best." Hetty took out an iron skillet, placed it on the stove, and threw the diced bacon inside the pan. Seconds passed and the fat began to sizzle. "When's this Social Service Department supposed to get here?"

Decker looked at Marge, who was still on the phone.

"Soon, I hope." The bundle in Decker's arms suddenly felt leaden. He realized the baby was sleeping and placed her gently over his shoulder. "How far along was Tandy in her pregnancy when she had her abortion?"

"Tandy told everyone it was six months." Hetty stared at the skillet. "But it was much earlier than that. Tandy and her overactive imagination. It wouldn't have worked."

"Who was the father?"

"Some crazy flouncy photographer. He was just as relieved by Tandy's abortion as I was. He wanted nothing to do with the kid." She paused. "Even if he *wanted* the kid, it wouldn't have worked. With *that* kind of father, no matter what you do, it won't work."

"By 'that kind of father,' do you mean a bisexual?"

"Yes. And don't start looking at me as if I'm from the Dark Ages. They can't be helped. They may start out with good intentions, but in the end they're not father material, no matter how hard they try. *I* know from experience."

"Your husband has AIDS, Mrs. Roberts?" Decker asked.

"Yes, Detective, my husband has AIDS."

Thirty-four

"HOW MANY TIMES DO WE HAVE TO GO *OVER* THIS?" Tandy flipped black satin off her shoulders. "I don't know anything about this baby!"

Marge felt hot and sticky underneath her cotton blazer. The interview room had air-conditioning, so the heat had to be a result of internal fuel. She felt sweat pouring into the pads underneath her armpits. It wasn't the first time she had conducted interviews that had made her perspire, but over the years she'd gotten smart. If she was going to sweat, she might as well prevent her jacket from requiring an expensive dry cleaning.

"Out of ten million people in the greater Los Angeles area, Marie Bellson just *happened* to choose *your* parents?"

"What can I tell you?" Tandy responded.

Silence.

That was cool. Pure control.

Tandy crossed coltish legs and lit a cigarette. Marge was surprised. She had figured Tandy for a my-body-is-my-temple type. Then she remembered: One addiction substituting for another. Was it smoking now?

"Any speculation as to why she chose your parents?"

Tandy shrugged.

Decker walked into the interview room and closed the

door. Tandy gave him a brief glance, then returned her gaze to her cigarette.

"What's in store now? Good cop, bad cop?" She crushed her cigarette into the overflowing ashtray. "I've been here over an hour, and I haven't told you what you want to hear. Why don't you guys give it a rest?"

"Just want to ask you a few questions," Decker said.

Tandy flicked an ash off the table. "Why don't you two compare notes so I don't have to repeat myself."

Decker studied the young girl. At the moment, she seemed crazy like a fox. She was one of the most exotic-looking females Decker had ever seen—dark and sleek and feline. The perfect femme fatale.

"No need to repeat yourself." Decker sat across from her and leaned his elbows on the table. "I've been watching you through the one-way mirror."

Tandy's eyes went to the reflective wall. "I was wondering why the mirror was so dark."

"Now you know." Actually, Decker had just walked into the station house not more than a minute ago, but he could surmise what Marge had talked about. They'd discussed the line of questioning as they split their assignments. It had taken Decker hours to finish up the paperwork on Henrietta and Geoffrey Roberts né Robles. While in custody, Hetty had secured a lawyer. Counsel was trying to spring Geoffrey on grounds of ill health. At last count, Hetty was in an interview room at the Pacific Substation, her attorney at her side.

Decker said to Tandy, "Do you want anything to drink? Maybe something to eat?"

Eat!

Tandy twitched nervously.

Eat! Eat!

The low one. The *stupid* one!

"Shut up!" she mumbled.

"Pardon?" Decker said.

Tandy twitched again. "Do I *look* hungry?"

A *sore spot.* He saw the twitch, saw the nervousness. Decker said, "Just a simple question."

"Like you don't have a reason for being nice," Tandy muttered. "I know what you're doing."

Control.

"You're trying to make me nervous," Tandy stated. "It won't work."

Decker was impassive. Then he said, "Sure you don't want something to eat?"

Control.

Eat!

Control!

CONTROL!

Tandy sighed. "Look, I *really* feel bad for what that poor girl went through. I know what it's like to lose a child. But at least she got her baby back."

"More than you got," Marge said.

"You're right about that," Tandy said.

"It's especially hard when it's your *own mother* who takes your baby away from you," Marge said.

Tandy snapped her head upward. "What else did *Mommie Dearest* tell you?"

"She told us you thought you were going in for a routine visit," Decker said. "That it was your first experience in a gynecologist's office. Otherwise you'd have known they don't put you to sleep."

"Must have been quite a shock to wake up and suddenly find yourself unpregnant," Marge said.

Decker said, "What kind of doctor would do such a thing?"

"What kind of *mother* would do such a thing?" Marge said.

Tandy blinked her eyes in rapid succession.

Eat! Eat, eat, eat—

Shut up!

"Tandy?" Marge said.

"Think you're going to *win* me over by beating me down?" she said softly. "Or do you just like nosing into other people's pasts?"

"No, we're simply wondering what kind of doctor would *do* such a deceptive, unethical thing," Decker said.

"I'm still amazed by your mother's action," Marge said.

"Not as amazed as I was." Tandy's voice was flat. "I wanted to kill her."

Marge and Decker exchanged looks.

Tandy lit another cigarette. "The office looked so clean and efficient. I thought to myself . . . 'This is going to be a snap.' " She let out a bitter laugh and lit another cigarette. Realizing she had one in her mouth, she blushed slightly and put them both out. Fury seeped into her eyes. "If you're so curious about my mother's motivations, why don't you question her?"

Decker said, "I sort of did just that."

Tandy paused. "What'd she say?"

That you were unbalanced, girlie. Decker said, "That she thought she was doing what was best!"

"That's a laugh," Tandy muttered.

"A mother deceiving her own daughter like that," Marge repeated. "You must have felt such betrayal."

"To say the *least*." Tandy flipped her hair off her shoulders again. "I know what you're doing. You're trying to build *rapport*! Get me to confess something. If you're looking for suspects, arrest my parents. They were the ones with the kid."

"Your parents are being dealt with," Decker said.

"That's good. I hope a judge locks them up and throws away the key." She was suddenly impatient. "Look, *Marie's* missing, not *me*! If I was going to kidnap a kid, do you think I'd be stupid enough to drop the kid off with my parents, then *stick around*?"

No one spoke.

Crazy like a fox, Decker thought.

Tandy said, "I haven't talked to my parents in years. I didn't even know they were back together again."

"Bet you'd never thought that would happen," Marge said.

"You're right about that," Tandy said. "Life's full of surprises. Anyway, *my* feelings about my parents have nothing to do with this kidnapping business. *I'm* still here, guys, in case you haven't noticed. I'm going about my daily life.

Marie's gone. And talk about motivation for wanting a baby. *Geez*, what can I say?"

"What can you say?" Marge asked.

"If you'd spent as much time on Marie as you did on me, you'd *know* that Marie's going through menopause. She's only forty years old. The whole thing was a real shock to her system. She probably flipped out."

Decker said, "Marie began treatment for menopause less than a year ago. If you haven't seen Marie in a couple of years, how'd you know about her condition?"

Again the twitch.

"I never said Marie didn't call me. But we weren't close anymore. Not like we used to be." Tandy smiled. "My choice. Marie turned out to be overbearing, just like . . ."

She stopped talking. Decker filled in the blanks. "Overbearing like your mother?"

"You said it."

"Marie looks like your mom," Decker said.

Tandy twitched. "So what?"

"Ever met Marie before you worked at Golden Valley Home?" Marge asked.

Kill her!

Shut up!

Kill her!

Marge repeated the question.

Kill her!

Shut up! Shut up, shut up—

"Tandy?" Decker asked.

"If you're asking do I know that Marie had an affair with my father twenty years ago, the answer is yes." Her eyes were moist and shiny—like newly lacquered ebony. "So *what*? My father had affairs with lots of women. He's a jerk . . . an evil jerk!"

"He had affairs with lots of women, but he fell in love with Marie," Decker said. "In fact, I do believe Marie was the reason your parents got divorced."

Tandy twitched. "I don't remember much. I was five years old."

"What do you remember?"

"Only that my life was falling apart . . . my mother's anger." She stared at the wall, then refocused on Decker. "It's history. And it has nothing to do with this baby. Either charge me or let me be." Her eyes glazed over. "Let me be in peace . . . please."

Once again Decker and Marge exchanged glances.

"How'd you find out about your father and Marie?" Marge asked.

Tandy blinked rapidly. "I just did."

"You just did?" Decker said.

Tandy bolted up from her seat and began to pace. "Look, I spoke to you guys without a lawyer because I didn't do anything wrong. But if you keep hammering away at my past, I'm going to walk out this door—"

"Why were you using Lawrence McKay's nursing license, Tandy?" Marge asked.

Kill her!

The high one.

She hated the high one!

The high one was malevolent. Malevolence. The wicked queen in Snow White. *Mirror, mirror on the wall—*

"Tandy, why were—"

"Stop!" Tandy whirled around and glared at Marge. "Just . . . oh, *now* I get it! It's dig-up-dirt-on-Tandy time. Maybe I *should* get a lawyer."

Decker pushed the phone across the table until it rested in front of Tandy's nose. "Be my guest."

Tandy stared at the machine. The room fell silent.

Decker said, "Your dad was evil, Tandy?"

Tandy looked at him blankly. "They both were."

"Your father and Marie?" Marge said. "Or your father and mother?"

"All of them," Tandy said softly. "They're all very evil people."

"Including Marie," Marge said.

"Including Marie," Tandy said.

"How did you find out about Daddy and Marie?" Decker asked.

"I just did."

"Did you recognize Marie when you saw her at the Golden Valley Home?" Marge said.

Tandy's eyes became sharp and focused. "Are you asking me if I recognized someone I last saw when I was five?"

"Why are you using Leek McKay's license, Tandy?" Decker said.

"Because it was *convenient*! I didn't want to have to go back to school just to learn things I already knew! Marie said I was better trained than most RNs she worked with. Why should I waste my time?"

"Because it's illegal to use someone else's license."

"So *arrest* me!"

Decker looked at the tape recorder. *She had him.* Yes, he could arrest her on the petty charge of impersonating a licensed professional. But the collar would make him look as if he were reaching. The woman was dancing around his traps. She was the sanest person he'd ever met.

"Look," Tandy said, "you have nothing to connect me to this kidnapping. You don't even have anything to connect me to Marie. The only thing you have is my parents with a baby that *Marie* kidnapped. Marie probably panicked and thought of old Geoffrey. Like you said, they used to be lovers till she dumped him. Maybe she thought she could play him for a sucker 'cause that's what he was."

"If you were only five years old, how'd you know Marie dumped your father?" Marge asked.

Kill her, the whore!

You're a whore!

Again Tandy's eyes blinked. "Mom told me."

"So you *knew* Marie was your father's lover when you met her at the home."

"No." Tandy shook her head. "No, I didn't. My mother never mentioned Marie's name. Just called her the whore. Mom always referred to her as the whore."

Consistent with the way Hetty spoke. Decker said, "So how'd you find out that Marie was the whore?"

"I don't remember."

How *did* she find out? Decker wondered. Was Marie's

name buried in her unconscious? Did it pop up when she actually met Marie again? Or did Tandy come across some tangible evidence of the tryst? Maybe while she was staying in Marie's apartment, she saw something. Yet Decker had *combed* Bellson's apartment and hadn't come up with a thing. He looked at Tandy. She smiled slowly.

Back in control!

"Look, even my parents aren't saying I have anything to do with this. So you've got *nothing* on me."

"How do you know what your parents are saying, Tandy?" Marge asked.

"If they implicated me, you wouldn't be floundering. Either arrest me or let me go."

"You falsified your credentials," Marge said. "That's illegal."

"So I won't work as a nurse anymore. Can I go now? Or are you going to charge me with impersonating a nurse?"

Decker was quiet. She fit the profile of a baby kidnapper—an unbalanced person who longed for a child. To wit: the pseudocyesis. But he had *nothing* on her. On her parents, yes. On Marie, yes. But nothing on her!

Maybe she *didn't* have anything to do with the kidnapping.

It was a little thing that bugged him. That one unanswered question. How did Tandy find out about her father's affair with Marie?

Surely, Marie didn't tell her. Why would she do that?

And she couldn't have come across something in Marie's apartment that clued her in. Decker had scoured the place. Nothing about Marie's past except some old books. No letters, no photographs in her desk—

Her desk!

The key under it.

The frigging lockbox!

He stood, gave a quick glance to Marge, then smoothed his mustache. "You know your apartment is being searched. We pulled the warrant."

Tandy shrugged. "Go ahead. You won't find anything."

Decker leaned against the back wall. "Sure you don't want anything to eat?"

Tandy twitched.

Kill him!

Shut up! Just go away!

The voice receded.

"No, I *don't* want anything to eat!"

"No need for the hostility," Decker said.

"I'm not being *hostile*," Tandy retorted. "I think I'm being very friendly, considering the circumstances."

"You ever been to Marie's apartment before, Tandy?"

"Of course I have."

"When was the last time you were there . . . in Marie's apartment?"

Tandy shrugged. "Maybe a year ago."

"You weren't there . . . let's say . . . four days ago?"

"No."

"What if I were to tell you I had witnesses who said they saw you there?"

"I'd say they were lying." Tandy's eyes were hot and angry. They met Decker's straight on. "You have *no* witnesses. 'Cause I wasn't *there*."

"You haven't been in Marie's apartment lately?"

"No!"

"You didn't come in and maybe rewind her phone messages?"

"No!"

"Tandy, would you take a lie-detector test for me then?"

Kill! Kill!

"Fuck you!" Tandy said out loud.

Decker was surprised by her vehemence. The girl blushed.

"Not you . . . never mind." Tandy twitched. "What do you *want* from me?"

"Sure you haven't been in her apar—"

"I already told you—*no*!"

"Which means if we search your condo, we're not going to find *anything* belonging to Marie. After all, last time you saw her was a year or two ago, right?"

That got her. Tandy turned pale.

Kill him!

The high one.

Kill him! Kill him!

Evil!

SHUT UP!

"Tandy?" Decker said.

She twitched and blinked. Her body became a series of small spasms. "Marie gave me lots of stuff. She liked me . . . loved me."

"Gifts are one thing," Decker said. "I'm talking about personal belongings of Marie's. Things like maybe a lockbox filled with letters and photographs—"

"So Marie gave me the box for safekeeping. So what?"

"Ah, so you do know what I'm talking about," Decker said. "You know about the box because you discovered it while you were staying with Marie during your so-called pregnancy? Of course, we all know you weren't really *pregnant*. Not like the first and only time—"

Kill him now!

Decker said, "The second one was all in your imagination."

Kill him!

No.

Yes.

No, you're not real!

Kill him. KILL HIM!

"Tandy, are you here?" Decker asked

A glow spread across the young woman's cheeks. "Marie *gave* me the box, and you can't *prove* any different!"

"Why would she give you her lockbox without the key?"

"Who says I don't have the key?"

"I have the key, Tandy."

"So she gave it to me without the key." Tandy shrugged. "She didn't want me looking inside."

"You're right about that, Tandy. I don't think Marie wanted you looking inside. Because the box held all her personal mementos, some of them very, very private—"

"Shut up!"

Decker leaned across the table. "But you snooped any-way."

"Shut up."

"You found it while you were staying at Marie's recovering from your shock at *not* being pregnant—for a *second* time."

"I don't have to listen to this." She closed her ears and began to hum. "I can't *hear* you!"

Decker yanked her hands from her head. "Tandy, Marie didn't *give* you any box. You *stole* it from her apartment."

"Shut! Up!"

"And we both know why Marie *wouldn't* have *given* you the box. It contained love letters and photographs of her and your father. Probably very graphic love letters—"

"Shut! Up!"

"Man, what *betrayal* you must have felt!" Decker added. "You thought you found an angelic mother in Marie, and irony of ironies, she turned out to be the very *bitch* that broke up your parents' marriage!"

Tandy jumped out of her seat and threw the tape recorder against the wall. *"SHUT UP! SHUT UP! SHUT UP! SHUT UP!"*

Decker stopped talking. Tandy grabbed her hair.

"SHUT! UP!"

"I'm not talking," Decker said,

"NOT YOU!" She sobbed openly. *"THEM!"*

Them? *The voices!* Decker realized. The panic seized him suddenly. The girl is *unbalanced*, you moron!

Decker said to the mirror, "Can I get Sergeant McKlintock in here?"

"I'll get her," Marge said.

Tandy threw herself at Decker, hugged him as tight as she could. *"MAKE THEM STOP! PLEASE!"*

She started to hyperventilate. Decker's heart did triple time. He shouted, "Get me Donna, damn it!"

The mirror answered, "She's coming!"

"MAKE THEM . . ." She sobbed and gasped, her lips taking on a bluish tinge. "MAKE THEM . . . STOP!"

A moment later, Donna McKlintock rushed inside the interview room. She had been with the department for twenty years, the last ten serving as the on-site consultant in psychology, having earned an MFC in night schools. Over the years, she had counseled many victims of crime—both civilians and cops. Decker hoped she knew her stuff. Solidly built, she took her strong arms and peeled Tandy off Decker's body. The girl immediately leeched onto Donna.

"Make them stop!" Tandy begged the psychologist.

Donna took a firm grip on the girl and began to walk her around the table. "You're safe here, Tandy. You're safe!"

"But *they're here!*"

"You're *safe* now, Tandy!" Donna reiterated. "While you're with me, I won't let anyone hurt you. And I won't let you hurt anyone, okay?"

"Then promise me you'll *make them stop!*"

Donna began to lead her out of the room. "We'll talk. While you're with me, I won't let anyone hurt you. And I won't let you hurt anyone!"

"Promise?"

"Promise." Donna led her out of the room. Decker looked at Marge, then ran his hand over his face. At times like these, practicing estate law looked downright tempting.

THIRTY-FIVE

INSIDE THE INTERVIEW ROOM, DECKER PACED. "I CAN'T *BE-lieve* I was that *stupid!*"

"Stop flogging yourself." Marge took a deep breath. "Need I remind you that someone was murdered?"

Decker stopped trampling the ground. "The body in the Honda was Lily Booker. Hennon made the I.D. this morning."

"So stop thinking about Tandy and start concentrating on the *real* victim!"

Decker said, "We still don't know that Tandy did it."

"We don't know she *didn't* do it. She certainly is *crazy* enough to do it!"

"What freaked me out was how fast she turned!" Decker exclaimed. "I thought she was being sly . . . clever." He blew out air. "Then all of a sudden . . ." He rubbed his hands together. His heart was still trotting.

Marge said, "For what it's worth, you put a whole new slant on the case with that lockbox thing. I'd forgotten all about it."

"So that's how Tandy found out about her father's affair. She was snooping in Marie's apartment and came across some pictures or letters. *So what?* We've got nothing substantial to tie her to the kidnapping and murder."

Marge said, "I think we got enough to book her. She has no real alibi as to where she was at the time of the kidnapping. And the baby was found in her parents' place."

"It's all circumstantial. They've stated that *Marie*, not Tandy, gave them the baby."

Marge rested her chin in her palm. "Want to hear my personal theory of what happened . . . for what it's worth?"

"Shoot."

"Last Tuesday, around midnight, Tandy goes to visit Marie at Sun Valley Pres."

"Why?"

"That is anyone's guess. Girl's nuts. Maybe a voice told her to go kill Marie. So she goes to Marie's assigned nursery—Nursery J. But Marie isn't there. As a matter of fact, no one is there—"

"Budget cuts," Decker interrupted. "Or so they claim. What a crock of shit!"

"Can we go on?"

"Go on."

Marge said, "So no one's there. Tandy takes one look at those babies and loses it. Her head starts playing tricks on her. She thinks about the baby she was forced to abort. She thinks about the pregnancy that wasn't real. Voices start telling her to do things. The impulses take over. She grabs a baby."

Decker said, "Then, to Tandy's surprise, Lily Booker walks in and confronts her."

"Exactly. Say a fight breaks out. Or maybe Tandy just lashes out. Who knows what was going through that girl's head?"

"She seemed so damn . . . *tormented*, Marge."

"Rabbi, that doesn't mean she can't do damage."

A good point. Lots of crimes are committed under delusion. Decker said, "Go on with your theory."

Marge took another breath. "So Lily confronts Tandy. Now Tandy's a strong girl, an iron pumper. She smashes Lily on the head and kills her. Wasn't there a big indentation in her forehead?"

"Yep," Decker said. "Hennon thought it was done with a hammer."

"And the frontal bones had been smashed, remember?"

Decker nodded. "Keep going."

"Okay," Marge said. "Then Marie walks in and sees what happened. Quickly, Marie thinks up a plan."

"Wait, wait, wait a sec." Decker held up the palm of his hand. "Marie walks in and finds out that Tandy has just murdered Lily and is in the process of swiping a baby. Suddenly, you've got Marie abetting Tandy in murder and kidnapping? *Why* would she do that?"

"Marie loved Tandy. Or maybe she just felt plain guilty over what went on between her and Professor Geoff. Marie was a martyr type."

"Don't buy it, kiddo. Maybe if Marie had been Tandy's biological mother . . . but she wasn't. I don't see Marie risking her neck to help a friend."

"Maybe Tandy was in the midst of a breakdown," Marge suggested. "Look how sorry you felt for her."

"But I wasn't looking at a fresh dead body."

"And you're positive that Marie isn't Tandy's mother?"

"According to Lita Bellson, it would have been impossible."

"And you think Lita's reliable enough to notice everything that went on in her daughter's life?"

"I think she'd notice if her kid was pregnant."

"Marie's a tall girl. She could hide a pregnancy."

"You're selling, Marge. But I'm not buying."

"All right," Marge said. "I don't know why Marie would help Tandy, but let's assume she did. Maybe Marie just panicked and didn't think rationally."

Decker hit his shirt pocket. The bottle was still there, thank you, God. He took it out and popped a couple of Advils into his mouth. Swallowed them dry.

"Marie helps Tandy," Decker said. "We've got two things going on. One, the baby. Two, the disposal of Lily's body. Even if Marie agreed to help Tandy dispose of the body, why would she let Tandy take the baby? If Tandy indeed took the baby?"

"Say Tandy was nuts. Maybe she wouldn't leave without the baby. Marie didn't want either one of them to get into trouble. She panicked and just wanted to shut Tandy up. So she let her keep the baby."

"Marge—"

"Let me just go on with my story, as fucked up as it is, okay?"

Decker nodded.

"So." Marge cleared her throat. "So Tandy takes the baby over to her parents' house, and Marie drives her car with Lily's body up to Angeles Crest. Marie pushes the car over the cliff, and Tandy picks her up later on. Marie splits town for good, tells Tandy she'll take the heat—"

"*Why* would she do that, Marge?"

"Because she thought she was Jesus Christ and was dying for Tandy's sins. I don't know!"

"But that's a big blank."

"Maybe she was atoning for the affair. Remember how Paula said she liked the parable of the prodigal son?"

"Okay. So even assuming Marie agreed to take the heat, we've got a few problems. Starting with the baby. It was *Marie* who took the baby over to Tandy's parents."

"According to Hetty, who'd be more than willing to let Marie take the blame."

Decker said, "Marie could be dead, for all we know."

Marge didn't speak for a moment. Then she said, "Well, I like my theory."

"Yeah, it sounds okay." Decker paused a moment. "You know what bothers me?"

"What?"

"Can you picture Marie and Tandy leaving the hospital with *both* the *baby* and *Lily Booker's body* unnoticed?"

"Everyone we interviewed said the place was short-staffed that night. You yourself said the hospital was a tomb."

"But it's the *physical element.* Even if Tandy is a big, strong gal and Marie is a nurse who knew the ropes, how did they leave the hospital carrying a dead body—a *bloody* dead body—and a squalling baby? Or even a sleeping baby, for that matter. That's a lot of weight."

Marge thought for a moment. "You're right. Lily was a big woman. Maybe they got help."

Decker suddenly grinned. "Who'd help them, Margie?"

"Can't be Daddy Geoff. He's practically an invalid. How about Mom? She's a toughie, to put it mildly."

Decker said, "Could have been Mom, but think about her physically, Marge. Hetty's a broomstick. We need someone strong, Marge. Someone who's used to toting deadweight bodies. And maybe someone who owes Tandy some favors."

Marge hit her forehead. "Leek McKay. I *told* you that guy was a scumbag! If he's gone because you played nice guy—"

"Don't say it, don't say it!" Decker ran his hands through his hair. "I've been doing nothing but fucking up lately!"

"Maybe it's sleep deprivation."

"It's bad work." Decker shook his head. "Marie's missing. I've got no idea where she is. Tandy's with Donna at the moment. She's not going anywhere. I've got nothing on tap. Might as well go get me some evidence."

Decker closed the door to the interview room and leaned against the wall next to Deputy D.A. Kurt Pomerantz. A moment later, a uniformed officer joined them both. Decker smiled at her. Nervously, she smiled back, her eyes focusing on a spot across the squad room. The blue was barely out of her teens, probably a rookie. Decker thought of Cindy. He hoped she'd gotten police work out of her system.

Pomerantz brushed his palm over his balding forehead and unbuttoned his jacket, exposing a sizable gut that came with beer-drinking and middle age. The deputy D.A. rocked on his feet as he talked. "I can tell you this much. Beltran's going to ask for all charges dropped in exchange for McKay's cooperation."

"McKay was an accessory."

"A phone call from the hospital to McKay does not a case make, Pete."

"It was made right around the kidnapping, Kurt. Fits beautifully into our time frame."

"It's a lousy phone call, Pete. McKay's a nurse. Maybe someone at the hospital wanted to consult with him."

"He's never worked for Sun Valley Pres. And who the hell would be calling him at *midnight* to consult?"

"Trace it to the nursery, your case'll look better."

"We're trying. It takes time." Decker paused. "We've also got bags of ash from Marie's burnt Honda. If McKay put the body into the car, he left some evidence transfer. Now, at least I know what to look for."

"Some evidence would be nice."

Decker said, "I think McKay'll bite. I think he'd love to get Tandy off his back. The girl had been blackmailing him for years to use his license. The girl is also psychotic— maybe even homicidal. I think he's afraid of her. I think he'd love to see her locked up and out of his hair."

Pomerantz said, "He's not going to screw himself just to get her locked up."

"It depends," Decker said. "Maybe having her loose would be worse for him than doing a little community work."

Pomerantz waited a beat. "True. I'll do what I can to put the squeeze on Oscar, but he's no dunce. You want a cup of coffee?"

Decker said, "I'll get it. What do you take?"

"Cream, no sugar."

Decker turned to the uniform. "Officer?"

"No, thank you, sir."

Decker stifled a smile and brought back two cups of coffee. A moment later, McKay's counsel emerged from the room. Oscar Beltran was Hispanic, in his early thirties, and had been with the Public Defender's Office for the last five years. Decker nodded to the rookie, and the kid turned to go back inside the interview quarters.

"Position yourself near the exit," Decker said.

The kid nodded and closed the door behind her.

Eyes upon the young patrol officer, Beltran said, "They keep making them younger."

Decker said, "What are you complaining about? You're not exactly an old fart."

"I feel like an old fart," Beltran said. "Must be the job."

"It's defending all those psychos, Oscar," Pomerantz said.

Beltran laughed. "Everybody's entitled to representation, Counselor."

"Ain't that lucky for old Leek McKay," Pomerantz said.

"Kurt, you're after the wrong person," Beltran said. "McKay's small time—a petty criminal."

"Ain't no petty criminals, Counselor," Decker said. "Just petty crimes."

"Are we going to dance, or are we going to talk?" Beltran said. "Without McKay, you don't have anyone for the Booker murder. We all know that, so let's not putz around."

"Putz?" Decker smiled. "I like your Spanish."

"In deference to you, Sergeant," Beltran said.

Pomerantz said, "We've got a phone call from the hospital to McKay, Oscar. It doesn't look good for your man."

"Kurt," Beltran said, "you don't have a case with a *phone call!*"

"Au contraire," Pomerantz said. "I think we can make a good one."

"Fine," Beltran said. "Make your case, and I'll see you in court."

Decker said, "Oscar, we know that *I* can get Golden Valley Home for the Aged to press a multitude of embezzlement and fraud charges against your client. And they'd stick like glue. Either way, McKay's going to get charged."

"Big difference between embezzlement and accessory to murder," Beltran said.

Pomerantz said, "Murder and kidnapping—"

"Murder only. He doesn't know shit about the kidnap—"

"So you say," Pomerantz broke in.

Beltran said, "You want to play poker, I'll call your bluff. Take what you've got to court."

"Fine, I'll call Golden Valley." Decker looked at Pomerantz. "Let's go for time, Kurt. I think we can get one to three—"

Beltran said, "Who's pleading this, Kurt? You or him?"

"The man used to be a lawyer," Pomerantz said. "Old habits are hard to break."

"C'mon," Beltran said, "you want to let loose a nutcase like Tandy Roberts, boys? I don't think so. You want her running around doing mischief when she should be in treatment? I don't think so. And without my boy McKay, you don't have anything on *her!*"

Pomerantz said, "Bottom line: What will you buy?"

"Everything dropped in exchange for cooperation. And I mean everything. No embezzlement, no accessory, no payback, no community service—"

"Suspended proceedings with probation," said Pomerantz. "First year served in county jail *if* beyond a doubt McKay is only an accessory. Because if it's murder, all bets are off."

"All charges dropped, Kurt."

"Why should we drop all charges?" Decker said. "At the very least, he'd get probation with embezzlement, Oscar."

"So charge him with embezzlement. You want his cooperation, Pete, all charges dropped."

"Suspended proceedings with five probation," Pomerantz said. "No jail time."

"No dice," Beltran said.

"Oscar, be flexible!"

"All charges dropped."

Decker remained stoic. He wanted to charge Leek McKay—the nurse deserved to do time—but he wanted Lily Booker's killer—or killers—even more. Maybe it was Marie. Maybe it was Tandy. Without McKay, he'd never know. If McKay had to go free in the bargain, he could live with that. None of the men spoke for a few moments.

Finally, Pomerantz said, "Suspended proceedings with one year probation. No jail time. With embezzlement, we could tie him up with at least two, maybe three, years probation, not to mention countless hours of community service and possible payback to the home. Go back to your client and ask him if what we have to offer is satisfactory."

Beltran tapped his foot, then nodded. "I think he'll go for it."

THIRTY-SIX

"**W**HERE'S THE CAMERA?" LEEK McKAY LOOKED around the interview room. "I don't see any camera."

"Behind the one-way mirror," Marge explained.

"Why am I being videotaped?"

Decker said, "The proceedings are being videotaped, Mr. McKay, not just you. It's for everyone's protection."

"I look lousy."

And he did. There was something especially pathetic about a big man withering in defeat. He reminded Decker of a bullmastiff he once saw in the vet's office, the muscled animal lying submissively on the floor, quaking at the anticipation of a shot. Leek had on a white shirt, tan jacket, and a pair of faded Levi's. His face was pale, his hair, though washed, was messy, and his hands were clenched knuckle white.

"I need a shave myself," Decker said. "Don't worry about it."

McKay said, "Tell the guy behind the camera to try to pick up the left part of my face. It's my good side."

Decker didn't answer, not knowing if Leek was serious. He continued reciting preliminary interview information into the tape recorder, ending by stating the name of each person in the room and his official title. Six people in a space inadequately ventilated for two. Everyone had circles under their armpits. He turned to Leek. "Do you want anything to eat or drink before we start?"

"Glass of water would be nice."

Marge topped a paper cup with water and set it in front of the bodybuilder. McKay drank it without pausing for air, then gave Marge a weak smile along with a hound-dog look. She knew he was trying to find an ally in her. Maybe he thought a woman would be more sympathetic. Little did he know what a hard-ass she could be.

Decker said, "Mr. McKay, we have a phone record of yours from PacBell." He stated the time and date of the call. "Do you remember receiving that call?"

"Yes."

"It lasted for five minutes and fourteen seconds."

"Sounds right."

"Who called you, Leek?"

"Tandy Roberts."

"And that's the same person as Sondra Roberts?"

"Yes. Tandy's her nickname." McKay focused on his hands. "She used to lisp as a kid. Sandy came out Tandy." He played with his water cup. "At least that's what she told me."

Decker said, "The caller identified herself as Tandy Roberts?"

"Just Tandy. She didn't even have to say that. I knew her voice."

"What did Miss Roberts say to you during the course of your conversation with her?"

"I don't remember word-for-word. She woke me out of a sound sleep."

"Tell us as best as you remember," Marge said.

"She said something like 'Leek, it's Tandy. You gotta come down here right away.' I asked her where 'here' was. And she said Sun Valley Pres. I asked her what she wanted, but she wouldn't answer. She sounded agitated over the phone. Breathing hard, gasping. Then Marie came on the line—"

"Can you identify Marie for the record?" Decker interrupted.

"Marie Bellson. She said they couldn't talk over the phone. That I should meet them at the hospital . . . in front of room four-something. I think it was four-sixteen. It was a room across the hall from a broom closet—a hospital utility closet."

"We'll refer to said room as room four-sixteen then," Decker said. "Did Tandy or Marie say anything else to you over the phone?"

McKay whispered something in his lawyer's ear. Beltran whispered something back. Out loud, McKay said, "Tandy told me she was in trouble, that she needed help. By trouble I thought maybe she had lost her purse or keys and couldn't get home."

Beltran nodded.

Pomerantz said, "You thought Tandy, who was gasping, had woken you up and had called you down to Sun Valley Pres at midnight because she had lost her keys?"

Beltran said, "May I remind Counsel that Mr. McKay is not on trial here. There's no reason to impugn the veracity of his statements. We are trying to cooperate with a fact-finding interview."

Decker said, "Did Tandy explain the nature of the trouble she was in?"

"No, sir, she did not."

"Did Marie offer any explanation?"

"No."

"And you went down to help Tandy?"

"Yes, sir."

"Without question, you went to help her."

"Yes, sir."

"And did you find her at Sun Valley Pres in front of room number four-sixteen?"

"Yes—well, no actually." McKay paused a moment. "I went to room four-sixteen and no one was there. Then, a moment later, Marie came out of the broom closet opposite room four-sixteen."

"Can you identify Marie once again for the record?" Marge asked.

"Marie Bellson."

"Marie Bellson came out of the broom closet opposite four-sixteen?" Decker asked.

"Yeah, she was hiding there. She pulled me inside."

"Did she shut the door?" Marge asked.

"Yeah, of course she shut the door. She had a dead body inside."

Beltran said, "Lawrence—"

"Mr. Beltran, call a spade a spade. There was a dead body in the closet. Scared the shit out of me. Marie was in the process of putting it in a body bag when I got there. I almost bolted on the spot."

"Why didn't you?" Marge asked.

"Because Tandy . . ." McKay rubbed his hands over his face. "She had dope on me. She was blackmailing me—"

Beltran said, "Lawrence—"

"The sergeant knows all this, Mr. Beltran. Can you let me get my story out?"

"I'm trying to protect you."

"Mr. Beltran, you said I'd get a year's probation tops. That nothing I'd say would make it worse on me. Is that true?"

"It's true, Mr. McKay," Pomerantz said. "As long as we're satisfied that your sole involvement in these activities was that of an accessory only."

"What does that mean?" McKay asked.

Decker said, "We need to be assured that you didn't know anything about the murder and kidnapping until after the fact, after the felonies took place."

McKay was breathing hard. "I swear on my mother's grave that I didn't know a thing until Marie pulled me inside the broom closet."

"Where was Tandy?" Marge asked.

"I don't know. I never saw Tandy. She was gone when I got there."

Pomerantz, Decker, and Marge exchanged looks.

"You never saw Tandy?" Decker asked.

"Nope."

"And even though Tandy wasn't there when you arrived,

even though you saw a dead body in the closet, you didn't run?" Decker said.

"I know that sounds crazy but . . ." McKay took a sip of water and looked at Decker. "Tandy had dope on me. You found out anyway. I should have saved myself some energy."

Decker was quiet.

McKay continued, "Tandy knew I was . . . investing . . . pocket money from the folks at the home."

"Embezzling, not investing," Pomerantz stated.

"Misappropriating funds," Beltran retorted.

"For godsakes, it was just *pocket* change. I know private nurses who *steal* behind their clients' backs. At least my patients *gave* me the money."

"Makes you a prince among men, Leek," Marge said.

Beltran said, "Lawrence, just go on with your story."

"Couple of the residents have big mouths," McKay went on. "That's not a problem, though. The elderly often confuse reality and fantasy. No one pays them any mind. But Tandy wouldn't let go. She started prying into my affairs to prove what I was doing. Tandy may be nuts, but she's not stupid. When she makes up her mind, she's relentless. Just like she is now with buffing. She wanted me, she was going to have me. Once she knew about my pocket change, I started doing favors for her."

Decker said, "Leek, describe the dead body to me."

McKay spoke softly. "It was a black woman. She wore a nurse's uniform. Her face had been bashed in." He buried his head in his hands.

"Did you know for certain she was dead, Leek?"

Beltran held up his hand and whispered something in Leek's ear. A moment later, McKay answered yes to the question.

"Did you take her pulse?" Decker said. "Did you check to see if she was breathing?"

"I just knew she was dead, Sergeant. Why else would Marie be putting her in a body bag?"

Decker said, "But you're a nurse, Leek. Wouldn't doing something like that be second nature?"

"Don't answer that," Beltran said.

"I've been a nurse in a geriatric home for five years, Sergeant," McKay continued. "I've been around enough bodies to know when someone is dead. They have a look . . . the eyes . . . the pupils . . . dilated. That vacant stare. I . . ." McKay held his hand to his mouth. "She was a mess. Her face had been smashed . . . front part of her skull, too. Her brains . . . you could see her brains. She'd been hit very hard."

"Hit?" Marge asked.

"Hit as in smashed up with a hammer." He shuddered. "I've seen more dead people than I'd care to remember. But I've never seen someone messed up like that."

"Was the closet a mess, too?" asked Marge.

"No . . . not . . . I don't remember. Maybe they cleaned it up before I got there."

Decker said, "Any idea who messed the body up?"

"Marie said . . ." McKay swallowed hard. "Marie Bellson said that she did everything. So I guess Marie was the one who did the bashing."

"Did she say she did the bashing?" Decker said.

"Not the bashing specifically. Just that she did everything."

"Who do you think did it?" Marge said.

Beltran said, "What he thinks is irrelevant."

"I'll repeat what you said, Counselor. This isn't a trial, just an interview."

"I said a fact-finding interview."

McKay blurted out, "I don't know if Marie would have the strength. But Tandy does. She's a *strong* woman."

Decker knew Leek meant Tandy was *strong* in more than one way. "How'd you get the body out to the car?"

"Marie and I loaded the body on a gurney and brought it to her car. No one really saw us. At that time of night, hospitals are empty, and no one pays much attention to anybody in an official uniform."

Decker knew that to be true enough. "Where'd you load the body? Front seat? Backseat?"

"Actually, we tried the trunk at first. But . . . we couldn't

... the limbs weren't pliable. So we put the body on the floor of the backseat."

Consistent with the evidence found. Decker had located Marie's I.D. ring in the backseat. She'd probably lost it while she was placing the body in her car. "When did all this take place?"

"I don't know. . . ." McKay closed his eyes and opened them. "Maybe one, two in the morning."

Decker said, "Leek, how'd you know a hammer did the damage to the body?"

"Marie gave me the hammer. She said get rid of it."

"Did you?"

"Yeah. I dumped it."

"Where?"

"In the canyon somewhere."

"Which canyon?" Marge asked.

"Somewhere in Angeles Crest." He cleared his throat. "Near where I . . . I pushed and burned . . . the car."

"Why'd you pick the spot you did?" Decker asked.

"It . . ." McKay let out a bitter laugh. "It was a private spot where Tandy and I used to go camping. We used to do that once in a while. She loved to camp." He paused. "I didn't mind. It was a lot less public than her spending the weekend in my place. I *hated* to be seen with her."

Decker kept his expression flat. "What was Sondra Roberts doing while you and Marie Bellson were loading the body inside Marie's car?"

McKay finished his water. "I told you Tandy had taken off. I never saw a baby. I never saw her. I didn't know anything about the kidnapping until I heard it on the news the next morning. That day, I spoke to Tandy at the gym—to ask about what the hell was going on. I didn't want to be involved in a kidnapping."

Decker nodded encouragingly.

"Tandy told me she didn't know anything about a baby. Why the hell was I bothering her?" McKay shook his head. "She acted like she never even phoned me. Like she wasn't even *there* that night. I don't know who took the baby. All

I know is that night, Marie was driving my car, following me up the mountain to get rid of the body."

"You drove Marie's car?" Marge asked.

"Yes. Marie drove mine. She wanted it that way. She knew I wouldn't crap out on her if I was driving the car with a body in it. She was right. She followed me to the dumping spot. I swear I don't know what Tandy was doing. News said the baby was found with her parents. So logic would say that Tandy took the baby to her parents. But I don't know that."

Decker paused, thinking about what he actually *had* on Tandy. So far, he could probably get a charge of accessory and make it stick. But with Marie missing, he had no sure-footed evidence to back up murder and kidnapping. Nothing to prove that *Marie* didn't do it. And maybe she *did*. He said, "You and Marie drove up the mountains in separate cars?"

McKay nodded.

"Did you stop at all?"

"Stop with a body in the car?"

"Stop for gas?" Decker asked.

"Oh, I get it." McKay clutched his hands tightly. "We did stop once. So I could steal a hose . . . from someone's front lawn."

"A hose?" Marge asked.

"You used it as a siphon," Decker said. "Less suspicious than buying containers of gas in the wee hours of the morning and more convenient. Then you doused Marie's car with gas from its own tank. Very good, Leek."

"I thought a long time to come up with that," McKay said. "I'm glad you're impressed."

The guy was serious. Decker gave him a weak smile.

McKay said, "I swear that nurse was *dead*."

"Where was Tandy?" Decker asked.

"I don't *know*! Why do you keep asking me that? She was gone when I got to the hospital."

"Where was the baby?" Marge said.

"I don't know anything about a baby!"

Marge said, "Tell me about you and Marie in the mountains. What'd you do?"

McKay looked at his hands. "We drove up to the mountains, I doused Marie's car with gasoline, then Marie and I pushed it off the cliff. It made a huge bang. Marie and I split as fast as we could."

"You left in your car?" Marge stated.

McKay nodded.

Marge said, "Can you answer the question yes or no for the tape recorder. Did you leave in your car?"

"Yes, ma'am, Marie and I left in my car. I drove."

"What'd you do with Marie?"

"Let her off in front of a building-supply place on Foothill. Her orders. That was the last I ever saw of her."

"And Sondra Roberts?" Decker asked.

"I don't know!"

"Something's bothering me, Leek," Decker said. "Lots is bothering me, but we'll start with one thing at a time. You said you pushed the car over the mountain around two, three A.M. Trouble with that one is that the car didn't burn until much later in the morning."

"I know."

"You know?" Decker said.

"I went back to the spot before I went to work at the home. You know . . . just to make sure." McKay sighed. "The car was wrecked but in one piece. I panicked. I found the hose I'd used the first time and took gas from my own car. This time I made sure. I threw a burning rag. . . ." He looked down. "Thing exploded like a nuclear bomb. I've never been so fucking scared in my life. The blast, the heat, the flames. I got out of there so fucking fast. I drove straight to work. Took a shower there." He smiled at Marge again. "Then I met you a few hours later. Pretty good job of hiding my terror, huh?"

"Very good," Marge said.

"I've done some acting. Actually, it was just playing volleyball on the beach for a beer commercial. But people in the business have told me I'm pretty good." McKay rubbed his face. "Like that matters, huh? You guys *got* to believe me. That black girl was *dead*! And I didn't know *anything* about the kidnapping until I heard the news. All I did was get rid of the body. Accessory. Like I promised you guys. That's it! I swear!"

Decker didn't speak for a long time. Finally, Beltran said, "Are we done?"

Decker looked at his watch. "Let's take a break."

"You're not finished with your questions?" Beltran asked.

"No, Counselor, I'm not."

"I don't think my client has anything to add to his statement."

"A few minutes?" Decker asked.

"Make it quick," Beltran said. "We've been cooperative. But now I'm getting impatient."

Decker nodded to Marge and Pomerantz. They followed him outside.

"What?" Marge said.

"We're still not there as far as Tandy's concerned," Decker said.

"What are you talking about?" Marge said. "We found Marie's lockbox in Tandy's condo just as you predicted, Pete. We've got Tandy as an accessory based on Leek's testimony—"

"But she wasn't at the hospital when Leek came down. We certainly can't pin her with murder and kidnapping."

Marge said, "Leek said that Marie wasn't strong enough to deliver those blows on Lily Booker's head."

"Since when is Leek an expert in forensics?" Decker said.

Marge turned to the D.A. "What do you think?"

Pomerantz answered, "Tandy, for all her outbursts, never admitted to anything. Her parents said Marie dropped off the baby. We have Leek's testimony and some circumstantial evidence, but without Marie, we can't do much to Tandy. Too much reasonable doubt."

Decker smashed his fist into a waiting palm. "I'm *pissed*. She's going to walk with probation, I just know it. The girl is crazy. Probably *homicidal* crazy. She needs treatment!

And she needs to be *confined* while she's in treatment! We can't let her out on the streets, and that's what's going to happen unless we have more dope on her. We *can't* let her walk!"

"Think McKay has anything to do with Marie's disappearance?" Pomerantz asked.

"You mean do I think McKay killed Marie?" Decker shrugged. "Who knows? I'll tell you this much. I think McKay knows more than he's letting on. I just *feel* it. The trick is how to get it out of him without Beltran pulling the plug."

"Soon as he realizes we're fishing for something bigger than accessory, he's going to pull the plug," Pomerantz said.

Decker kept hitting his palm with his fist. "Why did Leek *agree* to help Tandy out? Surely, he had to realize that embezzlement is a far less serious charge than being an accessory to *murder and kidnapping*. How'd she talk him into coming down to the hospital at midnight and helping Marie dispose of a dead body?"

Marge said, "She obviously has a lot of power over this guy."

"Lots and *lots* of power. I've got to believe she has something *bigger* on him than just embezzlement!"

"Like what?" Marge said.

"I don't know!" Decker punched his palm again.

"Why don't you ask him?" Marge said. "As if he'd tell?"

"Funnier things have happened," Decker said. "Why don't *you* ask him, Marge? He seems to like you."

"Fine." Marge led the men as they came back into the interview room.

"What now?" Beltran asked.

"Couple more questions," Marge said. "Please just bear with me, and then we can call it quits."

"I can get out of here?" McKay asked.

"You discuss that with your lawyer."

"But you said no jail time," McKay began to protest.

Beltran said, "Lawrence, let's finish up this interview,

and then I can work on the bail, all right?" To Marge, he said, "Can we get on with it, Detective?"

"Leek, something's . . . it's all right if I call you Leek?"

"It's fine."

"Leek, all of us here can't really understand *why* you helped Tandy out."

"I told you she had dope on me."

"Leek, there's a mighty big difference between embezzlement and accessory to a murder."

"So what are you saying, Detective?" Beltran asked.

"I'm just trying to figure out why he'd give Tandy— a girl who'd been blackmailing him for two years— ammunition to use against him."

"My client's motivation for accessory is irrelevant."

"Maybe I was trying to get on her good side," McKay said. "You know . . . pick up where we'd left off now that she looked so good."

Marge said, "You'd want to pick up with a person who'd been blackmailing you?"

Beltran said, "I fail to understand where this is leading."

"Yeah, maybe I *would*!" McKay said. "She looks real good now."

"As I recall, didn't you say she was a little off?" Marge said. "You said it repulsed you to have sex with her."

"She looked and acted different back then," McKay insisted. "She was so fat, I couldn't even *tell* she was pregnant."

Decker threw out, "That's because she wasn't."

"What?" McKay whispered. "What'd you just say?"

Beltran said, "I think we've had enough of this interview—"

"Wait a minute!" McKay shouted. "I want to know *why* you said that, Sergeant!"

Decker paused. It was an offhand comment. By McKay's reaction, he knew he'd touched upon something big. "When did she tell you she was pregnant, Leek? Was it around two years ago . . . September, October?"

McKay opened and shut his mouth. "How do you . . . ?"

Beltran said, "Sergeant, I'm putting a stop—"

"She wasn't pregnant, Leek." Decker turned to Marge. "That was when she went to the doctor with her pseudocyesis—her false pregnancy."

"That's right," Marge concurred.

"False pregnancy?" Leek cried.

"Let's go, Mr. McKay," Beltran said.

"No, wait a minute!" Leek rose to his feet. "Just wait a *fucking* minute! What do you mean, Tandy *wasn't pregnant*?"

"Mr. McKay, I strongly advise you—"

"Shut up!" Leek shouted. "Just shut up and let me talk to this guy for a second. Let me figure something out, okay?"

Beltran bit his lip and folded his hands.

McKay sat down and said, "I'm sorry, Mr. Beltran. But this is really, really important. What do you mean Tandy *wasn't pregnant*?"

Decker said, *"When* did she tell you she was pregnant?"

"Around . . ." McKay exhaled into his hands. "Around two years ago. Halloween time—just before or just after. I remember because she told me at the home's big Halloween party. I almost threw up on the spot."

Marge said, "Leek, as of November, two years ago, Tandy Roberts was not pregnant. When she told you, she may have thought she was. But she wasn't."

"You can *prove* that?"

"We have proof."

"Holy fucking shit!" McKay blanched. "I got *screwed* for nothing!"

Decker waited.

"I can't *believe* . . . all this time." McKay kept shaking his head. "Shit! That little . . ." He looked at Marge, then at Decker. "She told me she got an abortion. You mean to tell me she was never pregnant?"

Marge said, "As of November two years ago, Leek, she was not pregnant."

Leek wiped saliva away from his mouth. "She told me she was pregnant. She swore . . . she wanted to have the baby. I told her no way I'd do anything with her ever again if she didn't get rid of it. She was fat! She was crazy! I didn't want to be connected to this girl for life!"

The room was silent.

"I told her if she ever wanted to see me again, she'd *have* to get rid of it." McKay clutched his shaking hands. "She kept stalling and stalling. And then finally, around Christmastime, she announced to me that she was too far along to get rid of it. That it ..." Again, he wiped his mouth. "That it would be considered murder. Because the fetus was viable on its own." He lowered his chin against his chest. "She said she'd have to find a doctor who'd be willing ... she'd have to do it illegally."

Beltran said, "Lawrence, I don't want you saying any more."

"It doesn't matter now," McKay said. " 'Cause if she wasn't pregnant, her whole story was *bullshit*!" He looked up at Marge and Decker. "Unless you're lying to me."

Decker said, "We're not lying, Leek. Go on. What happened after she said she'd have to do it illegally?"

"I told her ... to do it illegally. And I gave her a lot of money to do it illegally."

McKay looked at his empty paper cup and squashed it.

"She said it would make us both murderers because the baby was viable. I said do it anyway. She made me sign this piece of paper. I don't remember exactly what she had typed out. Something that said I ordered her to do it ... to get rid of it. In case she got caught. I was so desperate for her to do it, I signed the paper." He wiped his mouth a third time. "She's been making me *pay* ever since."

Decker nodded. McKay looked up. "I've got some other information for you."

Beltran said, "Lawrence—"

"Let me handle this, Mr. Beltran. I'm in *control* now. In control for the first time in two years."

"What kind of information?" Decker asked.

"If you want to hear it, I want you to drop everything against me," McKay said. "And I mean *everything*! I want to be able to walk off the witness stand a free man. I've had enough shit hanging over my head."

"Tell me what you have, and we'll think about it," Pomerantz said.

"Not good enough."

"I can't help you if you won't help me."

"Let me talk to him first," Beltran said.

"No games, please," McKay insisted. "Yes or no. You want to hear what I have to say. It's good. I guarantee you."

"Leek, I can't make a deal on that basis," Pomerantz said. "Help me out. Give me a hint."

"It's about Marie Bellson."

Decker looked at Marge, then at Pomerantz, but said nothing.

Beltran said, "Lawrence, if you were involved in any way with Marie's demise—"

"Marie's not dead!" McKay said. "At least so far as I know. *I* certainly didn't kill her. You want to hear what I have to say?"

"Give me more of a hint," Pomerantz said.

"C'mon, Mr. Pomerantz!"

Marge said, "Leek, we're trying to help—"

"Okay. I think I know where she might be."

"Good Lord," Decker said. *"Where?"*

"All charges dropped," Leek said.

Decker looked at Pomerantz. Pomerantz said, "If it pans out—"

"Uh-uh," McKay said. "She may have split from where I think she is. I can't be sure of that."

"How about this, Counselor?" Decker said. "How about . . . if it can be shown that Marie *was* where Mr. McKay thought she was, we'll drop charges against him."

Pomerantz was quiet. Decker kept a neutral expression, starved for information on Marie. They needed something! Tandy had to be locked up. She was *dangerous*!

Finally, Pomerantz said, "All right. If we can show that Marie Bellson was at any time at the location pinpointed by Mr. McKay, I'll drop *all* charges pending against Mr. McKay."

"Right on!" McKay clapped his hands. "Could you have done any better, Mr. Beltran?"

Beltran smiled wearily.

"Spit it out, Leek," Decker said.

"Two days after the kidnapping, Tandy cornered me at the gym. She wanted me to write a letter of recommendation for Marie Bellson, using the home's stationery. Tandy wanted *me* to write it and sign it, because if this clinic called and asked for Mr. McKay at the home, there'd be a real person there to take the call. Turns out that it was unnecessary. No one called. At least to my knowledge, no one called."

"Did you write the letter?" Decker asked.

"Of course!" McKay asserted. "I still thought I was an accessory to murder—the *abortion murder*, not the black lady, Booker."

"Where'd you address the letter, Leek?"

"To a clinic in central California, not far from Berkeley but more inland. Where all the immigrants work on the farms. I wrote this wonderful letter saying what a saint Mary Whitson was. She was using the name Mary Whitson."

"Whitson's her mother's maiden name," Marge said.

"Do you remember the *location* of the clinic?" Decker asked.

"Spanish-sounding town. Tecale or Tecome or Tecate. Something like that. It had a rural route address. That much I remember."

"Do you have the exact number?"

"Not on me. But I can retrieve it."

"Retrieve it!" Decker said.

"You bet, Sergeant!" McKay broke into a smile. "Anything to help Tandy fry."

THIRTY-SEVEN

MARGE SLAMMED DOWN THE RECEIVER AND CLAPPED HER hands. "They *got* Bellson!"

The entire squad room broke into cheers. She stood up and gave Decker a high-five. "The bastard was right on the money. McKay's going to walk, the lucky little sucker!"

"She was where he said she was?"

"Twenty miles south. The address McKay wrote to was a post office. The town's sheriff was able to pinpoint the exact location of the clinic. And she *was* using the name Mary Whitson. The locals were very unhappy. Seems Marie spoke Spanish and had amassed a following in just a few days."

"She was an experienced nurse," Decker said. "Can't take that away. Did she offer resistance?"

"Nope." Marge patted Decker on the back. "Think you can smile? We're almost there."

"Almost, but not quite." Decker paused. "Well, I'll tell you one thing. I ain't about to give her kitten back. Poor little thing almost starved to death."

"Keep the kitten, Pete." Marge chuckled. "In the meantime, how about if I start the paperwork. And you can take the afternoon off and tend to your wife and kid and kitten."

"It's a good offer, Rabbi," Hollander said. "If I were you, I'd take it." He bit into a bagel loaded with cream cheese, then held it aloft. "I bought this in your honor. I wanted to practice being ethnic for your party on Sunday."

"Practice makes perfect." Decker walked to the middle of the floor and announced, "Regarding my baby's party on Sunday . . . everyone's invited."

Again a round of rowdy cheers.

Decker said, "Food, champagne, and beer on the house, but you've got to stay and listen to a half-dozen rabbis sermonize about the wonders of God and my kid."

The room filled with boos and hisses.

Decker laughed. Marge slipped his jacket over his shoulders. "Go home."

"I want to talk to Marie," Decker said.

"We probably won't get her in until tomorrow, Pete. Go home."

Decker didn't move. "We found out Leek's motivation for helping Tandy. He thought she had him on some ridiculous murder charge. But why did Marie help Tandy? What was *her* motivation? It *can't* just be guilt about the affair with Tandy's father?"

Marge turned him to the door. "Why don't we ask her once we have her in custody?" She gave him a gentle shove. "Go home!"

Walking through the door to his house, Decker heard the TV blaring at head-splitting volume. To his utter shock, he saw a medium-sized sturdy man staring at the tube. His hair was thick and dark, his ruddy complexion spotlighted by a sunbeam. The man wore jeans and a white shirt, sleeves rolled up to expose thick tanned forearms.

Dad!

Lyle Decker was posed two inches from the box—hence the overdrive decibel level: Dad was hard of hearing. Grinning, Decker jogged to his father and turned him around. They exchange hugs.

"What are you *doing* here?" Decker asked.

"What?"

Decker muted the volume and raised his voice. "What a great surprise! What are you doing out here?"

Dad said, "Your mom said it's time we come out and see our new granddaughter. See the old one, too. So we came out."

"You *closed* the store, Dad?"

Dad shrugged. "We're old now. Life is short. Besides, when Mom says come out, we come out."

Decker laughed and shook his head. "Where is Mom?"

"Baking and cooking with your wife, your big daughter, your mother-in-law, and the baby nurse—all of them been chatting like magpies. Speaking of pies, they're baking lots of pies for your party. Apple, strawberry, cherry, apricot, and peach. No boysenberry. Fresh is too expensive. Smells good, don't it?"

Decker became aware of his nose. "Yes, it smells very good."

"Your barn's a mess, Son."

Decker smiled. "Yes, it is."

"I bought some two-by-fours. Figured I could make myself useful as long as Mom dragged me out here."

"Dad, you don't have to do that."

"Heck, it's better than sitting around, listening to the ladies chirp." He patted Decker's back. "You got a beautiful little girl, Son. Two of 'em. Good Lord, Cindy's big and wonderful. You and Jan did something right."

Decker slapped his dad's back. "Good role models. Let me say hello to everybody. Then I'll meet you in the barn."

"Your boys are out there now. I got them sortin' nails. It's okay if they help?"

"It's fine."

"Good. Put some meat on their bones. Especially the younger one. He's as skinny as a stick."

"Jake's thin but healthy."

"Yeah, he's a wiry guy. But a little muscle wouldn't hurt him none." The old man looked over his son. "You still look good."

Decker smiled. "The yearly physicals force me to stay fit, Dad."

"Don't do much for your brother," Lyle said. "He's got a gut on him bigger than a sumo wrestler. You come out to the barn when you're done with the womenfolk. And get outta that suit. Can't fix a barn in a suit."

"I'm aware of that, Dad."

The elder Decker smiled. "Good to see you, Son."

"Good to see you, too."

Dad walked outside. Decker was about to turn off the TV when he saw a promo for the six o'clock news—a tearful and joyous Lourdes Rodriguez being handed a pink-blanketed bundle. Matty Lopez was at her side. He looked happy, but less so. Impending fatherhood had suddenly become a reality for the teenager.

Decker switched off the picture and went inside the kitchen. As per his father's lament, the place was as noisy as a chicken coop. Mom was as no-nonsense as ever, her salt-and-pepper hair tied in a bun, a starched white apron neatly covering her dress. Her weight was perfectly proportioned to her five feet eight inches—as it had been all her life. Ida Decker was a slender, strong woman with busy hands and an opinion on everything.

"How's it going, ladies?" Decker asked.

The women broke into high-pitched welcome squeals. His mother smiled at him, the corners of her eyes webbed with crow's-feet. Decker smiled back and gave her a warm embrace.

"I don't believe you're here." Decker turned to Rina. "Did you know about this?"

"Of course I knew about this," she answered. "I wanted it to be a surprise."

To his mother, Decker said, "I can't believe you actually came."

"Your wife invited us out, so we came."

"I've invited you two out at least fifty times over the past twenty years," Decker said. "You never once came for me."

"Oh, don't give me that nonsense," Mom said, a gleam in her eye. "I came for the wedding."

"Gee thanks, Mom."

Rina gave Decker a peck on the cheek. "Talk respectfully to your mother."

"Yes, you talk nice to her," Magda answered.

Decker said, "I'm getting out of here." He glanced around the room, saw Hannah sleeping in her cradle. He bent down and gently kissed his daughter on her nose. "Are they teaching you early to be a female chauvinist?"

"Peter, you're talking too loud," his mother scolded. "You're going to wake her up. And furthermore, you're going to make our cakes fall."

Cindy beat her chest. "Go fix a barn and be macho, Dad."

"Good idea."

Decker left the room, and no one said good-bye. Too wrapped up in pie dough. A moment later, Cindy came to his side and gave him a hug. "Isn't it nice to have everyone here?"

"It is . . . in theory."

Cindy slugged him playfully. "You're such a cynic."

"Only when I'm around this many women."

"You know what, Daddy? I've finally figured out who Grandpa and Grandma remind me of."

"Who?"

"Uncle Henry and Aunt Em from *The Wizard of Oz*."

Decker laughed. "Yeah, I suppose they do a little."

"A *lot*," Cindy said. "What I want to know is, what happened to Dorothy's parents?"

"Read the book."

"Poor little girl raised by her aunt and uncle, her only friends three goofy farmhands. Where were the parents? Did they die in an accident? Were they murdered? Did they *abandon* her? Where *were* her parents?"

"Some people just have lousy parents, Cin," Decker said.

He thought of Lita Bellson. A self-proclaimed shitty mother. But at least she'd never abandoned Marie.

And in turn Marie didn't abandon her.

He paused.

Auntie Em . . . Uncle *Henry*!

Marie turned out to be the stable, dependable one . . . like my first husband, Henry.

The dependable one!

Decker bit his lip.

Only she *wasn't his*!

Decker felt a surge of adrenaline. "I bet that's it!"

"What's it?" Cindy asked.

Decker checked his watch. Plenty of time before the Sabbath started. He kissed his daughter's cheek. "Honey, can you do me a favor? I've got to run somewhere. Can you tell Grandpa I'll come help him in the barn in about an hour?"

"Sure. What is it?"

Decker held his daughter's shoulders. "Cin, you see the news promo on TV? The one of Lourdes Rodriguez getting her baby back?"

The teenager's face lit up. "She's got Caitlin back?"

"Yep," Decker said. "Watch the promo if you can get away from the hen party. It's really touching. And then pat yourself on the back. You deserve as much of the credit for their reunion as anyone else on the case."

Cindy's eyes moistened. "That was a real nice thing to say, Daddy. Thank you."

"You're welcome."

"I'd make a good detective, wouldn't I?"

"You quit college, you're dead."

"Just tossing out ideas, Dad."

"Save your tossing for salads."

Lita Bellson sat in the sunroom, eyes upon a drawing of a pair of stick figures holding hands. They were girls, wearing triangles for skirts, their faces aglow with smiling mouths disproportionately large for the heads. Decker tiptoed over to the wheelchair and placed his hand softly upon Lita's shoulder.

"Nice, sunny afternoon," he said.

"Nothing but sunshine," Lita said. "I hate it. I hate Los Angeles. Weather never changes. Like this place . . . like my life now. A curse to live this long. Now, with Marie and Leek gone, I'm all alone . . . double fucking curse. I wish I was dead. Even spumoni ice cream don't mean much to me anymore."

"It all comes around in a circle, doesn't it, Lita?"

"I guess. Life and death ... death and life. One big fucking circle."

"I suppose someone might think there was biblical justice in your living all alone in your waning years," Decker said. "The one who abandons in the end gets abandoned. Some people might find that ... interesting."

Lita didn't speak for a long time. When she did, it was barely above a whisper. "I never abandoned anyone. He took her from me. I just didn't bother to put up a fuss. Felt I owed him that much ... for all the misery I put him through."

"Lots of affairs, Lita?"

"I never painted me as a virgin. Not to anyone, certainly not to Henry."

"Henry, your first husband."

"My only husband. I never married Marie's father."

"What was Henry's last name?" Decker asked.

"Henry Tollan. Nice guy. He couldn't live with me, couldn't live without me. Finally married me. Thought a child would change my ways. It didn't. It never works that way."

"Why didn't you put up a fuss when he took her? After all, *Henrietta* was your daughter, too."

"Guess I felt I owed him that much. Maybe I felt Hetty was better off without me." She shrugged. "It's all ancient history."

But it wasn't. Sins of the past were responsible for sins of the present. Decker said, "Did you try to keep in contact with Hetty at all?"

Lita shook her head. "No husband, no child ... I got what I wanted ... a clean break."

"How old was Hetty when you walked out of her life?"

"When he *took* her, you mean. She was five. I insisted that he wait till she had her fifth birthday. I made her a pretty dress that I wanted to see her in. I took a picture of her in that dress. I wanted something to remember her by."

"Is that how Marie found out she had a half-sister? By the picture?"

"They don't call you detective for nothing."

"How old was Marie when she found out?"

"Sixteen. She used it against me. Said she was the kind of person she was because I was the kind of person I was. She was wild because she liked the boys. But you know kids. They use one excuse or another to crucify their parents."

"Did she go to Berkeley to be near Hetty?"

"To be near Hetty, to be near the hippies, to be near the drugs, to be near the sex and the communes. Of course, *Marie* told me she was going to find the mother she never had."

Lita laughed softly.

"So right away she messes things up—carrying on with her own half-sister's husband." She closed her eyes. "I felt bad for Hetty. Really, I did. First I go ahead and mess her up. Then her sister goes ahead and messes her up. She was always kind of a fragile kid. I heard later she had a breakdown—her and the kid. Hetty had a kid—a daughter, I think. She was little when it all happened. That's what got to Marie more than anything. That the kid suffered. That's when she started looking to Jesus. I told her, don't put the blame on me for this one. I may have screwed up in my life. But I never fucked any of my sisters' husbands."

There was a long, reflective moment of silence. Lita was back in another world. And Decker thought about this one.

No wonder Marie took Tandy under her wing when they met up again as adults. Marie looked upon their relationship as a second chance. An opportunity to cleanse the soul.

The prodigal daughter.

And it might have worked for her except that Tandy had come across a lockbox containing old photos and love letters. Fragile to begin with and still swaddled in grief over the loss of her family and aborted baby, Tandy had never fully forgiven her mother or her father. After reading the letters, seeing tangible proof of her father's affair with her aunt, she wasn't about to absolve *anyone*. For a while, weight lifting helped keep the voices away, but it just wasn't enough.

Deep emotional hurt never really goes away. It always leaves a scar, even if it fades to the faintest of spots. Trouble brews when the pain refuses to heal, left as an open wound just waiting to abscess. And it doesn't take much steeping if the person is unbalanced to begin with.

"Know who your granddaughter is, Lita?"

Lita opened her eyes. "Who?"

"Tandy Roberts. She's Hetty's kid."

"Tandy, the fat nurse who used to work here?"

"Yep."

"She's Hetty's kid?"

"Yep."

"You don't say."

"It's the truth."

Lita was quiet for a moment. "I can see that. Tandy was strange. A little like Hetty. I always got along with Tandy. I felt sorry for her, but I liked her, too. I'm glad I got a chance to know her, even if I didn't know she was my own blood. Sometimes things work out for the best."

"Sometimes they do."

"Can you wheel me out of the sun? I'm gettin' hot."

"My pleasure." Carefully, Decker wheeled the old lady to one of the dining tables. "Anything else you need, Lita, before I go?"

"You going to visit me again, handsome?"

"No, Lita. I don't think so."

"I can dream." The old woman shrugged. "What time is it?"

"About four-thirty."

"Dinner's not until five."

"That's only a half hour away."

"It seems like a year when you got nothing better to do." The old woman picked her head up, and their eyes met. Lita's face was as hard as stone, as craggy as a mountain ridge. "Think you can get me some spumoni?"

"I'll do my best."

She gave Decker a conspiratorial wink. Then she said, "Think if I'd had boys, I would have been a better mother?"

"I don't know, Lita."

"Maybe." Lita waited a while before speaking. "But probably not. Like I always freely admitted, I was a shitty mother."

THIRTY-EIGHT

HIGHLIGHTED BY THE MOONLIGHT STREAMING THROUGH the barred window, Marie's face appeared blue and skeletal. Her bony hands rested in her lap, pressing her cotton prison gown between her legs. Her legs were bare and crossed at the ankles; her feet held soft shoes. She refused to turn when Decker entered the cell, refused to acknowledge his presence. His questions fell upon deaf ears.

"Marie, you're not helping Tandy by protecting her," Decker said. "Marie, she's *sick*! She needs medication. She needs *help*! If you take the heat for her and allow her to go back into society, it's a sure bet she's going to do more damage!"

Silence.

Decker scratched his head. "Don't you give a solitary damn about *Lily Booker*?"

Still staring at the window, Marie finally spoke. "I care."

"Then how can you allow her murderer to go free? Even if the murderer wasn't in her right mind?"

"I am the murderer."

"Taking the rap because you feel guilty about a twenty-

year-old affair won't change the past, Marie. It won't help
Tandy, either. You want to help her, stop trying to atone for
your sins. Your prodigal-daughter bit won't play well in the
courtroom."

"I killed Lily Booker."

Decker felt his blood boil. "We're bringing Tandy to
trial, Marie. No one is going to believe you murdered Lily,
then dropped the baby off with the Robertses ... or
Robleses. Because Leek never *saw* you with the baby."

"Leek's an embezzler and a liar. His testimony is tar-
nished."

"Marie, *no one* will believe *you* murdered Lily Booker,
given Tandy's history. So save everyone some grief and tell
us what really happened."

"I went crazy," Marie said. "My hormones went out of
control and temporarily blocked my rational senses. Everyone knows what hormones gone awry can do."

"So that's your brilliant defense, huh?" Decker bit back
sarcasm. "I talked to your doctor. Your hormones were in
check. There was nothing wrong with your mind that a cat
couldn't take care of. Tandy was the one out of control.
Tandy's *voices* weren't in check. Tandy was hearing voices,
do you hear me? She was *delusional!*"

Marie didn't answer.

Decker began to pace. "The high voice, the low voice,
telling her to do things. Shrink says they were probably her
punitive parents or something like that. I've got to read the
report. I'm not a shrink. I don't claim to know all the technical mumbo jumbo. But I do know this. Tandy is a *sick
girl!* We've got lots of professionals who'll testify to that,
Marie. *Why?* you ask."

"I didn't ask."

"I'll tell you anyway. Because everyone wants Tandy
treated! Because everyone truly cares, except *you.*"

"I care."

"If you truly cared, you'd want the same thing."

"I did the murder," Marie stated flatly. "I took the baby.
I was old and childless, and I wanted a baby."

"So you're telling me you pounded poor Lily Booker with a hammer to get a baby?"

Marie was quiet.

Decker said, "It was Tandy who walked into the nursery with a hammer, Marie. You know it. I know it. She was probably out to get *you*. She never forgave you for screwing her father, breaking up her parents' marriage."

Again, Marie was silent.

Decker said, "She found Lily and that was good enough. She smashed Lily, took the baby—"

"I took the baby—"

"Bullshit!" Decker said. "Tandy took the baby. Then she realized what she'd done and took the baby over to her parents. For the life of me, I don't know why you let her take the *baby*! Helping her with Lily Booker was one thing. Poor Lily was already dead when you found Tandy with the hammer in her hand. But why did you let her take Caitlin Rodriguez?"

Marie didn't speak.

"Why?" Decker pleaded.

"I took Caitlin because, through my hormonal delusions, I thought she was in danger in the hospital."

"Danger?"

"I walked in on Lily when she was doing a heel stick on Caitlin. The baby was crying—screaming. Lily was hurting her!"

Decker thought about her words. "What? Tandy thought Lily was hurting the baby when she was doing a heel stick?"

"Not Tandy! Me! I saw Caitlin cry and got upset. Because babies cry when you do heel sticks. I tried to wrestle her away from Lily, but she wouldn't let go. So I struck her . . . too hard!"

"Marie, you've done hundreds of heel sticks. No one will believe that—"

"I was *delusional*, for the last time! And yes, Sergeant, they *will* believe me! Because I, like you, have a reputable psychiatrist's testimony."

Decker felt his patience burst. "Fine, Marie. Go nail

yourself to a cross, die for Tandy's sins, and rot in a jail cell. Meanwhile, your niece will remain tormented by imaginary voices and will probably wind up hurting someone else. If she doesn't hurt herself first. Goddamn it, don't you want to *help* her?"

A slow smile spread across Marie's face. "She has all the help she needs now, Sergeant. She found Jesus."

First it was sex, then drugs, then lots of gods, until she found Jesus.

Symptom substitution.

Fanatically loyal.

Decker didn't speak.

There was nothing left to say.

It was close to midnight when Decker walked through his bedroom door. Rina was nursing Hannah while attempting to write on a notepad. It was a juggling act worthy of the Ringling Brothers.

Decker said, "Can I help?"

"Unfortunately, no. You can't nurse the baby, and you can't check off my food list."

"Why can't I check off your food list?"

"Because you don't have any idea of what I have and what I don't have."

This was true.

"All set for tomorrow?" Decker asked.

"I think so." Rina gave him a big grin. "Peter, I'm so excited. I think you should make a speech."

"A speech?"

"Yes, a speech."

Decker sat down on the bed. "Why don't you talk?"

"Me?"

"Yes, you. People would rather look at you than me."

"Peter—"

"I'm serious. Go on, Rina. Give Mike Hollander a thrill."

She laughed. "All right." She looked down at Hannah, who was busy with her midnight snack. "She is so beautiful, isn't she?"

"Yep." Decker snuggled next to his wife and child and

put his arm around Rina's shoulder. It was time to stop and smell the roses. Maybe Tandy wouldn't get the help she desperately needed. Maybe no matter how hard Pomerantz worked, the jury would believe Marie—that she was delusional and had masterminded everything. Maybe Marie really would die for Tandy's sins.

Some things are just out of your control.

As if to imply that some things are in your control.

Control may be an illusion, but it's the illusions that keep you sane.

Decker hugged his wife's shoulder. "She's gorgeous, like her mom."

Rina kissed his cheeks. "This is nice, isn't it?"

Decker let go with a full grin. "Darlin', it don't get much better than this."